A GATHERING OF GHOSTS

A GATHERING OF GHOSTS

KAREN MAITLAND

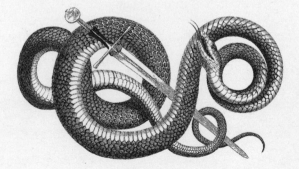

REVIEW

First published in Great Britain in 2018 by
HEADLINE REVIEW
An imprint of HEADLINE PUBLISHING GROUP

1

Cataloguing in Publication Data is available from the British Library

ISBN 978 1 4722 3587 9 (Hardback)
ISBN 978 1 4722 3588 6 (Trade paperback)

Typeset in Adobe Garamond Pro by Palimpsest Book Production Ltd, Falkirk, Stirlingshire

Printed and bound in Great Britain by CPI Group (UK) Ltd, Croydon CR0 4YY

Headline's policy is to use papers that are natural, renewable and recyclable products
and made from wood grown in well-managed forests and other controlled sources.
The logging and manufacturing processes are expected to conform to the
environmental regulations of the country of origin.

HEADLINE PUBLISHING GROUP
An Hachette UK Company
Carmelite House
50 Victoria Embankment
London, EC4Y 0DZ

www.headline.co.uk
www.hachette.co.uk

I shall see a world I will not like – summer without blossom;
kine without milk; women without conscience; men without
courage; conquests without a king; woods without mast; seas
without fish; faulty judgements of old men; false precedents
of judges. Every man a betrayer, every son a destroyer . . .
An evil time.

The Prophecy of the Morrigan from
Cath Maige Tuired (The Battle of MaghTuireadh).
Irish, *circa* ninth century in its written form

Soften your tread. The Earth's surface is but bodies of the
  dead,
Walk slowly in the air, so you do not trample on the
  remains of God's servants.

Abu al-Alaa al Maarri, eleventh-century poet
and philosopher, born AD 973

Cast of Characters

Hospitallers' Priory of St Mary, Dartmoor

Prioress Johanne – sister in the Order of the Knights Hospitallers of St John of Jerusalem and elected head of the Commandery of St Mary

Sister Fina – sister of the Order of the Knights of St John and keeper of the Holy Well

Sister Clarice – bookkeeper and steward

Sister Basilia – infirmarer, in charge of the infirmary for the sick and elderly

Sister Melisene – hosteller, responsible for the hospitality for travellers and pilgrims

Goodwife Sibyl – lay servant who cooks for the sisters

Meggy – local widow and lay gatekeeper of the priory

Sebastian – disturbed patient in the infirmary

Father Guthlac – a blind patient in the infirmary

Brengy – the stable boy

Dye – a kitchen scullion and sister of Brengy

Hospitaller Brothers

Knight Brother Nicholas – warrior-monk and steward of the Knights of St John

Brother Sergeant Alban – groom and non-military serving brother of the Knights

Hob – a carter from Buckland

Commander John de Messingham – preceptor of the Knights of St John at Buckland

Lord Prior William de Tothall – head of the Knights of St John of all England, based in Clerkenwell

Knight Brother Roul – Knight Hospitaller from Clerkenwell

Villagers on Dartmoor

Morwen – young cunning woman, daughter of Kendra

Kendra – blood charmer and former keeper of the Holy Well

Ryana and **Taegan** – Morwen's elder sisters

Deacon Wybert – local parish cleric

Tinners

Sorrel – woman with a withered arm

Todde – seeking his fortune as a tinner

Master Odo – owner of the tin-streaming works

Gleedy – Master Odo's right-hand man

Eva – cook for the single tinners

Chapter 1

Hospitallers' Priory of St Mary, Dartmoor
Eve of May Day and Feast of Beltane, 1316

That night, of all nights, Sister Fina was late. If she had arrived on time to close the holy well beneath the chapel, perhaps she might have averted all that came after, but she hadn't. And it was Sister Clarice who was to blame. Never let that woman start talking if you're in a hurry.

'Could I beg a moment of your time, Sister Fina?' she'd say. But it never was just a *moment*.

Sister Basilia, who wouldn't hear a bad word said about any soul, not even if they'd murdered every child in Widecombe, once told her fellow Hospitallers they should be thankful for Clarice's *gift* of words, as it pleased her to call it, for she said the pedlars and merchants were so battered down by them they gave her what she wanted at half the price just to get away. The other sisters had rolled their eyes, for Basilia was cheerfully determined to see God's blessing in everything, even a burned bun, which vexed them even more than Clarice's nagging.

That night, Clarice's *little word* was about the extravagant

1

use of candles, or was it beeswax polish? Probably both, Sister Fina couldn't remember. She'd long stopped listening, though that hadn't stopped Clarice talking, and by the time Fina eventually hurried across the priory courtyard it was already dark. She'd had to light a lantern to avoid tripping over the abandoned pails and pitchforks littering the cobbles. The priory cat, which was ignoring the mice and hunting for scraps of roast mutton, hissed as the sister's heavy black skirts clipped her tail. Fina giggled, for the little beast sounded just like Clarice sucking her breath through her teeth at the wanton waste of yet another candle. But it served the old steward right: if she hadn't lectured her for so long, Fina wouldn't have needed to burn one.

Even though the buildings surrounding the courtyard gave some shelter, the cold wind almost ripped the cloak from Fina's shoulders as she picked her way towards the chapel. But it sounded even louder inside, as if the devil was beating his tail against the stone walls in a violent rage, furious that he'd been shut out. Fina glanced up at the tiny stained-glass window above the altar. She was always afraid the wind would blow it in if the rain didn't smash it first. Basilia said that the casement was too narrow to come to any harm, but Fina took care not to stand too close.

Fina was the youngest of the eight sisters at the priory and taller than all of them. Her shoulders were perpetually hunched as if she was trying to make herself shorter, but her red-raw bony hands and feet looked as if they'd been intended for someone twice her height, and she'd been given them by mistake.

She hurried across the stone floor, the cold seeping up through her thin leather soles, and locked the pilgrims' door at the opposite side of the round chapel, which allowed worshippers to enter the church without going through the priory. She didn't want any villagers slipping in while her back was turned. Then she ducked beneath the low arch of the doorway that led to the well. The narrow stone staircase spiralled down into the darkness and, far below, she could hear the splashing of water in spite of the roar of the gale outside. But even before she'd taken a step, something made her draw back.

The rock walls of the staircase always glimmered for they were covered with a fur of delicate green moss that radiated a strange emerald-gold light whenever the candles were burning below, like glow-worms twinkling on a summer's night. Pilgrims gasped in awe when they first saw it. When they thought no one was watching, some scraped their finger-nails down those walls to steal what they imagined to be a strip of precious gold, but they found themselves grasping only a handful of wet mud. That gave them a fright, thinking St Lucia had turned gold into dirt to punish their thieving. Fina had been tending the well daily for a year or more and the golden light was as commonplace to her as a loaf of bread, but what she saw that night certainly wasn't. The walls were glowing with a ruby-red light that throbbed and pulsated like a beating heart. She felt as if she was staring down into the belly of the hill slashed open. The rocks were bleeding.

The sight so terrified her that she almost slammed the door and fled, but she was more afraid of her prioress's tongue. That woman's glare could freeze the sun in the sky. Fina forced herself to examine the walls again. But she could make no sense of what she saw. Was the red glow coming from a fire in the cave below? She sniffed, but there was no smell of smoke and, besides, there was nothing much to burn down there, except the St Brigid crosses left by pilgrims

3

or the rags they dipped into the holy water. And Prioress Johanne always insisted those filthy offerings were cleared away nightly.

Still clutching the lantern, Fina slowly descended the uneven stone steps, holding herself tense and ready to retreat at the first sign of flames. The holy spring gushed out of a gap between three rocks in the wall and poured into an ancient stone trough, just long and wide enough for a man to lie in, as if he was in his own coffin. Fat yellow candles burned on the spikes that had been driven into the rock on either side of the spring. The melted wax dripped down the rock face to form frozen waterfalls at the base. But when Fina reached the point on the stairs where the interior of the cave became visible, she thought she saw something red glowing at the bottom of the trough, as if a scarlet flame burned beneath the water. It was there only for the blink of an eye. Then it was gone, and soft yellow candlelight flickered across the rocky floor once more.

Ducking under a low jag of rock, she stepped down into the cave and edged towards the spring, thinking that a pilgrim must have thrown a jewel into the water, which had caught the light, but there were only the usual bent pins and silver pennies in the trough, nothing else, except a few stems of the creamy-white flowers of may blossom floating on the surface – another offering from a villager that would have brought a frown to Prioress Johanne's brow if she'd seen it.

Some village girl had probably been using the flowers to sprinkle herself with the spring water in the belief that on the eve of May Day it would turn her into a beauty. As a child, Fina had watched the servant girls in her father's manor house do such things and was almost tempted to copy them now, but her prioress's face rose in front of her, like an archangel with a flaming sword. She'd never be able to hide such a sin from her inquisitorial gaze.

Fina scooped out the dripping flowers, crushing them in her fist. A stray thorn pierced her palm and she winced, glancing guiltily up at the painted wooden statue of St Lucia above the well. The saint knew her thoughts and was punishing her.

Averting her eyes, Fina searched the cave for what her prioress called 'rubbish' – a bandage stiff with dried blood, a three-armed cross woven from rushes, and a crude doll fashioned from reeds and wrapped in a white rag. By now, Fina knew all of the little holes and crevices in the cave where the local women tried to hide such things, and it didn't take her long for the cave wasn't large. There was room for only four or five people to crowd in around the well, though mostly they came in ones and twos.

The figure of St Lucia, patron saint of the blind, stood in a niche above the spring, for the sisters had dedicated the well to her. The long wooden dagger in her hands pointed menacingly at the pilgrims as if she meant to kill any sinner who despoiled it. Johanne had had the statue installed there when she had been elected as prioress eight years ago, to remind everyone that they should pray to the saint that the waters might heal them. No one ever dared say as much to the prioress, but in truth only the sisters of the Knights of St John and a few of the pilgrims ever offered their prayers to her at this well.

Old Kendra and her tribe of daughters, who once were the keepers of the spring, called it Bryde's Well and they'd cursed the whole priory on the day it was blessed for St Lucia. Prioress Johanne had forbidden them to come near the place, but the villagers who crept down to the cave still

5

whispered the old name and made their prayers and offerings of clooties, pins and three-armed crosses not to the saint gazing down at their spring, but to the ancient one, the stone face that stared out at them behind the spring through a veil of water.

The prioress had not brought her to the holy well. That face had been watching over the spring centuries before the first Hospitaller sisters had set their dainty feet upon the moors a mere thirty years ago. Compared to that ancient carving, the sisters were no more than blades of grass beneath an ancient oak.

Fina tried never to look at the stone carving, though the face always drew her gaze, like a viper lying coiled in the corner of a room. It was hard to make out the features beneath the cascade, especially in the flickering candlelight. Basilia said it was a woman's face, with ears of wheat sprouting from her eyes and mouth. Melisene was sure it was the face of the sun, with tongues of fire leaping from it. The prioress said it was the face of a she-devil, who now lay crushed beneath the holy feet of St Lucia.

But Fina saw a skull surmounted by a warrior's helmet, with burning spears shooting from it, and when she was alone in the cave, she saw those spears dance with flame and the skull turn to stare at her. Even though she tried to convince herself it must be a trick of the candlelight flickering over the twisting water, even though she knew the demon had been crushed, still she could not shake off the feeling that the she-devil was very far from dead.

She shivered and, taking care not to look at the stone carving, rolled up the black sleeve of her kirtle. Clenching her jaw against the cold, she plunged her arm into the icy water to scoop out the glittering silver coins from the bottom of the pool. Even the bent pins had to be collected, for whenever they had amassed a boxful, they were sold to be melted down for their silver. But it was like trying to snatch minnows with your bare hands. The pins and coins were never where they appeared to be under the water. Over the past months, Fina had learned the skill of catching them, but that night, perhaps because she was still unnerved by the red glow she had seen, her fingers were as clumsy as those of an old woman with palsy, and the ripples she made as she lunged for them only sent them drifting further away. She gave up. She was hungry for her supper. The prioress would not come down here so late. She'd try again in the morning.

She blew out the candles on either side of the spring. Shadows closed in, like a pack of wolves, and only where the feeble light from her horn lantern flickered over the walls did the moss still glow with a green-gold haze. Once the light was gone, like the water, the moss turned black. She hurried up the stairs and into the safety of the chapel, slamming the door to the staircase behind her, as if the darkness might come bounding after her.

As the door banged, there came a yelp of fear. Fina spun round. The chapel had been empty when she'd gone down, she was sure, just as she was certain she'd locked the far door leading to the outside. But now a little boy was standing by the stone altar, gripping the corner tightly in both hands, turning his head this way and that, as if trying to see what had made the sudden noise.

He looked seven or eight years old, his tangled black hair curling over the top of a brown homespun jerkin. Fina thought he must be travelling with a family who'd taken shelter in the pilgrims' hall for the night and, as children

7

do, had gone exploring and somehow found his way into the chapel through the door from the courtyard, which she'd left unlocked.

'What are you doing in here, child?' She took a few paces towards him, intending to usher him out. 'The holy well is closed for the night. You—' She broke off. He was cringing, his arm raised over his face as if he expected a blow.

She held up her hands to assure him she meant him no harm. 'We'd best get you back to your kin before they start to fear the wisht hounds have taken you.'

She'd meant it as a joke, but he seemed even more terrified.

'Come,' she said, as gently as she could. 'Supper will be served soon and you don't want to miss that. There'll be a good hot soup. Well, the soup will be hot, at least.'

Good was not a word anyone bestowed on the cook's meals in the pilgrims' hall. Even when he did flavour the pottage with herbs or a bone stock, all you could ever smell was burned beans. That man could scorch water. The sisters always gave heartfelt thanks that Goodwife Sibyl cooked for them.

Fina raised the lantern, more to let the child see that she was smiling than to study his face. Only then did she realise the boy wasn't looking at her. His head was turning from side to side, as if he couldn't understand where her voice was coming from. His eyes were as dark as the peat-black bog pools, clear and unclouded. Twin reflections of the flame in the lantern blazed in the wide, bright pupils, but he couldn't see that light. He was blind.

She touched his shoulder and he started violently. Then his fingers inched up to grasp hers. He clung to her with a hand as cold as the water in the well below, yet his touch

8

seared too, like ice sticking to bare skin, and she had to force herself not to flinch.

It took Fina and the boy some time to reach the pilgrims' hall, though it was only across the corner of the courtyard. The child was afraid to move. He stumbled on the cobbles and kept stopping abruptly whenever he thought he might bump into something.

That evening, only five people occupied the long, narrow chamber where travellers in need of a night's shelter ate at the scrubbed table and slept on the straw pallets on the floor. Two were pedlars, the others a master cordwainer and his pregnant wife, the last an old woman who, from her torn but costly gown, looked as if she had once known better times. But none recognised the boy or remembered seeing such a lad with anyone on the road.

Leading the child out into the courtyard again, Fina pulled him into the infirmary, which stood alongside the pilgrims' hall, where the sick, the frail and those travellers in need of many days or weeks of rest were cared for. There were a dozen beds and most were occupied.

Sister Fina's gaze darted at once to the far corner, where Sebastian sat curled on a heap of sheepskins as far from the fire as he could get. He'd been there longer than any of the others, longer than most of the sisters, and though he wasn't an old man, the hair that tumbled down his back was white and his limbs thin as worms, every joint swollen and twisted at odd angles. He was staring at a crucifix in his lap, clumsily rubbing the wounded hand of Christ with the tip of a finger, as if he was trying to soothe the hurt. Fina was relieved that he appeared quiet and calm tonight. She did not want him frightening the boy, for Sebastian would sometimes

9

cower and scream, as if he was being tormented by all the demons in Hell. Many of the servants whispered that he was possessed but, curiously, it was often Prioress Johanne who calmed him when he was seized by these evil spirits. Although Fina couldn't begin to imagine how, for in her experience the prioress was more formidable than a legion of devils and more likely to scare someone out of their wits than into them.

Sister Basilia, the infirmarer, was at the other end of the hall, apparently giving instructions to one of the female servants. There was a mulish expression on the maid's face, and she folded her arms sullenly, staring at the long table on which the remains of supper still lay – burned mutton broth by the smell of it. Basilia kept smiling as if she was quite certain the woman would do whatever she was plainly resisting. She reminded Fina of a plump, eager spaniel, always wagging her tail and jumping up, convinced that everyone she met wanted to be friends.

She broke off as she caught sight of Fina and bustled over, while the servant seized the opportunity to escape, collecting the wooden bowls from the table with ill-tempered bangs and clatters.

Basilia beamed down at the child still clutching Fina's hand. 'And who have we here?' She gave the black curls a vigorous pat. The boy shrank back. She chuckled. 'Shy little fellow, isn't he?'

'Not shy, Sister.' Fina hesitated, then guided him to an empty bed. She prised his icy fingers from her hand and pressed them to the straw mattress. 'There . . . a good, warm place to sleep. Can you feel the wall behind? You stay here. I'll be back in a moment.'

The boy stood where she'd left him, his hands dangling,

his head turning this way and that to follow the many voices and clatter of dishes, but he made no attempt to touch anything around him.

Fina returned to Basilia and drew her aside. 'I found him alone in the chapel. He's blind, but I don't believe he can have been so for long – he has not learned to use his hands to discover where he is and he can't follow sounds, as Father Guthlac can.'

She nodded towards an elderly man sitting close to the fire, his fingers and lips moving as he recited his paternosters, counting them off on his string of beads. But his mind seemed not entirely focused on his devotions, for he cocked his head, listening to the chatter around him, smiling at this, frowning at that, occasionally calling a remark mid-prayer. His sight had faded gradually over the years, but with the help of his deacon he'd still been able to perform his duties as parish priest. Like most, he had never been able to read much Latin and had always gabbled the services by rote, so his parishioners scarcely noticed when darkness had closed in upon his world.

Basilia glanced over Fina's shoulder at the boy. 'Who brought the poor mite here?'

'I don't know, but someone must have. He can't have found his own way in. He's not even able to cross a room alone. He can't tell me where he came from or who he is. He hasn't uttered a word. I don't know if his kin have abandoned him to our care, or they mean to return for him, if he can be healed.'

Basilia regarded her with sad, reproachful eyes, as if she'd betrayed their faith in thinking that St Lucia might not perform a miracle. 'Imagine leaving a child when he needs you most. What mother would do such a thing?' She puffed

11

up her chest like an indignant hen. For a moment Fina thought she would march over to the boy and gather him up in her arms, like a baby.

They all knew that it was Basilia's greatest sorrow that she had no children. But with a litter of lusty sons to provide for, in addition to his daughters, her father had been able to offer land enough only for one of his girls to acquire a husband of suitable rank.

'Maybe he has no mother,' Fina said. 'And no one else can spare food for him. The famine is biting hard and if he can't work . . . You see how he is. He can do nothing for himself.'

'But he can learn,' Basilia said firmly. 'And there's no one better to teach him than Father Guthlac. He'd still be out tending his flock, if his poor swollen legs would bear him up.'

She lumbered over to the boy, seized his hand and dragged him towards the old priest. In her eagerness, she didn't watch him closely enough and the lad collided with the corner of the table, setting the remaining bowls and spoons on it rattling.

Father Guthlac turned his head towards the sound. 'Who's that?' he called. 'Don't know that tread. I reckon they've been supping too much mead by the way they're crashing about.' He chuckled to himself.

Basilia took the boy by the shoulders and steered him close to the old man. 'A boy brought to us, Father Guthlac. Sister Fina believes he's newly blind and no one's shown him how to get about for himself. We thought you might teach him.'

The old priest raised his hand to silence her. 'Come closer, boy.' He extended a wrinkled hand and grasped the child's sleeve. The boy tried to pull away, but Father Guthlac had dealt with a good many little sinners in his time and held him firmly by the shoulders. He lifted the boy's arm by the cloth and ran his hand down it until he found the fingers. The old man stiffened, hunching forward in the chair and sucking his breath in noisily through his teeth. His hand darted to the boy's face, running lightly over it, like a spider.

Then the old priest gave a cry of horror and jerked his hand away, as if he'd been stung. His sightless eyes flashed wide in fear. Seizing the staff beside him, he struggled to his feet, his paternoster beads slithering to the floor. He tottered backwards, crossing his breast as if the devil himself had risen up from the ground in a cloud of sulphur. Clutching the corner of the table, he brandished his staff towards where Basilia and the boy stood.

'Drive him out!' he shrieked. 'Drive him out from these halls now.'

'Father Guthlac!' the infirmarer protested, wrapping her arms protectively across the boy's chest. 'Whatever has possessed you? He's a little boy, a helpless child. Didn't you hear me tell you he's blind?'

'If you don't put him out this very hour he'll destroy us. Destroy us all! I know what you are, boy. You may fool those who can look but don't see. But I can see you, boy – see you plain as sin. Be gone, foul creature of darkness!'

Fina rushed forward to try to quieten the priest and help him back to his seat, but he was waving his staff so wildly she was forced to retreat. The servants and the patients who could move had backed away to the corners of the hall as if they were afraid the blind priest might charge towards them. In the corner, Sebastian was moaning in fear. He shrank against the wall, trying in vain to cover his head to protect himself, but he could not raise his poor twisted arms.

13

Fina tried to placate the old cleric. 'Father Guthlac, we can find the boy somewhere else to go in the morning. In any case, his kin may have returned by then. But he'll have to stay here till daylight. The gates are locked for the night.'

The old man's mouth twisted in fear and rage, a stream of grey spittle trickling from the corner of his mouth. 'You want your sisters to be alive come cockcrow, then heed me, Sister Fina. You take that demon, bind him tight, and throw him into the sucking mire. For I give you fair warning – if that boy sleeps beneath this roof this night, not one of us will be spared the curse he'll bring down upon our heads.'

Chapter 2

Sorrel

That was the day I knew I had to go, though I'd no notion where or why. I only knew I felt the urge flooding my veins, as swallows sense the icy grasp of winter stretching out to crush them, even before the first leaf has fallen, and know they must fly before it's too late. *Too late!* Yes, that was the ghost that had come to haunt me. Every dawn for months I'd woken in dread knowing that something was wrong, so very wrong, but what? *She* gave me no answer. She spoke no other word to me, as if I was talking to the wind or the sun or the moon. She said nothing but *Come*.

I was kneeling furthest downstream from the rest of the village women. The bailiff's wife always squatted highest upstream so that no dirt or lye from the others' washing could touch hers. That was her spot by divine right and no one dared usurp it, even though that day she wasn't with us. The lowest place was left for me. No one wanted water from my clothes near theirs for fear that my misfortune might flow on to them. The river carries curses from one person

15

to another, like the wind carries dust from one man's field and blows it into another's eyes.

But I was used to my neighbours drawing away from me, glad of it really, for then I need not join in with their prattling, though I could hear them bellowing to each other over the rush of the water.

'Don't know why we're bothering to wash these clouts,' one shouted. 'The rain'll never hold off long enough for them to dry.'

'To stop the menfolk bellyaching that their breeches are stinking and lousy,' her neighbour replied. 'Spend half our lives doing things just to stop them complaining.' She ferociously pounded her husband's shirt with a stone as big as her fist, as if it was his head she was battering.

'You'll never get rid of the lice,' another called, 'no matter how long you hold them under the water. Cunning little beggars. I reckon they're the only beasts left in this village that aren't starving.'

I scrambled on to a wet boulder that jutted into the water, and used my chin and my good arm to twist my shift into a rope, slapping it against the rock. It would not get as much dirt out as scrubbing, but the cloth was so threadbare it would fall apart if I rubbed too hard.

The river was running high and would run higher still, if we didn't get a dry spell soon. A year or so back, the boulder I was sitting on was so far clear of the water that on a hot day you could spread your linens on it to dry. But it had been months since we'd glimpsed even enough blue sky to make a cloak for the Holy Virgin. The village children talked about summer as if it was some fanciful tale a storyteller had invented.

A sudden surge of water smashed into the rock, which

16

shuddered beneath me. The river swirled and foamed around the boulder, tugging at it as if it meant to tear it free and send it sailing downstream. The sky was darkening. A chill wind wrapped itself around me, breathing ice on to my wet skin. Another squall was coming in. But upstream, the women chattered on, like the babble of water over stones.

A dark red flash in the river captured my gaze. I thought it might be a flower, though I couldn't make out what kind. The current swept it towards me. It spun on the surface, drowned and rose again, then was tossed from one side to the other, as the eddies caught it, until it bumped against the boulder on which I sat and was trapped behind it, trembling as the spray buffeted it. Now that it was close, I could see what it was – hound's-tongue. Its crimson petals are beautiful to look at, but it stinks like dog's piss and poisons sheep or cattle if they swallow it. I reached down to fish it out before it could do any harm.

But as my fingers stretched towards it, the water around it began to turn red, as if the petals were bleeding into it. The stain widened and spread till it touched the riverbanks. I snatched my hand back and jerked upright. For as far as I could see, above and below me, the whole river was blood red. But the women were still pounding their clothes in it. Red liquid ran down their arms and dripped from their fingers. Scarlet droplets glistened on their faces. The shirts they were scrubbing were stained crimson. But the women were still washing, still chattering, still laughing.

I scrambled to my feet, leaping back to the bank. 'Stop! Stop! The river— Can't you see?'

Their hands froze half in and half out of the bloody water.

17

They stared at me, then at the river and back at me, gaping as if I was making no more sense than a cawing crow.

'The water! It's full of blood! Look at it!'

They looked. Then they dropped the sodden scarlet clothes on to the bank and came hurrying towards me. I pointed down into the bloody water and they gazed slack-jawed.

Then one laughed and snatched up the dripping flower, waving it at the others. ''Tis only a sprig of hound's-tongue.'

'You want to keep that.' One chuckled. 'You put that inside your shoe on a journey and no dog'll come nigh you nor bark at you.'

The finder rolled her eyes. 'Blood, indeed. A flower, 'tis all. You blind, as well as crippled, Sorrel?'

'Hound's-tongue.' Another snorted. 'If you ask me she's been bit by a mad hound. First sign it is, being scared of water.'

'Then she'd best keep this. They say it cures that too.' The woman tossed the stinking flower at me. It caught in my hair and I felt drops of water from its sodden petals trickle down my cheek. I pulled it out, and stood there foolishly clutching it.

They were laughing, but I could see the fear in their eyes as they stared at me. I was afraid too, but I made myself glance down. Under the leaden sky, the river was as transparent and colourless as the tiny elvers that wriggled through it.

Drops of rain began to splatter on to the rock. The women hurried off to gather up their washing and hasten home. They glanced pityingly at me over their shoulders as they walked away, and I knew they were whispering about me.

The wind snarled, tearing at my skirts, dragging the bindings

18

of my hair loose and whipping the strands around me. The branches of the willows snaked across the water towards me, as if they were trying to hook me and pull me away from the river into an air I couldn't breathe. The clouds were bruised purple in the sulphurous light. At any moment, the storm would break over me. I should run home, but I couldn't move.

Come, you must come to me.

It was the wind playing tricks on my ears, as the river had done to my eyes.

Come to where the fire burns.

It was one of my neighbours. She was coming back to urge me to hurry to the byre I called home.

But I didn't turn my head, for I knew I wouldn't see anyone walking towards me. It was not a neighbour. It was not the wind. I knew that voice. I'd heard it calling to me since I was nine summers old, but until now only in my dreams. Was I asleep? I felt the sharp sting of rain against my face. Was I running mad?

Fire and water wait for you. The time is now.

The foul reek of hound's-tongue burned my nostrils. I stared down. My right hand was balled so tightly into a fist I could no more move its fingers than I could those on the withered left. I had to will it to open. Slowly, painfully, my fingers uncurled. The mangled red petals of the flower lay in my palm. They had stained my skin scarlet.

A flash of lightning startled me into looking up. On the opposite bank a fox, a black fox, stood motionless, its head turned towards me, ears pricked. We stared at one another. Its brush streamed out in the wind, like a flame from a blazing torch. The animal reek grew stronger till I was almost choking. And I knew that, even if I let the flower drop, it would not leave me. The smell was in the air, in the water, in the beast that stood watching me.

Come! Come to where the fire burns in my heart.

A growl of distant thunder rolled across the sky. The black fox had vanished, but its stench still rode upon the wind.

Chapter 3

Prioress Johanne

A sudden chill drenched my skin as if the door to my chamber had been flung open and a cold wind had barged in. The sensation was so intense that I glanced behind me, but the door remained firmly latched. I poked at the sluggish fire, trying to prod it into a blaze. Exhaustion: that was why I felt so cold. My head throbbed. I longed to beg Sister Clarice to retire for the night and discuss the accounts in the morning, but my steward was one of those women who never needed more than an hour or two of sleep and couldn't understand why others wasted so much time in their beds.

Clarice ran a crooked finger down the column of figures she'd inscribed on the parchment. The numbers stood erect in such straight lines that not even a master mason with a plumb line could have schooled them better. 'At least our calves are fetching twice what they did last year,' she announced, with grim satisfaction. 'The farmers who graze their cattle on the lower pasture lost many beasts because of the rain and floods, but we've been spared the worst up here.'

She thrust aside the parchment and pulled another towards us, impatient to move on. She was a small, compact woman, but her black kirtle was tight about her. She had not so much as a pinch of spare flesh on her frame, but saw no reason to squander cloth on folds her body would not fill. She had come late to the Sisters of the Knights Hospitallers. She and her husband had, as donats, made a generous gift of land and money to the order, but had continued to live in the outside world. Clarice had managed her husband's warehouses and properties while he travelled through Europe buying and selling merchandise for his cargo ships, but after his death from a fever in France she had made her full profession. I sometimes found myself wondering if that had been wise, for Clarice was unaccustomed to consulting with others, much less having her decisions questioned. If I had not heard her take the oath I might have been tempted to believe that, while she had vowed poverty and chastity sincerely enough, she had omitted obedience.

She was still talking and now rapped her finger against another sum on the parchment, as if she was disgusted by its indolence. 'But the offerings left at the well are lower, far lower.' She stretched out this last phrase letting it vibrate in the room, as if she was an ancient prophet announcing the destruction of a wicked city.

I moved the candle closer, peering at the column with smarting eyes. 'Lower, yes, but only by a trifle, Sister Clarice. I am sure that will make little difference when set against the income from wax and wool.'

Clarice gave an exasperated sigh. 'The point is, Prioress, that the number of people coming to the well has increased so the amount collected from the offerings should have increased too, but it has not.'

22

'But the famine—'

A shriek echoed across the courtyard outside. We both jerked round. Someone was shouting and seemed to be in great distress. I struggled to my feet. 'Sebastian! I should see what can be done to calm him.'

'Didn't sound like him,' Clarice said. 'But, if it was, he's quietened now.' She scuttled to the door and dragged it open, peering out across the dark, rain-drenched courtyard. The wind roared in, scattering the parchments on my table and sending billows of smoke and sparks from the hearth swirling about the room.

'Sister, have a care for the fire,' I protested, kneeling down to gather up the documents before the wind blew them into the flames. But before I could rise again, I heard another bellow as, somewhere, a door opened and slammed.

Clarice flattened herself against the wall as Sister Fina came hurrying in, tugging a small boy behind her. Clarice latched the door while Fina stood coughing and flapping ineffectually at the clouds of smoke. In spite of the weather, she had not fastened her cloak, which was trailing wet and muddy behind her. The drenched skirts of her black kirtle clung to her legs.

'What's the commotion? Sebastian again?' Clarice demanded, before I could utter a word.

'It was Father Guthlac,' Fina panted, wiping her wet face on her damp sleeve. 'The boy . . . I never expected . . . how could I? After all, he's just a little boy.'

'Calm yourself, Sister Fina,' I said firmly, in an attempt to remind both women that *I* was prioress and they were standing in *my* chamber. 'Why don't you and the boy come closer to the fire and dry yourselves, before you get the ague?'

Up to then the child had been half hidden behind Fina.

23

She grasped him by the shoulders and guided him gently towards the hearth. Although he was not in any danger of being burned, he shrank back as he felt the warmth, holding up his hands to shield his face as if he couldn't understand the source of the heat.

I wondered if he might be simple. Sadly, there were many such children born to villagers in those parts. They would rock back and forth, or shriek uncontrollably at the sight of something as commonplace and harmless as a feather. Changelings, the local people called them. They swore that pigseys stole human babies and left their own strange offspring in their place. But the boy's expression was not vacant like those children's. As he turned, he blundered into a stool and I realised he couldn't see, not even the flames of the fire that were dazzlingly bright in the dimly lit room.

'Who is this child? A villager?'

Fina gnawed her lip. 'I found him alone in the chapel, Prioress, when I was closing the well. He won't tell us his name and no one in the pilgrims' hall recognises him. I thought perhaps Father Guthlac might help him, being blind himself, but as soon as he touched him . . .' She twisted her long fingers as if she was attempting to plait them.

'Oh, for goodness' sake, spit it out, Sister Fina,' Clarice snapped. 'Prioress Johanne and I have a great deal to discuss.'

'The accounts can wait until the morrow, Sister Clarice,' I said firmly. 'Don't let me detain you if you have things to do.' My eyes felt as if they had been skinned. I couldn't even look at another column of figures much less make sense of them.

I was relieved as I saw Clarice scuttling towards the door,

24

but instead of opening it, she plumped herself down on a narrow bench beside it and folded her arms as if to make plain she was waiting for an explanation.

Fina glanced at the boy, who had backed as far away from the fire as he could and was crouching in the corner. She edged closer to me, lowering her voice, though in that small chamber the child could hardly fail to hear her, unless he was deaf as well as blind. 'Something about him seemed to upset Father Guthlac. He started yelling that we'd draw a curse down on us all if we let him stay. He said . . .' Fina swallowed and dropped her voice to whisper '. . . he said we should drown the boy in the mire. He's a priest!' she added, in a shocked tone, as if that fact had somehow escaped me. 'He's always so kindly and placid. What should we do, Prioress?'

'Do? I think that is plain enough. Unless you want the whole priory to be kept awake you had better keep the boy well away from Father Guthlac. I imagine his shouting has also alarmed the other patients. Is Sebastian distressed?'

She shrugged.

'Keep the boy out of the infirmary,' I said. 'We want no more disturbances for our patients.'

'But, Prioress, suppose Father Guthlac is right? They say the blind have the gift of second sight, and the boy did appear in the chapel after I'd locked the door. How could he have got in there unless by dark magic? And there's something else . . . When I opened the door to the well, the rocks . . . they were running with blood.'

'Blood? Whose blood?' I demanded. 'Has someone been hurt?'

Fina was twisting her fingers again, like an anxious child. 'I didn't mean . . . Not real blood, but the rocks were glowing blood red. In all these months I've been sister of the well, I've never seen such a thing.'

'Sister Fina, you are not an unlettered cottager! What you *think* you saw was a reflection of the candlelight on water, nothing more. You know the walls glow when the candles are lit. As for the boy being in the chapel, I dare say he was crouching in a corner when you came in as he is now, afraid to move or call out since he couldn't see who was walking about. But if you are going to take fright at shadows, perhaps I should appoint another sister to take charge of the well and you can work in the kitchens. In my experience plucking chickens and pounding dough is a sure cure for any strange fancies of youth.'

From her perch by the door Clarice gave an impatient snort. 'The boy got in because she neglected to lock the pilgrims' door properly. It wouldn't be the first time I've found it open after she swore she'd closed it. You don't attend to what you're doing, Sister. Always daydreaming. The prioress is right, some honest toil in the kitchens would soon set your head firmly back on your shoulders.'

Fina opened her mouth to protest, but I was in no mood to listen to an argument between the two. 'It matters not how the boy got into the chapel. Our duty is clear. He is a child without kin, at least until a relative claims him, and as such we are pledged to give him shelter and care. He shall stay here until we see if St Lucia, in her mercy, will intercede for him. Eventually he can be sent to one of our brothers' priories to be—'

I was interrupted for the second time that evening by a rapping at my door. How many more people were going to come charging in tonight? Could no one solve the slightest problem without running to me?

Clarice rose to unlatch the door. The gatekeeper, Meggy, edged in, a ragged piece of sacking grasped tightly over her head against the rain. Her florid cheeks glistened with water, and more dripped from the end of her broad, fleshy nose. Some in the priory muttered that the widow was too old for such a post, but she'd spent most of her life ploughing the family's own strip of land and helping her late husband in his blacksmith's forge, hefting iron, pumping the furnace bellows and holding the heavy carthorses. Years of such toil had left her with brawn enough to deter most unwelcome intruders. Besides, I knew that she had nowhere else to call home now.

'Prioress, Hob and his lad have come from Buckland with the supplies.'

'At this hour?' The carter usually arrived in the morning in time to unload his wagon and eat in the pilgrims' hall at noon, before setting out again. For reasons I had never understood, Hob always refused to stay overnight, preferring to sleep in the stables of inns or even on the open road rather than in our warm hall.

All our wine, with goods such as parchment and black cloth, which we could not purchase from the local markets, was delivered to us from the commandery at Buckland along with any messages from the preceptor of the Knights Hospitallers there, John de Messingham. But I had noticed in these past months that letters sent out by the Lord Prior, William de Tothall at Clerkenwell, intended for all the priories of the English order were dispatched to us through Buckland, instead of straight to my hand, which annoyed and alarmed me.

The commandery at Buckland was small, the number of professed brothers seldom rising above seven, but the community of sisters in the nearby preceptory of Minchin Buckland had, of late, swollen to almost fifty professed women and dozens more lay servants as, one by one, Lord William had persuaded the priories of sisters across England to enter the cloister at Minchin Buckland and live under one roof, with the knights at Buckland tasked with the noble duty of protecting and serving them. Although, if you asked me, *guarding and gaoling them* was a more accurate phrase.

But we would *not* be joining our sisters to sit sewing and praying for the souls of our brothers, of that I was determined. We were needed here, caring for those who crossed the moors, for they were fraught with peril. Outlaws hid among the rocky tors and deep valleys watching for vulnerable travellers. Seemingly lush swards of grass concealed mires that could suck down men and horses alike. Bone-chilling mists descended without warning, sending men wandering in circles till they died of cold or exhaustion.

'Hob has more sense than to risk crossing the moor at night,' I said. 'What's brought him so late to our door?'

Meggy shrugged her broad shoulders. 'Slow journey, Hob says. Up to their hocks in mud all the way, they were. Said they spent more time digging the wagon out than riding on her.'

'Tears of Mary!' Clarice muttered. 'They could have had their throats cut on that lonely track when it's as black as this, especially if the cart got stuck. There are more men turning to robbery every day, desperate for food since this famine took hold. Why didn't he and the boy take shelter for the night?'

'I reckon he'd a mind to do just that, but the knight riding with them was determined to press on to reach here. Asking to see you, he is, Prioress. I told him you'd not be best pleased to be disturbed. "Priory's locked up for the night," I said. I'd not have let him through my gate at this hour, save that he wears the cross of your order.' She gestured with her chin towards the white *cross formée* on the shoulder of my left sleeve.

'A brother Hospitaller? Here? Did he ride with the wagon to guard it?'

'If he did,' Meggy muttered, 'it was a foolhardy thing to do. Hob knows how to slip past any trouble quietly without drawing attention to himself. Folks see his cart being escorted by a knight with his white cross flashing out in the dark for all to see and he might as well have the King's herald marching in front of him bellowing, "Here's a fellow wants robbing."'

'If Commander John de Messingham sent a brother from Buckland, he must have had his reasons for doing so,' I said sternly. It did not befit a servant to question the actions of the Knights of St John.

All the same, I confess that I was a little curious too. The brother was probably on his way to board a ship at Fowey to voyage to the Citramer, our order's heartland on Rhodes, for every Knight of St John who held office was obliged to serve a season there or on our ships in the Turk-infested Aegean. But an unsettling thought burrowed into my head. Had the knight come to collect the responsions that every priory was obliged to pay to the mother house at Clerkenwell? But that money was not yet due. My stomach lurched. Why would he have come to demand it early?

'Where have you left our brother?'

'Sister Melisene took him to the guest chamber.' The expression on Meggy's face made plain that, had it been up to her, the knight would have cooled his heels out in the rain. 'There's a groom with them. He's supping with the knight. I told Hob and his lad they could bed down in the pilgrims' hall, seeing as how it's half empty.' She grinned. 'Hob's not best pleased about spending the night here. Said he'd sooner be on his way, but I told him, I said, "There'll be no unloading that cart this side of dawn. Sister Clarice will want to check every last keg and bundle, and she'll not be of a mind to do that in the dark." Isn't that right, Sister?'

Clarice gave her an approving nod.

'Then I had better find out what brings this knight to our door,' I said, reaching for my cloak.

'But what shall I do with the boy?' Fina wailed.

I'd almost forgotten she was there. The boy had not moved out of the corner where he was crouching, though he leaned towards us as if he was listening. I grasped his little hands and pulled him to his feet. His fingers lay limply in mine, cold as a corpse's. I examined his face carefully, feeling his arms and ribs. He offered no resistance.

'He's pale and thin, but not as emaciated as most children who've taken to the road in search of food.' I straightened. 'Give him something to eat and put him to sleep in the pilgrims' hall. And ask Sister Basilia to give Father Guthlac a sleeping draught to calm him. He can recognise faces by touch and it may be that something about the boy's features reminded him of someone he once knew. If it was a person he thought dead, the shock might have caused him to utter such wild words.'

Fina began, 'Father Guthlac said—'

But I cut her off. I had no time or patience to listen to more wild talk about boys appearing by magic and rocks bleeding. 'I'm sure Father Guthlac's reason will be restored by morning,' I told her firmly. 'He may even be able to tell us who the child is and where he lives.'

When I ventured out into the courtyard I walked the long way around so that I could pass beneath the casements of the infirmary. I stood for a few moments outside listening, but all seemed quiet within. The rain had eased into a fine wet mist, but the wind dashed it so hard against my skin that I was soaked before I'd reached the door of the lodgings that were reserved for highborn guests and clergy. I tucked stray strands of wet hair beneath my black veil, hoping I did not look quite as bedraggled as I felt.

Inside, two men were seated at either side of the table, fishing rabbits' legs from a dish of egurdouce, and gnawing them so voraciously that I would have sworn they had not eaten for a week. They clambered to their feet as I closed the door behind me, wiping the thick wine sauce from their fingers to their napkins and inclining their heads somewhat curtly.

'I am Knight Brother Nicholas, late of Buckland,' the older of the two said.

He had the appearance of one who had been forged of steel, not flesh, from the silver-grey of his close-cropped hair and the stubble on his chin, to the hard, angular bones of his face and rigid stance. I suspected that though his knee might bend when he prayed to God, his back never would. A single glance at his hard-muscled frame and corded neck told me he had known battle.

'This is Brother Sergeant Alban, my groom, also late of Buckland,' he added.

The groom, a bow-legged, wiry fellow, shuffled awkwardly and glanced shrewdly up and down the length of me through narrowed eyes, as if he was appraising the worth of a horse in the marketplace.

'I heard a man shouting earlier. If someone is causing trouble, I'll soon put him to rout.' Nicholas gestured towards his sword, hanging from a peg on the wall next to his cloak.

'That will not be necessary,' I said firmly. Why do men think a sword or a bow is the answer to every problem? 'It was merely Father Guthlac. Until recently he was the parish priest here, but now, in the winter of his life, he's being cared for in the infirmary. Something distressed him, but he is usually a mild-tempered man. I doubt he will disturb you again.

'But you said you were late of Buckland, Brother Nicholas? Then I assume you are journeying to join our brothers on Rhodes. God speed you both, and grant you safe passage. But it must be a matter of some import that forces you to travel by this route. Have you a message for us?'

Even as the words left my lips, I knew the question was foolish. Neither Commander John nor the Lord Prior of England would waste the services of two members of our noble order to deliver a message that could as easily have been carried by the carter. Hob had often carried them before and, since neither he nor his son could read, they could be entrusted with letters even of a delicate nature.

'We're not bound for Rhodes, Sister,' Nicholas said, 'which I deeply regret, but for which Alban here is profoundly grateful. He doesn't lust for the sea as his mistress, do you, Brother?' He jabbed at the groom's stomach with the point of a knife still dripping with red wine sauce.

The groom scowled and muttered something under his breath, but all the while his gaze kept darting back to the plate of rabbit, like a starving ferret.

'This is our journey's end, Sister,' Nicholas announced with a cold smile. 'The Lord Prior of England has commanded us to serve the order here in the Priory of St Mary. I have come to relieve you of the heavy responsibilities you have had to bear. You need have no more anxieties. I shall take charge now.'

Chapter 4

Hospitallers' Priory of St Mary

The fire spat petulantly in the hearth and the wind rattled the door and shutters, but even these sounds were less deafening than the chilling silence that had descended upon the guest chamber after Brother Nicholas's announcement. The speech he had been rehearsing ever since they had set off had withered on his tongue before he'd uttered a single word of it.

The summons to attend his commander at Buckland had filled him with elation. The arrival of two new brothers from Clerkenwell was a sign that two of the existing brothers were to be moved on, and Nicholas had prayed, with considerably more devotion than he had for many years, that he would be one of them.

All the men at Buckland grumbled that they had become little more than servants and bodyguards to the sisters of the Knights of St John, who complained almost daily about the brothers allowing their livestock to wander on to the sisters' land or not providing them with the provisions or wine they claimed they were entitled to either in sufficient quantity or

34

quality. Nicholas would have been eternally grateful never to spend another moment in the company of those demanding harpies.

He was aching to return to the Citramer, to be back in the fight against the Saracens, with the blood and sweat of battle in his nostrils, hoofs thundering beneath him, and on either side his brother knights, their mouths roaring death, their eyes shining. He longed to be sitting round the fires at night reliving the glory, his belly full of good wine, the smell of roasting meats mingling with the scents of rose, amber and musk, which clung to the skin long after aching muscles had been soothed by silent, dark-eyed maids.

So certain had he been that he was to be sent back to Rhodes that Commander John had been obliged to repeat his instructions twice before Nicholas had grasped them. His fellow knight was indeed to set sail, but Nicholas had served far longer in the Citramer than most, and fighting in that heat took its toll on the body.

'Let young blood fight the Saracens,' Commander John had said. 'The order has a far more subtle and insidious enemy to defeat here in England, one that threatens our very existence. Think of it as a mission behind enemy lines,' he had added, with a smile. 'The task will be simple for a man of your talents and it will take no time at all. And if you succeed, as you surely will,' he spread his hands, 'then Lord Prior William will undoubtedly wish to send you back to Rhodes, not as a fighting man this time but as a commander. And, believe me, Brother Nicholas, you will need all your wits and cunning to uphold the English cause there among all those knights of France. Prove your talents in this matter, Brother, and you will rise.'

Nicholas's dealings with the sisters at Minchin Buckland

35

had led him to believe that flattery, combined with his authority as a man and a knight, was the best way of handling women, and with fifty noble, literate but bored sisters pitted against seven overworked and harassed brothers, it was his only weapon. But his commander had assured him that managing the eight women who were alone up here on these remote moors would be as easy as bridling a well-schooled mare. The sisters would be overjoyed to have two men to protect them.

Commander John had nudged him in the ribs and winked. 'Next time I see you, Brother, you'll be twice your girth. They'll be falling over each other to make sure you have the tastiest dishes and softest linen.'

His commander had been right about the food: the rabbit in egurdouce, which was even now congealing in the dish, was delicious, but the expression on the prioress's face told him she was as far from overjoyed as it was possible to be.

Prioress Johanne was a small, neat woman with a straight, narrow nose, and startlingly vivid blue eyes, rendered all the more piercing by the black veil that covered her hair and hung in damp folds at either side of her sharp cheekbones. She held her head so upright, that her neck, not covered by any wimple, seemed to elongate even as he watched. Steam was rising from her wet clothes in the heat of the small room, so that she looked like some avenging spectre rising from a tomb.

'Here!' she finally spat at him. 'And precisely what do you intend to take charge of here?'

Alban dropped back into his chair, making clear that he wanted no part in this conversation by stuffing his mouth with large sops of bread dipped into the rich sauce.

Nicholas's belly was rumbling and he had to fight hard

to drag his gaze from the dish. Couldn't the woman have given them an hour or so to eat before she had burst in? 'Sister Johanne, my orders—'

'Prioress,' she said, enunciating each syllable in a voice as brittle as ice.

He ploughed on, ignoring the interruption. He was damned if he was going to allow her to correct him like some errant schoolboy. 'I am ordered to take over the stewardship of the priory and to oversee the running of—'

'Sister Clarice is our steward. I can assure you that she is more than equal to the task, having run her husband's warehouses and estates for many years before making her profession. She has never once failed to collect the produce and rents owing to this priory, nor, as I am sure the Lord Prior would be the first to acknowledge, failed to deliver a perfect reckoning to Clerkenwell. I shall compose a letter to the Lord Prior and Commander John, which you may deliver to Buckland, thanking them for their care, but explaining we have no need to deprive the order of the valuable services of two brothers who, I am sure, are needed to serve in the fleet.'

Nicholas could contain himself no longer. He reached over to the pot in front of Alban and stabbed one of the rabbit's legs savagely with the point of his knife. He dragged it out, tearing at the flesh with his teeth and gulping it down. He took a certain satisfaction in watching a spasm of disgust and annoyance flash across Johanne's brow. *You can stamp and frown as much as you please, Mistress, but this is a battle I am going to win.* When he had finally stripped the leg of its meat, he waggled the bare bone at her. 'Your sister may have found it easy enough to collect the rents and tithes in times past, but the longer people stay hungry, the more obdurate they'll become. It'll take more than the pretty face of a woman and her sweet tongue to persuade them to hand over what they owe. Believe me, Prioress, half the commanderies across England cannot raise enough to send the responsions that are due to Rhodes.'

'If, on your own admission, our brothers in the other commanderies have not persuaded their tenants to pay their rents, whereas we have, it must be self-evident that Sister Clarice's "sweet tongue" has proved considerably more effective than those of our brother knights. Perhaps you would like Sister Clarice to give them some instruction on how it should be done.'

An angry flush spread across Nicholas's cheeks. 'And perhaps you would like to read the Lord Prior's direct orders, Prioress.'

He snapped his fingers at the groom, who reluctantly laid down the bone he was gnawing and fumbled in a leather scrip, finally thrusting a roll of parchment into the knight's hand. Nicholas slid it across the table towards Johanne. 'I take it you are familiar with Lord William's seal and signature.'

The prioress unrolled the parchment using only the tips of her fingers, as if she was handling a soiled arse-rag. As her gaze marched over the letters, Nicholas watched the muscles of her jaw clench so tightly that he fancied he could hear her teeth splintering.

'I am sure I need not remind you that you and your sisters have taken a sacred vow of obedience, as have I, and we are all subject to the Lord Prior's rule.'

Johanne's blue eyes glinted as cold as winter ice. 'And may I remind you, Brother Nicholas, that prioresses, unlike commanders, are not appointed by the Lord Prior but elected by their own sisters.'

Nicholas slammed his fist on the table, jolting Alban's elbow so that the sauce-soaked bread he was about to pop into his mouth slid half across his face. He wiped it on the napkin, cursing under his breath and darting furious glances at the knight.

Nicholas, trying to hold his temper in check, ignored him. 'Doubtless you are aware that the other communities of our sisters in England have been compelled to move to Minchin Buckland where they can be kept safely cloistered under one roof – all except this one. If the Lord Prior should decide to close this priory and move you to Buckland too, you would no longer be prioress. So, if you value your independence, *Sister* Johanne, you had better learn to bend your neck before it is broken for you.'

'Do you dare to threaten—'

'I make no threats, Prioress.' Nicholas held up both palms in the mocking gesture of a man who shows he is unarmed. 'I merely offer you my humble advice.' He stuffed a hunk of bread into his mouth with one hand, while pouring wine into two goblets with the other. He offered one to Johanne, who curtly refused it.

'You must forgive me, Prioress. It's been a long, cold journey and my tongue grows sharp when my backside is aching from the saddle. Years of riding in stinking, sweaty armour in the heat . . . Well, let us just say that it gives a man sores that nag at him worse than any scold who was ever sentenced to ducking.'

'I will ask Sister Basilia to make up an ointment for you.'

'Ask her if she'll rub it in for him too.' Alban chuckled.

'I'm sure Brother Nicholas does not need the assistance of a woman to find his own arsehole,' Prioress Johanne said sweetly.

Alban's jaw dropped, revealing a mouthful of half-chewed rabbit.

'I will leave you to your rest, Brothers.' Johanne inclined her head curtly. 'We will discuss this matter further in the morning.'

She stepped out into the darkness of the courtyard, pulling the door closed. She had barely taken a step when it opened again and Nicholas slipped out behind her.

He pressed himself close to her to be heard over the wind. 'I fear that we have not made the best of beginnings, Prioress, but I must obey my orders and you will find it a good deal less painful to help me to carry them out than attempt to fight me. Do I need to remind you that it's been but seven short years since the Knights Templar were first interrogated in England and their treasures plundered, even though the order had believed itself safe here? Indeed, when the perse-cutions of the Templars began nine years ago in France, many fled to England to escape the torture and burnings, believing the Inquisition would never come to these shores. But come they did. Now there is no country left on God's earth in which those heretics and sodomites may hide. I've heard men mock the Dominican Inquisitors as *Domini canes*, the hounds of God. But all good jokes are built upon a savage truth, for when hounds are in full cry they will tear to pieces any beast that crosses their path, whether or not it is their quarry.'

'And what has that to do with this priory?' Johanne said. It was too dark for Nicholas to see her expression, but her tone was as sharp as a freshly honed blade.

'Since the Pope gave so many of the Templar lands to our order, there are rumours that the greedy eyes of the kings are now turning towards us. If they attack us, they will gain the lands and property of both orders at a single stroke. Our

Lord Prior is determined to ensure they have no excuse to cast us into the same prisons where so many Templar knights lost their lives. He has eyes everywhere, searching for the smallest spark of corruption, heresy or sorcery in his order, and if he suspects so much as a glimmer of it, he'll grind the guilty beneath his boot before they can ignite a blaze that will burn us all on the heretics' pyre.'

'Are you suggesting—' Johanne began indignantly.

'I suggest nothing. I merely wish to remind you that the sisters from the other priories were not gathered together in Minchin Buckland merely for their safety but to ensure that no whisper of scandal attaches itself to them.'

'Because they are the weaker sex?' she said. 'Have you forgotten, Brother Nicholas? It was the *Knights* Templar who stood accused of immorality and heresy, not their sisters.'

He spread his hands. 'As you say, Prioress, the weaker sex. And a fortress is only as strong as its weakest wall. As every defender knows, that is the wall you must shore up first.'

'Don't you mean shut up?' the Prioress snapped.

A satisfied smile creased the corners of the knight's mouth. The arrow had struck its mark. 'Sleep well, sweet Sister,' he murmured, as he strode back into the darkness.

Chapter 5

Sorrel

I must have been six or seven days upon the road when I finally met the one she'd sent to guide me. Now that I think on it, he was a strange one to send, for he didn't even realise he was her messenger. No more did I, at first.

I'd been searching for a place to shelter for the night, for though I couldn't see the sun behind the leaden clouds, the grey light was fading and bedraggled black rooks were massing in a small coppice of trees around me. Dusk was swiftly approaching. My legs ached and I was dizzy with hunger. While I still had enough daylight to see and strength left, I had to build a fire and cook the few wild worts I had been able to glean from beside the track as I'd trudged through the rain. If I didn't, I'd simply sink down in the mud and fall asleep, no longer caring whether I ever struggled up again.

But just when I despaired of finding shelter, I emerged from the trees and saw a drovers' hut and pinfold a little way off the track. The pinfold was no more than a clearing of sodden earth and mildewed weeds, surrounded by a broad bank. A stone trough stood in one corner, fed by a spring that flowed out of the bank and spilled over on to muddy stones beneath. By the look of it, no sheep or cattle had been driven this way for many a month – part of the bank had fallen away and one of the walls of the tiny wattle hut, which huddled next to it, had blown in. Still, half a shelter was better than none, and I'd little fear that any drover would be needing it. Since the famine had taken hold, few had any beasts left to sell and those that still lived were so weak they could scarcely be driven a mile to market without collapsing.

The earth floor of the hut was slimy and wet, but at least the roof gave some protection from the wind and rain. I wedged the sagging wattle wall upright, as best I could, and gathered a few stones to set a fire on. With my flint and iron and few precious wisps of dried flax, I managed to get a flame burning and tried to coax it into a blaze, but the wood I had gleaned along the way was so damp that the fire gave more smoke than flame. I set my pot of water and worts over it, but there was scarcely enough heat to warm my numb fingers, much less the iron pot. For the hundredth time since I'd set out, I asked myself why I'd left my village. I'd precious little there but at least I'd slept warm and dry.

I didn't know where I was going or even where I was. A week ago, that hadn't seemed to matter, for by the time I'd left the riverbank that morning, I'd had only one thought in my head – that I must go. It was all I could do to stop myself running straight out of the village and keep running until my legs could no longer move. Had I finally gone mad? Yet I knew I would go mad if I didn't follow that voice. I felt like a dog barking itself into a frenzy and leaping against the chain, almost choking itself in its desperation to break free and reach the one who was calling it.

I'd gone straight from the river to my father's cottage and bundled the few things I would need to survive into a small iron cooking pot that had once belonged to my mother. My father was, as usual, dozing by the fire. He grunted and cursed me as I tiptoed about gathering what I needed. He didn't open his eyes to see if it was me who had disturbed his rest. But for once his curses made me smile. I'd been raised on them, weaned on his scorn, you might say. It was almost comforting to hear the old goat swear at me for the last time. It was like a parting kiss or a dying blessing. For I was determined that, even if I starved or froze on the road, nothing would make me return.

My father constantly told neighbours and strangers alike that he should have smothered me when I was a babe, as soon as it became plain that my left arm, which had been wrenched from its socket when I was dragged from the womb, would never mend right. I can move it a little, use the back to help balance things, but there's no strength in it. My hand hangs withered and useless, like a rosebud that's been half broken off its stem.

When I was little, I would try to pull my arm off when no one was looking. It felt as if it didn't belong to me, as though the limb of some dead animal had been sewn on to my body. But at other times it seemed almost alive, a giant leech that had fastened on to my shoulder. It was swelling, bloated and full of blood, while the rest of my body shrank and shrivelled, like a dry leaf. I'd tear at the arm, bite it and scream till I was exhausted. But no matter how I hated it, I couldn't rid myself of it. I'd found out, earlier than most, that crying changes nothing.

And I'd learned to do with one hand what other women could do with two, including take care of my brother and the old goat, which I'd done ever since he'd driven poor Mam into her grave.

I'd turned in the doorway and watched my father scratch his belly in his sleep. He'd stir himself when my brother trudged home from the fields. They'd sit, the pair of them, either side of the hearth, drinking ale and grumbling about why their supper wasn't ready. I wondered how long they would wait before hunger drove either of them to look for me. And how many days would pass before they realised I wasn't coming back.

I wouldn't return, but where was I going? Ever since I'd left the village, the voice that had been calling to me so insistently had stayed silent, and the dreams I'd had in the few brief hours of sleep I could snatch, huddled in the wind and rain, were not of fire and flowing springs, but of Mam sitting on the threshold of our cottage in the summer sun, plucking pigeons. I was exhausted, soaked and starving, traipsing through mud and rain to reach some place I knew not where or why. What had I done?

I stirred the iron pot. The water was beginning to steam a little, but even if the wood burned long enough to soften the handful of blighted leaves and roots, I knew they wouldn't ease the hunger pains for long, probably only make them worse. And if I became too weak to walk . . . *Help me. Speak to me. Show me where to go.* I closed my eyes, trying to hear her voice. But the only sounds were the dripping of rain from the sodden thatch and the hissing of the wind. Even the rooks had fallen silent.

It was then that I heard the noise, not the voice in my head, but something outside. A distant clanging and clattering, like a ghost dragging chains. I shrank back. Mam used to tell me tales of tatter-foals that haunted lonely tracks

45

after dark, demons who took the guise of wild, shaggy horses and frightened travellers into bogs with their creaking and rattling, or else swept them on to their backs and carried them into lakes to drown them. Heart pounding, I peered out through the broken wattle and in the witch light saw a monstrous creature crawling down the track. I couldn't make out what it was at first, but then I laughed. It was nothing more than an ancient, swollen-kneed donkey ambling past. The noise came not from the poor beast, but from the shovels and picks strung from the wooden cradle on its sway-back.

Someone was leading the animal, though I couldn't see him clearly until he seemed to spot the drovers pen' and stepped off the track towards it. The donkey stubbornly resisted, until it caught sight of the water trough and bolted towards it, almost ripping the leading rope from his master's hands and rattling the tools so violently that the rooks flapped up from their night roost, cawing in alarm.

The man looked as if he'd not slept beneath a roof for weeks. His hair hung in long matted rats' tails and his clothes were so patched and dirty I reckoned even his lice had gone off to beg for alms. I'd have taken him for a beggar if it hadn't been for his donkey and all his tools.

Would he come to the hut? I pulled my knife from the sheath on my belt and held it ready to defend myself, though it was scarcely much of a weapon. My first thought was to slip out while he was occupied with watering the donkey, but the possessions I'd been carrying in the pot lay heaped in the corner, and my supper was just beginning to boil. I was ravenous. If I didn't get something hot inside me, I was afraid I'd not survive another night out in the cold and rain. I couldn't bring myself to tip it away. Besides, I had found the hut first: why should I give it up to him?

But if he did mean me harm, I daren't risk being trapped. If he chose to block the doorway, I'd never get past him. Leaving the pot simmering over the sulky fire, I crept out and crouched behind the bank.

The donkey, having drunk his fill, had turned his attention to the sparse patches of rank weeds and his master was sitting with his back to me on the side of the trough, pulling off his tattered boots. With a squeal of protest, followed by a sigh of relief, he dipped his blistered feet into the cold water. Mud and grass drifted from his filthy soles. But something else rose slowly to the surface. It was a single purple-red flower. It was crushed almost beyond recognition inside his boot, but I knew it, and it made my spine tingle. Hound's-tongue.

Come! Come to me.

He dried his feet on a bit of rag, then thrust them back into his worn boots. Without even a glance in my direction, he dragged the protesting donkey over to the more sheltered part of the pinfold and tethered it there, then edged towards the drovers' hut with a wariness that matched my own. He stood a few paces off and sniffed the air. The smell of wood smoke mingled with boiling worts gusted over the bank. His fingers slid to the hilt of the knife in his belt, as mine had done. But I sensed he was more afraid of being attacked than intending to do another harm. He glanced back at the donkey. Would he retreat and journey on?

The time is now. Follow. Follow.

'You're welcome to share my fire for the night, Master.' The words were out before I even knew I would utter them. *She* had sent him and I couldn't let him walk away.

He jerked round. His gaze darted to the knife in my hand, but instead of raising his own as most would have done, he

47

shuffled backwards a few paces. I slid my blade back into its sheath and gestured towards the hut.

He still hesitated, as if he feared I was leading him into a trap, but finally a broad grin split his long, thin face. 'Kindly offered, Mistress, and I'll not offend you by refusing. My friends call me Todde. I'll not trouble to tell you what my enemies call me,' he added, with a chuckle, 'for a woman with such a generous nature could never be one of them.'

It was only as I led the man across the muddy pen that I realised what I had done. I hadn't enough to fill my own belly, never mind his, and so little wood that the fire would surely die away before the hour had passed, if it hadn't already. Suppose he became angry and thought I had tricked him.

As soon as he entered, Todde crouched, pressing himself as close as any man could to the miserable fire as if he meant to suck all the heat from it. He stank like an old wet dog that had rolled inside the carcass of a rotting pig. He pulled out a battered wooden bowl from somewhere inside his jerkin and I tipped some of the herb broth into it. I found myself giving him a bigger share than remained in the pot for me, for Mam had always given the menfolk the largest portion of any food to be had, and I had learned to do the same. I felt a flash of resentment towards him and anger at my own foolishness. The few mouthfuls I had of the watery broth made my stomach cry out louder than ever. What had possessed me to invite this stranger to my fireside?

But when he had devoured every last drop, Todde rubbed his belly and, grinning, offered me his thanks. I stared at him slack-jawed: I'd never heard any man thank a woman in my life, much less me.

We sat in awkward silence for a while, rubbing our wind-chapped hands over the dying embers. Times had been hard for everyone since last year's harvest failed, and what precious seed had been saved for planting had rotted in the sodden earth or been gobbled by mice and birds that were as hungry as we were. Some folks from my village, the freemen, had packed up their families and left for the towns to see what work they could find. Most drifted back, saying it was even worse there. They'd been forced to sleep in graveyards and doorways – they couldn't find enough work pagging loads for merchants or scavenging bones for the lime-makers even to put food in their children's bellies, much less have any left to buy shelter for the night. They said the pilgrims' halls in the monasteries were full to bursting, and so many crowded to the alms windows when a dole of bread or broken meats was to be had that the food ran out long before those at the back could fight their way near enough to reach it. Many now tramped from village to village in the desperate search for work or to beg food. I guessed that Todde was simply another.

He scratched his armpit. 'Where are you bound, lass?'

I shrugged. It sounded foolish to say I didn't know and worse still to ask a stranger if he could tell me.

'Hunger driven you on the roads, has it? Aye, I've seen a good many along the tracks in search of food and work. But seeing as you treated me so kindly, I'll let you into a secret that'll serve you well.'

He lowered his voice, looking round with great exaggeration as if he was about to reveal where a crock of gold was hidden, though he could have stood on the middle of the pinfold and shouted it – there was no one, save me, to hear him.

'The King's decreed that any man has the right to look for tin on anyone's land as he pleases, without let or hindrance. There's not a sheriff or lord in the land can stop a tinner digging wherever he's a notion to, even if the land belongs to the Archbishop of Canterbury himself. But see now, it's pointless just searching anywhere. In most places a man could dig for a year and not find enough to make a sheath for a mouse's pizzle. But I know of a place where such quantities of tin lie just beneath the sod that a man can make his fortune as easily as scooping up coins spilled from a sack.'

'So where is this place of riches? Up there in the clouds with the angels, is it?' I said. My aching belly and light head were making me irritable. How could this help me? Had *she* really sent him or had the hound's-tongue been nothing more than a crushed flower that might be found in the shoes of a hundred pedlars, beggars and pilgrims to ward off savage dogs?

Todde grinned. 'You'd think you really *were* in Heaven if you saw the place. For with less digging than it takes to plant a row of beans, a man can become as wealthy as a lord. All you have to do is make a trench, then let water from a stream wash through it to sweep away the worthless gravel and leave the heavy tin. Then you pick it up, like you were gathering eggs from a hen's nest.'

Todde shuffled on his backside a little closer to me, and I found myself rocking away from his sour breath. 'It's where I'm bound right now,' he said. 'They call it Dertemora.' He frowned, then chuckled, striking his head with a palm. 'Whatever put that word on my tongue? Rain has rotted my wits. Dartmoor, that's the place.'

The fire smouldering on the stones burst up in a blaze, the flames clawing so high I was afraid they would set the hut ablaze, but Todde seemed not to notice. A shimmering ribbon of molten ruby gushed out from a brand and flowed down into the heart of the fire as if a spring was spouting from a rock.

Fire and water wait for you.

The voice was so clear, I thought someone was standing behind me. I whipped round, but the doorway was empty. And when I looked back at the fire it was no more than the heap of smouldering embers it had been a few moments before. But I knew. In that moment, I knew that this was the place I had to reach.

Todde was still talking: '. . . soon as word spreads every Jack and Jill in the country will be heading up to those moors to claim the richest seams. So, you want to get yourself there as fast as you can.'

'Have you not eyes to see?' I snapped. Lifting my withered arm, I let the useless hand dangle in the glow of the dying fire.

'Aye, I saw it,' he said softly, and a spasm of what might have been pain flickered over his face, as if it was his own arm that was hurt.

'So!' I demanded furiously, angry with him for making me show my arm, like some whining beggar. 'Even if I was to find a seam, how would I keep it, much less work it? With strapping men desperate to make their fortune, even a woman with two good arms couldn't hold a claim against them, especially if there's no law against any man digging where he wants.'

'Maybe you couldn't. But I reckon there must be more wants doing in a tinners' camp than digging. Same as reaping the grain. There's some that scythe and some that gather, tie and stook the sheaves, and others that keep all the hands fed. Haven't you noticed the pedlars and merchants haven't

51

been coming to the villages these past months? They know there's few can afford their prices now. I reckon they must all be flocking to sell whatever they have on Dartmoor, for that's the only place where men have money enough to buy. They live off the fat of the land, those tinners.'

A sly smile creased the corners of his mouth. 'But, now, here's the thing. When those tinners come back after a long day's work bone-weary, their bellies roaring for food, they'll not want to go out again to find wood for the fire, fetch water or pluck a chicken. They'll want a good hot meal on the table afore their backsides touch their stools.'

Todde nudged my cooking pot with the toe of his mud-caked boot. 'If they're earning a king's ransom, I reckon there's a fair few who'd be willing to part with a good measure of it to someone who could put hot food in their bellies night and morn, and maybe fetch them wood enough for a warm fire to sit by of an evening.'

I stared into the ash of my tiny fire. Now that the heat was gone the wind, blowing through every broken slat in the walls, sliced bone-deep through my wet kirtle. I couldn't remember how it felt to wear dry clothes. The rain never stopped. If what Todde had said was true, there would be dry dwellings, blazing fires and good food where a host of men and women were tinning. Fetching and cooking for tinners couldn't be worse than tending my father and brother, and I'd be paid in coin, not curses, for my trouble. If I tried to survive on the road alone, I'd soon be too weak from hunger and cold to continue searching. If she was calling me to this place, then surely she was showing me a way to live. With food in my belly and warm shelter each night, I could continue to search for her and I would find her. I had to.

Chapter 6

Hospitallers' Priory of St Mary

Brother Nicholas was dreaming that he was struggling in the sea, trying desperately to swim to the shore, but seagulls were attacking him, diving at him, pecking at his eyes, and shrieking loud enough to make his ears bleed. He jerked awake and the birds vanished, but their cries did not. It took a few moments for his fogged brain to remember where he was and even longer to grasp that the noise was coming from the courtyard outside, and they were not the cries of gulls but of women.

He groped for his cloak, which he'd laid over the bed for extra warmth, stumbled to the door and dragged it open. He peered out cautiously. The courtyard was crowded with people standing in small groups staring at the far end, though what was arousing their interest he was unable to see without stepping on to the muddy cobbles. He realised his feet and legs were bare. He shivered.

'What hour is it?' he called, but if any heard him, no one replied.

An overexcited pedlar's dog began to herd a paddling of

squawking ducks towards him, their wings flapping wildly. Still unnerved by his dream of the gulls and not wanting the creatures to invade his chamber, he slammed the door and sank into a chair. The chamber was freezing. The fire was nothing more than ashes, and there was no sign of any servant bearing breakfast or even water in which to wash his face.

He had overslept, and the burning in his belly, the sour taste in his mouth and dull headache convinced him that the cause was too much strong wine on a stomach that had been far from lined with solid food: by the time Nicholas had returned to the guest chamber, Alban had devoured every fragment of rabbit and every morsel of bread. There wasn't even a spoonful of sauce left in the pot.

In a foul temper, Nicholas had clambered into the narrow bed with the intention of rising early to question the old priest in the infirmary before he tackled the prioress again and began the tedious process of examining the priory's ledgers. Commander John had told him that the procurator at Clerkenwell was convinced there was something wrong with the account records he was receiving from the priory, not that he could put his finger on what was amiss. Nicholas had been ordered to ferret it out, whatever *it* might be.

He already had a shrewd suspicion of what he might uncover. Farmers and millers always tried to hide the true worth of their land and stock, so they could pay less rent and hand over fewer beasts and sacks of flour. It was the same the world over – Cyprus, Rhodes, England: the local people tried to cheat the order if they could. But a seemingly casual gossip with a long-serving parish priest might enable Nicholas to discover a little more about the true value of the lands, properties and livestock in those parts and the real wealth of the priory's tenants. Old men were always willing to talk for hours if they could find someone interested enough to listen, and Nicholas was interested.

Women were easily gulled and too soft-hearted. He'd wager his own horse that the farmers were handing their coins to Sister Clarice and rubbing their hands in glee that she was fool enough to charge them a fraction of what they should have paid. Little wonder she found it easy to collect the rents. Well, the tenants' days of ease were over. A seasoned knight was in charge now, and those thieving hands were about to be chopped off.

Nicholas plucked his hose from the crumpled heap of clothes and, with a shudder, tried to pull them on. They were still wet and stinking from the journey. He badly needed a fresh pair, but he couldn't see where his clothes chest had been put. Hob had plainly not troubled to unload the cart, and Alban had lacked the wit to retrieve his personal possessions from among the provisions.

It had been the journey from Hell. It had rained without ceasing, numbing limbs and faces, while the wind, slashing through their sodden clothes, had stung like salt on a flayed back. The loaded wagon had repeatedly become mired in the twisting ribbon of calf-deep mud that Hob had called a road. Both Nicholas and Alban had been obliged to dismount to help free it and they'd no sooner have it rolling forward again than it would start sliding back down the hillside or a wheel would become wedged behind a stone buried in the ooze.

Once they were up on the moors, they'd no longer been able to make night-camp for fear that the light from the fire would bring every outlaw in those parts swarming to them, like flies to a corpse. This shire was reputed to be one of the most lawless in England. Its inhabitants thought themselves so far from the sheriff's men in Exeter that they could rob and murder as they pleased and never be caught. Even the white *cross formée* on the breast of a knight's black cloak was no protection, these days. All the Hospitallers' garb meant to any man in England now was rich pickings.

Then, finally, as they had breasted a rise, Hob had stopped the wagon and pointed through the driving rain to where three or four tiny red dots hung somewhere in the darkness, suspended between Heaven and Hell. 'That,' he had announced, with grim satisfaction, 'is your new home, Masters, and may God have mercy on your souls.' He'd crossed himself. 'I hope you're praying men, Brothers, 'cause you'll need more than a sword to protect you up there. Other side of that priory stands the most accursed hill on the whole moor. Old 'uns called it Fire Tor, but some call it Ghost Tor. You can hear the dead whispering among those rocks. Hungry ghosts, they are. There's many has heard them talking, and some even followed the voices into the caves up there. Followed them in, Brothers, but never came out, for once you cross into the deadlands, there's no coming back.'

Nicholas shivered as he dragged his damp, mud-caked shirt over his head and struggled to thrust his arms through the clinging sleeves. He was still wrestling with his jerkin when Alban sauntered in, dragging a blast of cold air with him.

'It's well you're dressed,' the groom observed.

Nicholas grunted. 'In sodden clothes! Where's my chest? Hasn't that idle carter and his frog-witted son unloaded it yet? Go and chase them, and while you're about it, tell one of those servants to fetch me some breakfast, a good one too, seeing that I didn't get any supper.' He glowered at Alban.

The groom was leaning against the door, scraping mud from under his nails with the point of his knife. He was a scrawny, ferret-faced man, indifferent to people, but there wasn't a horse he couldn't calm and control in spite of having lost, as a lad, his left forefinger and half of the middle one to a badger cub. He didn't bother to look up until Nicholas drew breath.

'Be lucky to get anything to eat this side of noon,' he said morosely. 'All the servants and sisters are outside, chattering like a flock of starlings. There'll not be a peck of work done this day by my reckoning.'

'And the prioress allows this?' Nicholas said incredulously. If this was how the priory was run, then Johanne would find herself in a cloister in Buckland before the month was out.

'I reckon she's more to fret over than the servants just now. There's been a death, one of the patients in the infirmary.'

'So? That can hardly be anything unusual. Does work cease every time someone dies?'

'Aye, well, if the gossip in the courtyard is to be believed, it's not death that's unusual but the manner of it. There's some out there whispering *sorcery*.' A sly grin crept across Alban's face. It was not often he could render the knight speechless and he was evidently relishing the moment.

In spite of his thumping headache, chilled body, raging thirst and general ill-humour, a prickle of excitement and fear coursed down Nicholas's spine. He'd been sent to uncover financial mismanagement, but now it seemed there might

57

be a whole mess of corruption to be exposed. He grabbed his still-damp cloak and hurried out into the courtyard.

It was easy to guess which door led into the infirmary from the gaggle of people clustered around it. He forced his way through them and flung open the door. Prioress Johanne spun round, surprise and anger darkening her face as she saw who had entered.

The room was long and plain, save for a wall painting of the Blessed Virgin over the doorway, staring down with a dispassionate gaze. A fire blazed in the hearth in the centre of the floor. The reeds of the thatch above were blackened with smoke, which drifted among the rafters in sluggish grey clouds until it found its own way out. A row of narrow, but high beds were ranged down the length of one wall, each divided from its neighbour by a wooden partition to keep out the draughts. A scrubbed table and benches stood on the opposite side of the hearth, while an assortment of rough wooden stools, copper lavers and small iron-banded chests crowded together in the corners of the room. A screen woven from rushes had been set in front of a bed in the far corner. Nicholas could hear faint moans and whimpers coming from behind it. Evidently one patient was too ill to be moved, unlike the others: the rest of the beds were empty, the covers thrown back in disarray as if the occupants had been dragged out in haste.

Nicholas was puzzled. Many came to the infirmaries of St John in the hope of making a good death, and life carried on around them as they died. Indeed, it was right and fitting that it should, for it helped others prepare their souls for what must come to every man and to search their consciences for the answers to questions that would be asked of them in their final confessions. Why had these patients been removed?

Prioress Johanne and two more sisters of the order were standing close to the only other bed that appeared to be occupied, though Nicholas could not immediately see who was lying there. The plumper of the two sisters took a step towards him, as if she intended to shoo him out, but the prioress caught her sleeve and gave a slight shake of her head.

Nicholas strode towards them. 'I understand that one of your patients has died, Sisters. Brother Alban said . . .' He hesitated. Remembering the grin on Alban's face, he was suddenly afraid of sounding foolish. Suppose the groom had been joking. It wasn't something any normal man would find funny, but Alban had a twisted sense of humour.

Johanne moved, blocking Nicholas's path. 'There is no need for you to trouble yourself. As you say, the man is dead. The sisters will prepare the body for burial. Brengy, the stable boy, has been sent to the village to warn the sexton and Deacon Wybert to prepare for burial. All is in hand,' she said briskly. She gave a cold smile and took another pace forward, as if trying to ease Nicholas out of the door. But he stepped around her and, in a few strides, was at the bed.

The linen sheet had been drawn up to cover the face of the body lying beneath. After a lifetime of war, Nicholas was hardly a man to shrink from the sight of a corpse. He whisked back the sheet, exposing the gaunt face. An elderly man was lying on his back, his clawed hands raised to either side of his face, as if he had been trying desperately to push something or someone away. His milky eyes were wide open and his neck arched. His mouth gaped in a silent scream and his wrinkled face was contorted in an expression Nicholas could only describe as pure terror. He had seen such horror frozen on the faces of women and men who had been shrieking for mercy even as the fatal blow descended, from a knight's sword or a Turks' scimitar, but never on an old man who had died peacefully in his bed.

As he had done many times for his brothers slain on the battlefield, Nicholas grasped the wrists, intending to pull the arms down and cross them as a Christian should lie in death, but they were rigid, unyielding as stone, the flesh so cold it made his fingers sting to touch it. He snatched his hands away with a gasp. 'He's been dead for hours. Why was he left like this? Surely you know that a body stiffens and then it is impossible to straighten it. Who was watching these patients through the night?'

'That is the puzzle,' Johanne said softly. 'Father Guthlac has *not* been dead for hours.'

Nicholas stared at her. 'This is the parish priest? But I wanted to talk to him. You didn't tell me last evening that he was dying.'

'I had no reason to think that he was,' Johanne said. 'He was restless throughout the night, unusually so. Sister Basilia and Sister Melisene both went to comfort and calm him at different times, not least because the other patients in the hospital were distressed by his cries. Father Guthlac fell quiet in the darkest hour before dawn, and it was thought he was sleeping, but when dawn broke, he was discovered . . .'

'I found him like this, Brother,' Basilia said. Her plump hands were trembling and her eyes were red, as if she'd been crying. 'He was having terrible nightmares, but he had no fever or sickness, did he?' She turned in appeal to Melisene, who nodded silently.

'I tried to straighten his body. I made to close his mouth and cross his arms, but he was as stiff then as he is now, and cold as iron. There is no explaining it. The fire's been burning

60

all night and his is one of the closest beds to it, in consideration of his age, and he'd good thick coverings.'

'There's one explanation,' Melisene muttered.

'And one I do not wish to hear repeated, Sister Melisene,' Johanne snapped.

'What's this?' Nicholas demanded. 'If the sister knows what has caused this unnatural death, I insist on hearing it.'

'Father Guthlac was old, blind and frail. There is nothing unnatural—'

Nicholas pointedly turned his back to the prioress, raising his voice above hers. 'Come, Sister, what is it you wish to tell us?' He laid his hand on Melisene's shoulder in what he imagined to be a reassuring and encouraging gesture. She backed away in alarm, gazing in mute appeal at Johanne.

'Very well,' Johanne said. 'I dare say you will hear the rumours, anyway. Last evening a blind child was found abandoned in the chapel. When he was brought into the infirmary Father Guthlac became upset. As I said, he was an elderly man, and the old often become agitated by the slightest change around them. He was given a sleeping draught to soothe him.'

'Am I to understand he was poisoned with the sleeping draught, given too much or the wrong herb was administered?'

'I gave it to him and I've never made a mistake with my simples,' Basilia protested indignantly.

'It was the boy who did this,' Melisene blurted out. 'Father Guthlac said if we let him stay under our roof, he'd destroy us. Destroy us all! Those were his very words. And that boy was tormenting the poor old priest all night long. Punishing that sweet, holy man for speaking out God's truth.'

Nicholas stared down at the priest's corpse, the face still

contorted in terror. 'So, Alban was right,' he breathed. 'It was sorcery!'

'It was no such thing,' Johanne said firmly, glaring at Melisene. 'Brother, you are a learned man and you surely cannot believe that a frightened blind child, who cannot utter so much as a single word, much less a curse, would have the power to murder a priest when he wasn't even in the same room. The child is helpless. He cannot even find his bed unaided or feed himself without his hands being guided to the dish. Father Guthlac had become agitated, a state well known to bring about convulsions in those who are frail. Look at the way his neck is arched. That is doubtless why the body is so rigid.'

Nicholas eyed the corpse doubtfully. 'If this priest was indeed seized by a convulsion that is yet further evidence that *maleficia* is at work. The innocent are often thrown to the ground in such fits by evil spirits conjured by a sorcerer or a witch in order to prevent them from speaking the truth. I must examine the boy for myself.'

'I forbid you to do any such thing, Brother Nicholas.' The prioress's voice reverberated through the silent hall, like a watchman's horn. 'The child has been abandoned and appears to have only recently lost his sight. He is terrified. Interrogating him over matters of which he can know nothing will only frighten him still further. Besides,' she said, lowering her voice, 'any attempt to question him would be useless. As I have told you, he cannot speak.'

She took a deep breath, as if she was trying to hold her anger in check. 'You told me last night that the Lord Prior is anxious that nothing is spread abroad which could be used by those who seek to destroy the Knights of St John. The parish priest, Father Guthlac, was a good man, but the old

62

often lapse into strange fancies. I've known some who thought their own children were trying to murder them or that their wife was their mother. When men are dying their wits may flee their heads long before their souls depart their bodies. But I fear that if Father Guthlac's words were repeated outside this priory by one of the servants or travellers' – she glared pointedly at Melisene – 'there are some simple and unlettered folk who would believe them. The villagers still remember Father Guthlac as he used to be and they would be only too eager to see malicious witchcraft in his death. I am sure you would agree, Brother Nicholas, it would not be in the interest of any in our order to have the name of the Hospitallers coupled with that.'

She fixed him with a stare that had been known to stay the hand of even the most drunken or violent of men. And, to his surprise, Nicholas heard himself telling the prioress he would make it known that he had examined the body, and could assure the servants Father Guthlac had died in his sleep of nothing more sinister than plain old age.

Afterwards he convinced himself he had done it for the sake of the order. Neither Commander John nor the Lord Prior would thank him if tales of murder by sorcery at a Hospitallers' priory were spread abroad. A scandal such as that could be used to bring down the Knights of St John, as it had the powerful and wealthy Templars.

On the other hand, if a private report about the true manner of the old man's death were to reach the Lord Prior at Clerkenwell, it might prove the very weapon Lord William needed to force these obdurate women into Minchin Buckland and keep them safely cloistered there till they withered and died.

What better way to prove himself worthy of returning to

Rhodes as Commander Nicholas than to save the Hospitallers from disgrace and deliver the sisters to Buckland at one stroke? It would give him great pleasure to see the prioress stripped of her rank and forced to bend the knee, very great pleasure indeed.

Chapter 7

Sorrel

Todde was walking ahead of me on the narrow moorland track, dragging his donkey through the mire and deep icy puddles, while the poor beast tried repeatedly to jerk his head rope from his master's frozen fingers and snatch at a few blades of coarse muddy grass. The teetering stack of Todde's tools and Mam's cooking pot tied to his back clinked and clanked with every step.

I stumbled after them, gazing up at the iron-dark clouds swirling around the towering rocks, the black bog pools quivering under the lash of rain, the withered, stunted trees hunched and bent like aged men against the wind. I began to wonder if the sun had ever shone on these moors or ever would. Why had I been led to such desolation? Why had I ever listened to a voice in my head? I plodded on, my mind as numb as my face and feet, no longer bothering to pick my way around the deep ruts. My shoes were already so sodden and heavy with mud that another puddle would make no difference. Besides, the moor was as wet as the track – there was no avoiding the mire wherever you trod.

My flesh had turned into cold earth. My bones had become gnarled roots. I was a corpse melting back into the soil of the grave.

Somewhere overhead a buzzard screamed, like a cat in pain, but almost at once there was another cry, this time human. Three men were running down the hillside towards Todde and the donkey, long knives flashing in their hands. Before he'd a chance to draw his own blade they were upon him. One held him from behind with a knife at his throat, as the second grabbed the leading rope of the donkey, while the third straddled the path, staring towards me and tossing his knife from hand to hand.

'Take one step closer, woman, and we'll slice his throat from ear to ear. Then we'll come for you.'

Chapter 8

Morwen

'It won't do no good,' my eldest sister, Ryana, grumbled, but she might as well have saved her breath.

When Ma had been journeying in the spirit lands she'd have to do whatever the magpie or the other creatures told her, else we'd all suffer. Leastways, that was what she said. Taegan, the middle one of us three, reckoned Ma only did what she'd already made up her mind to do, and we suffered anyway. Once, when Taegan was only ten summers old, she'd dared come right out with it and say as much. Ma thrashed her for those words till she howled worse than the ghosts on Fire Tor. The beating didn't stop her thinking it, but it taught her to keep her thoughts from Ma's sharp ears, most of the time anyway.

Ma let Ryana argue with her sometimes, though never win, for she said Ryana would become the well-keeper when Ankow came to lead her own soul to the lych-ways. She said the gift always passed to the eldest daughter, but I watched Ryana whenever she said the spirits were talking to her and I reckoned she couldn't hear anything, just pretended to.

Not that it mattered: those black crows at the priory wouldn't let her or any of us near the well since they'd built the chapel over it.

'We'll go up to the Tor three nights from now,' Ma said. 'Moon will be nine days old by then, according to my reckoning.'

The leather curtain that served as door to our cottage was pulled aside to let the grey light of morning trickle in. Rain dripping from the thatch was blowing through the gap and collecting on the earth floor in a long puddle just across the threshold.

Ryana stared at it and scowled. 'How you going to see the moon, if it's pissing like this?'

'I seen what's coming,' Ma said. 'There'll be mist, but night'll be dry enough for what needs doing.'

She squatted on the edge of her low bed. The frame was larch poles lashed together, then criss-crossed with cords. It was light enough to move close to the fire on a winter's night, and when space was needed, it could be pushed back against the low wicker partition that separated the livier, where we ate and slept, from the shippon, where the goats were bedded. Ma pulled an old sheepskin from the bed and wrapped it around her shoulders. She always felt the cold after she'd been journeying.

Whenever I came back from journeying, it was as if I was seeing everything around me through a drop of water, which made it bigger and brighter. I'd see each tiny feather on a skylark's body, even if it was flying high above me, or watch a raindrop grow fatter and fatter till all the colours of the rainbow burst inside it before it ran down a leaf. I saw each shining buttercup and stone as if for the first time, looking right into them, the colours so bright they dazzled me, the grains in the pebble so sharp, they were bigger than a rock. I longed to ask Ma if she saw these things too. I wanted to share the colours and the things I'd seen with someone who understood, but I could never tell Ma that I journeyed. I wasn't the firstborn. I had no gift, no right.

'That bread done yet, Morwen?'

I started guiltily at the sound of Ma's voice and, wrapping my hand in the edge of my kirtle, dragged the flatbread off the hot stones set round the edge of the glowing peat fire. It was scorched and crumbled into half a dozen pieces before I could tip it into Ma's lap. It was mostly pounded meadowsweet and rush roots, and they never held together like flour. But since those black crows had stolen our well, there'd been few coins pressed into Ma's withered palms, not enough to buy flour from the village mill, and what little grain we sowed turned black and rotted afore the shoots were even halfway grown.

Ryana took small, quick bites from the edges of her bread, like a sheep nibbling grass. She looked like a sheep, with thick curly hair always falling into her eyes, big yellow teeth and a long face that rarely smiled.

Ma gobbled down the bread as hungrily as if she'd been walking all night, though I knew her wizened old carcass had never left her bed. Ryana was supposed to keep watch when Ma was journeying, see that her body came to no harm, for if someone were to wake her or move her while her spirit was gone, it would never find its way back. But Ryana always fell asleep, so it was always me who watched.

Ma licked the crumbs from her fingers and frowned. 'Tae's a long time fetching that water.'

When Ma had woken, that was where I'd told her Taegan had gone, but the truth was my sister had slipped out in the night, just as soon as she thought they were both asleep. She'd be in a byre somewhere with Daveth or his brother. Tae giggled that the lads shared everything, including her. But Ma would kill her if she found out. She'd forbidden Taegan to see the brothers. There'd been a bitter feud 'twixt her granddam and theirs, and probably their granddams before that, but Ma refused to speak of the cause. Don't suppose she could even remember. Besides, Ma reckoned men were only good for one thing and that was getting a woman with child. She'd told us to keep well clear of the whole tribe and trouble of them till we wanted a babe. Ma was staring suspiciously from Ryana to me, and I knew only too well whom she'd pick on to question.

Afore Ma could speak, I leaped up and pulled a sheepskin cloak around my shoulders. 'I'll go and find Tae. Maybe she's taken a tumble, ground's so slippery.'

Go and warn her was what I really meant, else Taegan would come sauntering back, blithe as a blackbird, without the water she was supposed to be fetching. She'd get a beating, all right, but I'd get a worse one for lying to Ma.

Outside, I snatched up a couple of pails and set off towards the stream that bubbled and meandered through the high clumps of sedges and marsh grasses. Clouds rubbed around the great rocks of the tor, like fawning dogs, and swirled down between the folds of the hills. The sound of two stones being struck together echoed through the rain. But it was only a stonechat – such a great noise for such a little bird. I glanced back at our cottage.

It had been built sloping sideways on the hill, so that water and animal piss would run out through the drain hole in the lowest wall of the shippon. At the opposite end, the highest corner of the cottage was formed around a great craggy boulder that stuck out of the ground, and at the back of that, among the smaller rocks, there was a cave. You'd not see it in passing, unless you knew where to look. In good times, we kept our stores in it. But since the famine, it was mostly empty save for Ma's tools that she used for her charms – a hag-stone, a hare's foot, feathers of owls, jays and magpies, the bones and skin of a viper, the skull of a badger and many other things the beasts and birds had given her over the years.

But there were other treasures too, things only Ma and Ryana were allowed to touch, especially the ancient white stone carved with the three women, their arms and faces pressed so tightly together that when I first discovered it – I'd been no bigger than a rabbit then – I'd thought they were all one creature, which in a way they were: the women were Brigid and her two sisters, who are one. The Bryde Stone, Ma called it. One night, when they thought I was sleeping, I'd watched Ma teaching Ryana how to feed the stone with milk from the cows and with wild honey. Ryana held it just as Ma showed her, but I could see she didn't feel it stirring in her hand or see the cold blue flame that burned around it, not like I did.

I dropped into a crouch and stayed very still. Through the rain and low cloud, I'd caught a fleeting glimpse of someone moving further down the hill. At first, I thought it might be Taegan, but if Ryana was the sheep-face of the family, Taegan was the cow, with a shaggy mane of ox-blood hair, and breasts and buttocks that, no matter how scrawny her face became when food was short, never lost their undulating curves.

As for me, Ryana said I was the scroggling of the family, stubby and skinny, the shrivelled apple left on a tree that isn't worth the picking. But I'd the reddest hair of all three of us. Once, I heard an old hag in the village say it was so fiery-looking that any man who touched my pelt would surely get his fingers burned. And he would too, I'd make sure of that.

A woman was toiling up the rise between clumps of heather, but as she came closer I saw she was altogether brawnier and much older than either of my sisters. A withered memory fluttered feebly inside my head. There was something familiar about her, but it died before I could revive it. She looked to be making for our cottage, for there was no other dwelling or road on this tor. She was taking the long way round to avoid the mire, but I could find a way through it, using stones and markers you'd never see, unless you knew what to look for.

I ran home like a hare and arrived before our visitor appeared above the rise.

'Woman's coming, Ma. Reckon she wants a cure.'

'How would you know, Mazy-wen?' Ryana sneered. 'She might want a curse.'

That was the name she'd tormented me with when I was small. She still used it whenever she wanted to remind me of how stupid I was.

Ma struggled up from the bed and took her place on a low stool behind the fire in the centre of the floor, poking it vigorously with a stick till the flames leaped and crackled. She liked her customers to find her there and be forced to peer at her through the smoke. She could make smoke form the shapes of birds and beasts, if she wanted.

'Fetch her in, Morwen.'

The woman was standing a little way from the door, her ruddy face glistening with sweat after her climb in spite of the cold wind. She was wearing a faded black gown, patched and worn but not homespun, like the village women. She shuffled awkwardly, evidently trying to make up her mind whether to come or go. Those who'd not come to Ma before often lost their nerve at the last moment. It was my job to coax them. I reckon even Ma knew I was good at that, not that she would ever say as much.

'Kendra knew you'd come.' I smiled encouragingly. 'She's been expecting you. She's waiting for you inside.'

Still the woman hesitated.

'No need to be afeared of her. She wants to help you.'

Finally, she seemed to make up her mind. Wiping the sweat from her nose with the hem of her gown, she ducked through the door.

I slipped in quietly behind her and crouched with my back to the rough stone wall. Ma would send Ryana for her journeying things if they were needed, but if she wanted fresh herbs, she usually sent me. Ryana could barely tell larks-claw from lungwort. But one glance at Ma's face told me something was wrong.

The woman was standing in front of the fire, her meaty arms crossed defensively, but Ryana was on her feet glaring at her, and Ma, crouching low over the flames, was spitting on the back of her fingers, as if our visitor had the evil eye.

Ryana turned on me. 'What you let her in here for? Don't you know who she is?'

'Morwen was no more than seven summers when last she saw her,' Ma said. 'That child's not been to our Bryde's Well since, 'cause Meggy wouldn't let us through the gate!' She thrust her hand towards the woman's face, her fingers clawed in a curse.

The woman staggered back a few paces, but she did not run out. 'I only do what I'm bade, as well you know, Kendra.

I was birthed on this moor same as you and my ma dipped me in Bryde's Pool just like you done to your chillern. But what can I do? You're blessed, you are, got three strapping daughters to take care of you if you're ailing. My man's dead and the only boy I bore who lived to be full-grown was taken to fight the Scots and I haven't heard so much as a whisper of him these past ten years. I've not a stick or stone to shelter under that I can call home. Those sisters of St John are good to me. Give me work, a warm bed, and a good bellyful of food – even give me their old robes while there's still plenty of warmth and wear left in them.' Meggy plucked at the faded black cloth.

'Gave you *my* work, that's what they did. Mine! Took the living from my family that's been keeper of that well since ever it first sprang from the rock.'

'It's Sister Fina who looks after the well. I'm keeper of the gate, that's all, as well you know, Kendra.'

'Aye, I know it well enough. I know you won't let us through it, not even when they're all abed.'

'I've my orders,' Meggy said sullenly, staring at the earth floor as if she was suddenly ashamed.

'So, if these women been so good to you, what you come to me fer, Meggy? They thrown you out?'

The woman glanced round and picked up a low stool. She set it opposite Kendra, on the other side of the fire, then squatted awkwardly on it.

'Ankow came for Father Guthlac's soul. I could tell someone had been taken when I woke with a shiver in the night. I knew for certain Ankow had passed through our gates, for a cold wind follows him wherever he goes. And when death's bondsman enters a dwelling, he never leaves alone.'

'That what you come to tell me?' Ma sneered. 'I saw black

Ankow galloping across the moors on that skeleton of a horse, with his hounds baying at his heels. I knew he was hunting souls. The magpie told me it was the old priest he was after. Good riddance, says I.'

I stared at Ma. Had she really known? She hadn't said, but she'd rarely tell me what she'd learned from the birds.

Meggy stared into the flames. 'Thing is, Kendra, it wasn't a natural death. That much every soul in the priory knows. There was a blind boy found in the chapel after dark that night. Abandoned by his kin, they reckoned, but I never saw him come through my gates, nor anyone leave that evening who could have brought him. Father Guthlac took against him the moment he came close to him, said the lad should be drowned in the mire, so as he could do no mischief. But the prioress wouldn't have it, insisting the boy stay. But his spirit hag-rode the old priest all night till he was worn to rags. You could hear his cries of torment all over the priory. Pitiful they were, poor soul. The boy's evil spirit left Father Guthlac at cockcrow and that was when the old priest died. He'd warned us the boy would destroy us all, and he was the first to be taken.'

She spread out her wrinkled hands before the blaze and lifted her head to look at Ma. 'Who is he, Kendra? He's not human, that's for certain, 'cause I never leave those gates when I'm on duty, save to piss, and when I do those gates stay locked till I return. No mortal being could have got in, unless they used sorcery to make themselves invisible.'

I expected Ma to send Ryana to fetch her stones or feathers, but she sat staring unblinking into the fire. Then her lips parted and her finger stirred. As the column of smoke drifted up, the heart of it began to swirl dense and dark. All of us leaned forward to see what creature might be hovering above

75

the flames. But it was neither bird nor beast that shaped itself in the smoke. It was the head of a man in profile, great beetle brows hung over deep dark eyes, craggy cheeks and a sharp angular nose. Then, like a wraith, it dissolved away, drifting up into the blackened thatch.

'You saw,' Ma said.

Meggy nodded, her face glistening with sweat from the heat of the fire. 'I saw, Kendra. And I've seen it afore on Crockern Tor, when there's a great storm a-brewing. I'd know that face like my own. But what does it mean?'

'The old man of Dertemora has protected these moors from danger since the day the tors rose into the sky and the first lark sang above them. Old Crockern senses danger, death. He's come to warn us evil has come to this place. The boy's eye is closed now. But if he opens it, malice will pour from it, like a river in flood.'

I'd seen old Crockern's face in the smoke too, plain as I saw Ryana dozing in the corner, but I'd seen something more. Someone was standing behind him, a shadow, but not of him. There was a woman in the smoke who wasn't Ma or Meggy or Ryana. I knew, like you know when a storm is rolling in, it was her that Ma should have been paying heed to. Ma should have listened to her.

'You must learn the boy's name,' Ma was telling old Meggy.

'He doesn't speak. And none knows who he is or where he comes from.'

'Bring me something of the boy's, something I can use to ask the spirits. But take care how you get it. He mustn't know, else he'll put you in the grave alongside the priest. You come to me on Fire Tor three nights from now. I'll make a charm that'll keep him from Bryde's Well. He must not touch that water else his middle eye will be opened.'

76

Meggy gnawed her swollen knuckle. 'Can you not give me summat to protect me now?'

Ma stood up and felt along one of the beams that supported the thatch, then pulled down a three-armed cross woven from reeds. I knew what she would do and, without waiting to be asked, I handed her the sack in which she kept her bits of wool. Ma said naught, but pulled out three strands, one black and one white as the sheep that had given them, and a third stained red with madder – Brigid's colours. She wove them sun-wise around the heart of the cross and held it out to Meggy over the flames of the hearth fire.

'Dip it three times three in Bryde's Well and put it under your pillow, along with a sprig of hare's beard to guard you from demons while you sleep. That's when he'll come to torment you if he learns what you're about.'

Meggy reached out, but let her hand fall without grasping the cross. 'Prioress says Christ's cross is all we need to protect us from the evil one. She don't hold with Bryde's crosses, specially this sort. Says it's pagan. If someone were to see it and tell her . . .'

'Then you'd best make sure they don't,' Ma said tartly. 'The four arms of his Christ's cross didn't protect old Guthlac, did they? And if you thought they would protect you, you'd not have come to me.' Ma thrust the woven cross bound with the three strands of wool at Meggy again and this time she took it, pushing it down inside her gown between her breasts, glancing uneasily behind her through the open door as if afraid she was being watched.

Ma held out her hand again, and Meggy fumbled in the small cloth bag dangling at her waist and drew out a silver coin, which she laid in Ma's palm.

'Three nights hence,' Ma said, as Meggy ducked out of

77

the door. 'And, remember, you'll not be safe till we know his name. Bring me something, do you hear? And whatever you do keep the boy away from Bryde's Well until the charm is ready. If his eye ever opens, there's not a soul on these moors will escape the darkness.'

Chapter 9

Sorrel

The long, sharp blade glinted in the sodden grey light, as the outlaw pressed his knife harder against Todde's throat. The whole world seemed to stand still, like a waterfall frozen as it crashed over the rocks. Even the wind held its breath. A single buzzard hung above the tor, its wings scarcely flapping, its clawed beak pointed down at Todde, who was hunched, motionless with fear. The bird watched as if it knew death waited below.

The outlaw glanced up at it and gave a harsh caw of laughter. 'Maybe I'll slice this little man's belly open, spill his guts, and he can have the pleasure of watching that hawk pick them over as he dies. Bird looks hungry for his supper, what do you reckon?'

From the grins on the faces of all three men, I was certain they'd have carried out their threat in a flea's breath and taken pleasure in it too. There was naught either Todde or I could do, save stare in dismay as the outlaws dragged the donkey to the top of the hill, every pick and shovel, pot and blanket that we'd owned along with it. For a moment, I saw the two men and the ass standing like grey rocks against the sky, then they vanished, as if someone had taken a giant cloth and wiped them away.

As soon as they were safely out of sight, the outlaw holding Todde whipped the blade away and kneed his backside, sending him sprawling face down in the mud. The robber took off after his companions and was gone.

Todde was bent double, shaking and retching, though his belly was empty. I thought it best to leave him be. Men don't like a woman to see them afraid, though I didn't blame him – only a mooncalf wouldn't be scared when he'd come that close to dying. He was straightening himself when I heard a shout on the track behind us. A man was trotting towards us on the back of a stocky little horse. In a flash, Todde had drawn his knife and was running back down the slope. He darted in front of me and stopped, his arms thrown wide as if he was trying to defend me. I stared at his ragged back. I couldn't imagine my own brother doing that for me.

'If you're thinking to rob us, you're too late,' Todde bellowed. 'Thieves just made off with all we had, so you'd best get on your way afore I do you some mischief.'

'Rest easy, sir,' the man said. 'I'm no outlaw, merely a hardworking tinner.'

Shaken though I was, I couldn't drag my gaze from the man's face. He had such a bad squint in one eye that it was staring into his hooked nose, and his pale, wispy beard did not conceal the absence of a chin. His mouth receded straight into his puckered neck. He looked like a plucked chicken.

He swung his leg over the saddle and slid off the horse. 'Saw them dragging your beast off, but I was too far away to help.'

'Caught me off guard, they did,' Todde muttered sullenly.

80

'But if you hadn't distracted me by riding at the girl, I'd have been after them in a flash and I'd not have stopped until I took back what was mine.'

The man shook his head sadly. 'It's as well you didn't catch up with them. You'd be lying out on that tor with a knife in your guts if you had. They've been known to cut a man's throat just for the fun of it. And it's not just travellers they prey on. They'll pick off any tinner who's fool enough to be working alone.'

Todde frowned and took a pace forward. 'Here, did you say you're a tinner?'

The man nodded. 'Gleedy they call me, on account of . . .' He pointed at his squint eye and laughed. 'Work for Master Odo. He owns the tinners' rights to the valley over yonder. There's dozens of men stream for him there. If you're looking for work in these parts, he might take you on.'

Todde shook his head vehemently. 'I'll work for no man. I know how it is – the master standing there supping while the men break their backs, then he takes all the tin they've sweated for and tosses them a crooked penny for their trouble. Well, he'll not be using me as his donkey. I'll stream for myself and what I earn I keep. I've got rights, you know. Can dig on any land I please that's not being already worked for tin, doesn't matter who owns it. That's the King's law,' he added, jerking his chin up as if challenging the tinner to disagree.

'I'll not argue with that,' Gleedy said. 'But how are you going to dig with no tools?'

'What's it to you?' Todde demanded.

Gleedy shrugged. 'Just being neighbourly. But I'm not one to force help on those that don't want it.' He made as if to climb back on the horse.

But I edged forward. 'Wait! You can't blame him for being chary after what's just happened.'

Gleedy lowered his foot and turned.

I grimaced at Todde, trying to make him see sense. 'Listen to him, Todde. You can't dig with your bare hands, and even if you could start streaming, it might be days or weeks before you found tin and then you've got to take it somewhere to sell. How are you going to eat till then?'

Gleedy nodded sagely. 'Master Odo doesn't need to go looking for men to hire. He's any number coming to him begging for work, 'specially now food is so scarce. Turned three men away just yesterday and they were all strapping lads. But, deep down, he's a heart as soft as a virgin's breast. If I was to tell him of your misfortune and how you've a crippled woman to feed, he might give you a chance. Worth a try, isn't it?'

I felt the heat of my fury and indignation rising to my face and had to force myself not to stalk away. Pride doesn't fill an empty belly.

Todde opened his mouth as if he would object, but Gleedy jumped back in before he could. 'I know you want to be your own master and so you shall, if you play it right. Master Odo would pay you a generous sum for each pound of tin you dug and that's a rich seam he's found. You'd be able to put food in your bellies and save a good bit too. So, by my reckoning, if you were to work for him a month or so, you'd easily earn enough in that time to buy the tools you'd need to set up on your own.'

Todde still didn't seem convinced, but clearly he couldn't think of anything better.

Gleedy told us to wait while he rode ahead to speak to the master. He knew how to handle Master Odo, he said, and it seemed he did, for a while later we saw him riding back with a grin as broad as a barrel.

'Master Odo's even got an empty cottage for you, all ready and waiting, it is. You come along with me.'

We followed him up the track, then turned off along a broad path, churned up by the hoofs of many horses. In the wettest places rocks, wood and bundles of bracken had been thrown down to make stepping-stones through the mire, but the mud oozed over the top when we trod on them. The track wound up a steep rise. I couldn't see so much as a byre, much less a cottage. Then I caught sight of a huge column of dense black smoke rising up from the other side of the hill, as if a great dragon lay coiled there.

Todde saw it too and yelled in alarm to Gleedy, 'Something afire over yonder.'

Gleedy reined in his horse and turned, waiting for us to catch up. He gave another of his wide grins, showing a mouthful of teeth so crooked and crowded, it looked as if he'd grown twice the number of any normal man.

'That smoke? It's from the blowing-house. New it is,' he added proudly. 'Every man used to have to crush the rock and find wood to burn the ore before he could take it to a stannary town. Even then it was worth only half its weight for it had to be smelted again there. Now it's all burned together and the fire's so hot it has to be done just once. That's Master Odo's doing, and it doesn't come cheap, I can tell you. When you think on it, those outlaws did you a favour. If you'd been working for yourself you'd have been put to four times the labour. Come on!'

His horse ambled on, evidently knowing the path so well that it was able to step on to tussocks of grass to avoid the worst of the mire. There were no sounds out here, save for the mournful cry of a bird and our feet squelching through the mud. I'd never known such quiet and a strange peace settled on me. I felt welcomed, wanted, as if the land had thrown a blanket of softest wool around me and gathered me up into its arms.

But as we breasted the rise, the noise that burst in my ears made me stagger backwards: iron hammers smashing granite, stones crashing into buckets, the whinnying of pack-horses, the shouts of men, the bellows of women and the yells of children. I had never heard such a violent clamour, even at St Stephen's fair. It was as if the ground had yawned wide before me and I was staring down into the pit of Hell.

Chapter 10

Prioress Johanne

Sebastian was quiet now. He had suffered another of his night terrors. I say 'night', but they came upon him just as frequently during the day. He'd shake and whimper, trying to crawl away from something only he could see, but his twisted, wasted limbs would not support him, and even the few feet he managed left him pale as death and sweating in pain. I held him in my arms, murmuring softly and stroking his long hair as he fell into an exhausted sleep. His hair and beard were as white as sea foam but soft and silky, like a baby's. He allowed the sisters to wash and gently comb them, but they could not cut them. He shrank in terror whenever he saw the glint of shears or a blade near his face, even if it was in my hands.

I laid him back on the sheepskin and watched him for a few moments to make sure he had not woken. Then I pulled the rush screen across to close off his bed and edged away.

The boy was sitting alone on a bed at the opposite end of the infirmary. I had ordered he be housed there after the death of Father Guthlac. Basilia could not keep leaving the

85

infirmary to tend him in the pilgrims' hall, and Melisene, the priory's hosteller, said he was making the other travellers uneasy, although when I pressed her she was forced to admit he had done nothing to disturb them. And that, it seemed, was the problem – he did nothing.

I knew Melisene wanted the boy out of her hall. She was accustomed to raucous pedlars, chattering pilgrims and old men-at-arms who ate heartily and drank deeply, but mostly, unless they were trapped by sudden snow or dense fog, these travellers were away about their business during the day, leaving the hall empty, so that she and the lay sisters could sweep, straighten pallets and mend fires in peace without, as Melisene put it, 'the idle getting under my feet'. But the child never moved, and that unnerved the servants. It wasn't natural, they muttered, especially not for a boy.

I walked down the length of the hall, pausing to speak with the other patients as I passed. When I reached the corner where the boy sat, I pulled a stool close to his bed and sat down. I took care not to touch him, fearing to startle him, but he flinched away as if he sensed someone was close to him. He looked even thinner and paler than I recalled, his wild dark curls framing a face that was as white as breath on a frosty morning, the skin almost transparent. Was he ill?

'I am Prioress Johanne. Do you remember my voice?'

He turned his blank stare towards me. The dancing candle flame glittered in the pupils of his dark eyes, like the sun reflected on the surface of a deep pool. His eyes were so bright and clear that, for a moment, I was convinced he must be able to see, but when I passed my hand close to his face, he did not blink or move.

Basilia came bustling over, an anxious look on her plump

features, as if she was afraid I'd come to find fault. 'The boy's been fed, Prioress, though he still makes no attempt to spoon anything down himself or feel for a piece of bread. He'll bite and chew it when it's put against his mouth, but . . .' she faltered, staring down at him, '. . . even the changeling children we've had brought here soon learn how to feed themselves. They're so greedy for food they'd snatch from anyone's trencher.'

'Perhaps those who had the care of him fed him like a baby.'

The boy's head was still turned towards me, but his eyes seemed fixed on some point behind me in the hall. His stare was so intense that, even though I knew he was sightless, I found myself looking round to follow his gaze, but could see only one of the other patients who lay tossing wildly and whimpering in her sleep, as if she was having a terrible dream. For a moment, I almost thought the boy was . . . I reproved myself sternly. The child had done nothing. He hadn't moved. The woman was doubtless in pain, which was making her restless. That was all.

'We cannot keep calling him *the boy*, Sister Basilia. He must have a name.'

'But he still hasn't spoken, Prioress. He can't seem to tell us who he is.' Basilia lowered her voice, her gaze flicking sideways towards him, as if she was afraid to look at him directly. 'He may have been born dumb, or whatever robbed him of his sight might have taken his voice too or his memory.'

'Then until we can find out who he is, we shall call him Cosmas after the great saint and physician who protects the blind.'

I grasped the child's hand, which still felt as cold as

granite. He jerked, but did not pull it from mine. 'Cosmas,' I pronounced slowly and clearly. 'You' – I prodded his chest to make my meaning clearer – 'will be called Cosmas.'

I watched his face for any sign that he had heard or understood. The candle flame still reflected in his black pupils, but I could have sworn that it had turned blood red. Startled, I dropped his hand and stared up at the candle guttering on the wall, thinking it must be smoking or tainted, but it was still burning yellow, and when I looked back into Cosmas's eyes that was how it burned there too, like any true reflection. The flame must simply have flickered in a sudden draught. What was wrong with me? I was starting to imagine things, like Sister Fina. I had spent too many hours lying awake, fretting over the arrival of Brother Nicholas. That was the cause. I rose and drew Basilia away from the boy, trying not to betray my momentary disquiet.

'How does he respond to his eyes being bathed in the holy well?'

Basilia's cheeks and neck flushed, and her gaze shifted to the painting of the Blessed Virgin on the wall, as if she was looking for divine protection or absolution. It was hard to know which.

'He's not yet been to the well . . . I would have asked Sister Fina to take him, but she's not come into the infirmary these many days and I had to stay with the patients. Poor things, they are still so distressed over dear Father Guthlac's death. They were all so fond of him – some of the older ones had known him since they were young . . . And we've all been so busy trying to make sure Brother Nicholas would not discover anything to find fault with.'

The longer she babbled, the more excuses tumbled out, so thick and fast that I knew none was quite the truth.

'I understand, Sister Basilia, but I insist you take Cosmas to the holy well tomorrow, whatever your duties here. I am sure the servants can manage the patients for the brief time you are absent. The boy was brought to us for healing and we must have as much faith as those who entrusted him to us. Ask Sister Fina to open the well early for you and take him there before the pilgrims are admitted. If he becomes distressed when the water touches him, it will not upset them. Do it, Sister Basilia. I will hear no excuses.'

The sudden rapping at my door sent my quill sliding across the parchment, leaving a trail of black ink. I hastily dabbed at it before it could dry, cursing. I was angry with myself for jumping like a guilty child: I'd no reason to feel shame. All the same I moved swiftly to the far corner of the room, where I had dragged my narrow bed away from the wall. A section of panelling had been lifted out to reveal a gap, just wide enough to squeeze through. The tiny chamber beyond had been designed as a private chapel and, should the need ever arise, a place of safety in case of attack. But it served another purpose now: it contained a stout chest standing hard against one wall, and it was into this that I slid the parchment and small bag of coins.

The knocking came again, more urgently this time. I stepped swiftly out, closing the wooden panel and pushing my bed back against it. Satisfied that all was safely concealed I pulled back the bolt on the door of my chamber.

Sister Clarice pushed the door barely wide enough to slip through, then shut it again, leaning on it and panting a little, as if she had been hurrying. Tiny beads of sweat glistened in the furrows of her forehead in spite of the chill weather. She reached into her leather scrip and pulled out a bag, which she held towards me with a triumphant smile.

'Three more rents collected, Prioress.'

'Did any complain?'

She grimaced. 'Master Rohese almost refused, saying that it was a week early, but I told him that if he waited until the due time then a brother knight would be collecting the monies owed. They'd search every corner and cranny of his byres and barns, and record everything down to the last egg and bale of wool to find reason to demand double from him.'

'Sister! You should not have said that. We don't know that Brother Nicholas has any such intention. No knight of St John would seek to take more from any man than was due to God and to his servants.'

As prioress it was my duty to defend the reputation of the knights of my order, but I would not have wagered a clipped farthing on the truth of it. Unlike most of my sisters, I had served on Cyprus before the order's headquarters was moved to Rhodes and I had seen at first hand the cruelty and arrogance of some of my brother knights, which had given the people of that isle good cause to rise against the Hospitallers, though I would never have breathed as much to a living soul, not even to Clarice.

The sister's sharp chin jerked up at my reprimand, and there was the same flash of fury in her dark little eyes as there had been when Nicholas had demanded she surrender the priory's accounts.

'It is no sin to speak the truth, Prioress,' she retorted indignantly, 'and I said no more to Master Rohese than I believe. I was forced to sit with *Steward* Nicholas, as it pleases him to dub himself now, as he went through my figures, and I can tell you he'd barely glanced at the records before he was claiming a property here had been undervalued or an acre of plough land there should yield twice more than I had recorded. He was accusing me of not checking thoroughly, not that he said it in so many words, but he might as well have done for we both knew what he meant.'

She snorted furiously, and then the corners of her lips twitched in a faint smile. 'But Master Rohese is no man's fool. There are many hidden valleys and oak woods on the moors. I suspect he'll already be moving some of his cattle and stores to places where a stranger would never find them. Not,' she added firmly, fixing me with a baleful stare, 'that I encouraged the tenants to do any such thing, Prioress.'

I fought back an answering smile. It wouldn't do to let Clarice know how secretly delighted I was, for I shouldn't be condoning such devious behaviour. But I was all too well aware that the moment Brother Nicholas had the rents in his possession he would have financial control of the priory. We would be forced to beg him for every farthing, like a servant asking their master for coin to pay the butcher. I could picture the smug satisfaction on his face as he debated whether or not to grant us a pittance, and the delight he would take in his power to refuse. He could and, I had little doubt, *would* make our work impossible and our lives unbearable. But so long as the coins remained in our chests and the keys on my chain . . .

'Thank you for your . . . efficiency, Sister Clarice. If I can deliver the responsions to Clerkenwell in full, using our own messenger, it may convince the Lord Prior that we can manage our affairs perfectly well and should be left here to do so.'

I found my gaze straying to where my bed stood against

the wall, guilt welling in me again. Was I breaking my vow of obedience or merely being a wise and prudent servant of God? It was a question I had wrestled with ever since I had become prioress, but not one on which I could seek guidance from any in our order or even from gentle, bumbling Father Guthlac. He had been a godly man of simple faith and I doubted such dilemmas had ever troubled his sleep.

Clarice crossed to the small fire and stood with her back to it, warming herself. With the flames flickering behind her steaming skirts, I saw again, for one terrible moment, the Templars burning on the heretics' pyres, heard the echo of those screams, smelt the stench of burning flesh. Brother Nicholas might have heard of the torments that had befallen them. But I had witnessed them. I had seen with my own eyes – would to God I had not – the once noble warriors blinking in the harsh light of day as they were dragged naked from their dark dungeons, seen the crowd spit at them, hurling insults and dung, where once they had thrown flowers. Sometimes I think it is a blessing to be blind, for then you cannot see those horrors again and again as if they were burned into your own eyes.

I knew far better than Brother Nicholas how quickly kings and crowds could turn. The Templars had lent money to finance half the wars and buildings in Christendom. They had fought and defended nobles and kingdoms. They had seemed as invincible as the Holy See itself. But how swiftly the hands of sovereigns that once had proffered coins and jewels could wield axes, ropes and flaming brands.

And the spinning of the stars in the heavens had brought us into a far more treacherous time than ever the Templars had known. When the populace starves and grows desperate, kings and bishops alike look for some way to turn aside the people's anger. Tether a bear for the hounds to rip to pieces, and the brutes will not turn on their masters. I shuddered, as if the dead had walked over my own grave. How could I protect my sisters from those flames if the Hospitallers were next to fall?

Chapter 11

Sorrel

The steep-sided valley was as raw as an open wound in a man's belly. The land had been stripped bare of grass, the earth and stones that had been torn from it lying heaped in great barren wedges of black and rust-coloured rubble at either side of a broad trench. A lake had been gouged out at the head of the valley, the water held back by a great wall of earth and stone into which a sluice gate had been set. Wooden channels ran from it in zigzags down the hillside towards the ditch at the bottom in which a line of men were digging. As I watched, a man standing by a sluice gate put a ram's horn to his lips and blew a single deep, mournful note across the valley. At once the tinners threw their shovels on to the bank and clambered out of the trench, only just in time before the man dragged on a rope to heave up the gate and a great gush of water flooded down the wooden leats into the ditch, pushing a tide of mud and gravel out into an old riverbed below.

At the top of the valley, directly below the lake, there was a large, square building, with roughly hewn granite walls and a slate roof from which a fat plume of tar-black smoke was rising into the grey sky. But Gleedy was pointing towards the lower end, where a score of tiny black huts were clustered.

'There now, that's where you'll be living, cosy as a flea in a king's bed. See how close to the digging it is? There's some workings on these moors where you'd have to trudge miles before you could start, but here it's just a lamb's skip and you're there, fresh as a skylark in spring, and no time wasted.'

I followed Gleedy and Todde down the sodden track into the valley. Everything was stained with black and red mud, from the faces and clothes of the men, women and children, who toiled with their shovels filling buckets, to the packhorses that stood, heads drooping, in the mizzle. The water in the river downstream of the ditch was so thick with it that it looked as if it was running with cow-dung instead of water. The mud had even hunted down the dandelions and the few blades of grass hiding among the cracks in the rocks to suffocate them too.

The tinners turned their heads to watch us as we picked our way round the spoil heaps, sidestepping the women with yokes on their necks who were heaving buckets of stones over to the granite blocks where the men were pounding them with iron hammers. A few muttered to each other, but I couldn't catch the words. A couple offered me weary smiles in exchange for my own, but mostly their faces were blank, indifferent.

The 'cottage' Gleedy led us towards turned out to be no more than a crude bothy on the edge of a group of others like it. The one he pointed to was lowest down the hillside and I knew at once that all the rain and piss from the neighbours' huts would run straight down into it. The walls were made from grass sods laid flat atop one another. But at least the cold earth floor was sloped, which was a mercy, for all the water had run into one corner, where it lay stagnant and black, like the rest of the valley.

'There's not even a shelf or bed boards,' Todde grumbled. 'You expect us to sleep on the wet earth?'

We'd been sleeping on nothing but mud for days, but I guessed that Todde was trying to cling to the one remaining snippet of dignity that had not been stripped from him by the outlaws.

Gleedy gave a high-pitched giggle. 'What would you want with a shelf? Those outlaws took all you had to put on it.' He tried to pull his features into a serious expression. 'You spread a good thick layer of bracken on the floor and you'll sleep like a babe at the breast.' He grasped Todde's shoulder. 'But, seeing as you've had a bad time of it, I'll tell you what I'll do. Master Odo keeps some stores 'case any should need them. I'll go there now and take a squint.' He laughed again and pulled down the bottom lid of his cross-eye in case we'd missed the joke. 'See if I can't find you a couple of snug sheepskins to rest your weary bones on.'

Todde ambled down to watch the streaming while I went to hunt for bracken and kindling to build a fire. I might as well have saved my aching legs. All the bracken had been stripped bare near the camp, and I was too afraid of stumbling into a sucking mire to wander far with the light fading. I found a few twigs but I knew they'd be too wet to burn unless I could borrow the heat of a neighbour's fire to dry them.

I heard the horn sound again, two notes this time, and by the time I found my way back, the mud-soaked women were trudging up to their huts, where they knelt to blow on the embers of glowing peats and coax them into a blaze.

Their menfolk squatted by the filthy stream, splashing water on their hands and heads. Dirt and sweat ran down their faces, leaving black trails on their skin, as if the devil's slugs had crawled there.

Gleedy had returned and was pushing a bundle of moulting sheepskins into Todde's arms. He caught sight of me, and beamed, his forest of teeth glinting in the darkness of the doorway. 'I've not forgotten you, Mistress. You'll be glad of this, I'm thinking.' He held out a rusty iron cooking pot almost burned through. 'I've slipped a parcel of dried mutton in there and an onion or two. Now, don't you be thanking me. Master Odo would never forgive me if your man was too weak from hunger to work come morning. Sleep sound.'

'He is not *my* man!' I blurted indignantly, and instantly regretted it when I saw Todde flinch. I'd not meant to hurt him – he had suffered enough blows to his pride that day. But, all the same, it was as well that it had been said. I had no illusions that any man would want a creature like me in his bed, but I'd not suffer myself to be in bondage to anyone again, as I had been to my father and brother. Todde had wanted to be his own master: couldn't he understand that a woman might want that too?

Gleedy grinned, gave a little bow and ambled away through the smoke of the cooking fires, swallowed by the thick grey sludge of evening.

'You want to watch what you take from Gleedy,' someone muttered behind me.

I turned to see a tall, handsome woman leaning on the corner of a hut.

'He'll not give you so much as a cat's turd for nothing. Deeper you climb into his purse, harder it'll be to pull yourself out.'

97

'What do you mean?' I asked, but as she spoke, one of the tinners slouched past. She caught my eye, giving a warning shake of her head.

The tinner scowled at her. 'Supper ready, Eva? My belly's roaring louder than a rutting stag.'

She waited until he had trudged further up the rise, then moved a pace closer to me. 'Just remember what I said, but don't speak of Gleedy or the master to any folk here. Those two have ears and eyes everywhere.' She gave a grim smile. 'Cheer up. You'll soon get the lie of this place.' She reached out to give my arm a squeeze, but it was my withered arm she grasped. She jerked at the feel of it, staring down at my flopping hand, and bit her lip. 'Ah, you poor creature.'

If any other soul had said it I'd have snapped at them, like a baited dog, but the haunted expression in the woman's eyes told me she'd scars aplenty of her own.

Eva's gaze darted to the twigs I was clutching. 'That won't warm a spoonful of water.' She jerked her head towards the huts higher up the slope. 'I cook for some of the men and chillern that has no women to tend them. My fire's up there by that old tumbled wall. If you bring along some of that mutton to add to the pot, you're welcome to join us, just for tonight, mind.'

Half a dozen men, three young boys and a girl, no more than seven or eight summers old, were already gathering around a bubbling cauldron, when Todde and I slipped among them. Eva had lit the fire close to an ancient stone wall that had half tumbled down, but was still high enough to give shelter from the wind, and she'd built two short, low walls out of the fallen stones to shield the fire-pit on either side. The great iron pot was balanced on top of them so it straddled the flames, but did not burn.

After several minutes of stirring, and calls from the men to hurry, Eva doled out the pottage into old wooden bowls. Some of the men had brought their own spoons made from mutton bones, the rest lifted the bowls to their lips and slurped, scraping the shreds of meat that were caught on rough wood into their mouths with black-rimmed fingernails.

It was hard to say what the pottage had been made from, for the fragments of meat, bone and herbs in it had plainly been reboiled so many times they'd no taste left in them. Most likely the cooking pot was never emptied. Eva just added whatever the day brought her, a bit of fat bacon, a handful of herbs, a lump of dried fish or whatever bird could be snared. But I would have gobbled a bowl of boiled mice that night. My belly ached for hot food. And everyone sitting around that fire likely felt the same for no one spoke: they were too busy eating.

As soon as the bowls were empty, most of the men handed them back to Eva and silently slunk away, too bone-weary to do anything but sleep. A few others sat on, talking to Todde, asking him where he'd come from and if he'd ever been streaming before. To hear him crowing you'd think he knew as much about tin as a master potter knows about clay. A flame of excitement flared in his eyes, as he boasted of the money he'd made in times past. He seemed more cheerful now that he'd a bellyful of hot food, as if he'd forgotten he'd had a knife held to his throat just hours before. But the tinners were grinning at each other behind Todde's back. They could tell he was talking through the seat of his breeches.

I gazed up at the moors. I'd thought I knew just how dark a night could be. Back home, when the moon was hidden by clouds and there was no light to be seen, save for the glow of a stockman's fire across the fields or a sliver of candlelight beneath a shutter, I had called that darkness. But it was only dark because the sun had gone. Here in this valley it wasn't simply that the light had vanished from the sky, the darkness there was alive, a great black river of malice that swept down the hillsides and filled the valleys, a chill, choking tide that could drag you down and drown you in despair.

I lifted my head and stared up at the top of the hill. She had called me to these moors, but not to this valley surely. This was not the place. It couldn't be. But where was I to go? What was I to do?

Why have you brought me here? Speak to me, I begged.

But only the wind answered and if it had words for me I couldn't understand them.

I shivered. Pulling my cloak tighter about my shoulders, I forced myself to turn my back on that desolate valley. But as I stared into the flames and smoke of Eva's fire, I glimpsed movement: something was glittering and swaying in the old stone wall behind the fire. I screwed up my eyes, trying to make out what it was. It must be the wind stirring clumps of grass or herbs growing between the stones.

Then the breath caught in my throat. Those were not grasses. They were the heads of vipers, their eyes gleaming in the firelight, their forked tongues flickering as they tasted the air. From every crevice and hole in the wall more heads were emerging, swaying back and forth, dozens of them. I scrambled to my feet, backing away in alarm.

The men's heads jerked up and one by one they followed my gaze, trying to see what I was staring at. Then a ripple of raucous laughter ran through them, and they nudged each other in the ribs, pointing at the wall and at my face.

'They's only long-cripples,' one man chortled. 'Nest in the wall, they do, and the heat of the fire makes them poke out their heads. They'll not come out to harm thee in this weather. Too cold and wet.'

'But on warm days you need to watch where you're treading,' another added, 'especially if you go barefoot. Moors are swarming with those creatures.'

'And you wants to give your bedding a good shake too, afore you lie down, creep in under the bracken, long-cripples do, looking for a warm place. Old Will got bit right on his cods one night. They swelled up and turned black as the devil's toenails. Could hear his screams all the way to Widecombe.'

The men, still chuckling, fell to telling tales about those they had known who had been bitten by vipers, blithely ignoring the dozens of glinting black eyes watching them unblinking from the wall.

But somewhere in the distance, a hound began to bay, another joined in, then another, their calls echoing across the moors, as if a pack of dogs were running after their prey. One by one, the tinners fell silent, tense, listening, straining to peer out into the darkness, and this time, I saw fear on every face.

Chapter 12

Morwen

My sister Taegan lay curled up asleep on a heap of old skins in front of the banked-down fire. Ma gave her a sharp poke in the ribs with her stick. She groaned and rolled on to her belly. Ma raised her stick again and cracked it down across Taegan's broad backside. She let out a yelp and scrambled to her feet, rubbing her eyes.

'Up, you idle trapes,' Ma said. 'We've work to do on Fire Tor.'

Taegan hadn't been asleep for longer than a cow's tail, having wobbled in after dark, her breath stinking of sour mead. She'd collapsed on to her sleeping place without bothering to drag off her gown, and was snoring before her face hit the skins. She scowled at Ma, rubbing her bruises. 'So, what did you wake me fer? I'm not Ryana, you blind old gammer.'

''Cause I'll be needing all three of you tonight. Ryana's already out fetching my tools. Morwen, you pick all the worts I bade you fetch?'

I patted the sack that was already slung over my shoulder.

102

I'd been searching for two days and nights, because some of the herbs could only be picked at dawn and others by moonlight if they were to be in their full power. And I remembered to give the earth some honey to make amends when I plucked the vervain, for that's a holy herb. Ryana never did.

Ma grunted. 'Bring water too, Morwen. Tae, you carry wood for the fire, and mind you bring enough to bait it till dawn this time, else you'll find yourself walking back to fetch more. Stir yourself, girl. Sun's not going stay abed for you.'

The wind was raw and chafing, driving the clouds across a waxing moon. A *duru moon*, Ma called it, when it was more than half full, for it opened the doorway into the kingdoms of beasts and spirits. It gave us little light that night, but such things never mattered to Ma. She always counted the nights of the moon, whether she could see it or not, notching them off with an iron blade on a gnarled branch she'd cut from the twisted oaks in the valley. She said you might as well try to empty a river with an acorn cup as make a charm or a curse on a night when the moon wasn't in the right phase to give it power. Some charms needed a waxing moon, others a waning, a full or horned moon. I tried as hard as I could to learn the ways, but some secrets Ma would only whisper to Ryana, not that she ever paid any heed.

We made a slow procession, winding up the slope to the rocks at the top of the tor. By day, there was barely a track to be seen, nothing that would lead a stranger up to that place, but at night the path shone out as clear as the streams that ran down the side of the hill. Ryana walked first and most easily for Ma's tools were light. Ma followed and, for all that she dug her staff into the ground to lean on, she was as sure-footed as the sheep that grazed the moor. I walked behind her with the wort sack over one shoulder, the heavy

103

skin of water over the other and the bundle of kindling sticks in my arms, which Taegan had thrust at me behind Ma's crooked old back. Taegan trailed behind, hefting a faggot of wood on her back, supported by a broad strap across her forehead. She'd heeded Ma's warning and was carrying as large a load as she could manage, though she whined like a chained dog all the way up.

In the last few feet before we reached the rocks the wind was so strong that I staggered under the weight of all I was carrying. I had to stop to steady myself. My eyes streamed. Here and there, far off in the darkness, blurs of red and yellow light shone like the eyes of beasts. They were the shepherds' fires burning far below in the valleys and the fires of the outlaws high on distant tors. Wiping my stinging eyes, I hurried up into the lee of the great towering rocks. Ma groped along in the darkness till she found the crevice between them and vanished inside. Ryana passed her the bundle of tools and squeezed in after her. But I hung back, listening. From deep within came a hollow knocking and a plaintive, high-pitched keening, as if many women were sitting deep inside the hill, mourning and weeping, throwing the melancholy notes from one to another, like the plovers that lived on the wind. Passing strangers and villagers, who heard the sounds, were always agasted and swore that Fire Tor was haunted by demons, or else it was the souls of the dead trapped inside, crying to be released. But I was never afeared: my skin tingled with excitement at the sound.

'Stir your arse, Mazy-wen,' Ryana called from inside. 'Ma's waiting.'

I pushed the water skin, herbs and kindling inside, then gathered up the wood Taegan had dropped and passed it through the cleft, stick by stick.

'Tell Tae to keep watch for Meggy,' Ma called, her voice echoing through the rocks.

'Fer why?' Taegan groused. 'It's so dark, I couldn't see a herd of white horses if they galloped over me. I've a good mind to go home.'

But I knew she'd not dare, just as I knew she would never set foot inside Fire Tor. When Taegan had reached her seventh birthday, Ma had tried to take her in, promising it as a great treat. But I reckoned that malicious cat, Ryana, had been whispering and pistering in little Taegan's ear, scaring the wits out of her, because later she'd tried to do the same thing to me. Ryana always sneered that when Ma had led Taegan up to Fire Tor, Tae had screamed and fought like a cornered weasel, even scratching and biting Ma's arms, rather than be pushed through that narrow gap into the dark, though she was so small she'd have passed through as easily as a mouse's whisker through a fox hole. Neither Ma's threats nor slaps had persuaded her to go in then or since, though I doubted she could have squeezed her fat udders through now, even if she'd wanted to.

I turned sideways and slid through into the space between the rocks. Inside it was so dark that my eyes ached. The blackness rippled towards me in waves. I felt for the wall of rock and slid down it, until I was squatting on the damp earth. The whispering spirits slithered around me in the darkness. They crept so close, I could feel them brushing my cheek and stirring my hair as they passed. Another voice began to sing. It was Ma keening softly with the spirits of rock and earth, begging them for the gift of fire.

There was a hollow click as she struck iron and flint. A tiny scarlet spark flashed out in the darkness, then yellow flame ran over the kindling, growing and leaping till a ruby-red glow filled the long, narrow cave, and the shadows of the spirits pranced around us.

The walls of the cave were formed of craggy rocks, with a huge flat stone over the top making a roof. At the far end, on the other side of the blazing fire, a narrow slab rose out of the earth, which was always kept covered with a long white woollen cloth.

Ryana was slumped against one wall, her bulging sheep-eyes half closed, yawning. Ma crouched before the flames, her head bowed, her grey hair tumbling loose down her back. She had spread her tools before the fire. She could do that by touch even in the dark for she knew them better than she did her own daughters – the white Bryde's Stone, a fox tooth, the hide of an unborn fawn, an ear of barley from a long-ago harvest, a raven's feather and the dried hind leg of a black dog.

Ma took a scallop shell that had been packed with dry moss and sprinkled with animal grease. She laid a burning stick from the fire to it. Sparks glittered across the moss and it began to burn with a bright yellow flame that rose steadily higher and thicker. Ma carried the shell into each corner of the cave, circling it there, muttering to the guardian spirits, before she returned to the fire.

Her wrinkled hand snaked out, and I passed her the water skin, watching as she poured water on to the earth in a circle around the treasures she had laid out. When it was complete, she hunkered down and took a small piece of dried meat from the bag that hung about her withered neck. It was the flesh of a red cat she had dried many moons ago. She chewed the dried meat, and when it was soft, she held it up in her hands before the flames, offering it to Mother Brigid, then laying it solemnly before the fire. Praying over each of her horny old palms in turn, she pressed them over her eyes and began to rock back and forth, singing with the voices in the cave, crying out to the duru moon to open the doorway and let the spirits come and go.

She tilted forward, rolling her head, her long grey hair flung out like a whip till it was inscribing a full circle in the air. The shadows on the walls were circling with her, spinning faster and faster, until it seemed that Ma was as still as a rock and the cave spun around her in a great dark vortex.

She turned her head, glaring back over her shoulder, and gave a savage snarl, like a wildcat, her yellow teeth bared, lips curled. She flung her arms wide and I saw red fur erupting through her skin, the glint of dagger claws on her outstretched fingers. Then, just as swiftly, they were gone. A long breath hissed from her open mouth, like the sound of rushing water, and she was limp again, bowed forward, her hands stretched out to the fire, and I knew that the spirit had passed through Kendra.

Ma held out her hand to Ryana for the worts I'd collected, but she'd fallen asleep in the heat of the fire. I crawled over and dragged the sack into my sister's lap, shaking her awake. While the charm was being woven, Ma would let only Ryana touch the herbs. Once I'd kicked her, my sister handed Ma the sprigs in turn, each bound with a strand of red wool. The murmurs in the cave grew louder, as if the sight and smell of the sacred herbs excited the spirits, drawing them closer, as the bloody carcass of a goat draws down the kites and ravens.

Ma lifted each wort in turn, singing its name and virtues to the mournful notes the spirits lent her.

Remember, Vervain, what you revealed,
Holy wort you are called, the enchantment breaker,
And you, Henbane, who call the ancestors to speak,
Call them to gather and call them to guard . . .

And so she continued, raising each sprig in turn before the seeing-fire – *bryony, wormwood, whortle, crow leek, corn-cockle, cleavers, adderwort.* Finally, she gathered them all together and bound them slowly, three times, with a strand of white wool as she sang:

Against demon's hand and dwarf's guile,
Against the elfin kingdom and the night hag's ride,
Against the fiend which flies from the west and the
    north, from the east and the south,
Against the eye of darkness that must not be opened.

Ma struggled stiffly to her feet and walked the bunch of worts three times around the seeing-fire, trailing them through the smoke. Then she stepped over the flames and through the smoke so that it swirled around her. Finally, she approached the cloth-covered slab at the end of the narrow cave. My stomach lurched. I knew well what lay beneath, but whenever Ma went to that rock, I felt as if I was seeing it for the first time. Ma nodded to Ryana, who lumbered to her feet and pulled the cloth from the ledge.

The corpse lay on its back, bathed in the blood-red firelight. The shadows of the spirits crawled across his chest. He was naked, his skin leathery, tanned to the colour of a thrush's wing, his hair and beard startlingly flaxen against his dark face. His lips had shrivelled back, revealing long teeth.

Beneath his chin, the skin had shrunk away from the long

108

gash across his throat, pulling it open as wide as a mouth. Ma had cleaned the wound in his neck and his corn-coloured hair, soaked in the blood that had poured from the skull-splintering blow to the back of his head. She had neatened his beard with her bone-comb and plaited a hag-stone into it. But she could not wash the look of shock and horror from his face.

Ryana had laid a river-polished black pebble on his fore-head and I had woven a bracelet for his right arm from the prickly twigs of the flying thorn that grew in the crevice of a rock without touching the earth. And it was to the hand of that arm that Ma now touched the bundle of worts. Then she pressed them against his bare feet, his head, mouth, breast and the withered worm of his pizzle and cods.

'Let me go, Kendra!' A voice as deep as a grave echoed around the cave. 'Bury me, burn me, release me from this torment of darkness.'

I stared up. The shadow of a man hung above me, grey, swirling, as if it was formed of smoke, except the eyes. His eyes were solid, living, burning like twin embers. The mouth opened wide as a scream and dark as a grave.

'Kendra, set me free from this misery and desolation. I beg you.'

Ma laughed. 'Not you. I'll never free you. You are Ankow. You were chosen. She gave you to me. See all the pains I've taken to keep your body safe. You should be grateful. You'll do my bidding till you come to carry me safe to the lych-ways, and then you'll serve my daughter, her daughter's daughter, till the sun and the moon vanish from the sky.'

His howl of despair and anguish made even the rocks tremble. I covered my head with my arms, feeling his wretch-edness stab deep inside me, but Ma only chuckled. She broke off a piece of the henbane and laid it below Ankow's naval. The curly golden hairs on his belly caught the fragile leaves and held them, like a spider's web. And the shadow vanished.

'Meggy's come.' Taegan's voice echoed through the cave.

Ma grunted and, taking the bundle of herbs, shuffled towards the narrow entrance, closely followed by Ryana.

It was left to me to cover the corpse again, extinguish the moss still burning in the scallop shell and collect the water skin, before finally emerging into the darkness. I shivered in the raw air after the warmth of the fire. Meggy and Kendra were already huddled in the lee of the rocks.

'. . . set the charm afire,' Ma was saying, 'and walk round the cave three times, so as smoke circles it. And mind yer walk round it with the sun.'

'Wasn't born with a goose cap on my head,' Meggy retorted indignantly. 'I know right way to walk.'

Ma snorted. 'No telling what queer notions you've picked up from those carrion crows you bide with.'

The gatekeeper bridled, but Ma ignored her and continued, 'As you walk, you must say the will worth, tell the spirits what you seek – "May this smoke keep him from the well as the flame keeps the wolf from the flock." And you've to mean it.'

Meggy shivered. 'Never fear, Kendra. There'll not be a charm worked that was ever meant more.' She glanced towards the east. 'I'd best hurry. There's not much time.'

Ma grasped her arm. 'This'll only keep the fiend at bay. If we're to destroy him, you must fetch me something I can use against him. We have to learn his name.'

Meggy nodded, tucked the bunch of herbs beneath her cloak and vanished into the darkness. Ma began to pick her way back down the hill, with Ryana and Taegan hurrying ahead, anxious to get back to their beds.

110

The echoes of the ghosts still whispered and sang through the cave. I turned to look back at the towering rocks. A red-orange glow danced and flickered through the crevices. The villagers said that whenever the heart of the tor was burning in the darkness it meant Ankow was riding up to the rocks on his skeleton horse, carrying the souls of those who had died. The fire would burn until dawn, and any who were awake in those parts would see the glow of those flames and tremble, afeared that, before the year was out, Ankow would drag them through that crevice into the lands of the dead.

Chapter 13

Hospitallers' Priory of St Mary

'Are you on your way to open the well, Sister Fina?' The words sprang out of the shadows, making the young woman start violently, for it was not yet dawn, and she'd thought the courtyard deserted at that hour.

Fina held up her lantern as Brother Nicholas stepped out in front of her, his black cloak billowing in the chill breeze. He was grinning, as if causing her to jump had amused him. The lantern lit his face from below, giving his hard features a wolfish, almost malevolent expression.

'You're about your duties early, Sister,' he added. He squinted up at the dark sky where as yet only a pale stain of light marked where the sun would rise.

'Sister Basilia wants to anoint a blind boy's eyes today with the water from St Lucia's well. But some of the pilgrims and villagers have heard . . .' She pressed her long fingers to her mouth afraid the words would escape if she didn't lock them in. Prioress Johanne had sternly warned all the sisters that they must be guarded in what they told the brothers about the priory, but Fina was certain the

112

prioress meant her. She was the one the prioress was warning and all the other sisters knew as much. Sister Clarice was always watching her, waiting for her to make a mistake, so she could go tattling to Johanne, trying to convince her that Fina was too young and stupid to be in charge of anything more than plucking chickens. The prioress had started to believe her. *An unlettered cottager*, Johanne had called her . . . Well, that was what she'd meant, anyway.

Nicholas had turned his head away from Fina, distracted by the sight of one of the scullions, Dye, emerging yawning from a doorway to fetch water. Her hair hung loose and tangled, and she was clad only in a torn shift that hung off one shoulder and barely covered her thighs. But the slattern seemed to hold more interest for the knight than Fina. She could sense he was about to walk away. He obviously thought she was too slug-witted to be worth talking to.

Words began tumbling from her mouth. 'Sister Basilia thinks it would be less frightening for the blind child if he was bathed in the well before the pilgrims arrive. The cave is so small, he might easily be jostled.' She offered Nicholas the small gift of information, like a tiny child might offer a feather or a daisy, knowing it was worthless, but wanting it to be accepted.

The knight took a pace or two towards her, so she was forced to look up at him. The hem of his cloak brushed her ankle as the wind gusted. His arm was so close to her breast that if she swayed forward his flesh would press into it. In spite of the breeze, she felt the hot flush on her cheeks and quickly lowered her eyes. *Why did he stand so close? He should not. He must not.* But she didn't step back.

113

'Pray excuse me, Brother. I . . . I need to unlock the door and light the candles.'

She tried to step round him but, whether by accident or design, he moved too, in the same direction and she found her way blocked again.

'Then allow me to escort you, Sister. It would not be gallant to leave you to stumble around in a dark chapel. You might fall and hurt yourself.'

'There's no need to trouble yourself, Brother. I've tended the well so often, I could find my way if I was blind.'

'Ah, but now that we brothers have arrived to protect you, you must allow us to assist you, else we shall feel we've made this tedious journey for nothing. Besides, I haven't yet had a chance to pray at this miraculous well of yours. You surely wouldn't forbid a brother knight his spiritual consolation when your sweet sisterhood exists to bring us such comforts.'

Something about the way his tongue lingered on 'comforts' made the back of her neck tingle.

'But the boy will probably resist having water splashed on his eyes. Your prayers would be disturbed by the commotion.'

'Believe me, I have offered some of my most devout prayers with a sword in my hand and men screaming all around me in the thick of battle. The squeals of one small boy will hardly disturb me. Come, I insist!'

He was not smiling now and the fingers that suddenly gripped her arm were not gentle.

They walked in silence across to the chapel door, where he released her. Frightened now, she fumbled with the bunch of keys that hung from a chain around her waist, praying that Basilia would come quickly, though she'd be no more help in getting rid of Nicholas than a puppy bent on licking

114

a robber to death. Besides, what was there to be afraid of? A brother knight of her own order merely wished to pray. That was all . . . all he'd said.

But the moment the door swung open Nicholas pushed into the chapel behind her, pressing so close she could feel his hard belly against her back. The single ruby light burning above the altar served only to make the darkness of the chapel more intense. Her hands were shaking as she lit the candles set ready on the iron spikes at either side of the door.

But Nicholas stepped away from her and curtly inclined his head before the crucifix hanging above the altar. Seeming to forget she was there, he began to pace slowly around the circular chapel in the space between the eight pillars and the outer wall, murmuring his *Aves* to honour the Blessed Virgin, as the sisters did in their private devotions. As silently as she could, Fina slipped across to the other side of the chapel and unlocked the door to the well. Now that she could see he was praying, her breathing slowed a little. What had she imagined could possibly happen?

But she had descended only two or three steps, when she heard footsteps approaching the door above her. It was customary to circle the chapel three times. Surely he could not have finished his prayers already. Panic gripped her once more.

'Wait!' she called. 'Let me light the candles below, then you will see a great marvel as you walk down.'

She hurried down as fast as was possible on the slippery, uneven steps. In the darkness below she could hear the gush and splash as the water poured into the stone pool. The spring was flowing strongly today. As she reached the bottom step, she lifted the lantern to light her way across the floor of the cave. She was about to take the last step down, but she snatched her foot back with a muffled scream. The floor of the cave was moving, heaving, as if the stones were alive and wriggling up out of the earth.

'I am still waiting for this marvel, Sister Fina,' Nicholas called, from the top of the stairs.

'I . . . cannot light the candles, Brother.'

She tried to think of some excuse that would stop him coming down. But it was too late – she could already hear his footfalls on the stairs. He'd evidently grown bored with waiting. She ran back up, taking the steps two at a time, heedless of slipping, and almost cannoned into him.

'The candles are wet, Brother,' she gabbled breathlessly, 'too wet to light, and the floor of the cave is slippery with water. The pool sometimes overflows when the spring gushes strongly. You mustn't soak your fine leather shoes. When it's safe, I will call you.'

She took a determined step up, though it meant pushing her cheek against his groin. The spiral staircase was only wide enough for one person to move safely and, as she'd hoped, he had no choice but to retreat back into the chapel to allow her to pass. As soon as she was safely through the door to the well, she locked it behind them and, on the pretext of fetching dry candles, she fled.

Her first thought was to warn Prioress Johanne, for she couldn't possibly open the chapel to pilgrims, not with . . . But as she was hurrying across the courtyard towards the prioress's chamber, she saw Basilia emerge from the infirmary, leading the boy by the hand. Fina had forgotten about them. There were only two other keys to the well. One hung in the prioress's chambers, for she had the key to every door in the priory, but the gatekeeper, Meggy, had the third, and if

Basilia went to the well door and found it was locked, she might fetch Meggy to unlock it. Basilia must not take the boy down there, not now, not today.

Fina picked up her skirts and ran towards the waddling infirmarer and the boy, intending to steer them away before they reached the chapel, though she hadn't any notion of what explanation she would give. But charging across a yard as slippery as a greased pig with mud and goose-droppings was bound to end in disaster. Fina had taken no more than a few paces before her foot slid from beneath her and she came crashing down. Spears of pain shot through her arm and knee as she lay in the stinking, wet ooze, wanting to clamber up, but too shaken to attempt it. Basilia dropped the boy's hand and hurried over, almost slipping herself in her haste.

'Sister! Sister, are you hurt?' She prodded and squeezed Fina, as if to discover whether she was fat enough to be slaughtered. The shriek Fina uttered when she touched her arm made her stop. Over Basilia's plump shoulder, she glimpsed Nicholas emerging from the chapel. He was the last person she wanted to see as she sprawled in the mud and filth. But he had evidently seen her and was approaching all too swiftly.

'Help me up, Sister,' she begged, dragging heavily on the infirmarer's arm. Fina succeeded in standing, but her knee gave way in a flash of pain and she almost collapsed again. 'Sister,' she whispered urgently, 'you mustn't let anyone unlock the door to that well . . . There is something down there . . . I must find the prioress . . .'

'The only thing you must do, Sister Fina, is to get that arm and leg attended to,' Basilia said firmly.

'Listen, please,' Fina begged.

'I have her, Sister Basilia,' Nicholas's voice broke in, and before either woman could protest he'd scooped Fina up in his arms and was striding across the courtyard towards the sisters' dorter.

Chapter 14

Prioress Johanne

'Whatever possessed you to gallop across the yard like a stable boy, Sister Fina, especially when it was so muddy?' I snapped, as soon as I reached the narrow bed on which she lay. 'Even a child would know to take more care.'

I hadn't intended my words to sound as harsh as they did, but my annoyance was partly born of guilt. The arrival of Brother Nicholas was occupying all my thoughts, so that I'd scarcely noticed how muddy and treacherous the courtyard had become. I should have given orders for it to be scraped and strewn with straw, but there was so little left that the servants were having to use bracken to bed the horses and could scarcely cut enough for that. The tracks were so wet that the horses pulling the sledges became mired to their hocks and it was easier for the servants to fetch what little bracken they could carry on their backs than spend hours dragging the exhausted beasts from the mud.

Fina blinked at me, then struggled to sit up, but I pushed her down. She was deathly pale, whiter even than the bleached linen sheets in which she lay. Basilia, with the help of two servants, had managed to wrestle her dislocated knee back into place. She'd also bandaged Fina's arm and, though our infirmarer believed it to be cracked, the bone had not snapped in two or pierced the skin. I guessed that she had given Fina something to dull the pain while they had dealt with her knee, for her eyes were unfocused, and when she spoke, her words were slurred.

'Unclean spirits. The devil's spirits, mustn't . . . he mustn't see.'

'Sister Fina,' I said sharply, intentionally so this time, trying to rouse her, 'are you speaking of little Cosmas again? You are a sister of the Knights of St John, not an ignorant village woman. He is just a child come to us for help, nothing more. You have been taught that our Lord himself said, "Whoever receives a child in my name, receives me." It is compassion and prayer the boy needs, not accusations of demons and sorcery. The draught Sister Basilia gave you has made you drowsy. I will leave you to sleep. We will speak again when you wake and I trust that by then your good sense will have returned.'

I hoped the syrup Basilia had given her was the cause of this nonsense and not the recurrence of the trouble that had afflicted her when first she joined us. She had come to our priory straight from her father's house. She had appeared shy and naïve, which was natural enough for any highborn young woman who had seen nothing of the world, but I also sensed a bitter resentment in her.

Not all of our noble sisters enter the order entirely by their own choice, though they must swear that they do. It is not unknown for their kin to persuade them that they have but two alternatives: to become a sister of the Knights of St John where they are comparatively free to travel and

120

work, or to enter a nunnery to be walled up in the cloister with little to do, save pray and idle away the weary hours in games and gossip. Though, if Brother Nicholas had his way, we would not even be offered that semblance of a choice.

But to a young woman who from childhood has dreamed of marriage and being mistress of her own house, even such freedoms as the Knights of St John can offer may seem like the bars of a cage. I knew that Fina saw me as an ageing prioress who could not possibly understand the torment and longings of youth, but I did. I had not made my profession in the order willingly, though my dreams had been very different from hers. But my own father had decided that placing two of his children in different orders was politically and spiritually expedient, for then the religious of two orders would offer masses for his soul when he departed this life, and Christ must surely regard one, at least, with favour.

It was the reason I had appointed Fina keeper of the well, although Clarice had warned me she was far too young. It was true she was immature and often given to strange fancies, but I hoped that such responsibility might help her settle in the order, even grow to love it as I had done. And it had appeared to work. St Lucia's blessed water had wrought a miracle. Fina had come to treasure the well, as fiercely protective of it as old Meggy was of her gate or Sibyl her kitchen.

I tried to assure myself that her wild words now were due to the shock of the fall and anxiety about who would care for her beloved well. When she was rested, she would doubtless be herself again.

I had already turned away when I felt the tug of a hand on my skirts. 'Not the boy. The well . . . go alone to the well.'

Fina was trying to drag herself towards the ring of keys

that lay on a stool near her bed. She almost tumbled out as she tried to reach them. She was becoming so agitated that I knew she wouldn't rest until she had them, so I placed them in her hand and, for the second time, pushed her back against the pillow. 'Lie still, Sister, or you'll do yourself more harm.'

But Fina grasped my hand and pressed my fingers around an iron key so hard that the edge bit into my flesh, making me wince.

'Alone,' the young woman repeated, her face screwed up in an effort to voice the single word.

I took care picking my way across the courtyard. I certainly didn't want to find myself lying in a bed with an injured back or worse. I'd given orders that the worst of the mud and dung should be scraped up, and planks and old sacks should be laid in front of doorways for people to walk on. Two of the servants, their skirts looped up to keep them out of the filth, were already at work with Brengy, the stable boy, and his young sister, Dye. They were shovelling piles of stinking sludge into a wheelbarrow. They paused to blow on their wet, cold hands and glowered at me, but I was used to that, and merely nodded. My duty was to manage the priory for the good of all, not to curry affection.

A thick rolling mass of granite-grey clouds turned morning to twilight. Inside the chapel it was almost too dark to see the pillars. The light from the lamp barely grazed the altar over which it hung. But as my eyes adjusted, I saw that the door leading down to the well lay open. Had the pilgrims been admitted? I crossed to the door through which they would enter the chapel, but it was still bolted.

Footfalls sounded on the stone floor behind me and I

turned to see the redoubtable form of Meggy lumbering away from the well door, lantern in hand. She started as she caught sight of me in the shadows, and guilt flashed across her face.

'Should you not be at the gate, Goodwife Meggy?'

'Heard poor Sister Fina had a bad fall. Didn't know if she'd opened the well for pilgrims. Went down to see if candles had been lit.'

'You could have asked one of the sisters to do that.'

'Didn't want trouble them. 'Sides,' she added, with a mulish shrug, 'my niece is these two years married and still not with child, so I said I'd fetch some holy water from the well for her, so St Lucia will grant her a babe.'

'St Lucia is not known for such miracles. Your niece should light a candle to the Blessed Virgin and ask her for a son.'

Before I had banished the cunning woman and her tribe of daughters, barren women had come to bathe naked in the spring, not seeking a blessing from a holy saint of the Church but to ask some pagan goddess to make them fecund. Some still tried, and one had fled dripping, without stopping to pull on her gown, when the sisters had surprised her. I was fond of Meggy. She was a loyal soul and, in her own way, good and honest, but she was still a villager at heart. No matter how often I had reproved her, she still could not entirely shake off the superstitious ways of the moorland people. I had little doubt that if any of the spring water were to be given to Meggy's niece, it would be the old goddess who would be invoked, not St Lucia.

I was just on the point of reminding Meggy for the hundredth time that she was a gatekeeper in a Hospitallers' priory, and that the order did not employ those who prayed to idols, when I noticed that the candle flame in the lantern she was clutching was guttering wildly. Her hand was trembling. 'Are you ill, Meggy?'

The woman shook her head, glancing behind her at the open door leading down to the holy spring.

'Is something wrong with the well? Sister Fina seemed to want me to inspect it. Did you see anything amiss?'

She made a strangled noise as if she was about to speak, but had choked on the word. She thrust the lantern into my hand. 'Been coming to the well since I were a girl and old Kendra's ma was keeper of it. I've never seen anything like this afore. You take a look for yourself, Prioress. Don't know how we'll get them out, unless they've a mind to go.'

'Get who out?' I demanded. 'Is someone down there?' I edged towards the door and dangled the lantern inside, but all I could see were the first few steps curving down. I strained to listen for any sound of movement below, but heard only Meggy's ponderous footsteps retreating across the chapel floor behind me.

The gatekeeper paused, grasping the latch of the chapel door. 'Old Father Guthlac was right. There's a curse come to this place with that boy and it'll not lift till he goes.' With that she wrenched open the door to the courtyard and was gone.

Taking a deep breath and a firm grip of the lantern, I edged down the first of the uneven steps. The craggy walls began to twinkle with the familiar green-gold shimmer. Normally, the sight filled me with a wondrous joy and peace, but today I was too anxious about whom I might discover below to see the beauty of it.

I'd reached the point on the stone steps where I should have been able to see the glow from the candles that burned beside the spring, but the only visible light came from the lantern I carried and the glimmer from the walls. The trickle and splashing of water grew louder as I descended, but I could hear nothing else. No voices or feet rattling loose stones on the cave floor.

I paused on the second to last step. The lamplight had caught a flicker of movement. At first I thought the water in the pool was overflowing and had flooded the cave. I lowered the lantern so that the light fell on the floor. But it wasn't water rippling across the floor. It was frogs, hundreds of glistening green-gold frogs. There were so many that they were climbing over each other, eyes bulging, throats pulsing in and out. The stone trough was heaving with them, all jostling to find space. Even as I stared, more crawled out over the lip of the pool, and they'd no sooner leaped to the floor than another wave clambered out behind them.

I had seen tiny froglets in the damp cave before, but they had vanished into the cracks and crevices of the rocks as soon as light fell upon them, and there'd never been more than two or three at a time. Frogs were generated from the filth of mud and slime, and there was certainly enough mud up on the hills after all this rain to breed a plague of them. If I'd seen them out there on the moor, in that desolation of sucking mires and black pools, I would not have been surprised. All the foul creatures of the night dwelt in those bogs. But that the pure, holy water of the well should spawn such vile beasts, the very symbols of sin and wickedness, was unthinkable. Now I understood what Sister Fina had meant when she spoke of evil spirits. Words from The Apocalypse of St John pounded in my head, accusing, flaying –

de ore pseudoprophetae spiritus tres inmundos in modum ranarum sunt enim spiritus daemoniorum. From the mouth of the false prophet, three unclean spirits like frogs, for they are the spirits of devils.

I hastily made the sign of the cross. We would have to close the well to pilgrims until a way could be found to cleanse the cave of such an abomination, but word must not get out. If it became known that the very water that was meant to heal and bless had generated a swarm of evil spirits, the pilgrims would never return. But what reason could I—

I jerked around at the sound of a low whistle. Brother Nicholas was standing on the stairs behind me, staring down over my head. Swiftly I raised the lantern in front of me, trying to plunge the floor of the cave into darkness, but even as I did so, I knew it was too late. The knight had already seen all that I had wanted to conceal.

'So, this is why Sister Fina was so anxious I shouldn't visit the well this morning.'

He pulled the lantern from my grasp and, crushing me against the wet wall, squeezed past me. He descended a few paces, peering at the heaving floor and the frogs swarming out of the trough. He raised his foot and stamped on two of the little creatures that were trying to crawl up the steps. They screamed as they died. He ground their corpses beneath his boot, scraping off the gory remains on the edge of the stone step.

'At least we know they're made of flesh and blood.' He gave a mirthless laugh. 'So, what has brought this plague upon your house, Prioress Johanne? I assume the pilgrims don't usually have to share their holy water with these foul imps. Some might be tempted to think God is punishing your stubbornness, like he punished the pharaoh of Egypt. But then frogs are a sign of heresy too, are they not? If the Lord Prior learns of this . . .'

We both knew I did not need him to complete that threat.

'On the other hand, Prioress, with no pilgrims bringing offerings until our little friends have departed, dear Sister Clarice's ingenious accounts might, in the end, prove accurate. Wouldn't that be a curious justice? Perhaps that's why you have been visited with such a plague, Prioress. She claims the offerings are low, so to keep her from the sin of falsehood, Our Lord is ensuring that they are.'

Brother Nicholas thrust the lantern back at me with a triumphant grin. 'I should make sure you close the door when you leave. You won't want Satan's imps infesting the entire priory. You'll find that much harder to conceal.'

Chapter 15

Sorrel

I heaved the bucket of wet tailings into the barrow and watched as the lad dragged it up the slope of the spoil heap and tipped it over the edge. *Tailings?* A month ago I'd not even known the word existed, but in the past few days I'd had to learn fast.

The tinners thought it great sport to talk in a language only they could understand. *Carry that to the bundle*, they'd say, then crack their sides laughing as I set off in the wrong direction. I'd asked the women what I was meant to do and they'd sighed and rolled their eyes, as if I was a moon-touched bairn, but they'd shown me how to tip the gravel on to a long, sloping stone slab where the water separated it into *heads*, which contained the heavy tin, and *tailings*, the lighter waste. They'd warned me they'd only show it me once, mind, for they couldn't afford to lose time teaching me instead of earning.

But Todde, being a man, wouldn't ask. The first time, he filled the buckets with the useless stones instead of the tin gravel. The tinners winked and grinned to each other but said naught. They let him heft those buckets all the way up to the crushing stones and watched him pound the gravel till the sweat streamed off him. Only when he'd hauled the broken stone up the slope and into the blowing-house did a bellow of laughter break out from the men below, nearly as loud as the blast of the horn.

The stoker came storming out, railing at the miners. 'Spit-frogs! Nugheads! Suppose you think that's funny, do you? If I'd not seen what this codwit was up to, his dross would have ruined the firing and it'd have had to be done all over again. Fuel doesn't come cheap, you know. Master Odo would have taken the cost from all our wages.'

'He will anyhow,' one man muttered darkly.

'Can't expect us to watch Todde like a babby,' another called up. 'He said he were old hand at tinning.'

'Well, you'd better make sure he learns to be and fast too, else we'll all be going hungry.'

Give him his due, Todde swallowed his humiliation and was learning. His arms were strong, and though he'd still a way to go afore he matched the skill of the experienced tinners, he was the last to set his hammer down when the horn blew at dusk and the first to lift his shovel at crack of day. The tinners began grudgingly to nod their approval behind his back.

At night, after we had gulped down the few mouthfuls of our meagre supper, I had taken to wandering up to Eva's fireside to get warm. Most days I was lucky if I could gather enough kindling and dung to keep the cooking fire alight long enough to heat the pot. Neither Todde nor I had time to cut and dry peat on the moor, which most of the tinners' wives burned, for we had to spend what hours of light there were trying to earn money. The dried mutton Gleedy had

129

given us was now no more than a lingering flavour in water that contained only herbs and a handful of dried peas I'd borrowed from Eva. She was a good soul and I'd often catch her slipping a piece of meat or dried fish into the hand of one of the small children who'd creep up to her hut after the tinners had gone in the hope of a bite. It was a pity she had no bairns of her own, for she'd have been the best of mothers.

She would glance up when I hesitantly approached, jerking her head towards a place close by the fire, as her way of saying I was welcome to share it. Mostly we sat in silence for, unlike the women I'd known back in the village and the tinners' wives, she never gossiped about others. Neither did she talk about her own life or worries. She spoke only when she needed to, as if words were precious coins that should not be wasted on fripperies.

But I reckon she did have troubles, for when she was passing by my hut, a day or so after we arrived, I noticed a great purple bruise on her cheek. I asked her if she had slipped in the mud, but she shrugged and trudged on up to her cooking fire by the ruined wall.

A tinner's wife watched her until she was out of earshot, then nodded towards her retreating back. 'I'll wager a man gave her that. It's not the first time I've seen her with a black eye or a cut lip. Cook their suppers and warm their beds for them, and that's the payment you get.'

I wasn't surprised by the bruise. Father had given them to Mam often enough. It was what a man did once he'd got a woman to wed him. She was his then, to use as he pleased, like a beast he'd bought at market. But all the same I was puzzled. I wondered which of the tinners who gathered around Eva's fire she'd taken as her lover. I scrolled through their faces in my head. I couldn't think of one I'd want in my bed, not that any man would want me, as my father had constantly reminded me. But I wondered why Eva put up with such treatment, if she wasn't married to the man. There were plenty of others to choose from in the camp.

While Eva never grudged me a share of her fire I felt bad that I'd nothing to offer in return. Then one night, after the tinners had gone back to their own huts, she settled down to pluck a few snipe she had snared. I picked one up, wedged the carcass between my knees, and swiftly ripped out the feathers with my good hand, neither tearing the skin nor leaving any shafts. I caught Eva watching me out of the tail of her eye. She said nothing, so I took up another bird and worked on, silently plucking and handing them to her to be gutted and dismembered ready to be dropped into her pot. Later, as I walked down to my own hut, I heard hurrying footsteps behind me. I felt something soft and cold thrust silently into my hand. It was one of the plucked snipe. I turned to thank her, but she had already vanished into the darkness.

Each night after I dragged myself away from the warmth of Eva's fire, I had to return to the misery of the cold, wet hut I shared with Todde. He was usually snoring by the time I crept in, for I tried to stay out until I thought he would be sleeping. I did not feel completely at ease sharing a hut with him. Sometimes, I'd wake in the night and listen to him breathe, watching his chest rise and fall. Once his fingers had lingered when they'd accidently brushed mine as I was handing him a bowl. I'd snatched my hand away and he'd dropped his gaze, staring at the ground as if he'd never seen it before, his face flushed. I still didn't know what to make of him.

131

Shivering, I wrapped myself in one of the damp, stinking sheepskins Gleedy had given us. My legs ached with the cramp, and my toes swelled and itched for my feet never seemed to get dry, but in spite of that, sheer exhaustion always dragged me into sleep. I dreamed of black mud and grey water.

Even trapped inside the mire of those dreams, I knew I must find the woman who had called to me. I was desperate to hear her voice again. Every night I begged her to speak to me. But she had fallen silent and I couldn't rouse her, couldn't reach her. Some nights, I was sure she was hidden just out of sight along the track. If I could reach the next bend in my dreams I would find her, but my feet were gripped fast in the mud and, as I struggled to free myself, I was jerked awake into another ash-grey dawn by the shrill blast of the ram's horn echoing across the valley.

Don't leave me here in this valley. Speak to me. Show me how to find you!

The sun was sinking behind the ridge above the tin workings and a dark tide was seeping up the valley before the ram's horn sounded the two notes to signal the end of the long day's hard toil. The bairns were the first to throw down their tools and escape. Older children began plodding up to their parents' huts, carrying the little ones, who were already falling asleep, utterly exhausted after a day of fetching and carrying, filling buckets and sorting through gravel. But all who wanted to eat had to work.

I rinsed the grime from my face and hands in the puddles left in one of the wooden leats. I'd soon discovered that they were cleaner than the river into which all the dirt from the gravel washings and the filth from the camp were emptied.

Using my teeth, I pulled off the mud-soaked rag wrapped around my fingers and dangled my hand in the icy water, sucking in my breath with a hiss as it touched skin rubbed raw and weeping from the rope handle of the bucket. I'd always thought the skin on my right hand was as tough as tanned cow's leather, but I'd not spent long days at home lugging heavy buckets full of wet earth and stones.

'You best stir yourself else it'll all be gone,' a woman called, over her shoulder, as she scurried by.

I glanced up. A straggling procession of men and women were making their way along the valley towards the blowing-house. The whole camp seemed to be on the move. I hurried to catch up with the woman, trying not to slip in my haste.

'Where they all going?'

She frowned at me, as if she thought I was mocking her. She glanced down at my withered hand, and her frown lifted. 'Course, you're the woman came with the squab. Don't you know what day it is?'

I shook my head and she gave a weary smile.

'Aye, well, can't say as I blame you. One day's same as another here. But it's Saturday, when old Gleedy doles out our wages and opens his stores so we can buy what we need for the week, seeing as how we can't get to market. But flour and beans have been real scarce lately, so you'll have to hurry if you want any.'

I scrambled after her as she toiled up the muddy track, my spirits lifting. At last I'd receive some money for my toil and, best of all, buy something to put in the pot, a good measure of beans or peas, flour to make flatbread, perhaps even a little meat. My belly ached for solid food after the watery soup I'd been eating. I remembered the excited gleam

133

in Todde's eyes that night in the drovers' hut when he spoke of the merchants flocking to sell to the tinners. *They live off the fat of the land, those tinners do.* I'd seen precious little fat since we'd arrived, but perhaps tonight we would eat well.

The choking smoke and metallic stench from the blowing-house billowed down to meet us, wrapping itself around us in the damp air. The door was open and a heavy, scorching heat blasted out into the chill night. A fiery glow lit the inside, turning the faces and clothes of all blood-red, as if we were staring into the maw of a roaring dragon. Outside, a great waterwheel churned, pumping the giant bellows for the furnace. But the tinners and their womenfolk were already hurrying past it towards a lower stone building, hidden from the valley below by the blowing-house in front. Two huge hounds had been chained to one side of it, and were straining at their spiked collars, leaping and barking savagely at all those coming towards them, though their leashes were too short to allow them to reach anyone. I fervently hoped their tethers were strong.

I edged in through the open door and found myself gawping like the village mooncalf at the sight inside. Gleedy was standing towards the back of the long building, surrounded by more kegs, boxes and sacks than I'd ever seen, even on market day. Sheepskins were piled on shelves next to cats of salt. A tower of buckets teetered precariously next to a stack of shovels. Bundles of rope and cord swung from the hooks on the beams beside several ladders, a swathe of axes and barrels of every size.

In what little free space remained, men and women had formed a straggly line in front of a broad oak table. A hunched, pimple-faced youth was perched on a stool behind the table. A ledger, a small brass-banded wooden box, a guttering candle and a dish of ink and quills were crowded so near to his elbows it was a wonder he didn't send them all flying when he moved. As each person came forward, he consulted the ledger, then slowly counted out coins, which he laid in a row close to him, as if he feared they'd be snatched away before he'd finished. Only when the person had made their mark in the ledger on the spot where he pointed did he slide the coins towards them.

Eva was hovering near the table, and the men I'd seen eating at her fireside on the first night each handed her a few coins as they passed. She looked more cheerful than most of the men and women, who scowled as they scooped up their paltry wages and hurried towards the stores. A couple of men argued with the lad, insisting he look again at the sum written in the ledger, but he jerked his head in Gleedy's direction and shrugged. Still grousing, but under their breath, the men made their marks.

Gleedy seemed too busy to notice the dark looks he was getting from the men near the table, or maybe he was indifferent to them, for those tinners he was dealing with seemed equally disgruntled. He was emptying a measure of withered peas into a small sack held open by one of the women. The coin she proffered vanished instantly into the deep leather pouch dangling from the belt around his hips. He beckoned to another woman and two rushed forward together, shoving each other in an effort to be served first. In the time it took to say a paternoster, he'd sold half a dozen salted sprats from a barrel, a handful of iron nails, a battered cooking pot, a length of rope, some dried beans and a small measure of rye flour to different customers, without once pausing to think or search for anything. Several times, though, he shook his head, showing empty barrels and sacks, and I realised my

135

neighbour had been right. There might be plenty of nails and shovels to be had, but you can't fill a belly with those. I would have to make haste to claim what I was owed and buy whatever food I could.

But before I could join the queue in front of the table, someone began shouting and my belly lurched. I recognised the voice only too well.

'All the graffing and crushing I've done, and you're saying that's all I have to show for it!' Todde bellowed. 'Don't you think you can cheat me, boy, just 'cause I'm newly come.'

He reached across the table and seized the lad's jerkin, hauling him up off the stool so that his toes were barely grazing the floor. The boy struggled to prise the great fists off. Todde dropped him and he tumbled backwards over the stool, letting out a high-pitched yelp, like a kicked puppy.

Gleedy strode across, elbowing people aside. 'What's all this?'

Todde rounded on him. 'This lad of yours is trying to get me to make my mark in that book to show I've had all that's due to me. Means to fob me off with a tenth of what I'm owed and he'll slip the rest into his own purse. I know his sort. Just 'cause he can read, he reckons he can gull us. But I wasn't hatched in a goose's nest. Here!' He brandished a notched stick in Gleedy's face. 'I've got the tally of every bucket I've fetched to the blowing-house and I've been keeping my ears and eyes open. I know exactly what they're worth.'

Gleedy took the stick and counted, then pulled the ledger towards him. 'See for yourself. What's written in the ledger exactly matches your tally, every last bucket.'

'Then why is this little arse-wipe only giving us this?'

Todde pointed to the few coins that now lay scattered across the table.

'That's what's due to you after what you owe has been paid.'

'Owe? I owe no man.'

'Sleep out in the open on the moor, do you?' Gleedy asked.

Todde frowned in bewilderment, but I caught the looks the other men were exchanging around him, and before Gleedy had said anything more, I suddenly understood what Eva had been trying to warn me about that first night.

'You sleep in a snug cottage, isn't that right? So there's rent to be paid for it, not to mention the sum you owe for the dried mutton and onions you've been stuffing your belly with and those sheepskins keeping you warm. Then there's the hire of the buckets, picks, hammers and shovels you've been using and wearing out. And there's taxes to be paid to the King on every ingot of tin that leaves here, afore it can even go to market. Fact,' he said tapping the ledger. 'What you owe Master Odo comes to more than twice what you've earned this week. So, by rights, the lad shouldn't be giving you anything. But I told him to pay you enough to buy a bit of food for your pot. "Can't work if they're starving," I says. You can pay the rest off each week, till you're clear.'

Todde had turned scarlet with rage. 'You thieving bastard! You never told me that!'

Gleedy shrugged. 'Only a fool would think he'd could use another's man's tools to work another man's land, then keep all the profits.'

'And it takes a bigger fool to think I'd stay,' Todde retorted. 'You can tell Master Odo he can work his own land. I'll not pay him for the pleasure of doing his work.'

Gleedy grimaced in the mocking way the mummers do when they're pretending to be sad to make a crowd laugh. 'I see now I should have explained to you how a free man earns a living. You being a villein, you'll not have worked for wages afore.'

The blood drained from Todde's face and his eyes bulged, as if Gleedy was pressing his hands round his throat. 'I'm no serf,' he spluttered. 'I was born a freeman. I'm a tinner!'

'You are now and living under the King's protection. Long as you remain a tinner, your old master can't touch you. But if you was to leave here with no tools to prove your trade and no claim on any land, the lord who owns you would have you dragged back at the horse's tail. And if you are the villein they've been hunting, he'll have you hanged for a thief too, 'cause you didn't run empty-handed, did you?'

Todde was shaking his head violently, but couldn't utter a sound.

Gleedy patted his shoulder. 'But don't you go losing so much as a peck of sleep over it. Long as you stay here, you're as safe as if the King's own guards were standing watch over you. You're in good company too. Half the men and women here are runaways. But they know their old masters can't touch a hair on their heads, leastways providing they don't make trouble and get themselves thrown out.'

I felt as stunned as Todde looked. I'd realised from that first night in the camp that Todde had never seen tin-workings before, much less been a tinner. But most men boast of skills they don't have. It had never occurred to me that he was a runaway, a bound man. Men who flee their manors and masters usually run with little or nothing. He had had tools and the donkey! There would be a price on his head, and anyone in the land could claim it whether they delivered his head with or without the rest of him. My face must have betrayed my shock, for Todde looked anguished as he caught sight of me.

'I swear there's not a word of truth in it, Sorrel,' he protested. 'That bastard's tongue is as forked as a viper's. He's been lying to us from the start. It was no chance meeting we had with him on that track. He was waiting for those outlaws to rob us. He probably pays them to do it.' He pointed towards the stores. 'It's how he gets all that. I reckon if you searched back there you'd find all my tools and your pot too.'

Fury gathered in his face and he twisted round to face Gleedy again. 'I'm right, aren't I? Those outlaws, they *are* in your pay!'

Two men were edging up behind Todde. Gleedy's eyes flicked towards them. I could see what was coming.

'Todde, leave it!' I pleaded, but he ignored me.

Gleedy laughed. 'Mine? You think cut-throats like that'd answer to me?' He pulled a comic face, exaggerating his squint. 'Rob me blind they would.'

The tinners laughed far more heartily than the feeble joke deserved. Gleedy sauntered away, as if the matter was settled. But Todde hadn't finished. With a bellow of fury, he launched himself at the retreating back, but had taken no more than a pace before his arms were caught by Gleedy's two henchmen, who pinned him against the wall. One drew back his fist aiming it at Todde's belly, but a burly tinner caught his arm, shaking his head.

'He'll be no use to Gleedy if he can't work, will he?'

The two men hesitated, glancing at Gleedy, but he was already serving his next customer. Reluctantly they let Todde go. Men and women averted their eyes and began talking loudly again, determined to pretend nothing had happened. But the tinner who'd saved him laid a firm hand on Todde's shoulder.

'Like your woman says, let it go. Be grateful he left you with enough coin to buy a bite. Seven days is a long time to go begging for scraps from neighbours when you've naught in your pot, and he's been known to do that and far worse to men that cross him once too often.'

Chapter 16

Hospitallers' Priory of St Mary

Brother Nicholas lifted his gaze from the accounts ledger as the candle flame snuffed itself out, leaving only a wisp of smoke. He rubbed his dry, smarting eyes, surprised to discover it was already dark inside the chamber. He'd been working by the light of a candle all afternoon: little daylight found its way over the high wall and in through the tiny casement, still less when the day was as leaden and grey as this. It must be later than he'd realised.

He'd been chasing the capricious figures from one parchment roll to another, but it was like trying to catch a shape-shifter by the tail. He was sure the accounts were not correct but, like the procurator at Clerkenwell, he could not pin down exactly where they were wrong. Money was missing, he was almost certain of that, but if it was, then from where? How was it disappearing, and into whose purse? The sisters were not spending it on living in luxury, if the food being served was any measure of that. So how far had the corruption spread? Were they all conspiring in this theft, if indeed that was what it proved to be, or was it just that crafty old

141

hag Sister Clarice? She'd certainly been extremely anxious that he should not examine the books.

The prioress had told him that Clarice had managed her husband's warehouses before she joined the order. And she had certainly gained the skills of bookkeeping, Nicholas had to admit. In fact one might say she had learned the art rather too well. Just what other lessons had she learned from some of the less scrupulous merchants and sea-captains? But he would uncover the truth. He refused to be made to look a fool by some withered old vecke, who should be spending her dotage sitting silently in a cloister, sewing altar cloths or whatever it was that nuns did.

The door of the priory's small guest chamber was flung open and slammed shut with equal vigour, sending a violent blast of glacial wind whirling around the room. The draught snatched up the parchment Nicholas had earlier laid to dry on the table and sent it spinning to the floor. But he was too busy trying to keep the quills from being blown into the embers of the fire to notice where his letter had landed, until he heard the ominous crunch of parchment and glanced down to see it crushed beneath Alban's muddy boot.

'You frog-witted ox! I know you're used to living in a stable, but haven't you at least learned how to enter a room without wrecking it?'

'Why did you toss it on the floor if you didn't want it walked on?'

Ignoring Nicholas's splutter of curses and insults, he lumbered over to his narrow bed and flopped down on the thin straw mattress so heavily it was a marvel that the wooden legs beneath didn't splinter or the cords snap.

Nicholas retrieved the parchment and examined it with dismay and fury. Wetted by the sodden footprint, black ink was dribbling down the page. Every word the loutish boot had stamped on was obliterated. 'Look!' he spat. 'It's taken me half the afternoon to write this and it is not even fit for an arse-wipe now.' He crumpled it and hurled it savagely into the fire. He instantly regretted it and tried to pluck it out, but it was already burning, turning his carefully crafted sentences to smoke and ashes. He cursed again. He could at least have used the fragments that were not smeared to jog his memory. God alone knew when Hob's wagon would return from Buckland, but when it did, Nicholas wanted to be sure his reports were ready to be dispatched immediately with the carter.

Alban lay on the narrow bed, watching him indifferently. 'You're in a sour temper. Fleas biting your arse, are they? It's me that should be grousing. While you've been sitting warm by a fire, scratching away like some fusty old monk, I've been up to my oxters in freezing water, trying to clean a cartload of mud off your rouncy, then pluck the burrs and thorns from his belly and legs. Where have you been riding that poor horse?'

'You'll be up to your armpits in cold water again, this time head first, if I find so much as a mote of dirt on that beast. I was out at dawn, freezing my cods off in a gale, riding these blasted moorlands and trying to prise some sense out of toothless old gammers and their drooling offspring, all of whom do nothing but grunt and stare at you till you start to wonder if you shouldn't be talking to their hogs instead.'

Alban gave a sly grin. 'And there was me thinking we're pledged to be the serfs and servants of the blessed poor, whom we should treat as if they were our lords and masters.'

'If you want to serve the poor, you'll find them out there grubbing around in the mud and rain, believing they'll make their fortune by digging for tin in other people's dung heaps. It's not the poor I've been chasing for days, but those who feign poverty, those who think they can fool me by hiding their cattle or concealing their kegs in caves. Everywhere I go it's the same story.'

He twisted his hands into the mockery of a fawning man. '"God's chollers, sir, you've come all this way and got yourself fair drowned on the road, and all for nothing, seeing as how I've already paid the holy sisters. Can't ask me to pay the rent twice, now can you, sir?"

'They think that by paying those harpies half what is due to our order, they can cheat us out of the rest. And that's when I can find my way to their wretched little farms and watermills. Ask anyone round here for directions and they either pretend they can't understand you, or deliberately send you in the opposite direction. And if they can lead you into a mire or through an icy stream on the way, they'll do it and think it rare sport.'

He punched the lumpy straw mattress on his own bed as if it was a man's face. 'But they'll rue the day they tried to deceive me, as will that wily old embezzler Sister Clarice. There is more mischief to be uncovered here than a few missing rents. I can smell the stench of it. That boy they claim to be blind, for one. Sister Melisene was certain he sent a spirit to torment and murder the old priest. But the prioress maintains the boy is dumb and can't be examined. She's deliberately keeping him from me.'

Alban grunted. 'You want to be careful if you go chasing after little boys. There's some might start saying you have a fancy for them. I keep my ears cocked in the taverns and marketplaces. There's talk that the knights of the white cross are no better than the knights of the red, buggers to a man.'

In two strides Nicholas was at the bed. He grabbed the front of Alban's shirt, hauling the groom up till his face was inches from Nicholas's own. 'I'm no sodomite and no Templar.'

'Hold hard!' Alban protested, trying to wrench himself out of Nicholas's fists. 'I don't take kindly to those insults any more than you do. The last man I heard say as much, I knocked straight through a wall. I'm just telling you what's rumoured.'

'I know full well what's rumoured!' Nicholas bellowed, thrusting Alban back hard on to his bed. 'Ever since the Templars confessed to kissing each other's arses and pissing on the cross, half of Christendom has been whispering that the Knights of St John indulge in the same foul practices.' His fists were clenched so hard that his knuckles had turned white. All the honour, all the glory so hard won throughout the centuries by noble men who had pledged their lives and souls for Christendom, all that gave meaning and purpose to his own life had been turned to dust and dung in the eyes of men and God because of what the Templars had done. They had soiled the very title 'knight' and all it stood for.

He slumped back on to his bed. 'Those fools in France didn't act swiftly enough. They burned the Templars they caught, but they let half of them slip through their fingers and escape to foul our nest in England, and our king won't supply enough men to hunt them down. Says his coffers are bare and we all know why – he's been stuffing the pockets of his own little catamites. Even when they do arrest the Templars hiding here, they're not put to the rack properly, because thanks to King Edward's lily liver, there's no one in England competent enough to do it without killing them before they've uttered a word. They have to smoke out every last one of the Templars and burn them for the filthy vermin they are. Until they do, we will all be tainted.'

'Aye, but till that happens, you want to be careful not to set tongues wagging here 'cause women will use anything they can against a man if it serves them. More cunning than a skulk of vixens, they are.'

'They can try any trick they dream up,' Nicholas said. 'But I swear that before I'm done I'll uncover every festering sore that the prioress is trying to hide from me and she will pay dearly for them all.'

Chapter 17

Sorrel

As soon as I plodded up to Eva's fire I could see that something was amiss. Usually by this time she'd be threading her way between the men and children, collecting the bowls that had been scraped clean and hovering impatiently over those who were trying to make the pottage last by savouring every mouthful. But that evening she was crouching on a rock beside the fire, hunched over the flames as if she couldn't soak up enough warmth, caged inside her own thoughts.

On most nights the menfolk, though always weary, brightened as the hot food slid into their bellies, cheered by the knowledge that a few precious hours of sleep lay between them and another round of muscle-tearing work. They'd pick through the bones of the day, teasing each other, bickering or grumbling, and when there was nothing left to chew over, they'd dice, or play a few rounds of 'cross and pile', flipping a coin and betting on which side up it would land. The tinners gambled on anything and everything, even how far they could spit or piss. I reckoned they were in as much debt to each other as to Gleedy.

But Eva's mood had settled over the men, like a winter's fog lingering over a pool. She didn't glance up as, one by one, the tinners dropped their wooden bowls in a heap next to her and, with a wary glance, ambled off back to their own huts. As the last vanished, I slid on to a stone close to the fire and held out my hand to catch its warmth, rubbing the heat, like an unguent, over my aching knees. From below came the sounds of families settling in for the night: the babbling of voices, children yelling, iron pots clanging, and the rasp of whetstones as men sharpened tools ready for the coming day. A shower of scarlet sparks rose, like a flock of birds, into the darkening, smoke-filled sky as someone tossed another peat on to the embers of their fire. Still Eva didn't stir. Even in the orange-red glow of her own fire she looked pale, her eyes sunk into dark hollows.

'You sick?' I asked softly.

Her head jerked up, as if she hadn't realised I was there. By way of answer, she struggled up and bent to collect the bowls the tinners had discarded. I scrambled to my feet and went to help her, taking a pile from her hand. She stooped again to gather up the rest, but as she reached out, a cry escaped her and she remained doubled over, clutching her belly. I dropped the bowls I was holding and guided her back to the rock. It was only as I tried to ease her down that I saw the dark stain on the grey granite, glistening in the fire-light. The back of her skirt was soaked with blood. She stared vacantly, as if she couldn't remember what she was doing.

I laid a hand on her arm to try to get her attention. 'Your moon time come? You want me to find you some rags?'

She frowned, and for a moment I thought she would shrug and say nothing as she usually did. But even from that brief touch, I'd felt the cold clamminess of her skin. She was shivering too. She glanced around her, as if to make quite sure there was no other within hearing.

'I was with child. But three days ago he . . .' Her mouth worked silently as if she could not drag the words out from the mire of her thoughts. She gave a deep sigh. 'I fell. Soon after, the bleeding started. The babe swam away on the red tide. It was no bigger than a pea pod. But the blood won't stop. It grows worse.'

I stared at her helplessly. Cobwebs and puffballs wouldn't work on bleeding like this, even if I knew where to find them on these sodden moors. I'd never seen anyone staunch this kind of flow. I was the last of my mam's children, and no other women in our village would have wanted me near them when they were birthing their babes. Neighbours, who knew they were with child, would cover their eyes as I passed and shrink back between the cottages, for fear my shadow would touch them and their unborn babe would be maimed in the womb.

'Is there a woman in the camp who helps with childbirth? They might have the knowledge . . .' I began.

'Any woman who had such skills wouldn't need to dig in the mud for stones,' Eva said. She winced, pressing her clenched fists into her belly, as she braced herself against the pain. 'But before you came, there was a woman here living with one of the tinners. She'd been born on the moor. Her man . . . he made enemies. One night, he was found with a knife wound. Threatened they'd do worse to him next time. Pair of them wanted to leave that night, but the gash kept bleeding each time he moved.'

Eva paused, her breath coming in short shallow pants. I could see it was costing her dear to speak so much, but I knew she'd not be telling me unless the tale was important.

'The woman . . . daren't leave her man, afeared they might do him more injury while he lay helpless. But she told me there was a blood charmer, lived out on the moors. She begged me to take a clootie to her, get her to charm it. I did as she bade me, fetched it back and she bound it round the wound. I'd not have believed it, but . . . the bleeding stopped.'

Eva drew her knife from her belt, and cut a strip of cloth from her skirt. Struggling to her feet, she soaked it in the bloody patch on the rock. Then she thrust the wet rag into my hand. 'You'll take it? Take it to the blood charmer. There's none else who'd do me such a kindness here.'

Chapter 18

Morwen

Ma wiped her fingers round the inside of the bowl and sucked them to be sure she hadn't missed a drop of the rabbit stew. Ryana scraped the burned fragments from the bottom of the cooking pot, nibbling them with her long yellow teeth. We'd managed to make the rabbit stretch among the four of us for two days, adding more herbs, stale breadcrumbs and water each time we heated it, till even the remembrance of flavour had been boiled out of the bare bones. The rabbit had been payment from one of the villagers – he'd wanted to know where to find his horse – and had likely been poached from one of the warrens, but Ma never asked where her payments came from.

The clouds had been lying low all day on the moor, wrapping our cottage in a wet grey mist, like a soiled bandage. In the shippon, on the other side of the wicker partition, the three goats had settled down to sleep as if they thought it was already nightfall.

'Have to go foraging tomorrow, the lot of ye,' Ma said. 'And I mean proper foraging, Tae. Don't think you can disappear all day and saunter back with nothing to show for it but a bunch of thyme, else you'll not be getting a share of anything in the pot.'

Ryana glanced sullenly at Taegan, muttering low so Ma wouldn't hear, 'She knows where to get fed and it's not from our pot.'

Ryana and I both suspected that Daveth and his brother stole food for our sister from their own ma, but Taegan never brought it home to share after her nights in the byre with them.

There was a clatter as the goats suddenly scrambled to their feet.

Ma raised her head. 'Someone's coming.'

'It'll be old Meggy back with summat she's lifted from the boy,' Ryana said, looking interested for once.

Meggy had come to our cottage just the day before. It was plain to see the old woman was in a fair twitter, which I could tell pleased Ma. She'd not refuse to help Meggy, especially if it meant thwarting the black crows – besides, she couldn't afford to turn away any chance of payment – but she'd not forgiven her, and if we could give her a fright, Ma reckoned that was no more than Meggy deserved.

'Birds tell me they've closed Bryde's Well,' Ma had announced, as soon as Meggy had seated herself on the stool.

The villager who had brought Ma the rabbit had told her that.

Meggy had nodded. 'I burned the charm and said the words like you told me, Kendra.'

'Never fails if it's done right,' Ma had told her.

'But you didn't warn me what that charm would do,' Meggy had protested indignantly. 'Made my skin crawl when I saw it. Frogs, thousands of them, swarming all over the floor and walls. Water was so thick with them it looked like a mess of pease pottage. That kept the boy from the well, right enough, kept them all from it. But for how long Kendra?'

Ma had ignored the question. 'Yer fetch me anything from the boy?'

Meggy had shaken her head. 'They've got him in the infirmary. Don't even let him out in the yard by himself to piss, case he bumps into summat and hurts himself.'

'You could give him something,' I'd said. 'That'd be a reason to get close.'

Ma had glared at me and Ryana had cackled with laughter. 'What's she to give him, Mazy-wen, a slap?'

But Meggy wasn't laughing. 'Maybe I could . . . a toy or some such.'

'Have a care, Meggy,' Ma had cautioned. 'If it's summat of yours, he'll use it against ye.'

Meggy had looked more affrighted when she'd left than when she'd arrived, and Ma had had a good chuckle over that. All the same, she'd meant the warning to be heeded. Ma never ignored what the spirits had shown in her smoke. She might not admit it, but deep down I could tell she was as worried as Meggy was about what trouble the boy might bring to the moors.

Ma jabbed me in the ribs with her stick. 'Move yer arse, Morwen. Get yourself out there and see who's coming.'

'It'll be Meggy, I'm telling you,' Ryana said, but Ma ignored her.

I slipped through the door and crouched behind the great rock that formed the corner of our house where I could watch without being seen. The clouds were lifting as a chill wind gathered strength. A flock of starlings took flight, weaving and twisting, like a giant puff of smoke. I gazed up at them, trying to read the shapes they made – a spiral with three twists, a hound's head black against the darkening sky, and then they were snaking down towards the valley. A black hound, a wisht hound, in the sky over the Fire Tor! Should I warn Ma? I could already hear Ryana sneering, *Mazy-wen can't even read the signs of rain when it's falling.* I felt myself shrinking. Say naught. That was safest.

Someone was coming, but it wasn't Meggy. The dregs of light had almost gone and I couldn't see her clearly, but I knew the old woman's shape and the way she moved. This one seemed younger, a thin whip of a creature. She was trying to cross the stream using the stepping-stones, but she was slipping and wobbling, like a duck on ice, as if she was unused to balancing on such things.

I darted back inside to warn Ma. 'It's not Meggy,' I said, grinning at the sulky scowl on Ryana's face. 'Must be a blow-in, I reckon. She's not from the moor for she doesn't know where to put her feet.'

I darted outside again. The stranger was standing afore our threshold, staring at the cottage, her face half hidden under a bit of old cloth she'd wrapped about her head against the wind and wet.

'Is it Kendra you're seeking?' I asked, gently as I could.

'Is she the blood charmer?'

'Best on the whole moor,' I said, though for all I knew, Ma was the only blood charmer – I'd not heard tell of another.

Kendra had already taken up her place on the low stool behind the fire and had veiled herself in the smoke by the time I coaxed the stranger in.

The woman huddled just inside the doorway. Her eyes, blue as speedwell flowers, darted round as she stared at each of us in turn. She looked as frightened as a mouse dropped into a box of cats. Her face was gaunt and her homespun clothes worn and caked with mud. They were heaped in layers over her thin body, as if she was wearing everything she owned, though if she was, how would she warm herself come winter?

Ma studied her curiously, then beckoned to her with a crooked finger. 'Come closer, Mistress. Old Kendra'll do you no harm, less ye mean harm to her.'

The stranger took a pace or two towards the fire. She ignored the stool and squatted on her haunches. As she moved, I saw that her left arm was dangling, like a broken wing, the skin on the limp hand mottled and waxy.

Ma noticed it too. She gestured to it. 'Can't do nothing about that. If you'd been brought to me as a babe, maybe . . . but it's too late now.'

The woman started to say something, but she spoke so low I couldn't make it out.

Ma leaned forward. 'Speak bold, Mistress. There's none here to hear your secrets save us and the spirits.'

The woman's eyes widened and she glanced around as if she thought she might see imps hanging from the beams or peeping at her from under Ma's bed.

'I'm living at the tinners' camp. A woman there . . . a friend. She took a fall and lost the bairn she was carrying, three days since. The bleeding won't stop. She said you once charmed a clootie for a tinner at the camp who'd been stabbed and his wound stopped bleeding.'

I could see Ma preening herself. It always put her in a good humour to hear her charms had worked.

'Eva said you might . . . I don't know what to do, how to help her. I'm so afraid she might die.'

155

'And what do they call you, Mistress? Have a name, do you? Everything must have a name.'

'Sorrel.'

Ma licked her lips, as if she was tasting the sound of it. 'A healing wort, sorrel is, and one old Brigid marked for her own. Well, now, Sorrel, you brought a clootie from this friend of yours?'

Silently the woman held out a rag rusty with drying blood. Her fingers were smeared with crimson. She passed the clootie over the flames of the hearth fire to Ma.

Ma held it in both hands, inscribing a circle with it in the smoke of the fire. Her eyes half closed, she began to chant:

> *'Stone woman sits over a spring and water stands*
>   *still as ice.*
> *Earth dries up, skies dry up.*
> *Veins dry up and all that is full of blood dries up.'*

She raised the rag. 'It shall be so, till milk flows from a rock.' She held the clootie out to Sorrel. 'Go home now. Tell her to press this to the flow of blood and it'll stop.'

But I knew it wouldn't. Something had gone amiss. There was no power in the charm – I could feel it.

Sorrel rose, holding the bloodstained rag carefully, as if it was as fragile as a blown egg. She looked at me, afraid to speak directly to Ma. 'I've no coin, not till . . .' She trailed off, her face racked with misery.

'Can't pay in coin for a blood charming,' Ma said. 'Silver works against it, see. But food I'll take,' she added hopefully.

Sorrel gave a helpless shrug. 'I've none of that either.' She flinched as if she thought Ma might curse her or snatch the rag away.

156

Ma hesitated, but we could all see the woman was not lying. She'd known more hunger than we had, by the look of her.

Finally, Ma grunted. 'See you bring me summat when you have it, else my curse'll follow.' She fixed the woman with a gimlet eye. 'But don't you go telling anyone, else half the moor folk'll be looking to me to give them charms for naught.'

Sorrel nodded and gave her a grateful smile, then ducked out of the doorway and into the night. I followed, and as soon as we were a few paces from the cottage, I hurried to catch up with her, but she had already broken into an ungainly, lopsided run, plainly anxious to take the charm back to her ailing friend. But it wouldn't work, I knew it, though I couldn't tell her.

'You're newly come to Dertemora?' I called after her. It was a foolish question and had tumbled from me before I even knew what I was saying.

But she stopped. No, more than that. She jerked as if something had struck her violently from behind. She walked back to me. Her eyes searching my face as if I was someone she had once known, but had only just recognised.

'What did you say? What did you call this place?'

'Dertemora. That's the name for these parts.'

The clootie fell from her hand. She stared around her into the darkness, as if she'd been asleep and had just woken and was trying to remember where she was.

The wind bowled the rag across the ground. I ran after it and snatched it up. I cupped it between my palms, silently repeating the charm. I saw blood running down flesh and willed it to stop. I watched it dry and felt the cloth grow hot, then icy cold in my fingers. Eva's flow would stop now, I was certain, though I could never tell Ma what I'd done.

But when I pressed the clootie back into Sorrel's hand, I almost dropped it again as a great flash of heat and pain coursed up my arm. For a moment, as we both held the rag, it was as if the moors had vanished and the two of us were alone inside the darkness of the tor cave. I could see Ankow's corpse lying on the slab, could hear the dead prowling around us, their high-pitched keening circling me and this woman, binding us together with a rope of fire. But Sorrel was not alone: a great dark shadow was hovering behind her, a giant bird, its wings spread wide, as if they were hers.

The rag was jerked from my fingers and the two of us were standing once more on the wild moor. Sorrel's eyes flashed wide in wonder, staring into mine. 'You,' she breathed, so softly I half thought it was the sigh of the wind. 'You hear her voice too. But who is she?'

'I know you . . .' I began. 'I saw you before in the smoke.'

She half opened her mouth to speak, but a shout rang out from the doorway behind us.

'Morwen, get you back in here. Ma wants some worts fetching.'

I turned to Sorrel, but she was already hurrying away, only glancing round once to look at me. But once was enough. I knew she had felt the heat flash between us too, though plainly she had not understood it. Had she seen what I had? No . . . No, she had sensed something, but she hadn't seen it. She couldn't. Not yet. She didn't know how to see. There was a power in her that was not yet awakened and she didn't know it. But I did. And in that moment, I realised I'd been waiting all my life for her to come and find me.

Chapter 19

Prioress Johanne

The knock on my door was timid and Sister Fina's entrance into my chamber more so. She edged through the door, still limping, and stood more hunched than usual, cradling her bandaged arm. She stared at the corner of the table, but said nothing. She was always ungainly, but that morning she seemed more awkward than ever, like a broken statue, repaired with parts from a different figure. I urged her to sit, not from kindness but irritation at her shuffling.

Fina winced as she perched on the edge of a stool.

'I'm glad that you are recovered enough to leave your bed,' I said. 'Are your injuries mending?'

Fina nodded unconvincingly, but still didn't look at me.

'Sister Basilia says she urged you to rest in bed for another day or two at least for you've eaten almost nothing. Are you sure you are well enough to be up? You look pale.'

It would have been nearer the truth to say she looked hag-ridden, with circles under her eyes and a dark stain on her lip where it appeared she had been biting the skin.

159

'I . . . The day is long when I am alone in the dorter and all the other sisters are working. I'd rather be busy.'

'Reading, contemplation and prayer are our work too, Sister Fina, and even the most infirm of sisters can do that from her bed.' I felt a pang of unease as I said it. If my sisters were forced into the cloister at Minchin Buckland, reading and contemplation would be all the work they were permitted to do. I shuddered as I imagined the endless years stretching ahead, filled with nothing but attending services and praying for the souls of our brother knights, one day the same as the next, each year identical to the one before and the one to come. Yet if I could not convince the Lord Prior to let us remain, I might well find myself trying to persuade my sisters of the glories of just such an existence. Could I really bring myself to urge them to submit to that? I'd have no choice. The Pope would never release us from our vows, and even if His Holiness could be persuaded to allow us to join another order, there were none we could enter that would allow us to escape the prison of the cloister.

But if Brother Nicholas uncovered the truth, I would not be granted even the small mercy of the cloister. Maybe none of us would live to see Minchin Buckland. What had he said the night he came? *The Lord Prior has eyes everywhere, searching for the smallest spark of corruption or sorcery in his order, and if he suspects so much as a glimmer of it, he'll grind the guilty beneath his boot.*

And if that boot descended, what would become of those we cared for? Where would they draw their last terrified breath?

Sister Fina shifted on the stool. Even that small movement made her wince.

'Sister Basilia also tells me you have refused to take the syrup of poppy she prepared to ease your pain.'

'It makes me drowsy . . .'

'So, you'd rather bear the pain. That is to your credit, Sister Fina. Fortitude is a virtue we should all endeavour to acquire, and when you reach my great age, your back aches and your bones creak, believe me, you will have need of it.'

I laughed, expecting Fina to smile at the joke or assure me that I was not old. But Fina did neither. She probably saw a decrepit old woman when she looked at me, and on days like this, I felt it.

'Even if you were fit to work, Sister Fina, we have been obliged to close the holy well, as you must know, and I cannot tell you when we will reopen it to the pilgrims. That matter rests in God's hands.'

For the first time since I'd entered the room Fina's head snapped up and she looked at me directly. 'The frogs are still there?'

'They were this morning when I inspected it.'

'It's the boy . . . The boy has brought a curse on the well, hasn't he?' Fina demanded fiercely. 'Father Guthlac said he would destroy us.'

'The boy has not been near the well, Sister Fina. How could a mere child conjure such a plague when he cannot even dress himself?'

'Then why have they come?' she wailed.

God knew I had prayed for an answer to that question for many hours, but I had received none, unless I had closed my ears to His voice. Was this a punishment for my disobedience?

Fina was watching me, her thin fingers plucking restlessly at the folds of her black gown.

'If it is any comfort, Sister Fina, I observed several dead frogs among the living this morning. It may be that the rest

161

will also die, since there can be little for them to eat down there. But, for now, all we can do is wait and pray.'

Clarice, in whom I had confided, had suggested several remedies, each more drastic than the last. She seemed to imagine we were defending our priory from the Saracens, for boiling oil and fire had been among those she most enthusiastically advocated, even capturing a few herons and letting them loose down there to eat the frogs. But most of her suggestions seemed likely to inflict as much damage on the holy spring as the animals. If we'd been suffering a plague of mice, we could have laid poison, but who knew what might poison a frog? I suspected few people had ever had cause to wonder.

'But you have to drive the frogs out,' Fina insisted. 'You can't just wait.'

I was losing my patience with the young woman. Only that she appeared to be in so much pain prevented me from taking her to task as thoroughly as she deserved. 'Sister Fina, kindly remember that I am the prioress, and it is not for you to question me! But I will endeavour to believe that your intemperate words arise from a deep concern for the pilgrims who have undertaken long journeys to reach us. Therefore, to ease your mind, I will tell you that Sister Clarice has been kind enough to sit in the chapel and receive the villagers and pilgrims. If they should ask why the cave is closed, she tells them rocks have fallen and are being cleared. Thanks to the protection of the blessed St Lucia, not a soul was hurt. If they have brought an offering or some token to leave at the well, she takes it and assures them that it will be placed by the well as soon as it is safe to do so. In the meantime, she offers them ampullae of holy water, if they wish to buy them. So, you see, they are not sent away disappointed.'

'But how can she get to the spring to fill them? The frogs . . .'

'She does not need to go down there. They have already been filled,' I assured her.

'But how?'

I sighed in exasperation. 'The water in them has been blessed in the chapel, which is directly above the well. St Lucia will hear the prayers of the pilgrims if they are made in faith, so we must ensure they have no cause to doubt, Sister Fina.' I stressed 'doubt', trying to make her understand that the precise origin of the water need not be discussed with outsiders.

'So, you have made Sister Clarice the well-keeper now!' Her hands were balled in her lap so tightly the knuckles were white.

Given her wild outbursts since she'd entered my chamber, I was sorely tempted to say yes. But I reminded myself of why I had given the duty to her in the first place. I did not want her to sink back into the strange melancholy and wildness that had afflicted her before. The well had healed her then. At least standing guard over it might help her again.

'Sister Clarice is the priory's steward.' I was determined that whatever orders he had received, Brother Nicholas would claim that title only when I was in my grave. 'As such, she has work enough for three sisters and needs no more added to her burden. Just as soon as you are recovered, I will ask you to resume your duties as keeper of the well. For you are sorely needed.'

'I am recovered now,' she blurted out eagerly, and her eyes suddenly looked alive again. 'I can sit in the chapel and receive the pilgrims and villagers much better than she can.

Many of the villagers recognise me now and they know they can trust me with their offerings.'

'Are you sure you are strong enough?'

She nodded earnestly, in the manner of an over-eager child trying to convince their mother they can be trusted with an errand. It only increased my doubts.

'You will remember what to tell the pilgrims and villagers. Mention only the fall of rocks. No talk of the frogs or curses must escape the priory.'

She was already limping to the door, moving hastily but so clumsily I was afraid she'd take another fall.

'Sister Fina.'

She turned and regarded me warily as if she thought I was about to snatch her treasure from her.

'I would remind you again to be guarded in what you say to the two brothers. If Brother Nicholas finds you alone in the chapel, he may wish to speak to you.'

She flushed. Then her chin jerked up defiantly. 'I kept him from seeing the frogs. I wouldn't let him down there and I locked the door.' She gnawed the raw patch on her lip. 'But I don't understand why the brothers are here. And why shouldn't we talk to them? We've nothing to hide. We've done nothing wrong.'

'In spite of your good efforts, Brother Nicholas has discovered our troubles with the well.' I did not tell her that I had neglected to bolt the door behind me. 'But it is . . .' I hesitated. How could I make her understand the danger we were in?

'The Lord Prior has sent the brothers here because he is anxious about all of his priories in England. I am sure you will not have ever encountered any men or women of the Order of the Knights Templar, for it has been seven years

164

since any dared wear the red cross in England, and you cannot have been more than ten years old then and even younger when the order was attacked in France.'

'When I was little my older brothers played being Templar knights. They used to make the servant boys be Saracens so they could fight them. My brothers had to win because they were knights.' Her mouth softened into a smile, but it vanished almost at once and she frowned. 'But there are no more Templars, so why should the Lord Prior care about them?'

'Because there are many similarities between their order and ours. Over the past two centuries, the Templars gained much wealth and land across Europe, and they were answerable only to the Pope, no matter whose domain their land and castles were in. Their financial and military power made many uneasy, King Philip of France for one. Nine years ago, without warning, orders were given that all the French Templar knights were to be arrested on charges of . . .'

I swallowed the words I was about to utter. There was no need to shock this sheltered young woman by telling her the foul things they had been accused of. And what did it matter now? In Paris, the knights' Grand Master, Jacques de Molay, who had confessed under torture, retracted his confession and was burned alive as a relapsed heretic. He died promising that woe would fall on those who had condemned them, and before the year was out both Pope Clement and King Philip of France were dead. But their deaths came too late to save the lives of the hundreds of Templar knights they had destroyed.

'Prioress Johanne?'

I dragged my attention back to Sister Fina, standing

165

impatiently by the door. 'The knights were arrested on charges of sorcery and heresy, charges the Pope was forced to investigate since they had been levelled by a Christian king.'

She shrugged, as if all I was saying was of no consequence to her, the rambling tale of some old woman about things that had happened long ago. But it had been just two years since Jacques de Molay was so cruelly executed. The wind still carried his ashes.

I fought to hold back my temper. 'Can you not understand the danger, Sister Fina? Our order, too, has wealth and lands that others covet, and we, too, are answerable to none but the Pope. The Lord Prior fears we might suffer the same fate.'

'But they were heretics. We're not guilty of any crime.'

I wanted to scream at her, *Neither were they*. Their only crime was their arrogant belief in their own survival and their blindness to the jealousy of powerful men. But I dared not say any of this. It was heresy to defend anyone who stood accused of being a heretic, and even worse to proclaim innocent those who had been found guilty of such an unforgivable sin.

'Sister Fina, you must try to understand that the Lord Prior wants to ensure that no one can falsely accuse our order of wrongdoing. There are many, both outside our order and within it, who believe that women who are neither married nor under the rule and government of the cloister may be led into wantonness and heresy because our sex is more easily tempted, as the serpent tempted Eve. The Lord Prior believes that to silence any who might point the finger, all the women in our order should be cloistered so that none may accuse us of any sin.'

Fina's eyes flew wide with alarm and fury, as if I was

166

responsible. 'But my father swore I would not be forced to take the veil. I only agreed to my vows, because—'

I held up my hand to stem the flow. I was in no mood to listen to any more of her angry outbursts. Did she really imagine I would not resent this even more than she did?

'That is why I urge you to consider carefully anything you say to the brothers, Sister Fina. We must all do everything we can to convince Brother Nicholas that we are above suspicion. Such wild thoughts as you uttered just now, about the curses and the boy, will only fuel our brother's fire. We must guard our tongues, chew every word twice before we utter it to ensure we give him nothing he can use to drag us to Minchin Buckland. If he does, you will not be the keeper of anything, much less your beloved well.'

Chapter 20

Morwen

'Told you, Ma, see? They've lit a fire inside the stone circle and they've penned their horses in there too.'

Even Ma could not deny the evidence of her own eyes, though she'd not believed me when I'd told her. I was hurrying home after setting snares when I'd spotted the smoke in the distance, rising thin as a sapling into the evening sky. I was always careful to set my traps well away from any cottage or track for all the land belonged to the King and abbots, so they said, not that I'd ever seen an abbot tending a cow or a king planting a bean.

I'd known something was wrong. No one lived near that stone circle and the villagers only ever went to it on the eve of Beltane or Samhain and it wasn't the night for either of those bonfires to be lit. No one went inside that circle, save for those feasts, or let their beasts stray in there. If they did, it would call down a curse on their heads.

Ma rose from where she'd been crouching in the darkness and picked her way towards the stream. She didn't bother to search for the stepping-stones, but hitched her skirts up

168

to her scrawny thighs and splashed across. She'd gone bare-foot all her life, and her soles were as horny as the trotters of sheep. She was as surefooted as them, too. I followed and we edged around the knoll on which the stone circle stood, then crept up the slope on the far side so we could look down into it. Ma squatted, still as a grey heron watching for fish.

Three men, wrapped in sheepskin cloaks, sat on low stones around the fire pit, which they had dug in front of the queen stone, the widest and tallest of all the standing stones in the circle. One man was sharpening his long knife while another turned a wooden spit on which a couple of skinned hares were impaled. The wind was gaining strength again and I could smell the roasting flesh in the smoke gusting towards us. Ma would never kill or eat a hare: some cunning women could turn themselves into hares and you might slay a woman instead of a beast. But, though I'd never taken a bite of one, I couldn't stop my empty belly growling. The meat smelt as sweet as rabbit.

A skinny hound, which looked as ravenous as I was, prowled around the three men occasionally making little dashes forward as if it meant to snatch a carcass off the spit in spite of the heat of the fire. It retreated whenever one of the men aimed a kick at it.

The flames sent shadows and lights writing across the circle, and by its light I saw that the spaces between the waist-high stones had been stuffed with prickly furze bushes and old wicker hurdles to form a pen, in which a half-dozen squat little packhorses were corralled alongside the men, with a big-boned, muscular beast that was obviously meant for hard riding, though few in those parts could have afforded such a valuable animal.

'He's got his fat backside on the cup stone,' Ma growled in outrage.

A man was squatting on a broad stone that lay horizontally in front of the queen stone. It had in it a round hollow, as if an apple had been carved into the top, where milk and sometimes honey were offered to Brigid. No villager would dare touch the stone, unless they were making an offering, much less offend the spirits by setting their arse against it as if it were a midden heap to be shat on.

The hound must have caught Ma's fierce whisper for he wheeled round in our direction and came bounding up between the stones, barking and leaping, though he couldn't jump over the thorns. In an instant two men were on their feet, their knives drawn. The third, still seated on the cup stone, peered warily into the darkness. He reached down and felt for a bow and an arrow, sliding both on to his lap. The horses, alarmed by the dog, bunched together, pricking their ears and circling restlessly.

'Who's there? . . . If that's you playing the fool, Hann, I'll give you the drubbing of your life.'

One of the men thrust a torch into the fire and, when the end was burning, hurried across to where the hound was barking, holding the brand out over the stone. But the wildly gusting light fell on nothing but grass and rowan whipping in the breeze.

'Is there something in that bush over yonder? I heard there was all manner of beasts on these moors, hellhounds and wild cats.'

'Wild kitten, more like, if it can be hidden in a bush so puny and wizened. It's outlaws you want to be fretting about, not cats.' He glanced back at the man seated by the fire.

'You reckon we should send old Whiteblaze out, see if he can flush 'em?'

The man by the fire rose to his feet, the bow gripped between his fingers, though not yet drawn.

'Ma!' I whispered. 'If they let the hound loose and he shows them where we are . . .' Kendra knew charms that could make even strange dogs lie down, but they wouldn't work against arrows. 'Come away quick, Ma, afore they get that hurdle pulled aside.'

Keeping low, I wove down the slope, expecting Ma to follow, but instead I heard her voice riding the wind, like a hawk.

'That's a sacred circle, that is. You get yourselves and your beasts out of there else I'll make you curse the day your ma whelped you.'

One man let out a strangled squawk, like a hen that had been sat on. But the other thrust the burning torch in the direction of Ma's voice. Ma rose out of the grass, brandishing her staff, her wild grey hair fanning around her in the wind, her arms flung high and wide.

For a moment, the men just gaped. Then they burst out laughing.

'That's your hellhound, Jago, a mad old vecke.'

'It's you who reckoned it were murdering outlaws,' the other retorted. He put his hands in front of his face, rocking from side to side in mock terror, and sang out in a high-pitched voice, 'Have mercy on us, old woman. Don't hurt us!'

Ma yelled her threats again, but I could barely hear them over the raucous laughter and insults of the men, as they pranced around in mocking imitation of her.

I ran back to her, trying to pull her away.

'Look,' Jago yelled. 'There's another. You're right, there's a whole gang of those outlaws need taming. I'll wrestle with the maid and you can have the old hag.'

'Not if I get to the maid first.'

They tugged at the furze bushes jammed between the stones, cursing as they scratched and pricked themselves.

I shoved Kendra down the slope. 'Run, Ma, run.'

She hesitated, but even Ma could see that we couldn't fight these men, leastways not like that. We ran. Ma bounded down the hillside towards the stream, though I knew she'd not make for the cottage. She'd not want to lead the men there, but there were plenty of hollows and rocks she could lie low in. Ma knew the moors better than the faces of her own daughters. She could still run like a hare, but she couldn't keep it up for long, not like she used to. I raced off in the opposite direction, trying to draw the men away from Ma. I knew it was the maid they'd chase after, not the old hag.

It was hard going, tearing over the tussocks of coarse grass and heather, but I was more surefooted than the men lumbering behind me. They'd not see me in the dark. Then I heard the dog fall silent. It must have bounded free from the pinfold and was searching for my scent. Almost at once I heard the deep baying of a hound that had picked up a trail. But was it mine or Ma's? Maybe, if we were lucky, it was a deer's.

I ran on, trying to keep to the low ground, so the men wouldn't see me against the sky. I was making for a place upstream where the water had cut a hollow deep beneath the bank at the point where the river curved around a stand of wizened oaks. I knew if I dropped down into that and crouched beneath the overhang, the men could search all night and they'd never find me. But that hiding place wouldn't fool a hound and I could hear it behind me now, its baying growing louder, more excited. I risked a glance over my shoulder. The men were following their hound, stumbling over the uneven ground, the flames and the smoke of the torch streaming behind them in the night's sky.

'Find her, Whiteblaze! Harbour the little witch.'

The hound was running at full chase now. My back tensed. At any moment, I expected to feel the beast's hot breath on my legs, its sharp fangs sinking into my flesh. If Ma had been with me, we could have driven it off with her stave, but I had nothing save the small knife in my belt and dogs don't back off at the sight of a knife. Only if it sprang on me would the blade be of any use, and then only if I turned to face it afore it leaped. But it was the men who followed the hound I feared more.

A pain tore at my side. I was gasping for breath. My legs felt as shaky as if I had the ague. The hound was gaining. I could hear it ripping through the heather and the bushes behind me. A boulder jutted up in front of me and the rush of the water crashed suddenly on my ears. In my panic, I'd almost run past my hiding place. I slithered to the edge of the river and slid down. But exhaustion and fear had made me clumsy. My bare foot slipped on the wet rocks, and I plunged under the icy water.

Gasping and choking, I struggled to stand, but the rain-swollen current dragged me over the water-polished, slippery stones. I threw myself forward and managed to half crawl, half stagger into the hollow beneath the overhanging bank. In hot summers, when the streams were low, a gravel ledge was clear of the water, but now the river filled the whole bed, though it was shallower and a little calmer at the edge of the curve. I crouched in darkness, clenching my teeth to

173

stop them chattering as the freezing water swirled and frothed around my thighs.

Over the thunder of the water and the rumble of stones, I heard the hound scrabbling directly above me. It was so close, I could hear it panting. Then it did what it was trained to do: it began to howl, its cry carrying right across the moor. It had cornered the quarry, trapped the prey and now it was calling its masters to deliver the kill.

I could no more break out than a vixen could escape from its den when the dogs had found it. I knew I wouldn't be able to scramble out of the river on the other side: I'd been to that spot enough times to know that the bank was too high and slippery. I'd have to wade far upstream against the swift current and the hound would keep pace with me all the way.

I pressed my shoulder into the cold wet earth and tried to think of all the charms and curses I'd learned when I'd listened to Ma teaching Ryana. But I could remember nothing that would silence the barking of a dog. And even if I'd known where to run to, I wasn't sure I could move now – my feet and legs had grown so numb that I couldn't feel them, much less move them. Over the wind and water, I could hear the voices of the men, out of breath, but urging the hound to hold. I was shaking and, though I tried to tell myself it was just the cold, I knew it wasn't.

Then, suddenly, there came a whistle so high and sharp it seemed to pierce the wind, like an arrow through flesh. The dog's barking ceased and it began to whimper. The whistle sounded again, even more piercing than before, and this time the dog yelped as if it was in pain and I heard it crashing away across the dark moor, as if a pack of wolves were after it.

The men were cursing and bellowing for it. 'I'll thrash that brute when I get hold of it,' one yelled.

'Leave the wretched beast. Look for the girl. Whiteblaze was standing on the riverbank. He must have chased her in. She probably thought to make him lose the scent by taking to the water.'

I buried my face in my knees and tried to cover my arms with my wet hair, so he'd see no gleam of pale skin. I shrank back against the earth. They were walking up the bank. The black water turned to foaming blood, as the red flames of their torch passed over it.

Mother Brigid keeps the men from the river, as the flame keeps wolf from goat. But I had no herbs to burn, no charm to weave, only the will worth, only that.

They were almost overhead. If they stepped too close, too heavily, and the sodden earth gave way, they'd crash down on top of me.

'What's that?' one called.

My heart had risen so far up my throat, I thought it would choke me.

'There, look . . . something moving . . . A black beast.'

'It'll be Whiteblaze come crawling back.'

'No, no! Over there, by that stunted tree. It's twice his size. It can't—'

A shriek split the night, a terrible sound, as if all the force of the wind had been balled in a giant fist and hurled towards them. The men echoed it with their own fainter cries of fear as they fled back towards the safety of the stone circle and the fire that burned there. I was shaking with cold and fright, but I daren't leave my hiding place.

Above me, I heard something moving again. Had the men returned, the hound?

175

'Morwen?' A woman's voice, but it was not Ma's or either of my sisters'. 'The men have gone. But you best get home quickly, case that dog comes nosing back.'

I could barely stand and fell several times as I splashed along the edge of the river, battling against the slippery stones and current to find a place upstream where I could pull myself out. As I struggled to clamber up, I felt a hand grip my arm. I stared up. A woman was standing on the bank above me. It was too dark to see her face, but as she hauled at my arm, a tingle shot through me, brief and brilliant as the flash of a kingfisher on the river. It was the woman who had come to our cottage, the woman I had seen in the smoke.

I clambered on to the bank, and stood there dripping, my jaw so stiff I could barely unclench my teeth enough to speak.

'Sorrel, what . . . are you doing out on the moors?'

'Went to your cottage to leave some dried mutton for Kendra. Only a mouthful, it is, saved from my portion, but I'll bring more when I can.' She gave a brittle laugh. 'Don't want her curse to follow me. Eva stopped bleeding, like she said. She's on the mend now. I meant to thank Kendra . . . to thank you. It was you, wasn't it, made the charm work? I could feel when I took it from you . . . I can't explain . . . But I could feel it had . . . *changed*.' Sorrel slowly folded her fingers, staring down at her hand as if it still held the blood charm.

'Your sister said you and your mam had gone to the stone circle. But I'd heard a couple of tinners talking earlier. They said they were going to pen a horse they'd found in a circle of stones that was well away from their valley. They didn't want it to be seen by the master's henchman. I reckoned there might be trouble if you ran into them, so I started

176

after you. Wanted to warn you. Saw you run off and the men send that hound of theirs after you.'

'Someone whistled, sent it flitting.'

Sorrel chuckled softly. 'Learned that trick when I was a bairn. I was always afraid of the village dogs. Boys would set them on me to make me run. Thought it funny, the way my arm would flap about and throw me off balance so I couldn't go straight. An old man in the village, who'd been lame since he was a lad, saw the dogs leaping at me one day and sent them howling off by whistling. Taught me how.'

'And the shriek that frightened the wits from those men? You did that too?'

Sorrel shook her head. 'Not me . . . I mean, I don't think . . . No, I couldn't do that. I was so angry I wanted to, but how could I have done it? But then . . . who?'

We stared out into the vast hollow dome of darkness. In the distance, we could see the tiny glow from the tinners' fire in the stone circle. The wind rattled the bushes and shook the grasses. Clouds tumbled over each other as they charged across the inky sky, but nothing else was stirring – at least, nothing that was of this world.

Chapter 21

Hospitallers' Priory of St Mary

For the third time that morning, Deacon Wybert paused and glanced uneasily at his congregation in the priory's chapel, catching sight of their frowns and furtive grimaces. All through the mass his voice had grown ever more strident, the words gushing out of him like liquid shit from a man with the flux. Now he hesitated, staring wildly around.

Nicholas flicked his fingers impatiently, urging him to continue. The knight's evident annoyance only served to unnerve the village deacon even more. He stammered, lost his place in his head and could only recover by returning to the beginning of a lengthy prayer he had already said and reciting it again, for he'd learned the service by rote, listening to old Father Guthlac.

Nicholas gave a deep-throated growl, alarming several of the elderly village women, who edged away from him, as if he might drop to all fours and start biting. Prioress Johanne glowered at him. But he ignored her. He was impatient to see the mass ended, so that he could grab the deacon before he escaped again.

Nicholas suspected the man had been deliberately avoiding him: each time he'd called at his cottage, his housekeeper had sworn Wybert was in another village. Having been thwarted by Father Guthlac's untimely death, he was determined to learn what the deacon could tell him, but from the way the gibbering fool was muddling his way through the mass, Nicholas was beginning to think that wasn't going to be much. On the other hand, he was obviously easily intimidated so he might be frightened into letting something slip.

Something else was annoying Nicholas even more than the deacon's babbling. He glanced around. What was that infernal noise? It was also alarming the handful of elderly villagers and pilgrims who leaned wearily on the pillars at the back of the circular nave, exhausted from having trudged miles across the moors to reach the priory. Now they, too, seemed anxious for the service to be over and not just to claim the bread and meat that would be doled out afterwards.

Up at the altar, the deacon's hand shook as he made the sign of the cross over the silver chalice containing the wine, now transformed by his gabbled words into the Holy Blood of Christ. His prayer ended, he sank heavily to his knees on the cold stone, raising the sacred cup to his lips. But the noise he had been trying to drown grew louder in the silence, a dull but skin-crawling buzzing. Several villagers peered nervously up into the thick shadows of the thatched roof, as if they feared a swarm of bees or wasps might be hanging there.

Wybert lowered the chalice and glanced fearfully towards the door that led down to the holy well, whence the droning seemed to come. Was some evil spirit trapped there? The whole village knew Kendra and her daughters had cursed the sisters the day they'd turned them from the well. Could this be their revenge? Now that Father Guthlac was dead, would he be called upon to vanquish whatever was down there? He shuddered.

'Deacon Wybert, you must finish the mass,' Prioress Johanne prompted.

Startled by the sound of her voice, he almost spilled the consecrated wine. The buzzing was invading every crevice and corner of his skull, driving out all other thoughts. He raised the chalice again and took a gulp of wine, but panic made him gasp for air at exactly that moment. The burning liquid was sucked into his lungs, and he choked violently, coughing and flailing for breath. The precious Blood of Christ spewed from his mouth and ran in red streams from his nose as he fought for air. He fell forward on to his hands and knees. The chalice clattered on to the stone and rolled away, leaving an arc of crimson wine spreading over the flags.

Sister Basilia reached him first, pounding on his back with her broad hands so hard it felt as if she had broken his ribs. But, gasping and vomiting, he was too weak even to crawl away from her ministrations. As the other sisters pressed around him, the prioress retrieved the chalice from among the feet and set it safely on the altar.

The villagers and pilgrims crowded forward, their excited chatter obliterating the sound that, only moments before, had so perplexed them. This spectacle was far more enthralling than any strange noise, for if this man had been struck down by God at the very instant the Blood of Christ had touched his lips, he must have committed some terrible sin. At least, that was what the pilgrims were telling each other. The moor folk, though, were glancing in awe at the locked door to the well. Perhaps it wasn't God he'd angered but old Brigid herself, for hadn't he been standing on the very spot where her spring gushed out below his feet? But God or goddess, whoever had struck him down, they were determined to enjoy his gruesome demise.

The prioress was equally determined to disappoint them. She tried to clear them from the chapel – though at first not even her authority could prise them away from the entertainment.

Sister Melisene knew her customers better. She hurried to the door, flung it open and bellowed above the din that she was off to distribute the dole of food. The villagers hesitated, but empty bellies triumphed, and they limped and shuffled after her. The pilgrims were harder to disperse, but by the time the prioress had succeeded in closing the door behind them, the deacon was hunched miserably on the stone floor, his chest heaving painfully and his face still scarlet. Otherwise it appeared he would live. As silence fell on the group of sisters, the buzzing grew louder till it filled the chapel, blotting out all the sounds of life outside.

Nicholas, ignoring Wybert, was prowling around the chapel trying to determine where the noise was coming from. He soon realised it was loudest by the well door. But it certainly wasn't frogs croaking. He marched over to Fina and thrust out his hand. 'Give me your keys.'

She turned wordlessly to the prioress.

'I think you may find it more convenient to ask Sister Fina if she would be kind enough to unlock the door,' Johanne said evenly. 'The wooden bolt often swells because of the damp, but she has a way of coaxing it.'

Nicholas was in no mood to ask any of the women anything. He snatched the ring of keys from Fina's hand and advanced on the door with one thrust in front of him like a lance. He regretted his impulse almost at once, for no amount of wriggling would make the prongs connect with the slots in the bolt on the other side of the door and he had no way of knowing if he had thrust the right key into the hole or if it was merely as stubborn and obdurate as the women who guarded it.

The sisters watched in silence, though he could sense their supercilious glances to each other behind his back. His temper and frustration were reaching boiling point. But even he realised he'd been beaten.

'Like everything else in the priory, it would seem that you have arranged it so that this bolt will yield its secrets only to a woman. Sister Fina, will you please open this door?'

His humiliation was complete as the bolt slid back for her as smoothly as ale slips down a thirsty man's throat.

But as it swung open, both stench and noise charged out, smashing against Nicholas like a battering ram – the sickening reek of hundreds of rotting frogs and the buzzing of the thousands of blow-flies that swarmed over them. The iridescent green vermin crawled so densely over the steps and walls that the very rock itself seemed to be undulating. It was as if he was staring down into an open grave. For a moment, he saw – he *thought* he saw – the putrefied remains of a man lying on the stairs beneath the pall of flies, as if a corpse had tried to claw its way out of a tomb.

Clamping his sleeve to his mouth to stop himself retching, Nicholas backed away from the stairs, stumbling over his own feet in his haste to escape. But though he kept telling himself it was only the shadows cast by the candlelight and the heaving mass of greenbottles, he could not shake the ghastly image from his head. All the sisters had taken an involuntary step backwards, clamping hands over mouths and noses, their eyes wide with shock and disgust. Mercifully, the flies were too cold and lethargic from the chill of the cave to fly out in any number, though a few were escaping into the chapel.

Johanne recovered first and slammed the door shut. Clarice snatched up the first thing she could seize, which happened to be a white linen manuterge with which Deacon Wybert had dried his hands during the unfinished mass, and vigorously swatted the few flies creeping out under the door. Wybert gave a feeble squeak of protest at the desecration of a holy cloth but no one paid him any heed. He began furiously batting and brushing at his clothes and tonsure, as if he could feel the tiny creatures crawling over his skin.

'There must be thousands of them,' Basilia mumbled, through the hand she still pressed across her nose and mouth, for the flies might have been contained behind the closed door, but the stench had escaped to fill every corner of the chapel, making even the strongest stomach heave.

'That is hardly to be wondered at,' the prioress said sharply. 'Flies are born of corpses. Judging by that smell, it would seem all the frogs have died and the flies have sprung from their remains. We must—'

She broke off. Sister Fina's moans were becoming ever louder, as though she was about to start screaming. She was staring fixedly at the bottom of the door, where more flies were emerging from the gap between wood and stone. Johanne seized her arm, and turned her, dragging her a few paces towards the courtyard door.

'Sister Fina, go at once and fetch wet cloths to stuff around the door. Otherwise the chapel will be filled with flies.'

Fina stumbled towards the courtyard, darting horrified

glances back at the well door, as if, at any moment, the whole swarm would burst through it.

Nicholas strode after her and stood in the open doorway, gulping air. For once the smell of stable dung and burned beans from the pilgrims' kitchen seemed almost as fragrant as a summer meadow.

'I can't be expected to celebrate mass with that noise and loathsome stench,' Deacon Wybert said, clambering shakily to his feet. 'It's not seemly.' He stumbled past Nicholas and almost hurled himself into the courtyard in his haste to leave.

Nicholas tried to grab his arm. 'I want a word—'

The deacon gagged, then vomited, barely missing Nicholas's boots. He staggered out of the gate looking as if another bout might overtake him. Nicholas, an expression of disgust contorting his face, decided there was little point in trying to detain him. 'Lily-livered fool,' he muttered. 'A spell in the order would do him good. Our priest brothers sing mass standing knee deep in blood, with the screams of dying men and horses as their choir, and they don't stumble over a word.' He glared at Prioress Johanne. 'But your gutless deacon has a point. No one will attend services here while the place is swarming with more flies than a dunghill, and all the time the door to that chapel remains shut the order is losing valuable income. How do you propose to rid it of that vermin?'

'For the present, there is nothing that can be done,' Johanne said briskly, 'except ensure the well door is sealed as best we can.'

'Hare's gall in milk will kill them,' Basilia said. 'I always leave some dishes of that in the casements of the infirmary when the weather is warm.'

'I fear we would not be able to catch enough hares to dispatch as many flies as we appear to have,' Johanne said.

184

Basilia looked crestfallen, but instantly brightened. 'I'm sure I've read in one of my herbals that burning fleabane and willow herb together will drive them away. But I can't remember if it was dried or fresh. We use fresh fleabane to mix with the rushes, but that's to keep down the fleas, so perhaps dried—'

Her prioress stemmed the flow by laying a hand on her arm. 'Sister, it is a good thought, but I fear any attempts to drive away the flies will merely send them pouring into the chapel and then they'll be crawling over the kitchens and the infirmary. We must be patient.'

'Patient!' To Nicholas, the buzzing seemed to be growing louder. He was sure he could feel the stone beneath his feet vibrating as if the creatures were dashing themselves at the roof of the cave. 'How many plagues are we to endure? It appears you can't maintain a simple holy well, much less a priory and all its lands and tenements. May I remind you, *Sister* Johanne, that this priory belongs to the order and exists solely to carry out our ministry to the poor and sick, and to collect the revenues the Citramer so desperately needs. And if the one appointed to have the care of it is found wanting, she, with all those sisters who support her, will swiftly be removed, by force should that prove necessary.'

Chapter 22

Sorrel

That evening I did not go up to Eva's fireside, though I told Todde that was where I was going. Eva was growing stronger. Since she shared the food she cooked for the tinners, she ate better than most of the women in the camp and, unlike them, she'd time to snare birds and animals for the pot too. But though the bleeding had stopped even before I'd returned with the charm – I reckon it must have happened at the moment Morwen held the cloth – there was still something draining out of Eva day by day, as if her spirit was shedding invisible drops of blood or weeping tears that could not be seen or heard. Even after all we'd shared that night, she talked no more to me than she had done before. She never spoke of her lost bairn, even when I asked her, but I could see in her eyes the edges of her soul freezing over, like the ice creeping towards the centre of a pond. And I climbed up to her fire of an evening as much for her sake as to seek warmth for myself. But not that night.

Why did I lie to Todde? Why would he care where I went? I was nothing to him. There were plenty of women with two good arms in the camp. Why would he or any man look twice at me, save in disgust? But, all the same, I knew he'd try to dissuade me from going out on the moor at night. He'd not ventured out there himself since we'd arrived in the camp. Few of the tinners would leave the valley alone after dark, for fear of the hounds we heard howling across the moors. But I had to go, just as I'd had to leave my village and set out on this journey. Morwen held the answer I'd been searching for. She knew whose the voice was and why she was calling me. I was growing more certain of that each day.

It was already dark by the time I neared Kendra's cottage. A chill wind blew through the sedges and rustled every furze bush. I couldn't stop myself constantly turning my head, certain that some beast was creeping through the long grasses behind me. I should not have come. When I'd ventured to this place before, I had been fretting so about Eva that a herd of dragons could have roared past me and I'd not have noticed. But now I heard every scurry among the heather, heard the cry of all the birds winging towards their roosts.

Kendra's cottage squatted like a black toad in a cold puddle of moonlight. A flickering tongue of gold-red light darted out beneath the leather curtain that hung in the doorway as if it was searching for grubs. I stopped. What reason could I give for coming? I'd no food to spare. I didn't even know what I would say to Morwen if I could speak to her alone. It was madness.

As quietly as I could, I began to back away. The slippery wet stepping-stones in the stream glinted in the moonlight. The bubble and rush of the water seemed louder than when I'd crossed a few moments ago and I stared down, trying to balance myself. But as I stepped out on the other side I collided with something in the darkness that was both soft and hard. I almost pitched backwards into the stream, but a hand grabbed my arm and steadied me.

'I knew you'd come.' Morwen's eyes glittered so brightly, it was as if a candle burned behind them. She put a finger to her lips, nodding towards the cottage, then beckoned to me to follow. We climbed up the side of the stream. When the clouds hid the moon, Morwen didn't falter. She slipped around every stone and bush, every mire and mound, as if, like a cat, she could see as well at night as in the day. She darted ahead and I lumbered behind, slipping and tripping, until suddenly she vanished. I called out, terrified she'd been swallowed by one of the quaking bogs the tinners feared.

I breathed again, as I heard her voice, but I couldn't make out where it was coming from. Then the moon sidled out from the clouds and I saw that I was standing on the rim of a hollow on the side of a hill, as if a giant ladle had been plunged into the earth and scooped it out. A small pool, black and glistening, lay in its heart. I could just make out the figure of Morwen crouching close to the water. I stumbled down after her, squelching through patches of oozing mud that lay hidden beneath sodden grass.

She grinned, her teeth flashing white in the moonlight. 'I knew I could fetch you back to the cottage.'

'Fetch me? No, you didn't. I came looking for you,' I said indignantly. I'd had a lifetime of my father and brother ordering me to do whatever they pleased. I knew that was the way of it with men. But since I had walked away from them, I was determined to be commanded by no one.

'I can teach you how,' Morwen chirruped, oblivious to my annoyance.

She was as excited as a bairn wanting to show off some

188

new-found treasure. Before I could stop her, she was yanking at the cloth twisted about my head. My hair whirled out in the breeze.

Morwen seized my good hand and thrust a slender stick into it. 'Elder,' she announced. 'Ma uses it to summon spirits too.' She guided my hand, scratching three circles in the sodden earth, a small one, then a larger one around it and the third around that. 'You must offer the spirits something.'

'Ow!' I flinched as she tugged a few strands of hair from my scalp, and bound them rapidly around some worts. Even in the dark I could recognise one by its scent: rosemary. Mam had planted a bush of that near the door of our cottage, but it died the year she did.

'This is what I used to fetch you,' Morwen said happily. 'Rosemary to bind us, yarrow to call you, and rowan to guard against wicked spirits that might harm you on the journey or might appear in your guise to trick me.' She leaned over and dipped the sprigs in the black pool, sending ripples running outwards across its surface. She touched the dripping herbs to the east, south, west and north of each circle in turn, letting the water shower on to the earth, though if you asked me, it was so sodden, it scarcely needed that blessing.

'See, that's what you do, but all the time, as you do it, you must say the will worth, say it and want it more than anything else. See the person in your head walking towards you, like I saw you. And you came.'

She sat back on the wet grass and, though I couldn't see her expression, I could hear in her voice that her smile had faded. 'Ma says only the eldest daughter has the gift, been that way since first our granddams had the keeping of Bryde's well afore the black crows stole it from us. Ma was the eldest, and her ma too afore that. But I know Ryana can't journey or speak to spirits. She fools Ma into thinking she can 'cause Ma is so sure it's her that has the gift, not me. Ma won't let me speak of it. She says there's ways and secrets that can only be passed to the eldest, else the spirits will grow angry and take revenge. But you can feel them, hear them, like me. I knew it from the moment we both held that clootie. I can talk about these things to you. I can show you.'

'But before I came for the blood charm, you didn't know me to call me. It wasn't your voice I heard in my dreams. Whose was it? Why did she bring me here?'

Morwen didn't answer. Frustration and disappointment fermented inside me. I'd been so sure.

'I thought you'd know,' I burst out. 'When you said "Dertemora". I thought that meant you knew. It was a sign.'

'It's just the old name for these moors,' Morwen said. 'Everyone calls it that . . . all the villagers. Only the blow-ins, like the black crows and the pedlars, call it summat different.'

'The tinners call it Dartmoor.'

'Aye, that's it, but no one birthed in these parts would say it. It's not respectful. 'Sides, Old Crockern, the spirit who guards these moors with his wisht hounds, he'd not know it by any name save Dertemora. How could any ask him to protect it, if they don't know its rightful name? But . . .' she shuffled closer to me '. . . this voice of yours, what did it say?'

It was a night for whispering secrets so I told her what I had shared with no one. I sensed that she alone would not mock me or think I'd run mad. I told her about the river turning to blood, Todde and the hound's-tongue, and how, since I was nine summers old, I'd heard a woman's voice in my dreams. That day by the river I'd heard her again, but this time when I was awake. I told how I'd walked away from my village, my father, my life.

She listened in silence.

'Who is it that calls to me?' I finished.

For a long moment, she said nothing, then finally she murmured, 'Maybe Ma could see her face in the smoke . . . Maybe she could show you.'

I reached out to take her hand. 'I reckon you've more skill in your fingers than Kendra and all your kin before her. I know the answer lies with you. You can show me. I know you can.'

Chapter 23

Prioress Johanne

Even with the door to my chamber firmly closed, I could hear Sister Melisene shouting from the other side of the courtyard. 'Now you stop that at once,' Melisene bellowed, 'or I'll feed all the meat to the swine. They have better manners.'

I flung open my door and immediately regretted doing so, for the cacophony emanating from the other side of the priory gate was worse than that of a mob of drunken revellers after a Christmas feast.

'You heard the sister,' Goodwife Meggy shouted, through the small grid in the huge door. 'Kennel your tongues and stand quiet, else this gate stays shut.'

She slammed the shutter and took a step back, murmuring something to Melisene and the servant with her, who were both balancing baskets on their hips. But the clamour outside, far from abating, was growing louder. There were even thumps on the stout wooden door, as if people were hammering on it with their staves. I dragged my cloak about my shoulders and hastened across the courtyard, trying to avoid the worst of the puddles. 'What is happening out there?'

The gatekeeper folded her meaty arms, glowering at me as if I was responsible for the disruption at her gate.

'Tinners' womenfolk and their brats, that's what. They've the gall to come here begging for food. Claim there's none to be had in the villages round about. Got more sense than to sell it to them, that's why. Hid it where those thieving tinners won't find it. They'll need every bite they can find to fill the bellies of their own families, if this harvest is as bad as the last, which it looks fair set to be. Now those tinners have come here demanding alms, shoving our old folks and cripples to the back of the queue. It's not right. You ought to send them packing, Sister Melisene.'

The hosteller gnawed her lip. 'I don't like them elbowing the frail aside, but I can't just turn them away. Some of those children are so thin they look as if their arms would snap if you touched them, and the mothers are nearly as gaunt. But last time I took the meats out to them, the stronger children and some of the mothers just snatched it straight from the basket before I had a chance to share it among them.'

'Then it is up to us to see that it is distributed fairly,' I said. 'Fetch four more baskets and divide the food equally between the six. Meanwhile I will go out and speak to them.'

'That rabble?' Meggy said. 'Don't you turn your back on them else they'll have the clothes ripped off it.'

Behind me I caught the piteous cries of Sebastian through the casement of the infirmary. The noise must be carrying in to him as loudly as it had into my chamber. I had to fight the impulse to go to comfort him, but I had to trust one of the other sisters to do that. Better for him and the other patients that I dealt with this disturbance.

If Brother Nicholas heard this . . . Sweat drenched my body, and I felt as if I was standing in front of the great fire in the kitchen instead of out in the courtyard in the damp, chill breeze. I took a deep breath. Thanks be to the Holy Virgin, our troublesome brother was one problem I did not have to deal with at this hour. Meggy had told me he had ridden out on his black rouncy early that morning. I had cursed the news then, worried about where he might have gone and what he might discover, but now I was relieved. After the plagues of frogs and flies, I did not need him accusing me of being unable to carry out the most basic of the Hospitallers' duties – the dispensing of alms. If Nicholas sent word to Clerkenwell that we couldn't even deal with a few beggars, they would have me removed before the ink on the report was dry. And the thought of what they might discover once I was no longer there made me shiver. I gave myself a little shake. This was foolishness. They would discover nothing, and I would not relinquish my duty as prioress until the day they laid me in my grave. All the more reason to ensure peace was restored at our gates before Nicholas returned.

I tried to focus once more on the commotion outside, which, though it seemed impossible, was growing ever louder. I seized Meggy's stave, then told her to open the wicket gate in the great door and bolt it behind me as soon as I had passed through. The gatekeeper regarded me dubiously, as if I was intending to walk out into a pack of ravening wolves. 'They're just women, children and crippled old men,' I assured her.

'Savages is what they are!' But Meggy did as she was bade and opened the wicket gate, though barely wide enough for me to squeeze through, then slammed it shut again.

For a moment, I found myself almost agreeing with Meggy, for a crowd surged towards me, jostling me so closely, I could barely breathe. I felt small hands burrowing under my cloak, stealthy as those of professional cut-purses.

But almost at once a cry went up. 'That's not her. That's not the one as brings us meats.'

The rabble drew back a little, staring at me sullenly. I recognised a few faces, old women and a lame man who came regularly to mass. But as Meggy had predicted, a group of emaciated but belligerent women and children had pushed them roughly to the back and were keeping them there. Some of the children were pawing me again, stretching out filthy, spindly arms and crying out in the high-pitched wheedling voices that hardened beggars use to solicit alms.

'You will all be given something. But I will not tolerate the scenes of yesterday.' I seized one of the more persistent urchins by the wrist, dragging his hand from my skirt. 'You, boy, sit over there. You, and you, join him. I said, "Sit!" Get right down on the grass. No one will have a bite until everyone is sitting, and if anyone gets up again before they have been given their meats, they will get nothing.'

I sorted them into six groups. At first some of the boys remained standing defiantly, staring at me with mutinous eyes, some even jeering, but eventually their mothers pulled them to the ground, and finally those children who had come alone reluctantly followed. It took much heaving and groaning before some of the elderly women were able to lower themselves on to the sodden grass. I was sorry to force them to it and felt every twinge of the pain in those aching backs and swollen knees, but I could see no other way.

When all were seated, I called to Sister Melisene and to the servants who had gathered at the window in the gate to watch, ordering them to bring out the baskets. As they passed out the food, several of the tinners' women and children began to demand two, three, even four portions for ailing children and old folks back at their camp, but I shook my head firmly when the servants looked doubtfully at me.

A boy sprang to his feet and ran towards an old woman. He snatched the bread and mutton bone from her hand as he passed, racing off down the slope with it, the old lady's wails following hard on his heels. Three other children leaped up, and before any of us could stop them, they'd grabbed the food from those who had already received their share and run off. Seeing what was happening, the other villagers quickly hid their portions in their clothes or the sacks tied to their waists.

When they were finally convinced that the baskets were empty and no more was forthcoming, the tinners' families clumsily picked their way down the slope, plainly unused to walking over the boggy grass. We helped the old and infirm to their feet, and Melisene went to see what she could find in the kitchens for those who had been robbed of their alms.

An elderly woman, who came often to mass, hobbled up to me. 'You'll not have any meats to give soon, Prioress, if those tinners aren't stopped.'

'Perhaps next time we will have to take the alms they need to a place nearer their camp so that the villagers are not pushed aside here.'

The old woman shook her head till the wrinkled skin of her neck wobbled like a cock's wattle. 'You'll not be needing to take it closer to them for they're coming closer to you. Seen it with my own two eyes, I have. It's you who'll be begging for alms soon and you'll not get any from them.'

The rumble of hoofbeats distracted me before I could ask

what she meant. Brother Nicholas was cantering up the rise on his black rouncy. Its coat was glistening with sweat, and wisps of pinkish white foam stained the corners of its mouth. He had ridden the horse hard. The villager was still talking as he reined in dangerously close beside us, forcing me to pull her out of his path.

The old woman cocked her head, watching him slide from the saddle. 'Take more than him to drive them off. Kendra's curses have done no good. And if she can't banish them, no one can.'

'Drive who off?' I demanded in, I confess, a somewhat irritated tone. I was preoccupied with wondering which properties my brother knight had been sniffing around this time. But it was Nicholas who answered me.

'I rather think the goodwife is referring to the tinners. I found your cowherd trying to round up the cattle. It seems he was watering them at the stream when a gang of men and their dogs charged them, scattering the beasts in all directions. They claimed the cattle were trampling their bounding markers.'

'Bounding?'

Nicholas snorted, sounding not unlike his horse, which was pawing the ground and tossing its head, impatient to be taken to the stable. 'When the tinners want to commandeer a new site, they mark the corners of their boundaries by cutting turves and flipping them over, then lay stones at the edges of their claim. All they have to do then, it seems, is to inform their so-called tinners' court that they have placed their bounding markers, and provided another tinner hasn't already laid claim to that spot, they're free to start tearing up the land, digging for tin.'

'But those are our grazing rights,' I said indignantly.

'Were!' Nicholas said. 'I've seen their tin works in the far valley. Once they start digging here, there won't be a blade of grass left fit for grazing or water a beast could drink without poisoning itself.'

'That's what I've been trying to tell you,' the old woman cried triumphantly. 'They'll be doing to you what they done to us. Tore off my door to use as firewood, they did, and their dogs killed my last hen, while they stood and laughed. You mark my words, they'll be cooking their suppers on your threshold, if you don't stop them, and it'll be your cattle that they'll be stewing in their pots.'

Her rheumy eyes spotted Melisene returning with a small basket of food for those souls who'd been robbed, and she hobbled away to claim her share, though I did not recall seeing anyone snatch food from her hand. But perhaps I was mistaken.

Nicholas took a tighter grip on his restless horse's bridle, trying to hold the powerful beast in check. 'I wouldn't generally wager a dog's turd on any prediction made by some old village crone, but I'd gamble my own rouncy that she'll be proved right about this. Those tinners have the King's law on their side and it's the most badly worded statute that was ever drawn up since Nebuchadnezzar was crowned. Tinners could dig up this priory stone by stone, if they chose to claim there was tin beneath it. And claim it is all they need to do. According to stannary law, *their* law, no landowner may "vex or trouble them", which means, in effect, whatever they want it to mean. If a farmer so much as waves his fist at them or sets a dog on them to try to stop them digging up his crops, they say he has *troubled them* and can have him fined or worse. There's no court in this land that can curb their rights, unless King Edward chooses to change the law, and he won't do that while they're making the tin he needs for his wars, and lining his coffers with the tax they're paying on every ingot. He doesn't care who in his kingdom suffers, so long as he has enough money to lavish gifts on those pretty lads he has tumbling into his bed.'

'That is dangerously close to treason, Brother Nicholas,' I warned.

His mouth curled in contempt. 'So, now I am obliged to listen to a woman try to school me in my duty to the King. Perhaps, my sweet prioress, you'll not be so quick to defend your sovereign when those tinners have taken your livestock, your water and your land, and you discover that our illustrious king is too busy fondling his friends to spare a moment to restrain these marauders. We will have to deal with this ourselves. The Lord Prior will not want to cause trouble, but Commander John at Buckland itches for a fight. He'll not be so squeamish. I'll send word to him. A few well-armed knights and sergeants-at-arms riding down on those tinners without warning will soon put them to flight.'

The tinners might be wolves, I thought, but Nicholas was a fox of the most cunning breed. Crying *help* to Buckland to come to the aid of defenceless women unable to protect themselves all alone on the moors – the brothers would love that. It would be just the excuse they needed to herd us safely into the fold of the cloister, leaving Brother Nicholas free to dig as deep as he pleased into the affairs of the priory. He would not be content with our removal. Nicholas was an ambitious man, itching for command. He wanted to discover something, anything, to earn the gratitude and respect of the Lord Prior. And when a man is so determined to expose evil, he can take even the miracles of a saint and present them as the work of the devil.

199

I met his gaze levelly. 'If a farmer's raised fist can be counted a vexation to the tinners, Brother Nicholas, I can only imagine what offence they might take if a party of armed knights came charging down on unarmed men, not to mention their wives and children.'

Nicholas laughed. 'They'd have a tough time serving an appeal against us to bring us to their tinners' court, much less imposing a fine. You must name a man to charge him. Hard to do that when he wears no coat of arms.'

I tapped the white cross on my cloak. 'A Knight of St John may not bear his own arms, but he does bear the arms of Christ, and God's knights do not ride down famished women and children, who are the very ones we are all pledged to serve. I have seen those tinners' families today with my own eyes. What they do, they do because they are desperate.'

'As you will be if they are allowed to invade our order's land unchecked. You women are too easily deceived by a tearful beggar's brat. You do realise that their mothers pinch them to make them cry, don't you? The tinners I saw in the valley were not hungry, they were greedy for wealth, and if their women and children go without food, it is because their fellow streamers would see them starve rather than share what they have. They're a pack of dogs gone wild.'

'Perhaps so, but when the knights have ridden back to safety at Buckland, where do you think the tinners will come to vent their fury? If you bring men-at-arms from Buckland to this place, all you will succeed in doing is starting a war between this priory and the tinners, and if they are the wild dogs you claim them to be, our cross and our veil will be no protection. You will not send to Buckland, Brother Nicholas, not as long as I remain prioress here.'

'And how long will you remain prioress, Mistress, with no livestock and no lands to support you? You had best ensure that no more plagues beset your holy well, for you will need every bent pin those pilgrims throw into it.'

Chapter 24

Sorrel

'Listen!' Morwen said, tilting her head towards the rocks towering above her on the top of the tor.

But I was panting so hard the only thing I could hear was the river of blood thundering deep within my ears. I was used to working all day on an empty belly, bred to it, you might say, like the donkey which walks round and round, day after day, turning the grinding stone. I'd spent my life hauling water from the village well, hefting firewood, pummelling the washing and wrestling with our own small patch of stony land, but though that makes your back and belly as strong as a blacksmith's, it doesn't prepare your aching legs for climbing up a steep tor with a spiteful wind snatching the air from your mouth before you can even take gulp of it.

It was all very well for Morwen. Like all those who were born on the moors, every step she'd taken in her life must have been either up a hill or down, and she could bound up a steep slope like a cat up the thatch on a roof. But by the time I'd staggered to where Morwen was crouched at the top of the tor, sweat was crawling down my face, and I'd such a burning pain beneath my ribs all I could do was flop down on the wet grass and lie there. Great grey clouds rose up, one behind another, like walls of stone, but a beam of dazzling sunlight, thin and straight as a golden arrow, slipped between them, striking the twisted branches of a thorn bush that grew out of a crack in the rock above my head, catching the raindrops that clung to the leaves and turning them into a shoal of sparkling rainbow fish.

I pointed. 'Beautiful,' I gasped.

Morwen lay down beside me, her head nearly touching mine as we stared up at the rainbow fish darting among the waterweed of thorn.

'Some nights,' Morwen murmured, 'the moon turns all the rocks to silver. The sky's as dark and soft as a mole's pelt, full of great frosted stars. When the summer is dying, the hills burst into yellow and orange flames. The bracken burns red as a fox, and rowan berries glow like hot embers. And when Brigid brings the sun back in the spring, the black moor pools are so still and calm you can see the clouds in them as if the skies were below your feet 'stead of above your head. When I was little, I'd watch the birds in the sky drifting in the pool, as if they were flying through water. I thought if I jumped in I'd find a whole new world down there. Tried it once, but all I found was mud.' She sat up, frowning. ''Tis all mud now. The moor is hurting. Nothing's right.'

She rolled over and tugged at me like a fretful bairn till I sat up. 'But listen,' she repeated.

I couldn't hear anything on that high peak, save the roar of the wind as it flattened the tawny grasses, but as my heart stopped thudding from the climb, I began to hear another sound burrowing out beneath the wind's shriek, a hollow knocking, as if a corpse was beating against the stone walls of his tomb with his own bones. And voices too, but they were murmuring to each other so low that I couldn't make out the words, or maybe they were speaking in a strange tongue, for I could no more catch the meaning than grasp that shaft of sunlight in my fist.

Morwen was watching me intently, her flame-red hair gusting in the breeze, her great green-grey eyes hungry as those of a stray cat. I felt like a beast with a plump bird clamped between my jaws and she was judging how best to snatch it. I knew she wanted me to tell her something, but I didn't know what.

She shook her head impatiently. 'You hear them?'

'Who's in there? Your mam and sisters?'

Morwen grinned, showing a missing front tooth. 'Ma only comes here at night when there's a certain moon she needs for her charms. That's why I brought you here in daylight, 'cause I knew it'd be safe then.'

The voices inside the cave grew louder, though their song was so mournful it hurt like a fist reaching into your chest and twisting your heart. I ached with misery at the sound, as if I was watching someone I loved weeping at a graveside. I wanted to take away their pain, but I couldn't.

'I knew it. I knew they'd speak to you.' Morwen breathed the words softly, as if she feared to disturb them. 'Come on.'

She edged sideways through the crevice, though she was so slender I reckoned she could have walked in face on. Then she stuck her hand back out between the rocks, groping for mine. Our fingers interlaced and she threaded me through the gap till we stood hand in hand, listening to the voices swirling in the darkness. Our breathing slowed and, without meaning to, I found I was drawing in breath with her and letting it go as she did, so that it felt as if the damp, earthy air was entering me through Morwen's body. We had melded into one creature.

A cold, hoary light trickled through the crevice, like dawn breaking after a winter's night, and I saw we were standing in an oblong cave. The floor sloped down towards the entrance and was bare but for the ashes of a fire set about by blackened stones and a few sticks of scorched wood.

Morwen let go of my hand, crouched and carefully heaped fresh tinder on the little nest of feather-soft ashes. She struck a flint and iron together several times until a bright flash of sparks caught the pile of twigs and a fragile flame guttered along its edge. She blew down a hollow reed, until the tinder was ablaze, then added some of the charred sticks.

'Ma'll not see the glow in daylight, but we'd best keep it small.'

The firelight flickered over the far end of the cave, which before had been in darkness. A slab of stone was covered with a white woollen cloth, but it wasn't lying flat. It concealed something beneath.

'What's under that?' I was curious, itching to raise it and look, but I didn't want to offend Morwen by prying.

As she glanced up, I jerked my chin towards the slab. That gesture would have made my old mam give one of her fond, sad smiles – she said I started pointing with my chin long before I could walk: if my good hand was grasping a crust of sucked bread or a shiny pebble, I had no other hand to point with. Mam said it broke her heart to watch me, for she could see even then that I longed to seize the world with both hands. But I reckoned one hand is more than big enough to catch life by the tail, if you can make that fist strong.

Morwen's gaze sidled towards the cloth, but she didn't

look at me when she answered. 'I'll show you one day, but not yet.'

There was something under there that bothered her. I could sense it. I glanced back at the cloth and shivered, as if Morwen's unease had jumped across the space between us.

She made me sit facing her on the other side of the fire, the way I'd faced Kendra across the smoke. 'Look,' she commanded. 'Look into the fire, then you'll see. And you must say the will worth, like I told you down at the pool. You must ask the woman who called you in your dreams to speak again and show you her face. You must want it so much that you feel like you'll break.'

While my mam still lived, I used to stare into the flames every evening, but it seemed now that that was centuries ago, far back in the embers of my childhood. When had there last been time to sit still of an evening without falling asleep from exhaustion? But now I felt myself shrink down into that little bairn again, when I'd watched fiery boars thunder through charcoal-black forests of towering trees, and golden salmon leap over ruby waterfalls, and great black and amber birds hover over the bloody corpses of the slain. Those things were as familiar as my own cottage back in my village. But what I saw in the flames in that cave were not those creatures. This was an alien fire.

Gnarled and twisted oaks, wizened and shrunken, old as the tors and their spirits as dark. But they are not trees at all. They're wrinkles and veins, nostrils and eyebrows. They're the face of a man, an ancient man, with great cavernous sockets for eyes. A black hound leaps from one of the sockets, his coat aflame and crackling with bright ruby sparks. A second dog bounds out and . . .

I turn my head. A woman is sitting before the fire. I see only her back, only her outline dark against the leaping flames. She is weaving cloth on a loom of silver birch poles. She has spun the warp threads from soft rushes, green as spring, but as she picks the weft thread in and out of the warp, it shimmers and dances, crimson as rowan berries, golden as sunbeams. And I see it is not thread at all but living flames. She is weaving a cloak of fire.

Something darts across the cave. I catch it on the very edge of my vision. But I know if I turn to look at it, it will dissolve. I glimpse it again. It shines as though it has been cast from moonlight, yet it has a shadow at its core, a deep blackness.

I feel a tingle on my back. The skin on my shoulder-blades stretches and bubbles, as if maggots are burrowing out. They burst the skin, emerge quivering. They're attached to my body like my wizened arm, yet while that lies limp, they're uncrumpling, unfolding, blood is pumping through them, my blood. They're swelling, fluttering, and I can no more make them lie still than I can make the fingers of my left hand move. Shadows are gathering around me, drifting closer, like shoals of curious fishes. If I turn my head, they dart away, only to swarm close again when I stare back into the flames.

'Fire and water wait for you. The time is now.'

It's her voice. The one that called to me in my dreams and from the river.

'Come deeper into the fire, come. It will not harm you. It is cold fire, a fire of ice. It is my fire, come.'

Something lies beneath those twisted oaks, deep at the heart of that fiery core, a fox, a black fox. It doesn't look at me, yet I know if I walk towards it it will rise and run before me, deeper.

'Deeper.'

The whispers around me grow deafening, as if I'm being

sucked into the roar and crackle of the fire. The creatures of the shadows are flying at me now. Their damp grave-breath drifts against my face, their dead icy hands stroke my hair, and I know that if I let go I will float away with them through that sea of cold black flames.

'Let go. Come deeper. Come to me!'

My head jerks up and, with every last grain of will I possess, I push a single word into my throat and force it out between my lips. 'NO!'

The shadows rise, swirling around me, like a clamour of rooks. The whispers slither back through the cracks in the rock.

'What did you do that fer?' Morwen's voice held all the bitter frustration of old Kendra's.

But the green eyes that stared at me through the veil of smoke were filled with betrayal, like those of a child who'd had a juicy plum snatched from her hand before she'd taken a bite.

'Did you see . . .' I began, but I'd no words for what I'd seen or heard, so the question drifted down to the trampled earth.

Morwen glowered at me. 'What? What did you see? Tell me!'

I tried, but it was like trying to make a shattered pot whole again. The more I spoke, the less sense it made. Nothing was joined together, nothing I had seen had an ending. I was sinking down in nameless dread, knowing only that if I had taken one more step I would never have been able to return. It was as if I was gazing down into my grave – no, worse than that: I was staring through it into whatever living darkness lay beyond.

All the time I was trying to tell her what I'd seen and heard, Morwen sat with her knees drawn up to her chin, her arms wrapped round them, fists clenched. Her gaze was fixed upon the fire. She didn't glance at me once.

'Brigid. That's who's been calling you,' she said dully, after a long silence.

'Saint Brigid?'

'No!' she snapped. '*Our* Brigid. Her whose well the black crows have stolen. Mother Brigid of the fires and the sacred springs. That's who you saw. She made these moors with her own hands, sang the wells out of the earth and called the rivers to run to the pools. It was her you saw at her loom. She was weaving her mantle. She returns at Imbolc and spreads her mantle over the earth to protect the land and drive away the last snows of winter.'

Brigid, the old goddess. Some memory fluttered to life deep inside me. Mam used to spill a little milk for old Brigid sometimes, if the butter was stubborn and wouldn't come in the churn. The parish priest used to rail against such things in his sermons, but Mam said the old mother belonged to the women and was no concern of any man.

I'd not thought of it since I was a bairn, but now a picture came into my head of Mam tying a strip of cloth on a bush outside our cottage at sunset. It must have been winter then, for I remember the puddles were frozen and Mam's fingers were so blue with cold she had to keep blowing on them as she tied the knot. I'd thought it a strange thing to be doing – Mam was always careful to gather in before nightfall any clothes she'd put out to dry for fear they'd blow away or be ruined by beasts.

''Tis Brigid's mantle,' Mam told me, though I could see it wasn't even big enough to make a cloak for my wooden doll. 'This night Brigid rides through the village to bless the mantles of those who do her honour, and it'll bring good fortune to our home if she blesses it.'

Mam promised that next year she'd show me how to hang the cloth, but she never did, for by then she was dead.

Morwen's head whipped round, fury blazing in her eyes. 'You don't even know who Brigid is, do you? So why did she call *you*? I have the gift. Why not me? Why can't I see her?'

I could feel her hurt, but I didn't know what to say. I wished it had been her. I didn't want this. 'What does she need from me?' I asked, hoping that Morwen's pride would be soothed a little if she could teach me again as she had down by the black pool.

But my question seemed only to bait her anger. 'Why ask me? You should have asked *her*. She wanted to tell you. Why did you refuse to listen? I would have gone to her when she called. I wouldn't have run away like a – a – a sheep with a tick up its arse. You have to look into the fire again. And this time you must do what I told you. You have to want her to answer.'

'I'll not be told what I *must* do,' I said, as furious as she was now.

I scrambled to my feet and stalked towards the narrow cleft that led out of the cave. 'And I'll not conjure those creatures again.' I shuddered, still fearing their grave-cold fingers against my neck. 'If you've the gift, like you say, then you look into that fire. And while you're about it, you can tell this Brigid of yours to leave me be!'

Chapter 25

Hospitallers' Priory of St Mary

Brother Nicholas, striding across the courtyard, caught sight of the chapel door and stopped abruptly. Smoke! The chapel was on fire! He started to shout a warning, but realised even as the word escaped his lips that it wasn't smoke but steam. The sun had broken through the clouds, and a shaft of light shone full upon the door of the chapel. The wet wood steamed in the unexpected warmth. Nicholas tried to ignore the curious stares of the servants who'd been startled by his bellow and were watching his progress with undisguised curiosity, as if they thought he might start capering like a court jester.

It was hardly any wonder he couldn't recognise sunlight when he saw it, Nicholas thought morosely. It was as rare as cocks' eggs on this blasted moor. In Rhodes, the heat would be shimmering off the stones and the golden sun sparkling on a clear azure sea. Grapes would burst sweet on his tongue, and a girl whose silken hair smelt of damask roses and jasmine would be smiling at him as she poured his wine.

Mud squelched out beneath the sacking that had been laid in front of the chapel threshold, covering his boots with a stinking ooze of stagnant water and goose dung. He cursed vehemently, startling the servants a second time. The Lord Prior *must* send him back to the Citramer. He'd rot from the feet up if he was forced to spend another winter in this miserable realm.

But Lord William would send him nowhere if he couldn't even prove that the accounts drawn up by some aged crone were flawed, either through ignorance or, as he was beginning to suspect, by deliberate manipulation. But every time that suspicion crept back into his head, he found himself stamping on it. It was one thing to believe that women were fools and easily gulled, but that they would be clever enough to cheat the order was quite another, especially to do it so skilfully that neither he nor the procurator at Clerkenwell was able to uncover it. That was simply not possible.

Nicholas grasped the iron ring on the chapel door, hesitating before he turned it. Frogs and flies, bolts that would yield only to a woman's touch, what new plagues was that well about to spew forth? He was starting to think it was possessed of a malice all of its own. He pushed the door. The bright pool of sunlight outside made the chapel seem darker than usual and, for a moment, it appeared deserted. Nicholas was annoyed. He'd been sure he'd find her in here and, equally importantly, find her alone. He was about to stalk out again, when he glimpsed a movement in the dark shadows.

Sister Fina was emerging from the well door on the far side of the chapel. She halted when she caught sight of him and he thought she might dart back down, like the lizards on Rhodes, which scuttled under rocks if they caught sight of a man approaching. But instead she stood in the archway, as if, once again, she intended to prevent him or indeed anyone from entering.

'The . . . the well is open again, Brother Nicholas. The pilgrims will come today.' Her tone was wooden, rigid as her body.

'I was informed that it was to be reopened.'

Actually, he hadn't been told anything. But Alban had seen lights moving in the chapel after dark and had alerted him. From the shadows, he'd watched the prioress and her sisters spend half the night carrying a stinking soup of rotten frogs, maggots, dead flies and slime in relays of buckets up the steps to a pit outside the priory walls, there to be buried with lime, and all under cover of darkness. Darkness covers many sins.

They had sluiced the floor and steps with lye and lime, but he was sure he could still smell traces of the foul putre-faction creeping from the open door. Like the stench of heresy, it could not be washed away.

Nicholas closed the chapel door and strolled towards Fina. He was half amused to see the panic on her face as she retreated sideways until she collided with a pillar. She stood with her back hard against it, as if she was trying to melt into it.

'No need for such modesty, Sister. We're brother and sister in the same order, both sworn to chastity. It's no less seemly for you to be alone with me than with one of your father's sons.'

God's blood, surely she didn't think he was going to ravish her. She might be the youngest sister, but she was no beauty, though now he thought about it, he couldn't exactly decide why. It wasn't that any of her features was ugly, he decided, more that everything about her was mismatched. A nose too narrow for her face, eyes too pale for her dark hair, and breasts too small for her ungainly height. But he was prepared to convince her he found her more ravishing than the Queen of Sheba, if he had to. It wouldn't be the first time he'd bedded a woman to discover what he needed to know.

It had been pounded into him since the hour he first grasped a sword that the first and overriding commandment was to ensure the survival of the order. Nothing transcended that. If a knight must disguise himself as a Saracen to discover where an attack was planned or lie with a woman to learn what God's enemies were plotting; it was his duty to God and to the Hospitallers to do it. Such knowledge was as nobly won as any fight on the battlefield.

Nicholas glanced towards the closed door, then back to Fina. 'Sister, you collect the offerings left by the pilgrims at the well, don't you? I know what pilgrims leave as gifts at the shrines of saints, but I confess I've always been curious about what they bring to a well like this. Tell me, what's the largest sum you've collected in one day?' He laughed. 'I imagine they are quite generous, having toiled all the way up here.'

'Bent pins. That's what they bring. They drop them into the water and I collect them. Prioress Johanne says . . .' She pressed a hand to her mouth, like a guilty child, as if she had said something she shouldn't and was afraid she might incriminate herself.

Nicholas studied her carefully. *Now, just what is it that our sainted prioress says that you don't want to tell me?*

He stepped towards Fina, reaching out his hand. He fingered a stray lock of chestnut hair that had crept out from beneath her black veil.

'You have hair like silk. I noticed it before, and I should know. I've handled the finest silks in the markets of the Citramer.' He tucked the strand back beneath her veil, his fingers gliding over her cheek. 'Don't blush, Sister Fina. There's no sin in a knight giving praise to God for the lovely thing He has created. Indeed, it would be a sin to ignore it.'

Fina tried to move away, but he leaned across her, supporting himself on the pillar with one hand, which rested a breath from her face.

'You were telling me about the pins. It must be a tedious chore to collect those wretched little things day in, day out. And I dare say you have to clear up all the mess those pilgrims leave too, their bits of flowers and stinking rags covered with blood and pus. I've known warrior knights who wouldn't have the stomach for that. I only hope your prioress appreciates all you do for her. I doubt she'd bend her proud neck to lift a rag or fish around in freezing water for something as small as a pin.'

She nodded eagerly and seemed on the verge of speaking. That was the trouble with women: if you feigned the slightest interest in any mundane task they performed they'd insist on telling you about it in such tedious detail that you'd be begging for the mercy of the executioner's axe before they were done. And he hadn't come in here to listen to her babble about pins.

He stepped away from her, fixing his gaze on the bloodied head of the crucified Christ that hung above the altar. 'After dealing with all those villagers and beggars traipsing through here, it must be a relief for you to meet with the merchants and their wives who cross these treacherous moors on their way to and from the ports. Doubtless their offerings of coin and jewels are worth the trouble of collecting. If they've

215

endured the perils of the sea, they must be overwhelmed with relief to have been brought safely to shore, and those about to venture on board ship must be praying they don't perish. They're fearful going one way and grateful coming the other. I imagine it's hard to say which pays better.'

He laughed. 'Brother Alban reckons it's the merchants returning from the ports that pay more, thankful to be on solid land. I say it would be those about to set sail, for they're praying twice over – first, that they don't drown and, second, that if they must, their days in Purgatory will be short. But you know what a surly fellow Alban is, always insisting he's right. That weasel had the nerve to bet me that you collect as much as twenty shillings a day at this well when the merchants are returning. I said it was twice that sum when they're going out. I beg you to settle the wager for us, Sister Fina. And I pray you'll tell me my reckoning is nearest to the mark, for if I should lose the wager to Alban I'll be obliged to—'

He spun round as the chapel door opened and sunlight burst in, scattering shadows. But the light was blotted out moments later by the great bulk of Sister Basilia waddling through the doorway, gripping a young boy by one shoulder. She propelled him towards the edge of the stone altar, lifted his arm as if he was a doll and pressed his fingers on to the edge. His hand clasped the corner, like the claws of a little wren perched on a rock. The boy stared at Nicholas, with an unblinking gaze that the knight found both impudent and unnerving.

'Why have you dragged this village brat into the sanctity of the chapel, Sister Basilia?' Nicholas demanded. 'There's no service today and I was about to make my private devotions. I don't want to be disturbed.'

Basilia looked flustered. She glanced uneasily at the child, who hadn't moved from the altar or given any sign that he knew they were talking about him. 'Forgive me, Brother Nicholas. I didn't mean to disturb you. I shouldn't have dreamed of fetching him in here if I'd known you were at prayer. I hadn't expected you . . . That is, you don't often . . . But Prioress Johanne instructed me to bring the child here and bathe his eyes and tongue in the holy well, now that the flies . . .' She faltered, her gaze darting to the well door as if she feared a new and more terrible plague was even now gathering below.

She took a steadying breath. 'If St Lucia intercedes for the child, the holy well will cure him of his blindness and his dumbness too.' Her tone suggested she intended to be quite firm with the saint and leave her in no doubt as to the nature of the miracle that was required of her. 'Though how I'm to get him and a lantern down those steps without him falling and sending us both crashing to the bottom, I'm sure I don't know. I can barely manage to squeeze down that staircase myself. I can't see where I'm putting my feet and those steps are so worn and slippery.'

She stared pensively over her great belly. Her feet were remarkably tiny for a woman of her size. 'I know I shouldn't say it, but I'm always afraid I'll get stuck and won't be able to turn round. It's foolishness, I know, but those rocks seem to close in soon as I start on the steps.' She gave a nervous high-pitched giggle. 'If I'm to take the boy down, I fear I'll have to trouble you to help me, Sister Fina.'

Fina's eyes flashed wide in alarm and she took a pace back, as if Basilia had asked her to cradle a snake.

'Blind, you said.' Nicholas took a pace forward. 'Is this the boy who caused the death of the old priest?' He addressed

217

the question to Fina. But she made no answer, though he hardly needed one for her panicked expression spoke louder than a town crier. 'So, this is the little sorcerer.'

'Prioress Johanne says he is just a helpless child,' Basilia retorted, lifting her head defiantly, so that her many chins wobbled.

Nicholas studied the corpse-pale lad. He was as thin and frail as a prisoner chained for months in a dungeon. The prioress may have protested the boy's innocence, but she didn't appear to have given orders that he be treated well. He looked half starved.

Nicholas did not trouble to lower his voice. 'The devil may work through any creature. His imps take the form of frogs, foxes and goats, why not a boy? We have no way of knowing if the child has ever been baptised and had the devil cast out of him.'

Cupping his fingers under the lad's chin, the knight tilted the child's head towards the light from the door, passing his other hand several times across the boy's eyes. Then, without warning, he slapped the child's face. The boy yelped, trying to protect his head with his arms.

'Interesting,' Nicholas said. 'He can make sounds.'

He dragged the child's arm away from his cheek and wrenched open his jaw, tilting his head back until it seemed he might snap his neck. He grasped the boy's arm, pulling him round to face Sister Basilia.

'He has a tongue and it's not tied to the bottom of his mouth, like some I have seen. He does indeed appear to be blind, but I can see no reason why he shouldn't speak, except for obstinacy. I wager you could cure his dumbness far more swiftly and surely than by pouring holy water into his mouth. Arm yourself with a good switch and use it hard. Tell him

218

you'll stop only when he begs you to. That will encourage him to words. I'll gladly do it for you, if you've not the stomach—'

He broke off and stared down at the stick-thin limb that he still grasped in his great fist. The boy's arm was moving, but not because he was trying to struggle out of the knight's grip. He was standing motionless. Only his arm wriggled. It was undulating in Nicholas's hand as if the long, solid bones inside were now many tiny bones, as supple as a spine, as if the soft skin had hardened into scales, as if Nicholas was holding a writhing serpent in his hand instead of the arm of a boy. The boy's hand began to open, but it wasn't a hand, it was a head, with jaws that were stretching wide to expose two long fangs.

With a cry of horror, Nicholas staggered backwards, crashing into the pillar behind him. He stared at the boy's arm. But it was just an ordinary limb made of human flesh, no different from its twin – anyone could plainly see that. Yet he knew what he had felt.

The child was staring up at him, as if he could read every wild thought that was passing through the knight's head, as if he could see the shock and fear on Nicholas's face. A shaft of bright sunlight from the open door fell across the boy, the golden sparkle reflected in the twin pupils of those great, unblinking eyes. But even as Nicholas stared, the light that bathed the child turned to thick crimson gore. Nicholas pressed his hands to his eyes, convinced that he must have struck his head on the pillar when he stumbled and blood was running down his face, blinding him. He drew his hands away and examined his fingers, expecting to find them stained scarlet, but they were clean and the light that flooded through the door was as yellow as the sun itself.

'Whatever ails you, Brother Nicholas?' Basilia cried, waddling towards him. 'You've gone as pale as milk. Do you feel faint? You should sit down.' She tried to take his arm, but he shoved her away.

She was still clucking around him, when out in the courtyard a bell began to toll for the midday meal. She gave an audible sigh of relief. 'That's the noon bell. Cook will be putting the pottage on the table.' She waddled back towards the boy. 'No time for bathing now, young man. We'd best get you back to the infirmary else you'll miss your dinner. We can't have that, can we? You're already as skinny as a mouse's tail.'

She seized the boy by his hand and dragged him out behind her to the courtyard. Nicholas stumbled to the doorway, but a sound behind him made him turn his head. Fina was standing in the centre of the chapel, making the sign of the cross over and over again, as if to protect herself against something she feared. Had she seen that serpent too? Nicholas was certain that was one question he did not want her to answer.

Chapter 26

Sorrel

I hugged the threadbare cloak to my chest and paused to draw breath, staring down at the tinners' valley. The slopes of Fire Tor had been jewelled with rosy-purple heather and butter-yellow furze, but here on the hills every bush had been torn up for fuel or bedding, leaving weeping sores in the scalp of the earth from which the mud oozed in deep rivulets. The snide wind carried a fine mizzle, which, though you could scarcely see the drops, had already soaked through my hair and skin into the bones beneath. After the warmth of the fire in the tor, I was chilled to the marrow and my belly griped with hunger. Even the roots of my hair ached with cold. But though my body craved heat, I cringed at the thought of returning to the clatter and swarm of that valley. I wanted time to think about what had happened in the cave. I needed peace. I needed to be alone, but there was no chance of that down there.

Misery had wrapped around me, like a wet mantle, and spurts of anger kept rising inside me, not for Morwen but myself. Truth be told, I was as frustrated with me as she was,

221

more so. Why had I pulled back? Why had I not followed that voice, followed Brigid to the place she was trying to lead me when I'd had the chance? I'd been so close.

I'd left my home, my village, all I had ever known, and trudged to this midden, this hell, to follow that voice. All these weeks I'd been begging her to tell me who she was and what she wanted of me. All through the long, cold days and freezing nights I'd been trying to reach the place she was calling me to, and now, when every question was about to be answered, when I would finally see her, finally understand, I had fled!

Why can't we call that hour back, unsay what should not have been said, turn right instead of left, stay instead of running away? But time will not turn for us. Each moment melts, like a snowflake, and will not come again. And everything has changed because of it. The flight of an arrow is quicker than a breath, yet it takes a man from this world for eternity.

If I could have run back to that cave, I would have done it in a heartbeat. This time, I would have found the courage to enter the fire. Even knowing I could never return, I would have followed that voice. But it was too late. Morwen would have extinguished the flames. She would have walked away, and who could blame her?

Would Brigid simply abandon me here in this desolation? The thought terrified me, but I knew I deserved no better. Worse than that, I had driven away the only person who could help me find my way. Morwen would not summon me again, of that I was certain.

I jumped as the mournful echo of the ram's horn drifted towards me on the wind. It couldn't be that late, could it? The tinners would already be trudging back to their huts.

Would this be my life from now on? But where else could I go? Where else would I find work when so many were tramping the roads in search of it? Listless, I began to pick my way down the muddy track, weaving from one side to the other, trying to find a stone or a clump of rotting grass to step on, every muscle tense, fearful of slipping in the glutinous mud. The fires outside the huts had already been poked into life, their gusting flames huddled beneath the tiny shelters.

It was hard to see clearly through the smoke and mist, but there was no welcoming glow in front of my own hut. Couldn't Todde at least have mended the fire? After all, he practically sat on it half the night. The only time I ever got near its warmth was when I was stirring the pot.

I picked my way along the bank of the soup-thick, muddy stream. A figure was limping towards me. His pace quickened as he caught sight of me.

'Where have you been?' Todde snapped. He was annoyed, that was plain, and a wave of guilt overcame my irritation. Hunger makes everyone waspish and he'd spent the day shovelling and breaking stones, knowing he'd have next to nothing to show for it come Saturday. We were so deep in debt we couldn't afford to lose a single minute, and I had thrown away whole hours up in that cave, and for what? I couldn't have felt more wretched if I'd dropped a loaf of fresh bread into the mire.

He broke off, tilting his head as though he was trying to look at someone behind me. 'Where's Eva?'

His tone had changed so suddenly that it took me several moments to understand what he was asking.

'She'll be up at her fire by now, doling out the men's supper,' I said, feeling all the more guilty that I wasn't at my own hearth stirring our pot.

223

'Aye, well, that's just it, she isn't. Seeing as how neither of you were at your fires and no one had clapped eyes on either of you all afternoon, we thought you'd gone off together foraging, setting snares or some such.'

There was no reproach in his voice and I was grateful that he didn't add 'when you should have been streaming'. Not that I answered to him: he wasn't my kin. But, all the same, he'd a right to expect that I'd help pay back what we both owed.

'Did she tell you where she was going?' Todde asked. 'Her cooking fire's dead and her pot cold. Beans in there still hard as nails. Only thing blazing is the men and lads who want their food. They'll be spitting like a nest of weasels if she doesn't come soon.'

'She's a lover, one of the men she cooks for,' I told him. 'Maybe she's with him.'

Todde gave a snort of laughter. 'I reckon it'd have to be *all* the men she cooks for to keep her rolling in the hay so long. There's not a tinner in this camp who'd have the strength to keep a woman pleasured for so much as an hour after a day's graffing.' His grin vanished and anxiety furrowed his forehead. 'No, I reckon if the two of you weren't out together, then something's amiss. Maybe she's had a fall and done herself a mischief. Some of the tinners she cooks for were muttering about starting a search. I best tell them she's gone off on her own. It'll be dark soon.'

I glanced up at the sky. The sun had long sunk behind the tor, and the shadows were creeping down the valley. Had Eva collapsed somewhere? Maybe the bleeding had started again. Was that possible? If Morwen had stopped it with a charm, did she have the power to start it again with a curse – revenge for what I'd said and done?

224

Todde squeezed past me on the sodden track, and as he did so, he put his hands on my shoulders. 'At least you're back without harm. I was starting to fret. You ought not to go wandering on those moors alone, not with the pack of wild dogs that keeps howling and those outlaws. It's not safe for a lass like you, not safe for anyone.' He hurried away.

I didn't know whether to be glad he was watching out for me or annoyed that he thought I couldn't take care of myself. I realised he hadn't asked where I'd been or what I'd been doing, not that he had the right but that wouldn't stop most men. Todde was a strange one, all right.

I heard the commotion before I had even clambered up to Eva's hut. Most of the unmarried tinners and the children had wandered off to try to cadge food at neighbours' huts or join in the search for Eva. But the few men who still lingered were shouting and arguing with each other, as they stared balefully at the big iron pot of cold pottage. Exasperated, I elbowed them out of the way, got a blaze going, then hefted the pot on top to start cooking.

It took time to heat, for it was a large cauldron with enough in it to feed a score of men and children. I stirred the pot and blew on the fire, trying to make it boil quicker. All the while men and children kept wandering up, demanding to know if they could eat. I reckon some would have devoured it half cold, dried beans and all, if I hadn't slapped them away with the ladle.

I kept glancing up, expecting to see Eva hurrying up the rise. I couldn't understand what had happened. Even if she'd gone to fetch more peats for the fire or to check her snares, she would have left the pot simmering. She always began to cook long before the horn sounded, for she knew the men would be wanting to eat as soon as they had climbed up the hill. If she had set out on some errand, it must have been much earlier in the day and plainly she had expected to return by mid-afternoon to make ready.

Darkness filled the valley. It had stopped raining, but sullen clouds still covered the moon and stars, threatening to tip more water upon the sodden earth at any time they pleased. Voices drifted up from below still calling for Eva.

Was she lying on the moors with a broken leg, having slipped in the treacherous mud? If she'd gone foraging for herbs she could be anywhere in the vastness of that wilderness. She might have stumbled into one of the sucking mires or fallen from the towering rocks, or be lying unconscious with Morwen's curse upon her, the life-blood seeping out of her. I shivered in the cold wind. If she wasn't in the valley they'd never find her tonight, not in the dark, and by morning . . .

Holy Virgin, keep her safe. Let them find her before it's too late.

Chapter 27

Hospitallers' Priory of St Mary

This time it was not Sister Fina who discovered it but the pilgrims or, rather, an old woman and her daughter with a tiny, wizened child. They had shuffled into the chapel, and had grudgingly parted with a coin to visit the well. Meggy had recognised the old woman at once. They'd grown up together in the village. As children, they'd played in the woods and streams. As mothers, they'd gossiped as they'd pounded their clothes in the washing pool, while their infants clung to their skirts. As widows to men who had died long before their three score years and ten, they'd helped each other to lay out their husbands' corpses and lent a comforting hand as the bodies were laid in the earth. But that was a lifetime ago, another age, another place.

Now the old woman's cow was ailing, she said, and its milk had dried, as that of so many down in the boggy valleys. She knew she should have driven the beast up to the common pasture on the high moor for the summer, but too many of her neighbours had lost their animals up there these past months, stolen and butchered by the outlaws or driven into

227

such terror by the tinners' noise and their dogs that they'd run headlong into the mire or broken their legs tumbling over rocks. Her little granddaughter was sick too, wheezing so she could scarcely draw breath. But the old woman was sure Brigid would heal both child and cow, for when times had been better hadn't she always left a drop of milk or honey by her hearthside for Brigid before she'd blown out the rush lights at night? And she swore to do it again, if Brigid would only draw down the cow's milk.

Meggy had wanted to keep her old neighbour talking, learn all the news and gossip from the village, but the old woman had been chary, ill-at-ease, eyeing Meggy's black gown as if her friend had been replaced by a changeling. She wouldn't even meet Meggy's gaze. When the gatekeeper talked of the times when they had first been kissed at the harvest feast or when the boys had stolen their clothes as they bathed naked in the stream, she had shaken her head and muttered that she didn't remember.

Meggy, wounded, had reluctantly sent them into the chapel, but had warned them to tell Sister Fina they'd come to ask the blessing of St Lucia for the ailing child. They had done as they were bade, reciting the words as carefully as a charm, if unconvincingly. But they could have told Fina they were coming to buy a curse from St Lucifer, for their words fell like sand thrown at a closed door.

Fina had caught a flash of movement outside in the courtyard and had already turned from the two women before they'd finished speaking, fearful that Sister Basilia was bringing the boy back. She had not made another attempt to bathe his eyes, but Fina had hardly dared to set foot outside the chapel, not even to relieve herself, for fear they'd slip in. She had started to close the well earlier each day, relieved when she could put the key through the wood and feel the bolt slide into place, knowing it was safe again until morning.

Like a fly trapped in a jar, the image of the boy staring at Nicholas as if he was cursing him buzzed ceaselessly round her head, Nicholas backing away from him, the horror unfolding in his face. What kind of power did that child possess to terrify a battle-hardened knight? Sister Basilia must not bring Cosmas back to the well. If the boy ever set foot in the holy cave, he would destroy it, just as the old priest had prophesied.

It was all she could do to stop herself running to the chapel door and slamming it shut. Bolt it. Keep him out. Keep them all out, Brother Nicholas too, especially Brother Nicholas. For days, she had been picking over his questions and her answers, telling herself what she should have said, what he would have replied, until she could no longer distinguish memory from imagination. He had been trying to catch her out, trick her, like Prioress Johanne had warned her he would, but what had she told him? He should not have been standing so close. He should not have touched her. She couldn't think, couldn't remember. It wasn't her fault.

Their offerings of coin and jewels are worth the trouble of collecting. That was what he'd said. *Jewels and coin . . . jewels and . . .* He was accusing her of stealing. The merchants were *paying twice over.* He'd said that too. Once to the priory and again to her: that was what he'd meant. He was calling her *thief.* But she'd never seen any jewels. So, someone was sneaking in here, to *her* well, and stealing.

A shriek made Fina jerk upright. Then she heard the sound of worn shoes slip-slapping on stone. The young woman with the grizzling child on her hip rushed up the steps from the well. The older woman followed more slowly, panting hard. Her daughter flung open the pilgrims' door and hurried out of the chapel into the cold, watery light.

The older woman took a few paces, then staggered back, leaning heavily against the chapel wall, her hand clutched to her chest. 'Spring's running blood – blood!'

Fina shook her head, trying to clear her thoughts. 'No . . . No. I've seen the walls turn red once before, but it's the light. Prioress Johanne said it was a trick of the light. If you go right down to the bottom it vanishes. There's nothing red in the spring.'

'I have been right down and I tell you it's blood, not water, in that spring.' The old woman peeled herself from the wall and tottered towards Fina. 'Give me back my coin,' she demanded, holding out a cupped hand.

Fina gaped at her. 'But it was an offering to God. You can't take it back.'

Many villagers and pilgrims grumbled at being asked for an offering, but none had ever asked for its return. Even if the cure they sought did not seem forthcoming, they left their coin in hope, in faith.

'What can't this woman take back?' a voice thundered behind them. Brother Nicholas strode into the chapel.

Chapter 28

Hospitallers' Priory of St Mary

Startled by the sudden appearance of the black-robed knight, the old crone who was arguing with Sister Fina staggered a few paces backwards until she collided with one of the pillars. She gripped it hard on either side as if she intended to uproot it and hurl it over her head towards Nicholas if he came any closer.

He glanced from her to the equally alarmed Fina, trying to decide which of the two he was likely to get more sense from, not that sense was something he expected from any female.

Fina found her voice first and an ugly flush, like a rash, spread from her neck to her face as she stammered some kind of explanation, but it made no sense to Nicholas. The old crone, sensing her chance to retrieve her money slipping away, loudly repeated her demand. Nicholas's jaw tightened. He wasted no words on either of them. Seizing the old woman by the arm, he thrust her out of the pilgrims' door, slamming it so hard behind her that the saint in the stained-glass window trembled.

Fina was now standing in front of the doorway to the stairs, with her back to them as if she intended to prevent him from going down. That made Nicholas all the more determined to do so. Evidently, there was something down there that the sisters were again trying to conceal. He gripped Fina by the shoulders and dragged her aside. With a silent prayer that it wasn't another swarm of flies or some equally foul creature, he began to edge down the stairs.

Above him he could hear Fina babbling about a trick of the light and a red glow, but as far as he could see the walls glistened with their customary luminous greenish-gold. It was unnatural and a little unnerving, but he supposed it was all to the good that pilgrims should be awestruck upon entering the place, without the need for artful displays of silver and jewels that other shrines had to install in order to strike wonder into their visitors.

Nicholas ran his hand down the oozing wet moss on the wall, pressing against the stone in an attempt to keep his balance on the uneven steps. The stairs seemed even narrower than he remembered. It felt as if the walls were squeezing together, crushing his broad shoulders. Some might say it was to his credit that he ventured down at all, for he still expected to hear the dreadful buzzing of those flies. His skin crawled at the thought of them and several times he scrubbed at his face, sure he could feel them alighting on him. But there were no sounds except for those of his boots grinding grit against the stone steps and the water splashing far below.

As he emerged in the cave at the bottom, he found himself sweating in spite of the chill, damp air. And then he saw it. A thick, deep-red liquid was running out between the three rocks and splashing into a scarlet pool.

Each time Nicholas watched a brother priest say mass, the

cleric would raise the goblet of wine and proclaim that it had turned to blood, the sweet, precious Blood of Christ. Some priests in the order seemed convinced that what they drank *was* His Blood. Some saints had even declared they had knelt at Christ's feet and suckled it as it gushed from his side. The idea revolted Nicholas. He could only assume that those men had never seen battle, had never seen a man hacked to death. He had watched gore pour from the terrible wounds of friends and enemies alike, tried to hold men's guts inside bellies slashed wide open, and pinched tight the wounds in men's gurgling throats as the blood scalded his hand. Nicholas could attend mass only because what was in the chalice looked and smelt like wine and, though he could never admit as much even to his confessor, he was certain it remained wine.

But when holy water in a well turned to blood surely not even the most pious priest in their order would regard it as a blessing.

Take thy rod; and stretch forth thy hand upon the waters of Egypt, and upon their rivers, and streams and pools, and all the ponds of waters, that they may be turned into blood: and let blood be in all the land of Egypt, both in vessels of wood and of stone.

For a moment, Nicholas felt a tingle of exaltation, the kind that an inquisitor feels when he sees the first flame running up the robe of the heretic on the pyre. The wicked are punished. These obstinate women are chastised. God has vindicated the righteous.

But the full import of the words of Holy Scripture, which had bubbled into his head at the sight of the bloody spring, suddenly punched him hard. *All* the ponds, *all* the streams, *all* the vessels of water! It was one thing for God to have

233

cursed this well as a sign to the women, but suppose He had indeed cursed all the water in the priory, all the water on the moor. Suppose, as in Egypt, it had all turned to blood. When a man has known the desperate agony of thirst, while roasting in heavy armour in the heat of a battle as the sun beats mercilessly down, he might be forgiven for fearing that particular curse more than most.

Nicholas almost fled straight back up the stairs in his desperation to find out how far the scourge had spread. But something penetrated his brain and stopped him. He stared at the sluggish stream of blood gurgling out of the cave wall. Another image floated into his head, of crossing the courtyard at Buckland when the servants were slaughtering the pigs, sheep and geese for the great Christmas feast . . . the sharp frost sparkling on the thatch in the winter's sunshine, the white breath of the sweating men, the squeals and shrieks of the beasts, steam rising from the eviscerated carcasses of the pigs as they were hauled up on chains to drip from the beams, then the rivers of blood running between the cobbles to freeze in great scarlet puddles. And with that sight came the stench of dung, guts, singed bristles and, above all, blood, the unmistakable sweet-metallic smell of fresh blood.

This cave, like any battlefield, should be reeking of it, but it wasn't. The only thing he could smell was damp and the tang of a creek when the tide has gone out. He took a pace towards the narrow coffin-like trough, and scooped up a handful of the red liquid. He sniffed it. Not blood, but mud. Stinking red mud.

Chapter 29

Sorrel

I shivered, trying to burrow deeper into my cloak though it offered precious little warmth against the clinging drizzle. Below me, in the darkness of the tinners' valley, a single line of guttering torches flickered past the ditch and climbed towards our huts. The shadows of the men splintered into tiny fragments against the hillside, so that a swarm of rats seemed to scurry alongside the tinners.

One of the boys had been dispatched to the camp with the news that a body had been found. You could see he was not best pleased at being sent home before he'd had a chance to take a squint at the corpse, but he cheered a little when he found himself the centre of a crowd who were, for once, desperate to hear what he had to say. All the womenfolk had gathered around Eva's fire to wait for the men to return. And waiting was all we could do.

'Looks like they've got a body slung over that pack beast,' someone murmured.

'Holy Virgin, let it not be Eva,' I said. 'The boy said it

was so dark out there they couldn't be certain till they turned the corpse.'

'Could be a beggar starved to death out there. More dying every day.'

'They'd not be troubling to fetch a dead'un back here, if it wasn't one of us,' another said grimly.

One by one the women who had been squatting on the ground clambered to their feet, standing still and silent as owls, watching the procession of scarlet flames crawling towards us. They stepped aside to make a space as the man leading the horse drew level and tethered the beast to a post near the old wall. Those men who followed him said nothing and looked at no one, not even their own wives. They blew on numbed fingers with lips that were pinched and almost rigid from cold. Strands of hair snaked down beneath hoods and wriggled across foreheads glistening with rain and black sweat. Crouching at the fire, they stretched out their hands towards the flames, begging for warmth. Todde was hunkered down among the other men, his shoulders hunched, his hands clenched under his armpits. I could see he was exhausted – they all were.

The bundle dangling over the horse's back was shrouded in the patched cloaks of several men, and bound with straw ropes, but no one made a move to cut it loose and lay it down. Whoever it was, we couldn't leave them hanging there, like a sack of grain. If no one else would do it, I'd have to. I drew my knife and began to saw at the rope. But a hand on my shoulder tugged me back.

'Leave it be. That's no sight for women or chillern,' a gravelly voice told me. 'It's Eva, as far as we can tell. No sense in taking her down, when we'll only have to lift her back up for the horse to carry her to her grave.'

My heart seemed to shrivel in my chest. Eva – dead! I fought against the tears that threatened to choke me.

'But she should be washed . . . shrouded, made decent,' I protested. 'She doesn't deserve to be carted about slung over a horse, like carrion.'

'Carrion's about the right word for what's left of her. Foxes and birds have been at her. Nothing left of her belly. Chewed off her hands and feet too, and . . .' He swallowed hard and didn't finish.

'But how could she be dead? Foxes couldn't have killed her.'

The old tinner flapped his hand at me as if I was a squawking hen. 'Hush, woman. When the fire's out, there's no point asking if it was wind or rain that did for it. Eva's gone and there's no more to be said.'

'Good deal to be said, if you ask me,' another man retorted. 'She's been ripped to pieces, bones gnawed like she was a roasted sheep.' He stared over his shoulder at the impenetrable black tide that lapped around the camp. 'Whoever did this is still out there. Could take any of us next.'

'Hounds gone wild, I reckon,' a woman told him. 'Masters have died or driven them out to fend for themselves 'cause they've not got scraps enough to feed them. Dogs start roaming in packs and they get so crazed with hunger they'll hunt down anything that moves. I've heard them howling many a night.'

'And there's men gone wild too,' another tinner said, raising his head as he crouched by the fire. 'I heard tell of a family, ten of them, maybe more, used to lie in wait for lone travellers, picked them off one at a time, dragged them to their cave and killed them. Whole family would feast on the corpses. Didn't even bother to cook them, liked their meat raw. When the sheriff's men hunted them down, they found a heap of human bones and skulls in the back of the cave. Hanged the lot of them, they did, even the children who were barely old enough to walk because they'd have grown up to do the self-same thing. No cure, there isn't, not once they get a taste for human flesh. It's like when a dog's taken to savaging sheep.'

His gaze crept towards the corpse slung over the horse, then darted back to the safety of the fire. 'I reckon that's what we got ourselves up on the moor, a nest of those corpse-eaters. I saw the marks on that body and I'd swear on the devil's arse and the Holy Virgin both that they weren't dog bites.'

There was a rumble of voices, some agreeing, others telling him he was talking out of his backside.

'Either way, the tinners' court can't handle this,' the stoker from the blowing-house said, raising his voice above the rest. 'Even they've not got the powers to deal with murder. Coroner will have to be fetched, and if he reckons there's men in these parts feeding off human flesh, he'll call in the sheriff and roust men-at-arms to smoke them out.'

'No cause to go involving them.'

Heads jerked round as Gleedy slithered out from the shadows beside a hut. As if he'd dragged it with him, a vicious gust of wind tore across the fires, flattening the flames and biting deep into wet skin. The tinners shuffled uneasily. How long had he been standing there?

'That's Eva we found,' the stoker said, getting to his feet. 'And if someone's murdered the poor mare, we want to see them hanged for it.'

One of Gleedy's eyes flicked towards the horse and its burden. His face was drawn and haggard in the firelight, as

238

if he'd not slept. 'So long as they hang the right man, but those coroners aren't bothered about that. Fat and lazy as hogs in a mudbath, they are. Just want to collect as many fines as they can for the King's coffers. The more they collect, the more they can cream off.'

'That's the pot calling the pan burned-arse, if ever I heard it,' a woman whispered in my ear.

Gleedy gazed around at the faces, gaunt as skulls in the firelight. 'And if I go sending for the coroner, it'll be you and your families that'll suffer, and I'll not let that happen. Eva cooked for you and she'd never see any man starve even when he had naught. She'd not want to bring down trouble on your heads. We all know who it was, who did this. I warned Eva time and again only to use food from my store, but she would insist on foraging. You all know she was a bondswoman. I warned her that there's hirelings combing every inch of these moors with their hounds for runaway serfs and villeins to drag them back to their masters for a heavy purse. I reckon she got caught by one.'

Gleedy jerked his head at the woman who'd spoken of the wild dogs. 'Those are the hounds you hear baying. Those serf-hunters are watching this valley night and day for the chance to snatch back any runaway who strays beyond it. And they think it great sport to set their hounds on any poor wretch whose only crime is to want to live free. They enjoy watching them ripped to pieces, just like their masters love to see a hind's throat torn out by their dogs.'

I stared at the limp bundle hanging from the horse. So, Eva had been on the run from her master, just like Todde and, like him, she'd dared not leave the protection of the tinners. So why had she gone out there yesterday?

I glanced at Todde. He was staring fearfully at the moor,

doubtless wondering if a hunter out there was lying in wait to run him back tied to a horse's tail, battered and bruised, then deposit him, more dead than alive, at his lord's feet. Had Eva, too, stolen from her master? Was that why they'd hunted her down, or had the lord of the manor merely wanted her returned to make an example of her to deter others from following?

'All the same,' the stoker said, 'bondswoman or not, if murder's been done the sheriff ought to be summoned. Even a serf can't be done to death without a fair trial.'

Gleedy shook his head gravely. 'I want poor Eva's killer brought to justice as much as any man here. If I could lay my hands on the bastard who did this to that good woman, I'd string him up myself by his cods. But you all know, same as I do, that the sheriff will not risk losing his office by pointing the finger at any lord or his hirelings. Those coroners and sheriffs all have good parcels of land, and you know how jealous the landowners are of the tinners' rights. They'll not go looking for anyone else, my friends, 'cause a chance like this is what they've all been waiting for. Eva was working here, they'll say, so it must have been a tinner that killed her and dumped her body on the moor, hoping the birds would peck it clean. The sheriff will arrest any man in this valley who can't prove he was in plain sight of others every moment of yesterday afternoon – anyone who slipped away to shit, anyone going to fetch a tool or a swallow of ale. I know how they reason. He'll hang the tinner, drive his woman and children on to the moors to starve, and announce justice has been done.'

The men were glancing anxiously at each other. There must have been at least a few moments that day when they'd vanished from sight behind a spoil heap or were crouching down in the ditch scraping up the last handful of gravel.

Gleedy stared pointedly round us all. 'And there's a few among us I reckon wouldn't relish being examined too closely by any coroner or sheriff. Isn't that right, Toddy?'

Todde's eyes blazed in the firelight. 'Don't you go accusing me. I was here streaming same as everyone. Isn't that right, Sorrel?'

All the faces around the fire turned to me. I tried to speak, but the word wouldn't come. I stared at Todde and saw fear flash across his face as he suddenly remembered I hadn't been in the valley when Eva had gone missing.

Gleedy grinned, his swarm of teeth glistening, like maggots, in the firelight. 'Think how the justices will see it. Most tinners in the camp have their womenfolk with them to warm their cods. But Sorrel told me, the first day she arrived, that you weren't her man, quite adamant she was, as I recall. But the justices, they'll look at you and say, "Here's a fellow has needs, just like us, and if the woman he's with won't satisfy those needs, well, he's bound to get roused up." They'll say you forced yourself on Eva and killed her to stop her telling. There's plenty here will swear to it that they saw you attack me in the warehouse for no good reason. You've a hot temper on you.'

'I never laid a hand on her, you dogshit!' Todde launched himself towards Gleedy, fists flailing. But Gleedy had already stepped swiftly back behind the fire. Three of the tinners grabbed Todde, wrestling him away.

Gleedy held up his hands. 'Course you didn't,' he cooed, his tone as soothing and slippery as butter. 'We all know that. It was the men hunting runaways, like I said. But I'm just telling you how a sheriff would reason it.'

241

I saw looks passing between some of the women and glanced at Todde, uneasy now. I shook my head, trying to rid myself of the chilling thought.

He was still struggling in the clutches of the men who held him, but the fight had drained out of him and he looked as if he might collapse if they let him go. The men sensed it too, for they lowered him to the ground, where he sat, head in hands, rocking and groaning.

The men and women had all fallen silent. They sat round the fires hunched, withdrawn into their own thoughts, while the shadow of the corpse on the horse's back moved restlessly over them as the beast shifted.

In the wall behind Eva's fire, vipers' heads were appearing, swaying back and forth, their eyes glittering, their forked tongues slithering in and out between their fangs, tasting the chill night air. Then, far out in the great lake of darkness, a hunting horn sounded, vibrating across the hills, and at once came the howls of a great pack of hounds as they took up the cry to seek and kill.

Chapter 30

Prioress Johanne

'Tinners.' Sister Clarice flung the charge across our supper table. 'That's who's to blame for our well turning red. They're damming every river and stream and building their leats right across this moor. Not to mention pouring the filth from their workings straight into the water that the villagers use downstream. It's a wonder they haven't poisoned every man and beast for miles. Some of those streams coming from their workings are so thick with mud and silt you could walk dry-shod across them.'

'For once, I find myself obliged to agree with you, Sister Clarice,' Nicholas said. 'I've seen it myself. The water spewing from those workings is much the same colour as that oozing from the spring.'

He laid aside the beef bone he'd been digging into with his spoon, finally forced to concede there was not a shred of marrow left inside it, and was reaching for the last bone on the platter, which had been placed between him and Alban. But Alban's fingers were nimbler, even though he had

243

lost the two on his right hand, and he snatched it up. Nicholas glowered at him.

'But it's a holy well,' Sister Basilia protested. 'A healing well. The water is miraculous, pure. It gushes from the rock. It doesn't come from any of those rivers on the moor.'

Nicholas snorted, staring pointedly at the marrow bone Alban was burrowing into. I suspected the sergeant was well aware of the knight's hostile glances, and was taking a childish and somewhat malicious pleasure in having beaten his superior to the prize. Nicholas dragged his attention back to Basilia.

'Your holy water comes from the moors. Even you can't be so naïve as to think it flows from solid rock.'

Basilia flushed and stared down at her trencher. I knew I should have intervened, but in truth I was relieved that at least this discussion seemed to be silencing Sister Fina. These past few days, I never knew what wild words would suddenly burst from her. It wasn't so bad when we sisters were alone, but whenever Brother Nicholas was within earshot, I felt as if I was trying to stamp out sparks blowing across a field of dry corn, knowing that he was listening for the smallest thing he could use to destroy us. But for the moment, happily, he had launched into one of his many gory tales of the Citramer to prove his point to poor Basilia.

'Some years back, I found myself part of an army laying siege to a Turkish citadel. An old man had attached himself to us and sold us information, for he knew the area well. He'd been captured in his youth and forced to become a Mussulman upon pain of death, but he'd always borne a hatred for them. He was willing to work for us, though he was crafty enough to make sure he was paid first. Anyway, this citadel of theirs had plenty of wells inside and well-stocked food stores. And

244

they taunted us each day that we'd run out of supplies before they did, even waved their meats and bread at us from the battlements.

'But this wily old serpent sidled up to our commander and told him to send men out into the countryside to find some pigs, slaughter them and leave the carcasses to bloat in the sun for a couple of days. The soldiers cursed him with every foul plague they could think of. They craved fresh meat and thought it a wicked waste.'

Nicholas glared at Alban again, who was chewing a lump of beef, apparently paying no heed to his lecture.

'The commander even had to set a guard over the pigs to stop his men sneaking in and stealing a leg or two, and the guards were even more incensed when the carcasses began to rot. They were having to stand next to the putrid stench. But when the pigs were good and ripe, the old man told us to wedge them in a particular river where the water would wash over them. None of us could see what good that would do, except add to the stink and flies, but a day or so later everyone in the citadel was vomiting and sweating in agony. The poisoned water from the stream had somehow flowed into their wells.' He raised his hand as Basilia seemed on the point of interrupting again. 'You can call that another miracle if you want – the Turks probably called it a curse – but years ago, someone told me that all the streams, springs and pools in the world rise up from one vast lake deep beneath the earth.'

Fina raised her head, glowering at Nicholas as if he had grossly offended her. 'Hell lies beneath the earth, deserts of fire and vast howling whirlwinds where thieves spin for ever in the darkness,' she said, like a child reciting a lesson.

Nicholas frowned, evidently wondering if we'd missed the

point of his story. But the word *thieves* sent a shiver of danger down my spine. Why had she selected that particular sin?

I rapped sharply on the table, trying to divert her. 'The water in the courtyard well still runs pure and clear,' I said, with as much cheer as I could muster. 'And one blessing of this rain is that it is even higher than usual. So, we shall certainly not want for water. We must give thanks for that.'

Basilia beamed at everyone, nodding so vigorously that her chins wobbled like a calf's foot jelly.

But Nicholas glared at me. 'And if this filth seeps into the well in the courtyard?'

'We have cisterns and barrels that are filled only with rainwater. They cannot be polluted.'

Nicholas let out a snort of derision. 'Even on this accursed moor, it cannot rain for ever. You must bend your neck, Prioress, and send word to the Lord Prior to ask for the knights to ride to our aid. It is only a matter of time before our cattle and sheep are poisoned and those of our tenants. We have a duty to protect them and, besides, it is in our interest to do so. How will they pay their rents if they have starved to death?'

The eyes of every sister were fixed on me and they all seemed to be holding their breath. Even Alban had stopped eating.

I laid down my knife and fastened my gaze on Nicholas. 'I assure you that I am fully aware of my duties both to my tenants and to my order. I trust no one will ever have cause to say I have neglected either. I thank you for your concern, Brother Nicholas, but if you imagine that the tinners will be frightened off by a band of knights, you are much mistaken. They are tough men, not armed with swords, I grant you, but more than capable of cutting down a horse

246

and rider with such implements as they can weld. They will fight and they have the law on their side.'

A candle, guttering on a spike on the wall behind Nicholas, threw his face into deep shadow, but I did not need to read his expression to know the fury that was written there.

'As you yourself have already so eloquently pointed out to me, the tinners are answerable only to King Edward. They live and work under his protection. The Lord Prior is not an imprudent man. And, as you have also told me, Brother Nicholas, he is anxious not to give the King any reason to act against our order. I am sure Lord William is wise enough to realise that, should the tinners send word to the King that a group of heavily armed Hospitaller knights had ridden down upon a camp of defenceless men, women and children lawfully engaged in the King's business, injuring, if not killing, many, he would take that as an act of war against the Crown.'

'Defenceless!' Nicholas exploded. 'They are terrorising the villagers.'

'Even a king may be caught in a snare of words, if they are well twisted, especially if they are delivered by a limping old man and a child with a bandaged head, which you may be quite certain they would be. Besides, the King needs tin and he needs the taxes from it. He does not need the Knights of St John.'

My chair scraped back on the stone floor as I rose. The sisters hastily scrambled to their feet and it gave me not a little satisfaction to observe that Nicholas and Alban, who shared their benches, were obliged to stand too, as they were pushed back.

'There are those among us who feared that the frogs and the flies meant the end of our holy well, but those plagues passed. The spring will soon cease to flow red, of that I am certain. Have faith, sisters, and pray. This is but another test of our courage.'

I guessed that Clarice would follow me to my chamber, but I was in no mood for her talk of falling revenues. I hurried across the darkened courtyard, pausing only to listen outside the casement of the infirmary for any sounds that might tell me Sebastian was distressed. Mercifully all seemed quiet. I unlocked the chapel door and slipped inside, pulling the wooden bolt into place behind me. I did not light the candles. I did not want anyone to know I was there. I craved just a few moments of peace and solitude. I knelt before the altar, bunching my robe beneath my knees to cushion them against the cold, hard flagstones. The bowed head of the crucified Christ, hanging above me, glowed beneath a halo of soft light shining down from the oil lamp above.

How long could I contain Nicholas? I truly believed what I had told him that declaring war on the tinners would bring more danger and call down the King's wrath. That was always the trouble with men. They thought every problem and vexation in the world could simply be put to flight by the point of a sword.

But was Nicholas really so foolish? He knew we were deceiving Clerkenwell, although I was certain he had no real proof yet. Otherwise he would have acted. He was arrogant, and he was no bookkeeper, that much was evident, but he wasn't stupid. The more we thwarted him, the deeper he would dig. As the proverb says, 'Suspicion has double eyes.' But if he started a feud between the priory and the tinners, he would not need to prove his case to finish us. I had to prevent any report of his from leaving the priory.

I stared at the open hand above me nailed to the cross. The painted blood around the wound in his palm shone fresh, as if Christ was hurling it down upon us. 'Why, Lord? Why do you punish us with yet another plague on your holy well?'

Guilt burned in me. Was He punishing me for deceiving our holy order? But if we failed, if I failed and the priory closed, what would become of all the frail creatures we sheltered – our servants, Meggy and Sebastian? Who would care for Sebastian? He would not survive without us. It was my duty as prioress to protect those I had taken a sacred oath to serve.

But an insidious voice nagged in my head and it was one I couldn't smother. It whispered that I had once knelt before another altar, placed my hands in the lap of another prioress and, before my brothers and sisters, had vowed faithfully to serve the order of the Knights of St John of Jerusalem with my life. To honour one vow meant breaking another. What if there could be no right way, no sinless path, only a greater or lesser wrong? And which was the greater wrong? Who would tell me, when God refused to answer me?

If any of my sisters had come to me, I would have told her that her duty was obedience to the order, yet as their leader, as the one responsible for so many lives, was it not them I should put before all else? We were pledged to be the serfs and servants of the blessed poor. Should I say, 'I cannot protect you, because I have vowed to obey the order. My oath of obedience is more important than your survival. My soul is worth more than your life'?

I stared down at the cold flags, painfully aware that I was kneeling directly above the holy well. I must have faith! I had assured my sisters that we had survived the plagues of frogs and flies, which had seemed to spell doom for the well. We had prayed and they had vanished as if they had never been. Like the woman with the issue of blood who reached out in faith to touch Christ's robe, I had only to reach out my hand in faith and the spring would cease to flow red. I had only to believe it.

Chapter 31

Hospitallers' Priory of St Mary

Meggy sat on her stool, slumped against the wall, a snore escaping her from time to time as she drifted comfortably between dozing and sleep. It was not yet time to damp down the fire and huddle beneath the blankets, and she was enjoying the blessed warmth from the flames. It was the only time her feet ever seemed to be warm these days. Although a stone was heating on the edge of the hearth, ready to be wrapped in sacking and slid under the covers, it always cooled long before morning. But she counted herself lucky. The hut, though barely long enough to lie down in, was dry, the door solid, and her belly was full of hot pottage. As she knew only too well, there was many a widow, like her, who that night would be huddling hungry in a doorway or coughing her lungs out with a dozen others in a wet, lice-infested byre.

Meggy was dreaming of her son, not the stocky lad who'd marched off to fight the Scots, but years before when he was little, small enough to run beneath a horse's belly. They were in her husband's forge and her son was giggling as he tipped a box of horseshoe nails on to the ground. She was scolding

251

the lad and scrambling to pick them up before his father returned, but no sooner had she put some back in the box than the little lad scattered more. The nails were growing smaller and smaller, harder to gather, and there were so many. Now the boy was banging the tongs against the anvil, making it ring through the smithy. The noise would bring his father striding in, and the child would be in trouble.

Meggy jerked awake and, for a moment, she thought the sound she could hear was the echo of her dream, but it was coming from the gate. Someone was singing, not the plain-song of the chapel or the bawdy chorus of a drunken pedlar, but an eerie high-pitched keening, like the ghosts on Fire Tor.

She dragged her cloak about her shoulders and hurried out to the small gridded window. The rain had stopped for now, but thick clouds crowded against the moon, smothering the light. Meggy cursed herself. Roused suddenly, she had neglected to bring the lantern. She was on the point of returning for it when she caught a wisp of singing again, like a feather spun towards her on the wind. It was a woman's voice, she was sure of that, and it was coming from outside the priory. But who would be out there on the moors at this hour? A soul needing help? The sound certainly tore at your heart, like a woman grieving over a new grave.

She almost found herself drawing back the beam that braced the gate. But she knew the tricks the outlaws used. She slid back the shutter covering the gridded window and peered out. Torches were left burning on either side of the main gate to guide latecomers and the lost, at least until the midnight hour, by which time they had usually burned away. The insipid orange light clawed at the darkness, as the wind twisted and flattened the flames. But she could see no one

252

standing in front of the door, no grieving mother or shivering child.

A chilling thought gripped her. Was it the voices of the dead that had awoken her, the restless spirits that roamed the moor trying to find their way back to the villages of the living? The corpses of murderers, self-murderers and madmen had been thrown into those black, sucking mires for centuries, for they weren't welcome in hallowed ground. The souls of the innocent, too, wandered the lych-ways: the babies born maimed, left out to perish; the beggars dying alone, unshriven, their corpses lying out for the birds to pick their bones. Their ghosts would never lie quiet for they had no graves to rest in.

Meggy crossed herself, and reached for the shutter, struggling to slide it back over the grid, but the wood had swollen in the months of rain. As she fought with it, the wind gusted the flames of the torches, and as the tongues of light snaked out, for a moment they illuminated a tall figure standing motionless in the darkness, unmoved by the buffeting of the gale. Meggy glimpsed a bone-pale face, a tangle of long hair darting out like lightning bolts about the skull. She couldn't tell if it was a ghost or human, only that it was staring at her, as if it was her that it had come for. The wind gusted once more and both torches were extinguished, as if that spirit had snuffed them out. All the world was plunged into darkness. But the singing rose again, riding the wind, like a shrieking hawk.

Her hand trembling, Meggy caught the edge of the wooden shutter and heaved with strength born of fear. The wood slid home with a crash, and she turned, leaning her back against the great oak gate, trying to recover her breath. Then a cry escaped her.

The boy was standing behind her in the dark, empty courtyard, his blind eyes suddenly glowing ghost-green, like a wolf's in moonlight. His arms were stretched out towards the gate, as if he was trying to grasp the wild notes that were rising like a flock of birds. He turned his head slowly, until he seemed to be staring right at the door that led into the chapel. A sudden silence filled the courtyard – even the wind held its breath. Meggy had never seen such deep blackness, known such dark silence. She could no longer hear the low rumble of water in the cave echoing up through the stones or the wind crying on the moors. It was as if she was lying in her own grave, beneath the earth. No sight, no sound, only darkness.

And she could not know that in that moment the prioress's prayers had been answered – the spring had ceased to flow red. In fact, it had ceased to flow at all.

Chapter 32

Morwen

'But what does it mean, Kendra?' the old villager wailed.

Her tiny granddaughter lying at her feet gave a faint mew and tried to turn herself over, but the effort was too great and she flopped back, grizzling fretfully. There wasn't a peck of flesh on her and the floor of our livier was digging into her sharpened bones. I winced for her, knowing the pain of sleeping on the hard earth, but Ma and her visitor glanced at the small bundle indifferently, as if it was a kitten they might toss into a pool to drown. Neither moved to lift her.

'Whole moor is turning widdershins,' the old woman continued, ignoring her grandchild. 'I've never known such rain. I've not a wort or a pea that's not rotted or been gobbled by birds. There's not a single chick hatched by my hens this year that didn't die of the gapes even afore it got its proper feathers, and now I've only one old bird left, and I daren't let her out of my cottage for fear a fox'll snatch her or the tinners.'

At the mention of tinners, Ma spat into the fire. 'There's your answer. You want to know why all's gone amiss, it's those tinners penning their beasts in the sacred stone circle. Using cup stone as a seat for their filthy arses and pissing on the queen stone.'

I shifted on my haunches by the door. I'd not seen the tinners actually pissing on the great stone, but they probably did, for they treated the sacred circle worse than a midden.

'Tearing up the land, they are,' Kendra said. 'Dragging the streams from their natural beds.' She wagged her finger at the old woman. 'But Old Crockern'll have his revenge on any man who tries to harm Dertemora. He always does in the end. You dare to scratch Crockern's hide, the old man will break you, body and soul. You mark my words, he'll let loose his black hounds from their kennels in the woods and he'll hunt those tinners to the highest peak of Dewerstone and drive them over the edge. Smash on to the rocks below, they will, every man jack of them. And wisht hounds will be waiting to feast on them. There's many have fallen to their deaths there and their corpses never found.' Ma's eyes gleamed with satisfaction.

The old woman shuddered. 'Dewerstone's an accursed place. Still, I reckon it's no more than those tinners deserve.'

I shivered too, thinking of Sorrel. I'd been so vexed with her that I stormed and railed around Fire Tor loud enough that it was wonder Ma hadn't heard me down in the cottage. But after, I could have cut out my tongue. I'd thought she might come back to the cave, when her temper cooled, but by the time I went out she was long gone. It was my fault. I'd been journeying afore I even had words to explain it, thought it was natural, that everyone did it. But they don't, not even my own sisters. Too late, I realised that Brigid had brought Sorrel to the moor for me to show her how, but I'd driven her away.

I had to find her. I'd summoned her to come. But she was strong that one: if she felt it, she could resist it. I closed my eyes, silently calling her, pleading with her. But suppose she came back to the cave and I wasn't there. I had to get up to it. If only the old woman would leave, Ma and Ryana would fall asleep and I could slip out.

I peered around the old woman at the naked child lying between her and Ma's fire. They seemed to have forgotten the little mite was the reason her granddam had come. The girl whimpered. She was barely three summers old, but looked like a wizened crone. Her ma had run off in the night with the last sack of dried beans they'd had, or so the old woman said. 'Left me and the little 'un to starve to save her own skin,' she grumbled, spitting on the floor.

The little girl stared up from the deep pools of her eyes, her ribs fluttering in and out, like the breast of a trapped bird. I could tell she was finding it hard to breathe, lying flat on her back, but she was too weak to sit up. I had to stop myself darting over and lifting her, but Ma's staff lay within easy reach of her crooked fingers. She didn't take kindly to any interference when she was working.

Over in the corner, sheep-face Ryana was supposed to be making a powder to heal the sick child, pounding a roasted mouse in an ancient stone mortar, with dried lungwort plucked from beneath an oak tree. But Ryana's hands were idle and her mouth had fallen slack, as she listened to the two old besoms.

'Between the tinners tearing the lights and liver out of the land and the black crows nesting over Bryde's Well, is it any wonder Brigid is angry?' Ma said.

The old woman clutched at a small bag around her neck, fashioned from a scrap of grey rag, one of Ma's charms. She lowered her voice as if Mother Brigid herself might be eaves-dropping at the door. 'I swear on my husband's grave I saw the water in her well turn to blood right before my eyes. Now I hear tell it's run dry. That true, is it, Kendra?'

'It is!' Ma sounded as if she'd stopped up the well herself. 'Blood gushed out, as if someone stabbed Old Crockern in the heart. Three days and three nights it ran with blood, filled the whole cave. Then the gore turned to dust, like burned bones on a pyre, and a great wind filled the cave and blew it away. Not a drop of water has flowed from that spring since.'

I studied Ma's face. That hadn't been quite like Meggy had told the tale when she'd come to her, angry and afraid. But Ma said the birds had already shown her when she was journeying – leastways that was what she said to Meggy.

The old woman fingered the amulet around her neck. 'My grandfather used to tell stories round the hearth come winter, and he said the well ran dry once before. Year of the long drought, it was, when all the streams and rivers dried. Must have been when your granddam, no, your great-granddam was keeper of the well. She told the villagers the streams wouldn't flow again till the well did. Terrible cruel, they say it was, whole flocks of birds lying dead, like black snow, on the ground and they reckon you could hear the moaning of the cattle all night as they died. People, they died too, but silently, like the birds.' Wonderingly, she shook her grey head. 'Terrible cruel,' she repeated to the fire.

Ma nodded. 'My great-granddam, she sat outside the well fasting and praying to the goddess.' She reached over and poked Ryana in the ribs with her stick. 'You paying heed to this, girl? See that you do, but keep grinding while you listen. Your ears are stuck on your head, not your hands, so there's no cause to stop moving your fingers.'

258

Ma stared into the burning heart of the peat fire. 'My great-granddam didn't move from the spot for days. Her lips were so parched they cracked wide open and her skin sank down to her bones till folks thought she'd already died and it was a skeleton sitting there. Then old Brigid spoke to her and told her what she must do. Told her to catch herself a live long-cripple, and cut its head off on the cup stone, so blood would run into the cup, then anoint the queen stone and the well stones with the viper blood. Then she was to hang the body of the long-cripple in the branches of a twisted oak tree in the wood, high as she could reach. She did exactly as Brigid had bade her, and afore dawn the first cloud appeared, by midday rain was falling and by nightfall the well was flowing again, streams too.'

The old woman glanced towards the hide hanging in the doorway to keep the rain from blowing in. Drops of icy water were dripping from the bottom edge into the stagnant green puddle that oozed over the threshold. 'Isn't rain we need this time, that's for certain. Rivers are brimming over, land is sodden, but still the spring is dry.' Her voice cracked, brittle, fearful.

'Brigid is angry.' Ma spread her fingers in the smoke of the hearth fire. She shut her eyes, muttering to herself as she slowly closed her hand. The smoke vanished into her clenched fist, as if it had been sucked up. Kendra unclenched her fingers and the smoke slid out again, slithering up towards the blackened thatch above. 'Brigid's closed the water in her fist. Only when she opens her hand will the spring flow again.'

By the time I had managed to escape from Ma's cottage and run up the hillside, I was afeared that if Sorrel had come she would be long gone again, thinking she'd been mistaken and I'd not summoned her.

Ma had blown the pounded mouse and lungwort through a cow's horn into the little girl's throat, making her cough, but she was too weak to struggle. It would ease her chest, Ma said, help her to breathe. But still the old woman was in no hurry to leave. Why waste peats on your own fire when you could share the warmth of someone else's? She'd glanced pointedly towards Ma's iron cooking pot, evidently hoping she could share whatever might be there too, but in that she'd be disappointed. Unless Taegan returned with a bite of food from Daveth and his brother, the pot was likely to remain empty, save for a spider that had foolishly scuttled in.

Halfway up the hill, I was forced to stop to draw breath, though usually I could run all the way to the tor. The rocks above me were hidden beneath a dense fleece of clouds, and the grey mist rolled down towards me, clinging soft as lamb's wool to my skin, cutting off all the sounds from below of running water and the cackle of the ravens. I shivered. Hunger always made me cold. I took a gulp of air to call, and the grey fret slid like syrup down my throat.

'Sorrel?' *Please let her be there.*

She was sitting by the entrance, legs drawn up, her head resting on her arms. She scrambled to her feet, relief and misery mingled in her eyes. We stared at one another, both opening our mouths to speak, both stopping to let the other go first. In the end, nothing was said – nothing needed to be said. But something had changed and it wasn't our quarrel. There was a deep hole in her, a wound, like when a green branch has been torn from a tree.

I grasped Sorrel's cold, ragged fingers and pulled her gently through the crevice into the cave. Only when the gold and ruby firelight was lapping across the walls did either of us speak.

Sorrel kept her head bowed before the crackling wood, while the voices of the cave nudged each other and whispered at her back. In a dull voice, she told me that the woman I'd charmed the clootie for was dead – not from the bleeding, she added quickly. They'd found Eva on the moors, her body mauled by dogs. I remembered Ma's tale of Dewerstone and the wisht hounds, but it was hounds of men that had killed her, Sorrel said. Hirelings hunting for bondsmen or women who had taken off without leave.

'Maybe if I'd talked to her more. Maybe if . . . Why did she go wandering out on to the moors? She knew there were men searching for runaways.'

I saw the grimace of pain on Sorrel's face and leaned forward. 'The seven sisters spin the thread of life, that's what Ma says. Spin it and cut it. You and me, we don't hold the blade. No mortal does.'

Sorrel stared deep into my eyes. 'But I have to know why. Why did Brigid bring me here? I've dragged myself all this way to sleep in a hovel that's not fit for goats. I break my back for a mouthful of food and I'm so far in debt to the master of the tin works that I may as well be bound like Todde, for I can no more leave than he can, all because I thought I heard a voice calling to me. All because a flower fell into a stream. But I did hear her. I know I did. What does she want of me? I ran away before. I was afraid to let go, afraid I'd never be able to return. And I'm sorry, so sorry. But now, after Eva, I need more than ever to find the answer. You can tell, can't you? . . . You can see?' The words hovered in the air between us, commanding and pleading.

I gnawed my lip, hesitating. 'Not the fire this time. It's not the way for you. I shouldn't have tried to make . . . You're afraid of it. And you'll not find your way to Brigid through the flames, not alone, because fear'll pull you back. But you've a friend who's travelling the lych-way now and that opens another path for you. And there's one who journeys between life and death, between the place of the living and the place of the spirits. He walks in the shadow. But if you want his answer, you must walk with him.'

Chapter 33

Sorrel

Morwen did not explain what she would do – perhaps there weren't names for such things. I watched her groping along a dark, rocky ledge. Her hands closed around a lump on the craggy shelf, as though she was gathering it out of the rock and pressing it in her fingers, like a child moulds a snowball from a drift of snow. As she lifted it, I saw that it was a roughly hewn bowl stuffed with fat-soaked dry moss, fashioned from the same grey stone as the rock on which it had stood.

She set it down near the cloth-covered ledge at the far end of the cave that I'd noticed when she'd first brought me into Fire Tor. She pulled a burning stick from the fire and lowered it towards the bowl. Tiny scarlet sparks flashed across the moss, like a flock of coloured birds taking flight from the moors, then a flame shot upward growing in strength and height until it was the silky yellow of a buttercup.

Morwen turned, holding out her hand to me. I stumbled to her side across the uneven floor, sick with apprehension. She pulled me down so I was kneeling beside her. Then, grasping the edge of the white woollen cloth, she tugged it aside. I had to stifle a cry. The light from the bowl of burning moss flickered across the corpse of a man stretched out on the slab, but it could not penetrate the black hole in his throat. In those first few moments, I barely noticed his nakedness, or the blondness of his hair, or the withered lips drawn back over yellowed teeth. It was the wound that held my gaze. It seemed to yawn wider and wider as I stared at it, a gaping mouth stretching to devour me.

Had the body been lying there last time Morwen had brought me into the cave? Had I been sitting next to a corpse and not known it? I'd realised that something lay beneath the cloth, but I'd never thought . . .

There was no stench of decay, only of herbs and a bitter-sweet smell lingering about his hair. He was like the dead cat Mam dried in the smoke when I was a bairn and hung from the rafters to keep us all safe from sickness.

'Who is he?' I whispered.

Morwen lightly touched a bracelet of thorns that had been bound about his wrist. The nails on his hand were long and smooth, almost as black and shiny as the pebble that lay on his forehead. 'Ankow – he collects the souls of the dead.'

I knew what Ankow was condemned to do. But I'd never dreamed I'd see his face, not till he came to take me. Mam used to say his head could turn right round, like an owl's, so no soul could hide from him. But she said only the dying ever saw his face when he threw back his hood and reached out his hand to seize them.

Morwen stared down at him, a strange expression in her eyes that was almost pity. 'Brigid chose him for Death's bondsman.'

'She killed him?' My voice sounded tight and high. I could barely squeeze out the words.

264

Morwen laughed softly. 'Not her. Another killed him. She marked him.'

I must have looked as bewildered as I felt, for she smiled.

'It was two, three summers back. I was late coming home from foraging, near owl-light it was. The sun had already dipped behind the tor. I saw a woman standing near the track, behind a rowan tree. She'd her back to me and was watching the path, so I knew she was waiting for someone, but she was peeping out so cautiously that, at first, I thought she might be afeared someone was following her and that was why she was hiding. So I hid behind a furze bush. Then I saw him leading his horse along the track. The beast was lame, hobbling. The man was hunched against the wind, not paying heed to anything save the track in front of his feet, like some folks do when they've fallen into a mire-mood. He passed the woman without seeing her. Then, as soon as his back was to her, she called out. He must have heard her, for he pulled the horse up and started to turn. That was when she hit him a good hard blow to the head with her stave. The crack was so loud a cloud of starlings flew up from a tree close by.

'He lost his hold on the horse and collapsed on all fours. He was trying to get up again, but he was too dazed to stand. She grabbed his hair then, dragged his head back and cut his throat. He was on the ground, gurgling and grasping his neck. Blood was spurting out through the fingers of his gloves. I ran for Ma, but by the time we got back he was dead and there was no sign of the woman. But the corpse wasn't alone: there was a white cow with a red blaze between its horns shaped like a snake. It was standing over the body, guarding it.

'Ma knew it was Brigid's cow, for there's no cattle with

265

those markings in these parts. Brigid had chosen the man as Ankow, so we brought him up here and the cow followed and lay in front of the cave for three days and three nights while Ma prepared the body with honey and herbs, so she could smoke it.'

'You told no one about the murder? Did no one come searching for him?'

Morwen's brow creased in puzzlement, as if the idea had never occurred to her. 'Who would we tell? Brigid gave us Ankow to care for. That's Ma's business, that is, like her worts and charms.'

She reached out and grasped my good hand. 'Makes no odds who killed him. He's Ankow now. As long as his corpse stays whole, his spirit can come and go between this world and the deadlands, so he can help the newly dead find their way to the lych-ways across the moors that'll lead them safe to Blessed Isles. But if his body rots and vanishes back into the earth, he can't return here. That's why Ma has to keep it safe.'

Before I realised what she was doing, she'd pressed my hand on to the corpse's chest. It was cold and leathery. I tried not to pull away. I didn't want to see the scorn in Morwen's eyes if I flinched from a dead man. This time I had to follow. There might not be another chance. A corpse could do me no harm.

'He's Ankow,' she repeated. 'Walk with him.'

I tried not to look at the gaping black hole and the bared mustard teeth. 'How can I?'

I saw a flash as the yellow flame in the bowl glinted on a blade that had suddenly appeared in Morwen's hand. I almost sprang to my feet, but I knew, though I had no words to explain it, that she would never hurt me. I let her take my good hand and turn it palm up. Morwen lightly pierced the tip of my forefinger with the point of the knife, but it was done so swiftly I felt nothing, or maybe she could charm away pain. As if I was a doll made of rags, my hand lay limp in hers as she held my finger over the corpse and squeezed so that three drops of my blood fell into its mouth. They ran down one of its teeth outlining it in crimson.

'He must taste the blood that your spirit lives in,' Morwen said. 'Then he will know and remember.'

Afterwards, in my dreams, I would see a blackened tongue slide out between those teeth and lick them, savouring my blood.

Again Morwen pressed my hand to the cold chest. 'Now say the will worth, like I taught you when we spoke to the spirits. Ask Ankow what Brigid wants of you. You must want to hear the answer. But don't ask her, unless you swear to do what she commands.'

'But how do I know if I can until I know what she wants of me?'

'You listened to her voice before. You came 'cause you couldn't find peace until you did. You can go, if you want, leave now and never ask, though you'll never rest easy. But don't ask unless you swear to do her bidding,' Morwen repeated, 'else she'll take your life and your soul.'

I knew she was right. I had come all this way, drawn by a voice that dragged my spirit behind it as if it was in irons. She would chain me to her echo for ever and without mercy, until I stood and faced her. I closed my eyes and spoke the words, trying not to flinch from the cold, dead flesh beneath my fingers. I waited. I felt . . . I thought I felt . . . a throbbing against my palm, as if the dead man's heart was flickering into life, beating faintly then thumping hard, drumming against my fingers, but perhaps it was only the blood pounding through my own body.

My hand is sinking through that cold leathery skin, pulling me down behind it. I am dragged through white bone and scarlet flesh, where blood runs like purple fire through great pulsating veins, pulled through the heart's fleshy walls, thick as granite rocks, into a great dark cavern thronged with people, but they do not look at me. They do not even lift their eyes to look at each other. Each is the only creature walled inside their misery. They walk in single file through the cave, coming in from the darkness behind me, going out into the darkness in front of me; their faces swim at me like pale moons in a black lake. Some are as gaunt as skulls, others battered and bruised. There are ancient ones, wrinkled as the bark of trees, and those so young they have not known even a single day of life, a single hour. On and on they come and vanish, a great army of the dead.

One face looms out of the rest, a face I know and do not know, for her face is like a mask, a carving of a face I once knew. Only the eyes are alive, glittering like white flames.

Eva? Eva!

The twin eyes flicker towards me, the hands stretch out, as if begging me to catch hold of her and pull her from the line. As she lifts her head, I see her neck, see the marks.

Eva?

I stretch towards her, trying to touch her fingers, trying to snatch her back. But the eyes blink as if they know they are seeing something that isn't really there, a shade, a wraith, a ghost that might have been me. The face turns away and she is gone.

A voice cries behind me in the darkness, torn and rent by anguish, till it is but the ragged tatter of a human sound.

268

Let me go! Release me from this torment.

*I half turn, though I am mortally afraid of what I will see.
A grey shadow hangs in the darkness, the shape of a man, but
constantly swirling and re-forming, as if it is a creature so racked
with pain it cannot keep still. Its flesh is despair, and only its
eyes burn. The mouth opens, dark and deep, like a wound in
a throat.*

I beg you, set me free!

I felt two arms tighten around me and realised I was leaning
back against Morwen and tears were running down my
cheeks. I pulled away and scrubbed at them with my sleeve,
trying to control my trembling.

Morwen was watching me, shaking her head in bewilderment. 'You didn't walk. You didn't find her, did you? But
you were crying like a babe.'

'Eva, I saw Eva, she looked so lost, her face, I thought
. . . I thought she'd be whole again after . . .'

'In the Blessed Isles, she will be, but she's not reached
them yet. She still walks the paths of the newly dead. But
you knew she was gone. There's summat else,' Morwen
said.

'When she turned, I saw her neck, the marks on her throat.
She'd not been hunted down by the hounds. She'd been
strangled. She was dead long before the dogs got to her. The
serf-hunters wouldn't have throttled her. If they'd caught her,
they'd want to take her alive to claim the reward.'

Morwen shrugged. I could see the death of a tinner's
woman meant no more to her than the death of this corpse
in the tor. She was not cruel: she merely accepted that that
was the way of things. Extinguishing the bowl of blazing
moss, she sprinkled a pinch of the charred fronds on to the

269

man's chest. As I stared at the gaping black hole in his throat, I knew it was him who had pleaded with me.

I grasped Morwen's arm. 'He's in pain, in torment. He begged for release. How can we help him? We must.'

Her eyes softened, turning to the colour of fresh spring grass in the firelight. 'I know,' she said. 'But Ma'll not let him go. Brigid chose him, he must serve until—' She turned her head away from me, as if someone else was talking to her. 'The spirits are gathering, waiting for us. Brigid is calling them. Soon, it will be soon . . . I can feel it.'

'But what do the spirits say?' I demanded, almost shouting at her in frustration. 'Do they know why I was brought here?'

'Do the spirits know, Mazy-wen?'

I jerked around. Ryana was standing just inside the entrance, a look of malice and triumph on her long sheep-face.

'So, our little Mazy-wen has been telling you she can speak to the spirits, has she? She couldn't even charm a wart away. The gift only passes to the eldest and that's me.' Her mouth twisted into a sneer. 'Mazy-wen, Mazy-wen, doesn't have the wits of a squawking hen.'

Morwen stood up, facing her sister, her fists clenched. 'And you haven't even the wits to invent a new rhyme. You made that up when you had milk-teeth, and you still couldn't think it up without Taegan helping you.'

Ryana's grin vanished, and she slowly paced forward, pushing her face close to Morwen's. 'You won't think your-self so clever when I tell Ma you brought a blow-in to Fire Tor, one that's a tinner's bitch 'n' all. You wait, Ma'll thrash you till she breaks every bone in your body and she'll bring down such a curse on your head, you'll be tormented night and day until you drown yourself in the mire just to escape her. You're a traitor, Mazy-wen. You've betrayed Ma and all our kin. The spirits will never forgive you for what you've done. Never!'

Chapter 34

Hospitallers' Priory of St Mary

Meggy was jerked from her doze by the fire as something struck her on the knee and slithered to the floor. Claws scrambled over her head in the thatch and before she was even fully awake, she was already batting at her skirts. Mice again! There were always a few scurrying about, but these past days they'd been swarming in from the moors and fields, driven from their flooded holes and starving. Gnawing at everything, they were, from leather to candles. The cooks were at their wit's end trying to keep them from spoiling every keg and sack in their stores.

The rush lights in Meggy's little hut had burned away and the glow of the embers of her hearth fire in the centre of the floor barely illuminated the stones that encircled it. Meggy winced at the pain of her stiff legs as she hauled herself to her feet to light some more rushes, not that they did much to keep the mice from running over her, cheeky little beggars. She took a pace and almost fell headlong as she stumbled over something lying on the floor. The room was so dark she couldn't make out what it was. She stooped awkwardly to pick it up. It crackled beneath her fingers. She lit a rush candle in the embers of the fire and held the flame close to examine what she held.

'Bless my soul, a brideog.'

She sank back in her chair, cradling the little object. It was a doll made of rushes, which had been soft and green when it was fashioned but were now dry and brittle. It was clad in a crudely made gown, stitched from a scrap of white woollen cloth, now almost black with dust, smoke and cobwebs. A white hag-stone was strung about the doll's neck to prevent thieves and evil spirits from entering the home. The head had been gnawed. The mouse must have knocked it off the beam above her. She'd forgotten it was even up there. Dimly now, she recalled hiding the doll somewhere in the shadows of the thatch when she'd first moved into the gatekeeper's hut, along with a crumbling sprig of rosemary from her wedding day, an eel skin to ward off stiff joints, and even a torn scrap inscribed with words she couldn't read, but words once written could charm or curse and, whatever they were, it was bad luck to destroy them.

She knew the prioress didn't hold with such things, but she'd always kept a brideog in her cottage, as her ma and granddam had done before her. Brigid blessed the hearth and kept the family safe, the goats in milk and the chickens in lay.

As she fingered the little doll, a smile softened her lips, though she didn't know it. It had been on Bryde's Day when her husband, Arthur, had asked her to be his wife. She'd been no more than fourteen or fifteen summers then. All the unwed girls had gathered, as they did every Brigid's Eve, to sit with the new brideog doll they'd made until the fire died down. Then they'd raked out the ashes and laid their shifts in front of it. The next morning, they'd raced to see whose shift Brigid had walked over, leaving her ashy footprints on the bleached linen. Meggy had been delighted when she'd found her shift marked. She had been wed within the year, just as Brigid had foretold. It wasn't till long after her son was born that Arthur confessed he might have given old Brigid a helping hand: he'd crept into the livier that night and smeared ash on Meggy's shift so she would be persuaded to accept him.

Meggy chuckled to herself. Arthur had been well named for he truly was a bear of a man but soft as butter. She still missed him and she missed her lad. If only she knew what had become of her son. How could you mourn for him, how could you let him go, if you didn't know whether he was alive or dead? Hope was a cruel tormentor.

The old gatekeeper stared up at the low rafters, from which dangled sacks, lengths of cord, rusty cooking pots, a pair of deer antlers, a couple of broken snares. It was all that she'd managed to salvage from the house she'd once shared with Arthur. His blacksmith's tools and their few sticks of furniture had been sold long ago. She would have sold these bits, too, except they were so worn out no one would buy them. She scarcely knew why she'd kept them. Always banging her head on them, she was. But she couldn't bring herself to toss them on the midden.

Meggy had never been one to throw anything away, however worn or broken, for she knew only too well that tomorrow it might be all you had to call your own. It wasn't much to show for a lifetime of toil, but she'd a roof to shelter her, a fire to comfort her aching bones and food to put in her belly. At this moment, that was worth a king's ransom to her. There were many who didn't have a mite of what she had, the poor villager who'd tottered past her gate earlier that day for one.

For the hundredth time, Meggy cursed herself. She should have made the woman come in, dragged her in. Maybe in the morning after a warm night's sleep and a full belly, she might have seen another way. But Meggy knew better than most the cruelty of having the pride ripped from you when that was all you had left.

Dusk had already been circling the priory when Meggy had slipped outside to light the torches on the priory wall. Heavy amber clouds were pressing down upon the hills, covering the tops of the tors, and the wet wind that howled up the hill sliced through her, like a butcher's knife. She'd no mind to linger out there and was hurrying back inside when she'd caught sight of a hunched figure limping up the hill. Meggy's eyes were not what they'd been in her youth and she squinted into the fading light, trying to decide if it might be a pilgrim seeking shelter or, more likely, from the painfully slow and unsteady progress, a beggar. Best wait and see before she went to the trouble of bolting the gate, for it was getting harder and harder to ram that rain-swollen beam back into place, or maybe her old arms were weakening – she angrily dismissed that thought.

Meggy had hovered just inside the open gate watching the figure stagger closer. The pitiful creature looked so frail that Meggy feared the next gust might bowl her straight back to the bottom of the valley. As she drew level with the gate, Meggy realised she was probably no older than she herself was, maybe younger, but the woman had no more flesh on her bones than that of a corpse left a year in the gibbet. The only sign of life in her was in her eyes, sunk deep into the hollows of her face.

Meggy stretched out a welcoming hand. 'Here, come you

in and rest. Sisters'll find you a bite of food and a place at the fire.'

The woman had stopped, her hand clutching her heaving chest. She stared up at the walls of the priory, as if she'd thought it a trick of pigseys to deceive her, a castle of mist and smoke. Meggy had repeated her offer of food and warmth, but the woman had flapped her hand, as if shooing Meggy's words away.

'I'll not trouble you,' she wheezed. 'Never begged in my life. Least I can say that much . . . Reckon I'd vomit anything I tried to eat now, anyhow. Waste it'd be. You got bread to spare, you give it to the chillern. It's the young 'uns who need food now.'

She stared out at the desolation of grey, rain-soaked moors. 'When we were girls dancing so carefree, we never thought it would end like this. There's a curse come upon Dertemora, a terrible curse, and I'm not sorry to be leaving it now.'

'Leaving? Where're you bound?' Meggy had asked. The woman didn't look strong enough to reach the next valley, much less find her way off the moor.

But she didn't reply. Leaning heavily on her stave, she had turned and hobbled away. For a while Meggy watched her, puzzled and uneasy. The distant figure paused and raised her head, staring up at Fire Tor, invisible and cloistered behind a wall of cloud. Then the stave fell from her hand and she stretched out her arms towards the tor, like a child begging to be lifted up. Suddenly Meggy understood what she intended. *It's the young 'uns who need food now.*

Grief and anger blazed up in the old gatekeeper. Her own lifetime, all her memories, all her past happiness seemed to be hobbling away from her in that brave, frail figure. And it wasn't right – it wasn't fair that any soul should come to such a bitter and lonely end. Yet fear also laid its cold hand on Meggy's back, for she knew that if it wasn't for the priory she'd be taking that same walk and there'd be no one left even to remember her name. But as she watched, the cloud rolled down the hillside, like a great wave. The woman was gathered up into the mist and vanished.

A great bone weariness sank over Meggy. Her limbs felt suddenly twice as heavy as they ever had before. *When we were girls dancing so carefree, we never thought it would end like this.* No, she should have been sitting side by side on a bench with her neighbours in the summer sun, stretching out steadying hands as grandchildren pulled on their skirts, dragging themselves up on to their chubby legs while the parents toiled in the fields. That was how it should have been. That was how it had been for their mothers and grandmothers for generations before that. Why had it all vanished into the mist? Whole lifetimes washed away in the rain. *No, we never thought, did we, never dreamed, it would end like this.*

Tears gathered in Meggy's eyes. How many months was it since she'd last set foot in the village? She didn't belong there any more. Friends she'd known all her life stared at her whenever she returned, glancing sidewise at her black cloak as if she was collecting taxes or bringing bad news. They didn't meet her eyes when she spoke to them, and their little children stared unsmiling at her, hiding behind their ma's skirts. What reason had she to go back? Yet if the priory was closed by those knights or destroyed by that boy, where could she go now? Would she, too, end her days out there starving and alone on the tor?

Anger and fear grow unseen in the darkness like the wind. At first you only notice the shutters rattling or a branch

277

creaking, but as the night wears on it gathers strength till it has the power to rip the thatch from a roof or burst a door wide open. So it was with Meggy for the dregs of that night. She lay in her narrow bed, tossing this way and that, till anger had grown to rage and fear to terror. Even when she finally slept she was assaulted by dreams of the brideog, which had grown a long snout with sharp teeth and scurried about the blacksmith's cottage, gobbling every bite of food in the place, before scuttling up the wall to devour the side of pork hanging from the rafters. But Meggy suddenly realised it wasn't a joint of meat at all, but her own little son dangling there, and woke with a shriek of horror.

She lay sweating and trembling. Was the brideog falling on her a sign of anger from the old goddess? Was she being punished for neglecting her, turning her back on the old ways?

For the first time in many months, the fire in her hearth had died and no amount of fresh kindling, poking and blowing revived the flames. It was another bad omen. A body always feels more chilled after a restless night, especially one that has survived as many winters as old Meggy. So, grumbling to herself, she slipped out of the door of her hut, fire pot in hand, to fetch some burning embers from the kitchen.

A few servants were straggling in and out of doors bearing fresh peats and ewers of water. One of the scullions, Dye, was bent sideways trying to lug a heavy pail of piss and night soil across the cobbles. She had already spilled some over the hem of her skirt and on the rags that bound her feet and more of the foul liquid was sloshing out as she staggered forward. The girl was going to be soaked long before she reached the midden. The scullion gave a furtive glance around her, then tipped the contents into the shallow gully that ran down the middle of the courtyard. She jumped guiltily as she caught sight of Meggy watching her, but though the gatekeeper wagged a finger at her, Dye knew she wouldn't tell, and flashed her a cheeky grin as she scurried back inside.

It was only as Meggy was halfway across the yard that she saw the boy standing in the corner, deep in the shadow of the wall. Had he moved even a hand Meggy might have noticed him sooner, but he was as still as a grotesque on the church wall, with his cheek and ear pressed against the granite stones, as if he was trying to hear what they were whispering. Like Dye, Meggy glanced guiltily about her. All of the servants were about their work inside and the courtyard was deserted now, though she could hear Brengy, the stable lad, whistling as he tended the horses.

Meggy stepped closer to the blind child. 'What you doing out here, lad?'

When he gave no sign that he knew she was there, she made to touch his shoulder, but even as she stretched out her hand towards him, fury bubbled in her belly and clawed up into her throat. Why did he live, when somewhere out on the rain-drenched moor a good woman lay cold and dead?

He'll destroy you! He'll destroy you all.

He had already murdered the saintly old priest, and now he had destroyed the well. Cursed it with frogs, flies and blood, then stopped it flowing at all. Ice slid down Meggy's stiff old spine. She saw the boy again standing in the court-yard in the dead of night, his hands stretched out, summoning the spirit to her gate; she heard the unearthly keening rever-berating through the black empty sky; she saw his face turning towards the well as the water ceased to flow. Brigid's spring had kept the villagers safe and healed them since the first dawn had broken over the tors. That water had given Meggy a son. And this demon had destroyed it and he would destroy the priory too, for without the well the pilgrims wouldn't come.

Bring me something of the boy's, something I can use to ask the spirits.

Only Kendra could stop him and she must. Meggy had tarried far too long. The falling brideog was a sign. Brigid had sent it, and now Brigid had led the boy to Meggy. She must do it before it was too late. She might never get a second chance.

Meggy reached for the knife dangling from the sheath at her waist, not to stab the boy, no – as much as she loathed him, fear of what he could do to her would not let her hurt him – but simply to cut a lock of that curly hair or a snippet of cloth.

Take care how you get it. He mustn't know, else he'll put you in the grave alongside Father Guthlac. Gently now, quietly, before he senses anything amiss. He doesn't know you're there.

The old woman's grimed fingers trembled as they reached towards the child. What should she take?

Hair, take hair. It weakens a sorcerer's power. But will he feel the strength leave him?

The boy lifted his head from the stones in the wall, as if they'd whispered to him, warned him of danger. His arm banged against Meggy's hand. His eyelids jerked wide at the touch and, with an animal mew of fear, he started forward, his shoulder striking the rough stone wall as he staggered too close to it. The blow knocked him off balance and he toppled over, banging his knee against the shards of stones that were hammered sidewise into the courtyard floor.

The boy twisted himself into a sitting position, bending

over his injured knee, which was drawn up under his chin. His arms covered his head and face. He whimpered as if he expected blows to fall on him. The sight of a child cringing away from her twisted Meggy's guts. In that moment, as he was on the ground, he suddenly looked too helpless, too vulnerable to be feared. Maybe there was something about that curly head or that wordless cry that reminded her of another boy, before he was marched away and vanished into the first icy mist of autumn with a hundred other men and boys who never returned.

The courtyard was still empty and the tiny whimpers of the boy were no louder than a nestling's cheeping. No one else seemed to have heard him. Meggy hurried back inside her hut and found some clean rags and a jar of unguent Sister Basilia had given her last winter to soothe chilblains and chapped hands. She dipped the rags in a pail of cold water and returned to the boy. He hadn't moved. He just hunched, shivering, as if afraid to stir for fear he might fall off the world. Crouching, she wiped the blood from the bruised and grazed knee, then gently massaged the ointment over the torn skin. Her fingers were rough, the skin jagged. He winced but did not pull away, as if he understood she meant no hurt to him. Finally, she bound his knee with the dry rags.

She was helping him to his feet when a servant ambled out of the kitchens. 'Whatever has he been up to now?' She hurried across, holding her skirts clear of the mud. 'I only left him for the blink of a hen's eye. Set him against the wall where he'd be out of harm's way.'

'Took a tumble,' Meggy said. 'Grazed his knee is all.'

The servant shook her head, her expression flitting between annoyance and anxiety. 'Boys – always charging about! I tell you a herd of rampaging goats is easier to mind than any lad. And as for that one, he's . . .' She shuddered. 'Keep the butter from coming and make the cows run dry, he would.'

She seized the boy's sleeve, seeming unwilling to touch his flesh, but as she gave him a tug towards the infirmary, he pulled away from her and fumbled for Meggy's hand. He clutched it in his icy fingers, lifted it to his mouth and pressed a soft kiss in her horny old palm, before allowing himself to be hauled away.

Meggy stared down at her hand, still feeling the warmth and softness of the child's lips in it, as if she was holding a sun-warmed rose petal. Her throat felt uncommonly tight.

Something caught her eye, flopping back and forth in the breeze. It was stuck in the mud between the stones of the courtyard. She picked it up. A damp rag, the one she'd used to wipe the boy's knee. It was stained scarlet with his blood.

Bring me something of the boy's.

He had given it and didn't realise it had been taken. Just minutes before, Meggy would have been elated. But now . . . She stared down at her palm again. Maybe she should just rinse it clean. No need to go bothering old Kendra. Then somewhere far off, carried towards her by the breeze, she heard the tolling of the village bell, deep and melancholy, a death knell. Had they found that poor woman, or was it another soul taken from this world? Stuffing the bloody rag into the pouch at her belt, Meggy hurried towards the gate.

Chapter 35

Sorrel

I am standing on top of a towering tor. The great boulders beneath my bare feet are drenched in the crimson and purple light of a huge blood-red sun. Across a ravine there is another stack of rocks, even higher, and flat as a vast table. The sun is drifting down behind those stones, and they shimmer gold in its dying rays. Far, far below, the moor stretches in every direction, but it is already in darkness. Tiny fires, glittering like shoals of little fish in a black pool, mark the cottages and those who dwell in them. As I lift my gaze, I see that I am no longer alone. A little boy I do not recognise stands on the rock opposite me. He does not move. He does not look at me. I think he cannot see me. Maybe I am a wraith, a ghost.

As I watch, dark clouds are gathering in the sky, but as they roll towards the tor, I see that they are not clouds but birds, hundreds of them, thousands. All carry twigs and branches in their beaks. They drop them at the feet of the little boy. More fly towards us, black against the scarlet sun. The pile around the boy grows wider, higher, till he is standing on top of a great mound of wood. It glows gold in the dying light.

But it isn't glowing. It is burning. Tiny flames are shooting up through the pyre, like seedlings. They are taking hold, clawing upwards. The boy still stands motionless in the centre. The flames are writhing towards him. I try to cry out, to warn him, but no sound comes. Dark shapes leap from the wood, like mice from a burning hayrick, foul creatures, their bodies long and sinuous as weasels, snouts full of sharp teeth, eyes black as spiders. They are streaming over the rocks and running down the hillside, a great tide of them, pouring down on to the people below huddled around their fires. I hear the screams. I see the fires going out one after another as the wave of beasts spreads out from the tor and still the boy does not move.

I have to reach him. I have to stop this. The moor is writhing, shrieking in agony as the creatures swarm over it.

Then I hear it, hear her voice. Brigid's voice.

Protect the child.

I cannot see her. I cannot see. The sun has vanished. The flames die. All is darkness now. But the beasts are still swarming down the hillside. I hear their claws slithering over the rocks, smell the reek of death on their breath.

Protect the boy.

Who is he? Tell me! Tell me how to find him!

But she does not answer.

She never answers.

284

Chapter 36

Prioress Johanne

An explosion of screeches, yells and crashing metal jerked me from my morning prayers. I flung open the door of my chamber, then leaped back, covering my head with my arms as a dozen wings and claws flew straight at my face. For a moment, I could see nothing except a shrieking black snow-storm of flapping feathers and furious eyes. A great vortex of ravens, rooks and crows were swooping and rising in the courtyard, as if they'd been trapped there by some invisible net and were beating their wings trying desperately to escape.

The servants, brandishing brooms, ladles and frying pans, waded among the birds, trying to drive them off, but that only added to the creatures' panic and fury, and for a few moments, it seemed that they might succeed in driving the humans back into the buildings. Then above their cries came the clang of the chapel bell. The birds rose again in alarm, but as the bell swung back and forth, its great echoing gong proved too much even for them. They rose into the grey-pink dawn and flapped towards a distant tor, in dense dark cloud.

I leaned against the doorpost and muttered a prayer of thanks, trying to steady my breathing, but as I opened my eyes I noticed one of my sisters standing motionless in the courtyard, her arms stretched out in a cruciform, her head bowed. Black feathers, still drifting down in the breeze, brushed her face and caught on her veil and in the folds of her black kirtle. Around her lay the bodies of maybe half a dozen birds, some dead, others still twitching feebly, smashed out of the air by the servants' flailing brooms and pans.

Taking care not to slip on the fresh bird dung that now covered the courtyard, I hastened towards her. 'Sister Fina! Whatever . . . Are you hurt?'

Of course she was, I could see that. Scarlet blood trickled down her white face from several deep and livid scratches, and there were more on her long bony fingers, yet it was not those wounds that concerned me for I could feel the burning sting on my own neck where a bird's claw had raked me. No, it was that Fina hadn't moved. She still held her arms stretched out, like stiff wings. Her eyes were closed and she was so still that had she not been standing I would have assumed she had fainted.

'Sister Fina, look at me!'

The young woman slowly raised her head. Her eyelids, almost blue and transparent, opened suddenly, like shutters on a casement being flung ajar, but the tawny eyes beneath were as sightless as the painted eyes on a wooden saint, the pupils so small that they were mere dots. I caught hold of one of her wrists and pulled the arm down to its natural position at her side, giving its owner a little shake. Fina's other arm flopped down with the first, as if the two were attached by strings.

'The place for contemplation, Sister Fina, is in the chapel,

286

not in the middle of the courtyard. We are not nuns who make a show of public penance and humility.'

Sibyl, one of our cooks, clutching a heavy iron frying pan splattered with feathers and blood, shuffled towards us. She was scarlet in the face and sweating after her efforts, and the twist of cloth about her head was pulled rakishly askew, almost covering one eye. She glanced up at Fina, who remained statue-still.

'I reckon that tumble she had a while back must have scrambled her wits. Why didn't she get herself indoors when the birds started swooping?'

'Perhaps it happened so suddenly she was too frightened to move,' I said. It was the only explanation I could think of, but even that made no sense. Fear would surely have made someone cover their head with their arms, or cower in a corner, not stand there with their body and face exposed, like a holy martyr welcoming death. 'What on earth caused the birds to mob the yard like that?' I glanced anxiously up at three carrion crows, which had once more alighted on the roof.

Sibyl attempted to stuff the greasy grey locks of her hair back beneath her spattered head-cloth. 'That nuggin, Dye, caused it, that's who. You wait till I get my hands on her. I told her to take the scraps from last night's supper to Sister Melisene for the poor basket. I said, "There'll be beggars pushing and shoving round that alms window before alms bell has finished tolling, and the sooner we're rid of them, the safer we shall all be." So, I told Dye, I said, "You take the meats to Sister Melisene, so they'll be ready to dole out straight way, afore those vagabonds get themselves settled in front of our gate."

'But that girl's not got the brains of a dried bean. She goes ambling out of the kitchen, mindless as a headless herring, without even thinking to cover the tray. A bird swoops down from the roof to snatch at the bread, gives her a fright and she drops the whole mess of it, scatters bread and meats all over the yard. And before you can say "pickled pork", there's a whole flock of those vicious creatures swooping down. Dye came tearing in as if the wisht hounds was after her, as did everyone else in the yard. We all grabbed up something to drive them off, but her' – Sibyl jerked her head towards Fina – 'she just stood there, like she was St Cuthbert talking to the beasts. It's a wonder they didn't peck her eyes out, mood they were in. I've seen them do it to lambs as can't protect themselves.'

As if her words had indeed become flesh, her gaze fastened on a corner of the courtyard behind Fina and she gave a little cry. She scuttled over and returned to my side, the limp and bloody bodies of two chickens dangling by their feet from her fist. 'Look! See what those flying imps have done, murdered two of my finest laying hens.'

'Murdered.' Fina repeated the word clearly and slowly, as if it was one she had never heard before. 'He'll do it again. I have to stop him.'

We stared at her. Her eyes were alive now, bright, almost luminous in the leaden morning light.

Sibyl took a pace backwards, holding the iron frying pan like a shield across her chest. 'Blessed Virgin and all the saints . . . is she saying someone's been murdered?'

I felt a chill hand clutching at my heart, but I shook my head emphatically. 'Of course not! She is simply upset by the birds.'

I glanced back at Fina's pale face, her strange eyes. Could Sister Basilia have given her more dwale? But there was no reason to do so.

'The boy murdered Father Guthlac,' Fina gabbled. 'Sibyl says, he's calling up his flying imps to destroy us. You saw them. I had to pray against them. I had to drive them away.'

I glared at both of them in exasperation. 'Goodwife Sibyl knows they were just birds, not imps. She merely meant they were causing mischief, didn't you?' I said firmly, and ploughed on before she could argue. 'And, for the last time, Father Guthlac was not murdered by anyone! Cosmas never left the pilgrims' hall that night. You know as well as I do that he is blind. He can't find his way out of any chamber unless someone leads him. The child was asleep. How could he possibly have harmed anyone?'

In truth, I was not at all sure Cosmas had been asleep for, now that I thought about it, I'd never seen him sleeping, no matter what hour of the day or night I had visited the infirmary, but that was hardly a sign of evil.

Sibyl frowned. 'There's folk do say that when we dream our spirits leave our bodies and they travel to distant places—'

'But they don't kill anyone there,' I snapped.

Sibyl eyed me doubtfully. 'My uncle went to his bed hale and hearty, and he was found dead as boiled beef come morning, face all purple and swollen like he'd been strangled. Only a mouse could have got into his livier. And they reckon that's how the spirit came in, as a mouse, then murdered him. It was his brother that did it. Two of them had been butting horns like rutting stags for years and his brother wasn't the least surprised when he was told the news. Bold as a magpie, he said he knew already because he'd dreamed his brother was dead that very same night. That's as good as admitting it was his spirit who'd killed him.'

'But Cosmas has not killed anyone.'

'And you have proof of that, have you, *Sister* Johanne?'

289

Brother Nicholas peeled himself away from the cart he had been leaning against and covered the short distance between us in a few strides. I cursed silently. Just how long had he been standing there and what part of Fina's wild accusations had he heard?

My brother knight did not wait for me to answer, as if he had already dismissed anything I might say. Instead he took a pace closer to Sister Fina, almost pushing his bulk between us and deliberately turning his back to me. 'Was the boy out here in the courtyard, Sister Fina? Did you see him summoning those birds?'

Fina was staring at him stricken, obviously remembering too late that I had warned her not to speak of the boy or of sorcery in Nicholas's hearing.

'Brother Nicholas,' I said coldly, before she could reply, 'as I have already reminded Sister Fina, Cosmas cannot leave the infirmary unaided, and if one of the servants had brought him out here, they would hardly stand around idling to watch the child cast spells. The birds flocked here because, as Goodwife Sibyl told us, a scullion was clumsy enough to drop a tray of meats and scatter them all over the yard. There is no more mystery to the birds swooping down than—'

'Prioress!' Sister Basilia was standing in the doorway of the infirmary beckoning frantically. 'You'd best come. It's Sebastian. The commotion in the courtyard frightened him and nothing'll calm him. He's begging for you.'

I hesitated, torn between Fina and Sebastian. It was dangerous to leave my sister alone with Nicholas. He would not rest until he had bullied and cajoled her into giving him the answers he wanted, no matter if they were true or false.

But as Basilia called again, Nicholas turned towards her, his curiosity evidently aroused. I could not have him questioning

Sebastian. I walked swiftly towards the infirmary, hurling orders over my shoulder, which I hoped would give Fina and Sibyl ample excuse to scurry away to the noisy, bustling kitchen, where Nicholas would find it impossible to trap and question them.

The rush screen was pulled beside Sebastian's bed, but I could hear his cries before I reached him. Not the shrieks and screams that at times could carry right across the court-yard, but the quiet sobs of misery and despair that were far worse, for they drove knives through my soul.

He was lying curled on his side, trying in vain to hold his hands over his head, but lifting his arms was agony for him and his limbs trembled with effort. That he even tried was testimony to a pain that was worse than any his flesh endured. I could not even hold him without causing him hurt. So I stroked his soft white hair, now matted with sweat, as he thrashed to escape the noise from the courtyard.

'Let them die!' he was sobbing. 'Sweet Jesu, spare them this agony, let them die now! Let it be over. Make them stop! Stop!'

'Hush now. You're safe in the priory. Nothing can harm you. It was only the shrieks of birds you heard through the casement, fighting for crumbs in the courtyard.'

'Swords! Can't you hear them? It's begun. You must come away now. Quickly, quickly, before it's too late! The tunnel . . . we must reach the tunnel. Run!'

'Sebastian, try to listen. All is quiet. The banging and shrieking is over.'

But the courtyard was never really quiet except at night. Always someone was dragging a rake across the stones, clanking a chain against a pail, or banging burned fragments from an iron pot. I had grown used to it, but for a man like

291

Sebastian, lying helpless in his bed, tormented by his dreams, every clang, scrape and squeak must have felt as if a blacksmith was driving nails through his skull. How could he understand what the most innocent of sounds outside the wall of this infirmary signified when in his nightmares even a pail of water might be an instrument of pain?

'No one is attacking us, Sebastian. It was only Sibyl and the servants banging pans to drive off the crows. No one has come with swords into this priory. You are safe here.'

I prayed with all my soul that he was. But I had lied when I said none had brought a sword within our walls. For one man had, and he could summon a whole army against us. And there was no tunnel in this priory. No hiding place for us.

Sebastian's shoulders would no longer take the strain of holding his hands above his head. His arms collapsed in despair as if he had given up trying to defend himself.

Still murmuring promises of safety to him that I did not know I could keep, I smoothed the sheet on which he lay, gently lifting swollen joints and settling them again on folds of sheepskin to take the strain from them. I knew better than any of the other sisters at which angle each wasted limb should lie to give him more ease, for I had been tending him the longest.

But as I cupped my hand under his wrist to move his arm, his fingers suddenly seized mine, pulling me close to him. His eyes, sunk deep into their dark sockets, searched my face.

'Please, I beg you do what I have asked.' His breath was sour and cold, like an old man's, though he wasn't old.

'Lie still, Sebastian, try to sleep. I'll remind the servants to be careful and quiet. I know noise distresses you.'

'No!' He spat the word at me, tugging on my hand with all the strength he could muster. But his grip was so feeble and clumsy that a small child could easily have drawn their hand from his, but I did not.

'You must listen to me . . .' he croaked. 'I can't do it . . . You . . . It must be you.' But fear and exhaustion had already taken their toll. I saw that he had sunk into sleep.

Chapter 37

Dertemora

Meggy stepped out of the narrow wicket gate and dragged it shut behind her. The moment she left the safety of the court-yard walls, the wind leaped on her back, snarling and roaring, trying to claw her cloak from her. It took several moments of wrestling with it before she managed to untwist it and free her arms. The torches on either side of the gate were guttering so wildly that she had to feel for the hole where she could push the long iron key through the wood, and wriggle the prongs to slide the bolt into place. She'd persuaded Dye to listen for the bell. The girl owed her a favour and she knew it.

Meggy turned to face the wind, and though she kept her head down, her eyes watered and her nose dripped from the smart of its bite. But she'd been born and raised in these parts and to her, like all villagers, the wind was merely the great moor breathing. If it ever stopped blowing, they'd have thought the moor had died. But even Meggy was forced to admit it was panting hard and angry tonight. There was malice prowling out in the darkness.

Her fingers strayed to the rag stuffed into the pouch

hanging from her belt. It was stiff now with the boy's dried blood. Should she take it to Kendra? She hesitated again, half turning back. She'd watched them bring that woman's body down from the tor, slung over the back of a shaggy little packhorse, like a sack of grain, but the poor soul had been lighter than grain, just a sack of dried chicken bones, good for nothing, save dumping in the ground. Meggy had stood in the gateway, watching a man and a little boy leading the horse down the narrow sheep track, listless, stumbling, their heads bowed, but not in grief. What little energy they had left could not be wasted on useless feelings.

You got bread to spare, you give it to the chillern. It's the young 'uns who need food now.

Meggy had run inside and grabbed the first thing she could find in the kitchen, then ignoring Sibyl's outraged bellows, hurried out, calling to the man to wait. The boy's eyes had popped at the sight of the dead chicken, its feathers matted and crusted with rusty blood where the birds had mobbed it. He snatched at it with such a wild, ravenous expression, that Meggy was afraid he'd sink his teeth into the raw flesh and devour it like a fox. But his father pulled the bird from his son's hand and thrust it into a sack next to the sodden corpse. He said not a word to Meggy, as if she had struck him a final blow, the last of so many that he could no longer feel the pain. But his face turned briefly towards her, angry, bitter, ashamed.

If the priory closed, she would be driven out on to the moors, for she had nowhere else to call home, no one who would take her in. And when she died out there from cold and hunger, there wasn't a single person from the village who'd waste their time searching for her corpse. No one would bring her back to lie in the earth beside her husband, her mother and grandmother. The villagers would leave the ravens to pick her clean, like a dead sheep. She had only the sisters at the priory now. They were all that stood between her and death.

Worse than death, for what happened to those souls who had no priest to give them a Christian burial, no family or friends to set salt on the corpse to protect it from the torment of evil spirits? There was no rest for such souls, no Heaven, no Blessed Isles. They wandered for ever on the desolate lych-ways, haunting the mires and lonely tracks, trying to find their way back to the living, back to homes long vanished. She'd heard them scrabbling at doors in the night. She'd seen their white shades flitting over the marshes, no longer human, twisted into the foul creatures of darkness, neither living nor dead.

She'd seen her future, felt it when the boy had turned his face to Bryde's Well and destroyed it, destroyed the life blood of her mothers and grandmothers, which had poured out for them ever since the old goddess had first struck the rock and called the spring forth. Meggy had seen what that demon could do. She had stared out into the black desolation, listened to that dark silence. She knew what was coming for her.

It must be done. He must be defeated before it was too late. His blood had been delivered into Meggy's hand. Brigid herself had put it there.

Meggy dug her staff into the muddy track and turned her face towards old Kendra's cottage. Behind her, the burning torches beside the gate fought and lost their battle against the darkness that rolled over the priory, enveloping it like a sorcerer's cloak.

Meggy paused on the track, digging her stave into the soft ground to steady herself against the violence of the wind.

She strained to listen, peering through the dark. Now that her eyes were accustomed to it, she could just make out the outlines of the furze bushes and thorn trees closest to her as they shuddered in the wind. It didn't bend them, like it did the birches – they were too stiff and low to the ground – but tonight it was giving them a fair old thrashing.

She heard the sound again. It was more than wind in the grass and it wasn't the whistling of the ghosts up on the tor. It sounded like the barking of a hound, maybe more than one. Meggy took a firmer grip on her stave. The wind was tossing the sound back and forth across the hills, like a juggler, first, it seemed, on the right of her, then behind, next in front. She peered down the valley. She could see shapes moving. Were they just bushes blown by the wind, or were creatures running out there, quartering the ground? Her eyes were watering, blurring everything.

The sound came again, a deep baying of hounds on the scent of their quarry, but from behind her now. She jerked round, her heart banging in her chest. How close was she to Kendra's home? She'd thought she could walk this track blindfold, but she'd lost all sense of how far she'd come. She didn't know whether to turn back for the safety of the priory or make for the cottage. She took a step down the track, but at once changed her mind and started back the way she'd come.

The howling was closer now, she was sure of it. She broke into a limping run, but she was struggling up the slope and the path was as slippery as raw egg. She knew she couldn't keep it up for more than a few paces.

She slowed. Her breath tore at her throat. It was only the farmers' dogs howling their protest about being chained up, she told herself firmly. No reason for her to go tearing across the moor and risk breaking a leg. She should know better at her age. But still she hesitated. Perhaps, after all, it was wisest to return to the priory. It was a foul night and an old besom like her might easily slip in the mud or on a loose stone, and then where would she be? Lying out there in the cold and wind, that's where, and it might be hours before any soul found her, for that feckless scullion would saunter off to her bed without thinking to tell anyone that the gate-keeper had not returned.

The wind shrieked about her, driving thick clouds across the sky, like ships in a storm. Meggy dug her stave into the hillside and pulled herself up the track. Her legs were as heavy and stiff as fallen tree trunks now. A black shape moved on the hummock ahead of her. A tree? There wasn't one, not there, unless she was being pigsey-led. They did that, the pigseys, imitating bushes and rocks to fool you into thinking a track was familiar so you'd follow it and become so hopelessly lost you'd wander in circles till you died of exhaustion.

Meggy wiped her streaming eyes and squinted, trying to see if it was shadow or . . . She spun round as the baying sounded again, closer, much closer. A cloud peeled back from the moon. A thin shaft of snow-cold light fell on the earth and the shadow on the hummock reared up. The black horse and black-clad rider seemed to be staring straight at her. She couldn't see the man's face – she wasn't even sure he had a face. There was nothing beneath the hood of his cloak, save the shadow of the grave.

'Ankow,' Meggy whispered, but even as she breathed the name, the moon was swallowed again by the cloud and the figure melted back into the night. The pulsing notes of a hunting horn throbbed on the wind and at once the baying of the hounds excitedly took up the cry. Now she could see them, black streaks streaming towards her, bounding over rocks and crashing through bushes. She turned and ran down the hill, her throat afire, her breath ripping at her side. But even terror could not lend her speed enough. Four huge paws crashed against her back as the lead hound leaped towards her. The old woman was sent sprawling on the ground, rocks grazing her face and hands, though she scarcely recognised the smart of it for the weight of the creature on her back, its scalding breath against her neck, the globs of spittle falling from its jaws and running down her face. In an instant, the others were upon her, their claws raking her skin as they scrambled over her arms and legs, barking and yelping their excitement.

She tried to drag her arms towards her to cover her face but the hounds trampling back and forth over her kept her pinned down in the stones and mud. She was rigid with fear, expecting any moment to feel their huge teeth tearing at her flesh.

Holy Mother Mary and sweet Brigid, help me!

Dimly she knew that she should be making confession of her many sins in these last moments, but all she could pray was that she would not know the agony of being eaten alive. They were tearing at her side, scrambling against her ribs, snarling at each other as they tried to push their great heads beneath her. She tried to press herself hard into the ground to protect her belly.

The belt around her waist tightened as one of the hounds seized the pouch that dangled from it and shuffled backwards with it clamped between its jaws. Another sank his teeth into it and they pulled against the belt, dragging Meggy sideways over the sharp stones until she thought she would be cut in two. She screamed against the pain, but as a third beast tried to seize the little bag, it snapped from the belt and the three huge dogs tumbled over and over, yelping and growling in a tangle of teeth and fur.

An ear-splitting, high-pitched whistle stabbed through the barking of the hounds. The dogs stiffened, shaking their heads, but after a moment they returned to sniffing around her and trampling over her helpless body. The whistle came again, even more piercing this time, slicing through the darkness, like an arrow. The hounds lifted their heads and whimpered, and with a final kick against Meggy's thighs, they ran off.

Everything inside Meggy was urging her to scramble to her feet and flee before they returned, but she couldn't. She lay there, her arms and legs sprawled where the hounds had left them, as if their weight was still pinning her down. She couldn't feel anything. She couldn't seem to remember how to move even her hand, as if the beasts had torn her into tiny pieces and scattered them. Then, as she gradually became aware of the wind's roar, pain flowed back into her aged body: the smart and sting of the grazes from the stones and the scratches from the hounds' claws, the bruise on her side where her belt had been dragged into her flesh, the aching and throbbing of her chest and legs from where she had been hurled to the ground. Slowly, stiffly, she pushed herself to her hands and knees, and twisted herself round, until she was sitting on the sodden track.

It was only then that she saw a figure standing on the rock above her, like a giant bird, feathers fluttering ragged and wild in the wind. It was staring down at her as if it was about to swoop and snatch her up in its talons. Meggy gave a muffled cry, pressing her hand to her mouth, and tried to struggle to her feet, but her legs and arms were trembling. She was as weak as a nestling. The figure watched her impassively as she dug the stave into the ground and dragged herself upright. Then it turned and vanished into the night.

Chapter 38

Sorrel

I crouched by Eva's old fire pit, stirring the broth in her great iron cauldron. In truth, I needn't have bothered for the broth was so watery that there was nothing to burn. The handful of lamb's cress had turned to pulp in the water. One of the tinners' wives had told me that the white shaggy-mane mushrooms I'd found on the edge of the track were good for eating, but they had dyed the green broth almost black. Apart from some bulrush roots and withered thyme there was little else floating in the pot, save for a few strips of dried salt fish. It was not nearly filling enough to stave off hunger, but what else could I offer the menfolk?

The dried beans and meat that remained in Gleedy's store now cost more than a man could earn in a week. I had tried to lay snares as poor Eva had done, but I didn't know her secret places and, so far, mine had remained empty, except for one which had caught a fox, and that had been torn to pieces by beasts and birds, leaving only a bloody skull and a few bones.

Every night I walked up to Eva's hut to cook the supper

for the single tinners, as she had done, still half expecting to find her there, adding peats to her fire or worts to her pot. And every time I felt a stab of grief on seeing that the stone she used to sit on was empty, save for the dark stain of blood, which had never washed off, even in all that rain. Who had strangled her? Why? I couldn't imagine that anyone had held a grudge against her, not Eva. I'd lost the only two friends I'd ever had, Eva and now Morwen, for I doubted old Kendra would ever let her near me again. I'd lived friendless all my life, since Mam died. I should have been accustomed to it and I was, except that once you have found a treasure and had it taken from you, it leaves a gaping hole in you where there was none before.

A snatch of ripe meat drifted down the hill on the wind. All around, neighbours lifted their heads and sniffed. Rumour was one of the women had driven some ravens off the maggoty carcass of a hare. It was rank, exceedingly so, but she wouldn't share it. Some said sourly they'd not touch it anyway – might fill your belly and satisfy your cravings for an hour or so, but just wait till the cramps and flux began. You'd be wishing you'd stayed hungry. But, given half a chance, most would have snatched it from the woman's pot.

Although the shelter Eva had built kept the rain from the fire, the wind still forced its way through the smallest crack, stirring and swirling the flames, as if they were its supper. It was almost nightfall and the horn to end the day's work would soon be echoing over the valley, though it had seemed to be blown later and later these past few days. The men grumbled that they could scarcely see the spades in their hands by the time Gleedy gave orders to sound the signal. Tonight I was thankful for that, though, for by the time the tinners had trudged up here, it would be dark enough to mask the colour of the broth and at least it smelt a deal better than it looked.

I stared down the valley towards the hell-red glow of the distant blowing-house furnace. Beyond that there was nothing but a cavern of blackness, as if the land had fallen away into the void and everything – workings, moor and men – had simply tumbled into a dark abyss. Was Morwen out there somewhere on the moor, by the black pool, or sitting by her own hearth in her cottage? I was desperate to see her. My dreams had become so vivid I was afraid to sleep.

Who was the boy I'd seen? Did he live in this world? I'd heard Brigid's voice telling me to protect him. Was that what she'd called me here to do? But how could I, if I couldn't find him? Only Morwen seemed to know what my dreams meant, but I daren't seek her out for fear of bringing more trouble to her. I'd little doubt that Ryana had carried out her threat to tell the old hag.

The night before, I had stared into Eva's hearth fire, trying to journey as Morwen had taught me, though I was terrified that, without her, I would not be able to get back. I walked into the flames, trying to reach the heart of the fire where I was sure Brigid would be waiting for me. But at the centre of the fire was the moor, and I was standing on a rock in darkness, staring down at a pack of hounds streaking across the hillside. At first I couldn't see what they were hunting and then I saw it was a little black cat. I was so afraid those huge dogs would tear the defenceless creature to pieces that I whistled to drive them off. But instantly the moor vanished, like a candle flame blown out by the wind, and I was sitting by Eva's hut again. What did it mean? What did any of it mean? Without Morwen, nothing made sense.

I spooned some of the broth into my own bowl, clutching

the warmed wood in my good hand, so that the heat could seep into my skin. But I was too ravenous to hold it for long. I drank it swiftly and, for a few minutes at least, the hot liquid fooled my belly into thinking it was food and the gripping ache eased a little.

Something brushed my shoulder, making me jump. Gleedy was standing just behind me. The firelight gleaming up from below melted away his face, leaving only a forest of crooked teeth and the whites of his eyes hanging in the shadows. 'You swallowed that faster than my hounds gulp their suppers. Hungry, are you?' He dipped the ladle into the great iron pot and raised it to his lips, taking a noisy slurp, then letting the remainder trickle back into pot. 'Weak as whey. That wouldn't satisfy a babe, much less men who've been digging all day. The tinners will not be paying you for a belly full of water.'

'They know what you're charging for a handful of mouldy peas,' I muttered. I wanted to say more, a great deal more, but I had to bite the words back. I couldn't afford to anger him. There was no food to be had except what was in his stores, and he could charge whatever he pleased for it. If I couldn't even buy a little dried fish on Saturday, the men really would be eating water.

His fingers touched my bare neck. It felt as if a huge spider was creeping over my skin. I slapped his hand away and scrambled to my feet, stepping away from him. He studied me with a curiously amused expression. I couldn't be sure, because of his squint, but his gaze seemed to be wandering over every inch of my body. It made my skin crawl as if his fingers were still touching me.

'I envy the tinners on nights like this,' he said, 'with their women to cuddle up to, keeping them snug and warm of

305

an evening. There's me, all alone, at the other end of the valley. A pot stuffed full of tasty meats and a flagon of wine is well and good, but you can't really savour them when you've no one to share them with. Same as a bed, thick blankets, soft place to rest your head, but somehow you can't seem to get warm when there's no one lying beside you. I really miss my Eva on nights like this, grieve for her something terrible, I do. My bed's a lonely place without her in it.'

'*Your* Eva? What? *You* were her lover? I don't believe it.' I shuddered at the mere thought. Why would a woman as handsome as Eva even look at a creature like Gleedy? Of all the men in the camp she might have sought a little comfort with, it would surely never have been this slug. But . . . there was the bruise I'd seen on her face, the food she got from his stores to cook. What had Gleedy said to Todde? *Half the men and women here are runaways. But they know their old masters can't touch them, providing they don't make trouble and get themselves thrown out.* If Eva had been a bondswoman, she'd probably had no choice but to let Gleedy use her or be sold to the serf-hunters. Her babe! Was he the father? I felt sick.

From the other side of the valley came the long mournful wail of the ram's horn. In front of the huts, fires were blazing up as the women poked and blew on sleepy embers. The tinners would be climbing the hill hungry for their supper.

Gleedy scooped another ladle of broth from the pot, and held it high in the air, watching the liquid splash back down into the cauldron. 'I'm thinking a good wedge of fat ham would cook up a treat in that pot, maybe with some white peas. Can't you just smell them?'

'If you could cook wishes, beggars would eat like kings,'

I snapped. 'The tinners can't pay me enough to buy ham at your prices, and I'll not be digging myself more debt. Besides, I heard you say there wasn't so much as a strip of dried mutton left in the stores. And dwelling on what you can't have only makes the belly crave it more.'

Furtively glancing down towards the tinners' huts, Gleedy shuffled close to me again, catching my arm as I tried to move away. 'I always keep a little something aside for those who know how to ask nicely,' he whispered.

'Then you'd best offer it to someone else. I told you, I'll not be owing you any more.'

I tried to wrench myself from his grasp. I was desperately willing the tinners to arrive and come to my defence. Gleedy had hold of my good arm, and I hadn't the strength in my withered one to push him away. The wind gusted, shoving me hard towards him, as if it was his henchman.

'Did I say anything about money?' Gleedy said, with an injured expression, as if I'd grossly wounded him. 'Ask nicely, was all I said.'

At that moment, two of the younger tinners plodded up to the fire, juddering to a halt as they caught sight of me struggling in Gleedy's grasp. I was never more relieved to see anyone, but it was short-lived.

The two lads grinned at each other. 'Got yourself a new woman, Gleedy? Didn't take you long. Don't mind us, we'll just help ourselves.'

Gleedy ignored them and bent his face close to my ear. 'You be nice to me and I'll see there's always something hot and tasty in your pot . . . and not just this one.' He was still holding me tightly by my arm. But his other hand snaked down and he grabbed me briefly between my legs, winking at the two men, who roared with laughter.

I jerked my arm from Gleedy's grasp, almost smashing him in the face with my elbow. I was only sorry that I missed. I didn't know who I was more outraged by – Gleedy or the lads who were watching us, as if I was a dancing bear being goaded for their amusement.

'You might have been able to frighten Eva into your bed. But I'm no bondswoman. You can't threaten me.'

Gleedy spread his hands and gave a high-pitched giggle. 'You know me, I couldn't threaten a mouse. No, Eva and I had an arrangement. I helped her to set up her business. Sold her food cheap from the stores, so she could make a nice little profit. I took care of her. She never went hungry. And she was more than eager to show me her gratitude, as you will be as soon as you see all I can do for you.'

'Go on, you warm his cods for him,' one of the lads jeered. 'Keep him in a good humour and we'll all be the better for it.'

They glanced round as another man came lumbering towards us. He halted abruptly, frowning as he stared at the two of us in the firelight. But before I could yell out, he'd hastily retreated back into the darkness. It was then I realised no one was going to come to my aid. Why would they? There wasn't a man or woman in the camp who could afford to be on the wrong side of Gleedy. They'd not risk their hides to defend a woman who was no kin to them.

Gleedy watched the tinner back away, his lips gleaming wetly in the firelight as he grinned at me. 'Like you said, food's dwindling fast in the stores. I may have to start keeping what little I have for the tinners who've worked here longest and those with families. Only fair, that. You wouldn't want the little ones to go hungry.' He leaned over me. 'Course, you might be thinking, That makes no odds to a woman like me 'cause I can leave. Find work somewhere else, even though I'm a cripple and there's hundreds of strong men begging to be taken on. And you may be right. You may find some tender-hearted person who'll take pity on you, same as I did. But what you got to consider is those who can't leave, like your friend, Toddy.'

He gestured towards the dark expanse of the moors. 'Serf-hunters are lying in wait out there and they've got fat purses. And, these days, a poor man like me has to scrape a few coins together wherever he can, *sell* whatever he can, even though he hates to do it. Those hunters spend many a cold night out on the moor, so when they do finally capture their quarry, they think to have a bit of sport with him, pay him back for all the trouble he's given them. Well, I don't need to tell you that, do I? You saw what happened to poor Eva. But then maybe old Toddy means nothing to you. Why should he? In which case, you just forget all about it and sleep easy.'

Gleedy yanked me forward as we trudged up the rise towards the storehouse. His pace, far from slowing as we climbed, had quickened, like that of a small boy who could barely contain his impatience for a promised treat. His fingers dug painfully into my good arm, while my other dangled, helpless, by my side.

There had been times when I was growing up that I'd wept that no man would ever want to marry me. My father and the village boys jeered often enough at the useless lump of flesh hanging from my shoulder to convince me of it. I knew all men would be as repulsed by it as they were, and even supposing there was a man who was not, he'd never wed a woman with one arm, any more than he'd buy a horse with three legs. A wife was for work, like a pig was for pork. But Gleedy was not looking for a wife and I sensed that the very thing that might repulse other men aroused him. He was excited by the thought of a woman who could not push him away, a woman who could be easily overpowered even by a runt like him.

All the while he'd been dragging me down the hill, he'd been prattling about how grateful I'd be when I saw the food and other little comforts he could provide if I was especially nice to him. But now he fell silent, taut with anticipation, panting noisily, like a dog.

A thousand thoughts jostled and fought in my head. Would he try to make me flirt with him and coax him, like I'd seen tavern girls do, or would he force himself on me at once? I tried to picture his storehouse in my head, remember where things were. What could I snatch up and use as a weapon? Should I grab something as he dragged me through the door or pretend to submit to get him off guard and hope that I could find something to use while he slept? But what if I tried to hit him and missed? What would he do to me? And if I succeeded in knocking him senseless, what then? What would happen when he recovered? And if I hit him too hard and he died . . . I'd hang!

He was dragging me past the blowing-house. The heat from the glowing furnace rushed at us through the open door. Inside I glimpsed two men, their bare backs running with glistening black sweat as they ladled the molten tin from the stone trough beneath the furnace and poured it, shining like moonlight, into the moulds. I wanted to cry out to them, beg them to help me, but I knew it was useless.

We turned around the corner of the blowing-house into the bitter wind. The two hounds had been chained so that

310

their tethers would now reach the storehouse door. They sprang to their feet, barking and growling, making me jump back so violently that Gleedy, his fingers slippery with sweat, lost his grip on me. Impatiently he snapped at the dogs to lie down. But they took little notice until he reached into the pouch hanging from his belt and tossed them each a sheep's hoof, which they caught in mid-air and flopped down at once to gnaw.

Free from his grip I stared frantically around, desperate to run, but where could I go? I couldn't return to our hut. I'd have to make for the moor. I tried to move silently, but I was afraid to turn my back on him. If he let the dogs loose, they'd seize me long before I could scramble up the steep, slippery side of the valley.

Gleedy was dragging the growling brutes away from the storehouse door. I turned to run, but before I had taken more than a pace, a hand was clapped over my mouth from behind and a strong arm wrapped about my waist. I was dragged, struggling and kicking, away from the glow of the blowing-house and into the shadows. Hands forced me face down to the ground. A man's thighs straddled my back. I tried to wriggle free, but his weight was too great. Stinking, sweaty fingers still pressed across my mouth, half blocking my nose. I couldn't breathe. That became the only thing that mattered, trying to draw air into my lungs. My good hand was pinned under me. I managed to pull it free and grasp the hairy arm that was suffocating me. But strength was fast flowing out of me. Tiny golden sparks were bursting in my head. My body was drifting away from me. I lost my grip on his arm and lay limp.

I felt his hot breath on my ear and dimly heard a man's voice whisper to me to lie still and not make a sound. I didn't need to be told that: I couldn't move. Was Gleedy going to drag me inside or force himself on me out there in the mud?

The hand slid from my mouth, and I took a great gasp of cold air, though his fingers still rested on my chin, and I knew they'd shoot up again if I attempted to call out. The thick legs uncoiled from my back. The crushing weight lifted, but an arm tightened about my waist again, holding me down. Every muscle in my body seemed to have turned to bone.

'Playing games, are we, Sorrel? Hide and seek? And what'll be my prize when I find you?'

It took a moment to realise that Gleedy's voice was not coming from beside me. He was tramping around in the darkness, calling out first in amusement, then with growing impatience. Boots crunched over the stones just yards from me, and lifting my head, I caught a glimpse of his outline lit by the glow of the blowing-house, before a hand pressed me back into the mud.

'Keep down!'

I strained to hear if Gleedy's footfalls were coming closer, but it was impossible over the hissing and wheeze of the huge blowing-house bellows, the creaking of the waterwheel that drove them, and the clatter of the men inside.

The arm lifted from my waist and hauled me to my feet. 'Come on, this way and keep low.'

I found myself running and stumbling over stones and the stumps of bushes, with the sound of rushing water growing ever louder, until I was dragged behind a wedge-shaped heap of gravel spoil, where my captor finally released me and flopped down beside me in the mud. There was not a glimmer of light and I could see nothing of the man sitting beside me. I could hear him panting hard, though whether from the effort of dragging me or from excitement I couldn't tell. My own breath was tearing painfully in my chest. My legs felt as if my bones had melted away and I was sure I'd never be able to run again. But, all the same, I levered myself up until I was crouching, ready to spring away if the man made any move to touch me.

'What do you . . . want from me?' I groped behind me with my good hand, ignoring the scratches from the sharp gravel and thorns, as I swept my palm over the ground until my fingers closed around a weighty stone. Slowly, so he wouldn't detect the movement, I brought it to my side, ready to strike.

'Guessed he'd fetch you to his storehouse. Takes everything he buys or steals there.' The man was keeping his voice low, but I'd heard it many times before these past weeks.

'Todde? Is that you?'

'Who else?'

I could hear the cocky grin in his voice.

'Ought to be a special room in Hell for rats like him,' Todde muttered. 'I'd skin him alive, then cut out every twisted little bone in his body, one at a time, starting with his thieving fingers.'

I knew the smile had faded from his face for his tone was as bitter as ox gall. But I felt more angry than grateful. If Todde hadn't stopped me, I'd be safely up on the moor by now. Then his words penetrated my fear and anger.

'You guessed he'd take me to his storehouse? You knew what he was planning and you didn't trouble to warn me?' I tightened my grip on the stone.

'Been watching you and him, just in case, though I didn't really believe it. Even I thought a vile little weasel like Gleedy wouldn't go that far. And bairns imagine all sorts, don't they, always making up wild stories, especially the lads?'

'What stories?' I whispered.

'After Gleedy accused me of killing Eva, I did some asking around quietly, case they did fetch the sheriff. Wanted to be ready to defend myself. Nobody would say anything, though I reckon a few knew more than they were letting on. But I noticed one little lad, seemed to be acting a bit queer, especially when Gleedy was around. I got him on his own and bribed him with a strip of dried meat that I'd . . . found.'

Stolen, he meant, but that hardly mattered now.

'Anyway, the lad told me the day Eva went missing he'd sneaked away when he was meant to be picking over stones and gone up to Eva's hut. He said Eva used to give him a bite of food now and again. She was soft like that. But when he got up there he heard Gleedy's voice and hid 'cause he was afeared he'd be in trouble for skipping off. He saw Gleedy punch Eva, leastways that was what the boy claimed. She tried to get away, but that weasel put his hands round her throat and throttled her. He slung her over that horse of his and led it up the track. Lad didn't know if she was dead or alive then, but it was the last he saw of her. Gleedy must have dumped her corpse on the moor. Probably hoped it would be picked clean afore she was found and recognised.'

I saw again, with a shudder, Eva's face as her spirit walked the lych-way, the dark marks on her neck, the look of terror in her eyes, and I knew it was the truth.

'Course, the lad said nowt, not even when her body was brought back, 'cause he knew he shouldn't have gone up there when he was meant to be streaming, reckoned his father would give him a whipping if he found out. He was terrified of what Gleedy might do to him too, and with good reason.'

Eva's face hung in the darkness in front of me. Fury raged through me. Gleedy had used her and killed her. Todde knew and had said nothing to me, to anyone. At best, that made him a coward. At worst . . .

'I suppose you thought that if you snatched me from Gleedy, I'd be nice to you instead. Was that it? Or maybe you thought if I'd warm his bed, I'd warm yours after. Was that what you were hanging around the store for, to beg his leavings? That's what you've been after from the beginning, isn't it?'

I was only out there because of what Gleedy had threatened to do to Todde. I should have let Gleedy sell him. He deserved it. Instead, I had almost sold myself to protect this . . . this little toad. I heard the gravel grating under Todde's backside as he moved and nearly swung at him with the stone, but behind the spoil heap it was too dark even to see his head. But I was so filled with rage, I would have pounded it to a pulp.

'Won't deny I took a fancy to you the first day I clapped eyes on you. Hoped, maybe, in time . . . But I'd never force myself on you or any lass. Seen too many masters have their way with maids against their will. Makes me mad as a lynx in a trap to see a man do that to a woman that can't refuse him. My own brother was forced to send his new bride to the priest that had married them. Things weren't never the same between them after that, and when their first babe was dragged into the world . . . Well, my brother was never sure. I'd catch him looking at the child with this cold stare, and when the little lad would try to take his hand or cuddle up against him, he'd shrug him off as if the boy were a stray dog.'

There was silence between us, filled only by the wind and the water tumbling unseen.

'You can't go back to the hut tonight. The weasel's bound to go looking for you there.'

'You think it'll be any different tomorrow? I'll have to make for the moors.'

'You can't do that! It's not safe.' Todde lunged at me.

I suppose he might have been trying to seize my hand in the darkness, but it was my thigh his fingers closed around.

'It'll be safer than here! You're as foul as he is.' I pushed myself on to my feet.

Todde grabbed the hem of my skirt. 'I swear you'll come to no harm from me. You'll starve out there, if you don't die of cold first. There's tinners and outlaws crawling all over the moor. If they find a lass on her own, they'll do things to you that would make even Gleedy sick to think on. At least in the camp you'll not starve and I'll not let that weasel lay a paw—'

But I refused to listen to another of Todde's wild promises. 'Aye, I'll not starve if I let Gleedy have his way, at least until he loses his temper and I end up as hound's meat on the moor.'

Todde was no better than those tinners. I'd cooked for them and they had just stood by and let Gleedy drag me off. Worse, they'd egged him on, just to make their lives easier. *Warm his cods for him. Keep him in a good humour and we'll all be the better for it.* Was that how Todde reasoned too?

'You don't like to see a man force himself on a woman?' I snarled at him. 'No, I wager you don't unless there's something in it for you, and that's a belly full of food. Was that your game, hold me here, then deliver me to Gleedy yourself, so you'd make quite sure to get your share.'

I caught the tail of my name being shouted into the wind. Gleedy was coming back.

Todde heard it too, he already had hold of my skirt, now his other hand fastened itself around my ankle. I couldn't pull away from him. I daren't kick out, knowing if I did, he could easily pull me over.

Fingers grabbed the back of my neck. Another arm locked about my waist, so that I couldn't turn. Gleedy's body pressed into my back. I could feel his prick hardening against my thigh, his mouth hot against my ear.

'Seems I misjudged you, Toddy. You've done me a service catching this little cat for me. You'll not be sorry. I'll see you well rewarded. Always pay my debts I do, unlike some. But you'll have to wait till morning. I fancy I'll be a mite occupied tonight.'

I struggled, but I couldn't break free from him. His fingers had slid around my neck and were pressing into my throat, not hard enough to make me choke, but as if he wanted me to know he could throttle me just as easily as he had Eva, more so, for I had only one hand to fight with.

I was still clutching the stone in my fist. I smashed down as hard as I could against the knuckles of his hand on my waist, and felt the stone strike flesh and bone. Gleedy yelped and his fingers released their grip. I brought my elbow back hard against his belly, heard him grunt and felt him sag. But as I tried to step away, I slipped in the mud and fell to my knees. Gleedy didn't hesitate: before I could struggle up, he'd grabbed my hair and was yanking my head back so far I thought my neck would snap.

Todde was on his feet beside me. 'Let her go, you bastard!'

I felt rather than saw his fist fly past my face and heard the crack as it crunched into Gleedy's jaw. Gleedy crashed down, almost dragging me with him. Todde seized my arm and dragged me upright.

317

'Run!' he yelled. 'Run!'

I picked up my skirts and scrambled up the slope, slipping and stumbling. Behind me I could hear the two men shouting. There was a long-drawn-out scream, then nothing but silence and darkness.

Chapter 39

Prioress Johanne

'Brother Nicholas, I assure you that your letters have been safely dispatched to Buckland.'

My hands clenched in exasperation inside my sleeves, where I'd tucked them, not for modesty but to warm my numb fingers, since he and Brother Alban were, as usual, blocking what little heat rose from the meagre fire.

'Any reply there may be for you will be sent with Hob when he brings the next wagon of supplies, and we cannot expect him now until the first frosts harden the ground. The servants can't even use the sledges on the moor, for fear that the horses will get stuck in the deep mud and die of exhaustion. It is the same every year in the autumn. I grant you, this year the season has come upon us unnaturally early. But there is nothing to be done, except pray that rain will soon give way to ice. Though that will bring its own horrors,' I told them grimly.

As if to prove the truth of my words, a particularly vicious blast of wind rattled the shutters so violently that I began to fear the thatched roof would be lifted off.

Nicholas shuffled forward to the edge of the wooden chair and spread his fingers over the glowing peats, trying to snatch at the warmth. 'If my letters had reached Commander John, I am certain he would have dispatched a messenger with a reply at once, not trusted to carters and lumbering wagons.' He drained his goblet and stared pointedly at the flagon of wine that had somehow found its way to Alban's side. He gestured for it to be passed back, but his sergeant studiously ignored him.

'He can't handle the eighty hinds he already has in his herd, never mind chasing after the handful up here,' Alban muttered. 'You want your letters to be answered, Brother Nicholas, you should be sending them to Clerkenwell. They've men and good horses to spare as messengers. Don't have to rely on an ancient old gammer and his mooncalf son.'

Nicholas stalked over to seize the flagon. 'I have told Commander John quite plainly that unless he sends men-at-arms, this priory will be starved out long before winter sets in, let alone spring, because there won't be a single head of cattle or sheep left on our lands that the outlaws, tinners or thieving villagers haven't butchered.'

'And I told you, Brother Nicholas, that bringing armed knights here will simply start a war we cannot win,' I thundered.

'I trust even you will not presume to consider yourself more able than a knight commander of St John to decide how best to protect one of our order's priors.'

'I am prioress here. The safety of this priory is my responsibility—'

'Can't see as it makes any odds either way,' Alban cut in. 'It's not knights we need. This place is losing more kine to the rain and the packs of starving beasts than to tinners and outlaws. Kept awake half the night, I am, by packs of wild dogs howling out on the moor, and young Brengy in the stables tells me the foxes are growing so bold they attack the sheep in daylight. You want to tell the Lord Prior it's hunters and trappers are wanted here.'

A look of disgust settled on Nicholas's face as he tipped the captured flagon over his goblet, to see nothing but the gritty dregs slithering out. 'I would indeed have informed the Lord Prior of all that has befallen this cursed priory, Brother Alban, if the prioress hadn't sent the only able-bodied man who was capable of finding his way to Clerkenwell on some spurious errand to Exeter from which he still has not returned. And *if* he ever returns,' Nicholas said savagely, 'he is likely to find only skeletons sitting round the refectory table, since we will all have long since died of hunger and thirst.' He flung the lees of the wine over the fire. 'All, that is, except a certain brother sergeant, who will have died of a burst gut having devoured every last morsel of food in the priory and our corpses as well, I imagine.'

Nicholas picked up his cloak and swirled it around to settle on his shoulders as he strode to the door. 'I will bid you goodnight, Prioress, and retire to my chamber where, if I hurry and manage to get there before my brother, I might still find a goblet of wine left in the ambry.'

The door opened and slammed shut, letting in a blast of wind, which sent a dense cloud of smoke, peat ash and scarlet sparks from the fire swirling about Alban's head. He coughed violently and overturned the chair in his haste to back away, beating out the burning fragments that had fastened themselves on his jerkin and were smouldering in his beard. Eyes and nose streaming, he stumbled to the door and out into the cold, damp air.

I waited until the second billowing of smoke had settled, then sank back on the chair close to the fire, the seat still disconcertingly warm from Nicholas's backside. I should have returned to my own chamber and my devotions, but a great leaden weariness had settled on me and I couldn't summon the energy to take even that short walk across the dark courtyard.

I knew my chamber would be nearly as cold as the open moor for I'd given instructions that the fire should not be lit in there, in spite of the season. From now on, we had to save most of the fuel for the kitchens. We had not had a single full day of sun, much less the weeks of good weather needed, to dry newly dug peats. The only way of getting peat or wood to burn was to bring it in wet and try to dry what little we could beside those fires that were still alight. Food was scarce enough, but if we couldn't cook it we would surely starve.

Somehow the presence of the two brothers at meals always left me exhausted. What was the word Alban had used so contemptuously about our sisters at Buckland? Hinds? Yes, and the two men were like rutting bucks, always roaring and charging at one another. It should have been easier when my sisters were present, but I found myself in a constant state of tension in case one prattled some indiscretion, which Nicholas would pounce on. I found myself trying to listen to half a dozen different conversations at once, so I could step in and deflect the speaker if they were drifting into perilous waters.

Fina was the worst for, like a small child or a moon-crazed beggar, whatever thought came into her head burst from her lips. Without warning she would hurl some bizarre remark across the refectory table or toss it into the courtyard. She seemed to have convinced herself that all that had befallen the well of late was somehow an attack on her, because she was its keeper. Though I had succeeded in convincing her that it was dangerous to speak of Cosmas in front of the brothers, I knew I had been unable to persuade her that the little boy was not cursing the holy spring.

Clearly the responsibility for the well had become too heavy a burden for her and I was annoyed with myself for not realising it before. Several times I had been on the verge of informing her that, when the spring started to flow again and the well reopened, I would give the charge of it to another of the sisters. But that seemed to be what she feared most, that the boy was trying to drive her away from it, steal it from her. I feared that telling her I was going to give the task to another, far from easing her mind, would only increase her unreasoning hatred of the boy and, indeed, of me. Sometimes I caught her glaring at me with such malice, it seemed she thought I was as much to blame as the child for the spring drying up. Perhaps I was. Perhaps God was punishing me for my deception.

With every day that passed, word would spread like a ripple on the pond that the well was dry, and who knew if the pilgrims and their offerings would return even when the waters flowed once more? That would give Nicholas yet more to write about in his letters. Not that any of his reports had so far reached Buckland, for Sister Clarice had paid off the messengers before they set out and retrieved the parchments. She had even recruited the ever-loyal Meggy to keep watch for signs of any servant preparing for a journey in case our brother might try to dispatch them with one of his letters.

Nicholas could wait until his beard grew as white and long as winter, Buckland would not be sending any knights. And so long as I remained prioress, I would do all in my power to ensure they never did, if I had to burn a thousand reports or bribe a hundred messengers.

But even if our brother's reports never reached Buckland or Clerkenwell, how long could we keep going? The infirmary was filling with the frail and those made sick from starvation or eating grass to stave off the agonies of hunger. The old were being left at our doorstep by families who could no longer feed them, and the crowd begging for alms at the window grew larger and more pitiful by the day, but we had less and less to give them. I had talked glibly about Hob not returning until the ground hardened, but what if he never came back? The famine was not confined to the moor: the whole of England was suffering. The time would come, if it hadn't already, when Buckland had no food to spare for us.

If we had to survive alone and feed all those so desperately in need who came to us, the money Clarice and I had hidden would be our priory's only hope. I would have to send her out with a couple of strong servants to Exeter or one of the ports to see what she could buy from any ships that docked. The merchants were already exploiting the famine and charging a king's ransom for a sack of grain, but if anyone could drive them down it was Clarice. She knew how hard won every coin we possessed had been and she would not waste a single farthing.

But first we had to rid ourselves of our two brothers. Even if she managed to slip away without Nicholas or Alban noticing, Nicholas would demand a reckoning when she returned with supplies, and not even Clarice could disguise the fact that she had spent more than we had claimed to have. Nicholas had made it his business to learn the price that was charged for every pot, fish and nail in these parts and I knew he was watching every bale and basket brought into the priory, adding up what we were spending. He was determined to prove we had money we had not accounted for. That man could turn a saint to murder, and with every day that Nicholas was here, the guilt I felt at deceiving the order was slowly dissolving, like salt left in the rain.

My head jerked up as a blast of cold air struck my cheek. Had I been dozing? For the third time that evening, smoke and ash swirled about me as the door opened and slammed shut.

'I've been searching all over for you. You'd best come quick.'

Beating the smoke away, I struggled up to see Sister Clarice, her hand already on the latch, as if she was about to dash away again. My heart quickened.

'What is it? Don't tell me we've another plague of creatures down in the holy well.'

She shook her head. 'Sebastian.'

I didn't wait for more. We hurried out into the cold night air. Before we even reached the door of the infirmary, I heard the shrieks and crashes coming from inside, but the shouts were not the usual cries of Sebastian's night terrors. I ran the last few paces and burst in. I couldn't see him at first, but I could tell from the terrified glances of the other patients where he must be. Those who could walk were huddled together at one end of the room, those still in bed had shrunk beneath their blankets. Cosmas alone sat motionless on the end of his bed, as if he was deaf as well as blind. Basilia was standing in the centre of the hall, gnawing her lip, as she turned to me, her expression wavering between relief and fear. Tears welled in her eyes.

'We never thought to keep it from him.' She gestured helplessly towards the far end of the infirmary. 'Didn't think he could use it.'

I still couldn't see Sebastian, but hurried down to where he slept.

'Careful!' Basilia called behind me. 'He's not himself. If he doesn't know you, there's no knowing what he might . . .' Her words trailed off as I reached the furthest wall.

Sebastian sat curled on the floor, hidden by his bed, his head tilted sideways and his eyes squeezed shut. I stifled a gasp. His white woollen nightshirt was streaked with blood, and more oozed from beneath his fingers. At first, I thought he must have fallen and grazed himself, but there was too much blood for that. His shrieks had subsided into long, body-shuddering moans.

'Sebastian? It's Prioress Johanne. You know my voice, don't you? Open your eyes. Look at me.'

His eyelids fluttered open, but he wouldn't look up. 'Go! Go . . . away. I can finish this . . . want to finish this.'

'Finish what?' I laid my hand on his twisted leg. He was chilled to the marrow and little wonder, lying on the cold flags. 'Come, let's get you back into a warm bed. I'm sure Sister Basilia will have an unguent to soothe those fingers.'

I tried to take one of his hands in mine so that I could examine his palm. 'What have you been doing to them now?' I could hear myself speaking in the tone a mother might use to a little child. Sometimes when he was in the grip of a night terror it calmed him, but this time, he jerked furiously away from me.

'Leave me! Get away. I want this to end. In God's mercy,

let me finish it, if you will not.' He lashed out, flailing his arm, though the pain of doing so made him shriek. His elbow struck my cheek. He was too weak and the limb too wasted to do me any serious injury, but the bone was sharp and I jerked back.

The violent movement of his arm had unbalanced him and he rolled sideways away from the bed. It was only then that I saw what his thin chest had been covering. A long, sharp knife had been wedged into the gap between the bed and the wall, so that the blade pointed out into the room.

'Who left that . . .'

But even as I spoke, I realised what Basilia had been trying to tell me. Sebastian had wedged the knife there himself. He'd cut his fingers on the blade as he'd tried to thrust the handle hard into the gap. I could only imagine the pain and effort it had cost him. His joints were so crippled that on most days he could barely grip a piece of bread and raise it to his mouth, much less spoon broth from a bowl or comb his hair.

Sebastian began throwing himself from side to side, and at once I realised what he intended to do. He was trying to use his momentum to impale himself on the blade, for he had not strength or control to stab himself using his hands. I seized his shoulders, trying to drag him away from the knife, but for all that he was weak, he was in the grip of such a terrible agony of the mind that it lent him a strength even I could not overcome. I came close to being flung against the point of the blade myself in the struggle.

'Help me hold him!' I yelled.

I heard feet running down the flags behind me. Two hands seized Sebastian by the shoulders and dragged him roughly across the floor. I made a lunge for the knife, wresting it out

327

and sending it skidding to land at the feet of Basilia. Startled, I turned to see who had pulled Sebastian aside and found myself staring up into the face of Brother Nicholas. He was the last person on earth I'd wanted to witness this.

Sebastian lay trembling and helpless on the floor. Nicholas lifted him, sobbing and shaking, into his bed. Trying to suppress the tremor in my voice, I thanked the knight curtly, told him we could manage and need detain him no longer.

'You appeared not to be managing just now, but if you insist.' He stared down at the huddled figure, studying him carefully for a long time, before he finally turned away.

He strode towards the door, but as he passed the bed where Cosmas sat, his steps faltered. He glanced sideways at the boy, as if afraid to look at him directly, then swiftly and covertly, he extended the two fingers of his right hand towards him, making the horn gesture, which I had seen others use to ward off the evil eye. Then he hurried to the door. Surely Nicholas didn't still believe the boy to be a sorcerer, capable of conjuring evil spirits as he had accused him of doing that first day.

It took a long time to settle Sebastian. I tried to calm him while Basilia attempted to anoint and dress the deep cuts to his hands. At first, he resisted us both, but finally what little strength he had summoned was exhausted and he lay limp, staring blankly up into the dark shadows beneath the thatch, allowing us to move his limbs as if he had already passed from life to death. I winced for him as Basilia tried to close the wounds. How he could have had the willpower to keep pushing the knife handle into the crack while the blade sliced so deeply into his palms and fingers, I do not know, but he had lived constantly in such agony that perhaps he had barely registered this fresh pain.

Finally, Basilia forced a hollow horn between his lips, and tipped a sleeping draught into his mouth. He swallowed it. He no longer had the will to resist. Tears ran down the creases at the corners of his eyes, but they were not tears born of pain.

When the patients had finally settled quietly in their beds, I walked softly from the hall. Cosmas had been helped to bed and lay exactly where he had been put, but he was not asleep. He, too, lay staring up into the cavern of the roof above his bed. Firelight danced in his crow-black eyes. Did the child ever sleep?

It was only as I reached the door that the shock and horror of what Sebastian had tried to do fully engulfed me, and with it came such an utter weariness that I wasn't sure if my legs would bear me long enough to reach my chamber. For eight long years I had prayed that Sebastian would be healed, if not his body then at least that the torment of his poor mind would ease and he would stop reliving the horrors. But his despair was greater than ever. I felt as if a knife was being twisted inside my own chest knowing that he was in such agony of spirit he'd been driven to attempt such a terrible sin, one that would send him straight to the torments of Hell. He was so desperate to escape his own self, his own life, and I was powerless to ease that pain. Bile burned my throat, as I realised what he had been begging me to do the day the birds had mobbed the priory. He'd wanted me to help him end it then, but I had not listened, not heard him. I should have warned Basilia what he might try to do. I should have kept him safe.

I shivered as I shuffled outside. In my haste, I had not stopped to collect my cloak, and the wind cut wet and sharp through my kirtle. The courtyard was almost in darkness now. Most of the torches had burned away, and I had to tread carefully for fear of tripping. My foot sank into a deep, icy puddle I hadn't seen, and I cursed beneath my breath.

I was watching the ground so carefully I didn't notice the figure emerge from the doorway of the guest chamber until he was almost upon me.

'I trust the man is sleeping now?'

'Brother Nicholas! I thought you had retired long since. Yes, he is quiet.'

'But for how long? Our infirmaries, Prioress, are intended for those who are sick to have a place of rest and solace until they are well enough to leave. They are not fitting places for the mad or possessed. Next time it might be a child or even one of your sisters who is stabbed. Even cripples can summon surprising strength when they are seized by a fit of madness or by a demon, as you yourself discovered this night. Why has he not been moved to a monastery where there are monks with the strength and skill to deal with such unfortunates?'

'Sebastian is content here. He knows us now. It would distress him to live among strangers. We can care for him as well as any monastery,' I added firmly. I tried to step around Nicholas. 'You will excuse me, Brother, I am weary and in need of my bed.'

But the knight moved swiftly to block my way.

'Evidently Sebastian is neither content and nor can you care for him, if he was attempting to commit the unforgivable sin of self-murder to get away from this place.'

His words struck me like a blow to the stomach for they cut too near the truth. I had failed Sebastian.

I swallowed hard, grateful that it was too dark for Nicholas to see my face. 'Sebastian is tormented by night terrors. Sometimes the dark shadow of them pursues him even into his waking hours and he cannot shake off his melancholy. But, in future, we will ensure no knives are left within his reach.'

'Next time it might be poison, or hanging. There are a hundred ways a man might kill himself if he is not restrained. But there are those monks who devote themselves to caring for the possessed. They can bind him or shackle him in a cell where he can do no harm to himself or others. They can use whips and all manner of mortifications of the flesh to drive the demons out. Who knows? They may succeed in restoring him.'

It was all I could do to stop myself slapping Nicholas. 'He is not possessed! And he will be cared for *here*!'

Sebastian already suffered agony night and day, and this knight of our compassionate order was suggesting that more should be inflicted on him! I knew what they did to those they believed possessed. They suspended them in baskets over their dining tables to torment them with the sight and smell of food while denying them even a crust. They ducked them repeatedly in icy water until they almost drowned, and flogged them mercilessly so that the demons would flee their poor bodies. But they would have to hack their way through my body if they wanted to take Sebastian and subject him to that.

Nicholas pressed closer to me in the darkened courtyard, peering down into my face. 'But I am curious, Prioress. Why do you insist on keeping this particular man here in the order's infirmary? Why is it that when he becomes agitated it is you they fetch to calm him? I think, for once, you spoke the truth when you said he is not possessed. I have seen those like him before, broken in mind and in body. I know what the Holy Inquisition can do to a man.'

I'd been cold standing out in that courtyard, but the icy chill that enveloped me now came not from the bitter wind but from fear. 'You are mistaken,' I protested, trying to keep my voice low and even. 'The poor man has been crippled from birth. You've seen for yourself how wasted and twisted his limbs are. He cannot walk.'

'Few can, after oil and flames have been applied to the soles of their feet. I saw his scars. But Sebastian can consider himself fortunate. I hear there have been those whose bones have dropped out of their feet, when the torture has been applied too enthusiastically. As for his limbs – I suspect they were damaged on the rack or perhaps the strappado, if weights were also employed.'

Nicholas's tone was as cold and dispassionate as if he was talking about carving up the carcass of a hog instead of the agonies inflicted by the Holy Church on living men.

'The Inquisition serves Christ to root out heretics, Prioress Johanne. If Sebastian has indeed enjoyed their hospitality and survived, it can only mean that he has confessed to heresy. The guilt of his sin is what troubles his conscience and makes him cry out in his sleep, and the abject shame of his betrayal of Our Lord is what has driven him to try to take his own life, as Judas did.'

Nicholas glanced at the infirmary casement, then returned his gaze to me. His eyes glittered like wet granite in the light of the one torch that still burned.

'I believe you know exactly what manner of man you are harbouring in there. That's why you don't want him moved, for fear others will discover his guilt. You are sheltering a heretic, Prioress Johanne. Now, why would you do such a thing unless, of course, you yourself share those same vile beliefs? It seems those frogs were a sign from God, after all.

They were sent to expose the foul corruption and sin that lies in the heart of this priory. And I will not ignore God's warning. No sister, servant or patient will be spared if they are infected by this evil. Mark me well, *Sister* Johanne. I will see that every putrid canker in this priory is cut out and burned.'

Chapter 40

Sorrel

My first thought, as I crossed the rise at the top of the tinners' valley, had been to make for Fire Tor. It was a good shelter and I could make a fire, if Morwen had left wood enough, for my flint and steel were always in the purse at my belt. But the closer I got, the more I began to fear Kendra might have put a spell on the cave to stop me going in or that she might even be lying in wait for me inside.

The face of the corpse who lay inside Fire Tor kept rearing up in the darkness, the gaping wound in his throat stretching wider and deeper. I didn't fear to be alone with it, but I could not forget the terrible anguish in the spirit's voice, his pitiful pleading to be set free. Kendra had preserved his body and kept his soul prisoner. The old woman might reckon to make another corpse to lie with the first and trap another spirit in that cave to be her servant, especially if it was someone she wanted to punish. The thought of what she could do to torture a soul she held in her power made the torments of Purgatory sound like Paradise.

I crept instead towards Morwen's cottage, but all was in

334

darkness. Still, I was careful to keep my distance for fear that Kendra or Ryana might be watching for me, if the old woman had seen my coming in her smoke. But if Morwen had seen me in the flames, she would try to slip outside alone and come to me, as she had before. She'd surely know of a place I could take shelter, where no one, not Gleedy, Kendra or any outlaw, would find me. Morwen knew every rock and bush in these parts and who else could I turn to? I could never go back to the tinners' valley, that much was certain.

I huddled beneath a rowan tree to keep watch. But though I stared at the cottage for what seemed hours, no one slipped out through the leather curtain. The clouds surged across the moon. A wave of darkness broke over the cottage, then receded, exposing the tiny dwelling again, like a silver-grey rock in an inky sea.

I was exhausted. Cold burrowed deep into my bones. Every muscle stiffened. How could I tell Morwen that I was close by? We hadn't thought to invent a signal.

Will worth! Will her to come out. Charm her to come.

I'd no worts I could use, or any fire, but I plucked up grass in front of me until I'd cleared a small patch of earth. Then I drew three circles in it with a twig, as Morwen had shown me by the black pool. I unbound my head clumsily with my one hand, which in the cold had become almost as numb and dead as the other. My hair whirled about in the wind, as if each lock was a tongue darting out to taste the air. I tore a few strands from my scalp and, clamping a small stone between my knees, wound the hairs about it. I held up the stone to the darkness.

'Morwen, hear me. Morwen, come to me.'

Over and over I said the words, trying to pour all of my body and mind into them. But my strength was failing. I could scarcely keep upright. All I wanted to do was sleep, and still no one stirred from the cottage. I forced myself to sit up and try once more, daring this time to call upon Brigid to help me, as Morwen had done.

I'm kneeling by the edge of a deep lake. A horned moon is reflected on the water, the stars flash in it, so that for a moment I think I am looking up into the sky. A line of rocks, made silver in the moonlight, stretches out into the water, flat and just wide enough to walk upon. And I do walk on them, towards the centre of the lake. The water on either side of this causeway is getting deeper. If I slip, if I fall, I will plunge into its depths. But now the causeway begins to slope down into the lake. The rocks on which I'm treading lie just below the surface. My feet splash through water, soft as raw wool against my skin. The path slopes deeper. The water splashes my thighs and I stop. My feet will not stay down on the stone. I'm floating. I'll be swept off it.

I start to turn, trying to retrace my steps. But now I see where the causeway is leading. A narrow rock juts out of the lake. I think it is all rock, but now I see that a living woman crouches on the pinnacle. She's bound hand and foot. I can't see her face, but I know it's Morwen. If she moves, if she falls, she will sink, she will drown.

Kendra has put her there. Kendra will keep her there as she keeps Ankow bound to the paths of the dead.

Mother Brigid, help her! Help her to fight. Help her to break free.

The throb of a horn carried towards me on the wind. It sounded again, like the one that was blown in the tinners' valley, except this was coming from somewhere much closer than the camp. The tinners' horn wouldn't carry so far and it wouldn't be blown at this hour. I dropped the stone, ran towards a small clump of willow scrub and crouched there, straining to peer through the darkness. I could see shapes moving, but it was impossible to tell if they were wind-whipped bushes or men. Then I saw the flames of three torches, coming over the rise across the valley, heard the excited yelping of hounds. Gleedy and his two henchmen were tracking me with the pair of guard dogs he kept chained by the storehouse. The dogs had already caught my scent as Gleedy dragged me there – they'd easily find my trail.

Terror flooded through my body, and my legs, which had been aching with cold and weariness, suddenly found a new heat and strength. I fled, stumbling and tripping over the tussocks of grass. Ignoring the bushes that grabbed at my skirts and tore my skin, I ran without any idea of where I was going.

The clouds peeled away from the moon, and all at once the moor was bathed in a cold white glow. I glanced back over my shoulder. I could see the men now, the two dogs straining and panting on long leashes in front. They were making straight for the rowan tree where I had been watching the cottage. But, once there, they would quickly pick up my scent leading away. With the moon shining so brightly, they had only to look in my direction and they'd see me as plainly as I could see them. If the dogs had been off the leash and far away from the men, I could have whistled to drive them off, but now it would draw Gleedy and his men straight to me.

I dropped to my knees and found myself staring into two glowing green eyes. The creature was standing sideways, gazing right at me. For a moment, I thought it was one of the hounds, and then I saw it was a fox, a black fox, just like the one I had seen watching me back in the village when the river had turned to blood.

The beast ran a few yards away from me, then stopped again, turning its elegant head to look at me. I knew it was waiting for me. I scrambled to my feet and followed. It quickened its pace and I ran. Behind me, I could hear the voices of the men swooping towards me on the wind. The moon vanished behind the clouds. Dertemora was plunged into darkness. I couldn't see the fox and, for a moment, I thought it had gone, but it turned its head and the shining green eyes shone like lanterns in the night, drawing me on.

The fox was running towards a dark smudge of trees, tucked down in the fold of the hill. I tried to keep pace, but several times I slipped on the mud or caught my foot in the tangled stems of heather. But fear always dragged me up again, until finally I reached the trees and stumbled into the grove.

Twisted roots snaked over and around waist-high boulders, each covered with a shaggy coat of moss. It was impossible to run inside the wood, almost impossible to walk. The rocks were so closely packed together on the forest floor that I couldn't step between them, but had to clamber over. My feet constantly slipped off the wet moss into the deep, treacherous gaps between the boulders, which threatened to trap my ankles or break my toes. All the time I was scrambling deeper among the trees, the fox was bounding ahead. Every time I thought I had lost sight of it, the creature stopped and turned its blazing eyes upon me. Then, as suddenly as it had appeared, it vanished. I frantically searched this way and that, trying to glimpse a movement or a flash of shining green. But it was gone.

My leg plunged into a deep hollow between two rocks

and I realised that the space was just wide enough for me to squeeze in and sink down between them. I hunkered there, listening. From somewhere close by came a gushing and gurgling of water as it rumbled the stones on the bed of a stream. I could still hear men shouting and the excited barking of the dogs, but unless they were muffled by the trees, the sounds seemed to be growing more distant, as if the hounds had turned and were following another scent. The scent of a fox?

Chapter 41

Morwen

'You awake, Mazy-wen?' Taegan whispered.

'Course I am. Could you sleep in here?' I dragged myself up, groaning as my back scraped against the rock. It was as black as a bog pool outside, and I guessed that if Taegan had crept home, the night was half over.

Ma and Ryana had tethered me in the stone dog pen. My granddam had kept a watchdog in there years ago, afore it was killed by the King's men for they said it was a hunting hound. Ma had chained me with the old hound's iron collar round my neck, like a beast, so I couldn't lie down properly or stand up. The chain went through a hole in the rock and ended in a bar on the other side, which caught against the stone if you pulled it. Only if someone twisted the bar flat to the chain and pushed it back through the hole could you get free, but Ma was in no hurry to do that. And I couldn't reach it.

Taegan glanced towards the cottage, then squeezed her fat udders through the opening and dragged her arse in behind them. She squatted on the wet earth and pulled out something wrapped in a bit of old sacking from between her dugs. 'Here, Daveth give me this. I reckon you must be fair starved by now.' She shoved a small hunk of what felt like cold meat into my hand. I was dumbstruck. Taegan never shared what Daveth and his brother stole for her. I sniffed it, sure she must be tormenting me with something putrid, but it didn't smell rotten.

'You going to eat it?' she whispered.

'What is it?'

'What do you care? It'll fill your belly, won't it? Ma'll not give you so much as a bulrush root, till you cry and beg for it.'

My belly was so empty that I'd been pressing stones against it as hard as I could to stop the pains, but I snorted. 'I'll not be doing any begging if that's what she's waiting for.'

I could only make out the whites of Taegan's eyes, but I heard her laugh.

'I reckoned as much,' she said. 'Twin yolks in an egg you are, both as contrary as each other.'

I split the meat in two, wrapped one piece in the sacking and shoved it down the front of my own kirtle, then tore a strip off the other with my teeth. It was tough and stringy, horse probably, stolen definitely. Daveth and his brother could pinch an egg from under the backside of a goose without it giving so much as a squawk. But food was, mostly, all they thieved.

'Thanks,' I mumbled, as I chewed the last mouthful.

'Aye, well, you've covered for me plenty of times with Ma.'

'That she has!' a voice growled from outside the pen. Before Taegan had time to turn, a hand grabbed a fistful of her thick hair and jerked her backwards out of the entrance.

There came a slap loud enough to scatter crows, and a yelp of pain from Taegan.

'Seems to me you need a taste of what she's getting,' Ma yelled. 'Only got one loyal daughter and that's my Ryana. She told me you'd sneaked out again. Planning to let the little traitor loose, were you? Is that what you were doing skulking round here?' From Taegan's squeals, I guessed Ma was yanking her hair or twisting her arm. 'Answer me, you idle trapes.'

I heard the sound of wood hitting flesh and Taegan's squeals became shrieks.

'Stop that!' I yelled. 'You let her be! I won't let you beat her.'

Somewhere outside Ryana laughed. 'And how are you going to stop her, Mazy-wen? You're all chained up like the mangy little cur you are.'

I might have guessed Sheep-face wouldn't be far away, taking a malicious delight in any punishment the old hag meted out to Taegan or me.

Rage boiled up in me. I yanked violently at the iron chain, trying to smash it through the granite so I could get to her. I wanted Kendra's bones to turn to ice, her skin to itch without mercy as if a thousand gnats were biting her, her guts to sear in agony as if foxes were gnawing at her belly with their sharp fangs. I had never wanted anything so badly.

Brigid, Mother Brigid, help me!

Someone was shrieking outside, but it wasn't Taegan now. Ma was howling louder than the wind in a winter storm. 'Be gone! Be gone! Stop them, Ryana, help me. Drive them off!'

'What, Ma? What is it? There's nothing there, Ma.'

Ma screamed again and tottered in front of the opening where I was chained. She was lashing out wildly with her staff and flailing, all the while trying to cover her head with her free arm. Then I saw them. They were slithering out of the mire towards her, swooping down from the night sky, creatures with sharp leather wings and clawed talons flashing in the moonlight. They were fastening on her scraggy face, her scrawny arms, her wrinkled neck, her balding scalp. As soon as she dashed one away, it would haul itself back up her body, its claws clamped in her flesh, squealing in rage.

'It's her! It's Morwen! She's calling them!' Ma yelled.

She was howling every hex she could at me, but in that moment, I knew I was stronger.

'Stop her, Ryana, make her stop.'

But Ryana was staring fearfully at Ma, as if she thought she'd run mad. She couldn't see those creatures. She'd never been able to see the spirits or demons. I knew that. I'd always known that. And I laughed.

I felt the chain rattle and slither down my back. Taegan must have scrambled to the other side of the rock and released the bar. I tore it from my neck and crawled out. My legs were so cold and stiff I could barely stand, but I knew I had to run. Ryana was scuttling back to the safety of the cottage. Taegan had wisely vanished, leaving Ma leaping wildly about, as if she was dancing in red-hot shoes, beating and clawing at her own skin, and screeching every curse she knew at me. A great bubble of triumph shot up inside me. I had beaten her. Ma knew now that the gift was mine, not Ryana's. It had never been Ryana's. And it was stronger in me than it had ever been in Kendra. I was the keeper now.

Chapter 42

Prioress Johanne

Sister Clarice squinted anxiously down the hill towards the pinfold, but there was still no sign of our herd of goats the shepherd lads were supposed to be driving into it. The two of us had taken a walk outside the priory gates ostensibly to select those beasts to be slaughtered and salted for winter. Only outside the priory walls could I be sure that we could safely talk without being overheard.

I glanced at my steward. 'Brother Nicholas is no fool, Sister Clarice. I take it he has examined the accounts relating to our own beasts and the offerings left at the well?'

'He's raked every column, like a virgin maid combing her hair for fleas – only the copies of the ones we sent to Clerkenwell, of course. But he's seen our bee skeps and our cattle, so he knows – or our little ferret *thinks* he does – that they're not a true record. I've had the man pestering me from morn to night, insisting that there must be other ledgers. Sister Melisene says she saw him slipping out of our dorter when we were all at supper, and I'm sure my chest and bed have been searched, though I can't prove as much. But just

344

let me catch him with his hand in my boxes again and I'll chop it off, knight or no knight,' she added, in a tone of such grim determination that I was convinced she would carry out her threat if he provoked her much more.

I was always careful to lock the door of my own chamber, but I reminded myself that I must make doubly sure to do so, even if I was called away in a hurry to tend Sebastian.

I had never intended to deceive the Lord Prior over the money we obtained from our livestock and the well. When I had become prioress eight years ago, the income from these sources had indeed been meagre, and for the first few years, Clarice had sent faithful and accurate accounts to Clerkenwell, delivering a third of all we received to the Lord Prior as every priory was commanded to do.

But these last few years, as the farmers' cattle and bees in the lower valleys had sickened and died in the perpetual wet and cold, ours had fared somewhat better up on the high pasture. As meat, honey and wax had grown scarce, so the price they fetched in the markets and fairs of the towns had risen, which was a blessing, at least for those who had such goods to sell. And since I had dedicated the holy spring to St Lucia, the fame of the healing well had spread far beyond the moor, carried by those making their way to and from the ports. The pilgrims had come in ever-increasing numbers, and while few left the gold and jewels that the holy relics of the famous saints could attract, nevertheless their offerings amounted to substantially more than they had been in the beginning.

But I had begun to wonder if it was judicious to record the full amount of the priory's improved income in the accounts we dispatched to Clerkenwell. The Lord Prior and his stewards would see only that the priory's wealth was increasing and the responsions would likewise rise, which would naturally gratify them at a time when most other priories were failing to deliver: Rhodes was like a dog with worms, voraciously gobbling ever increasing sums of money to support the growing fleet.

But if the seasons changed again or cattle murrain struck, our remote priory would not be able to spare the third of what little income we might receive. The Lord Prior was not a man to take such misfortunes into account. I doubted he even knew, much less cared, that bees must have flowers or that cattle sicken. He would see only that we had failed – that *I* had failed. So, like the wise virgins, whose example Christ commanded His disciples to follow, Clarice and I had, so to speak, been setting aside a little of the oil that might be needed for our lamps in the future, so that, should disaster strike, the priory could survive while the sum we had always delivered could continue to be sent to Clerkenwell.

I had not kept back the money like some crooked tax collector or coroner, creaming off coins owed to my master so that I might live in luxury. It was simply prudence, good housekeeping. I had husbanded our money, so that we could shield ourselves and those defenceless ones we cared for. But I knew those at Clerkenwell would never understand that. They would regard it as nothing less than theft, and for such sums as were involved, Clarice and I could expect no mercy. The Lord Prior would make certain that we were stripped of our right to be tried in an ecclesiastical court, and if we were tried before the King's courts we would not escape with our lives. I might deserve such punishment, but not Clarice. I couldn't bear to see such a loyal friend end her days on the gallows in front of a jeering mob and know that I had brought her to it. Brother Nicholas had to be stopped.

As if she had read my thoughts, Clarice briskly patted my arm. 'There's one blessing, Commander John's tame ferret can't send any more of his letters out until Hob returns after the frosts have set in. And I reckon we'll see the back of our two brothers once and for all then.'

'But the moment Hob returns Nicholas is bound to ask why Commander John has sent no answer to earlier reports,' I said.

'If he brings no answer, which he won't since they never received them, it's my reckoning the brothers will decide to ride back themselves, so that Nicholas can speak to the commander in person. That'll buy us time, and if he's no real proof that any sums have gone missing, what with the famine raging, Clerkenwell will more than likely decide there's no point in digging further, for they'll have greater dragons to slay than us.'

I hoped she was right, except that it wasn't simply the missing money. There was Sebastian and what Nicholas knew, or thought he knew. It hardly mattered if he couldn't prove that the accounts we submitted were false, he had only to speak the word 'heresy' and all other crimes real or imaginary would be proved. Sebastian was all the evidence of that they needed. And if Nicholas realised exactly who Sebastian was . . .

There was much I had confided over the years to Sister Clarice. She probably knew more about me than my own confessor, but not this. No one knew of it. There are some wounds that can never bear the touching and some secrets too dangerous to share with even a trusted friend.

I gazed out disconsolately over the valley. The sodden grass and bracken, beaten down by the rain, were decaying where they lay and the slopes of the hills were the colour of dung.

Even the leaves on the trees sheltering in the folds of the land had turned from green straight to dull brown with none of the gold, orange and ruby I recalled from the autumns of my childhood. The rowan berries, usually a bright splash of scarlet, had, like the purple bramble fruit and blue whortleberries, shrivelled and fallen before they had ripened. Everything inside the priory – clothes, leather-bound books, walls and hangings – was covered with mould and stank of damp and mildew. Clumps of fungus, the colour of old bones, had sprouted around the walls of the courtyard and even sprung up overnight in the chapel. The whole world was rotting away.

Clarice took a few paces forward, peering anxiously down the hill. 'There's one of the boys coming now. Where's the other with the rest of the herd? If they don't make haste, the sun will be setting again before we have even the first beast butchered.'

We started down the hill towards the stone pinfold. A solitary lad was trudging along a sheep track below us, his bare feet so caked in mud, it looked at first glance as if he was wearing boots. Three goats hobbled in front, and in spite of the whacks he kept delivering to their scrawny back-quarters with a long, thin birch switch, they did not quicken their pace. At the sight of us bearing down on him, he stopped and half turned, as if his first impulse was to run away. But he seemed to think better of it. With a last push, he herded the listless goats inside the stone wall enclosure and slid the wooden board into place.

I would be the first to admit I knew little about the care of goats. I merely gave the orders that they should be cared for, but even I could see something was badly wrong with those pitiful creatures. Their hair was matted. They were painfully thin and limping from the hoof rot. They had patches of bald skin on their backs and necks, which in some places was scabbed, or raw and oozing, as if they had been burned.

Clarice reached the pinfold first and dragged out the wooden board. Without saying a word, she clamped the goatherd's ear between her thumb and forefinger, making him yelp, and dragged him inside the stone wall. She let him go, only to seize one of the goats by its curly horns and examine the sores on its neck.

'Rain scald!' she barked, releasing the animal and turning furiously on the lad. 'You were charged with the care of these beasts. Didn't you see the signs? If you'd got them under shelter and treated the scabs straightway you could have stopped this. You've tended goats since you were in clouts, didn't the older boys teach you how to cure it?'

The boy rubbed his ear, looking mutinous. 'Goose grass, devil's leaf and great bur, that's what you use. But great bur only grows where it's dry and the devil's leaf had all gone mouldy. Could only find a bit of goose grass. Not enough for all of them.'

'And just where are the rest of the herd and the other lad who's supposed to be minding them?' Clarice demanded.

Fear suddenly flooded the boy's face. He darted a glance at the entrance to the pinfold, but I was blocking his escape.

'Had your tongue cut out, have you?' Clarice snapped. 'Answer me, boy.'

He stared at the ground, tracing a triangle in the mud with his toe. 'Tinners and outlaws stole a few, but then last night . . . We penned the goats up, we did, in the fold. Me and Kitto sat outside the gate to guard it, same as always. We had a fire lit, but only a small one, mind, 'cause we were trying to dry the rest of the wood. It was Kitto's turn to

349

keep watch, but something woke me . . . a horn, then a pack of hounds baying answer. But no one goes hunting in the dark of the night. Kitto was nearly shitting himself. He reckoned it was Ankow riding cross moor looking to collect dead souls. He said if you heard the wisht hounds, it meant you'd be next to die. They were coming right down the hill towards us. Kitto, he opened the gate to the pinfold. I reckoned he was going to hide behind the wall, but afore he could get inside, the hounds were on us. Some went in through the gate, others they leaped clear over the top.

'Goats were bleating and the hounds were chasing them round. Me and Kitto, we only had our slings and staves. Couldn't fight that many dogs – besides, no one can fight the wisht hounds. So, we ran and hid. After a bit, we heard the horn again, closer this time, like it was calling the hounds, and they ran out and vanished.

'Kitto took off then. I reckon he hared it back to the village. I daren't move, case the hounds were still out there. Didn't close my eyes all night. First light there was this great screeching and cackling. I crept close to the pinfold. Couldn't hardly see the goats for this huge flock of crows, ravens, kites and buzzards all squabbling and fighting over the carcasses, pulling off great strips of meat. I fired my sling and yelled, but there was too many of them. They scarcely stirred.'

Helplessly he gestured towards the three goats. 'Found them wandering when I was on my way here to tell you – must have slipped out, when the hounds attacked.'

'More likely they were never in the fold and you'd lost them days ago,' Clarice said.

The goatherd looked as if he was about to protest, but thought better of it and simply shrugged.

Clarice looked as grim as I had ever seen her. 'I'd best

take some of the servants and see what can be salvaged. I'll wait here, Prioress, while you go to the kitchens and tell them to send the men down here. Ask them to bring moor sledges, so we can drag the meat back. The lad can show us where the carcasses are.'

The boy shuffled his feet. 'There'll not be much left after birds have been at them. And the goats have their throats torn out. It'll make you sick to your stomach to look at them. Best not go.'

'I can assure you, boy, my stomach is stronger than most and I've seen a good many beasts after dogs have mauled them.' Clarice eyed the goatherd suspiciously. 'Why do you not want me to see them? Will I find fewer carcasses than I expect?'

'Told you,' the boy said sullenly, 'the tinners, they stole some.'

'And if Kitto spreads the news of what's happened, the villagers will spirit away the remains of the rest.' She clamped a hand on his shoulder. 'On second thoughts, you and I had best go to find those goats now, boy. Prioress, can you send the servants down after us? Tell them to come with good stout staves and maybe a bow or two.'

I nodded. 'Perhaps our brother knights could help to guard those carcasses. Nicholas has been itching for an excuse to draw his sword. I'm sure I can see to it that the task keeps them safely occupied for the day.'

The goatherd stared from one to the other of us, evidently bewildered by the grim smiles that suddenly flashed between us. But I had underestimated Brother Nicholas.

By the time the servants and knights arrived at the pinfold where the goats had been killed, the villagers were already at work plundering the spoils, ignoring Clarice's orders to stop. As soon as they glimpsed Nicholas and Alban bearing down on them, they ran off down the slope, nimble as the goats whose remains were now slung over their shoulders. Apparently, Nicholas had charged after them and managed to give one of them a slash across the back with his sword, sending him tumbling head over heels. But the haunch of goat the villager was carrying had landed in a bog pool where it sank into the black ooze.

I had suggested to the servants that they might butcher the first sledge-load before going back for the next, pointing out that the cooks and scullions could start the boiling and preserving while they dragged back the next load. That way, Nicholas and Alban would be standing guard for the best part of the day in the rain and cold, for Clarice had left them keeping watch with only young Brengy, the stable boy, for company.

But late that afternoon, a clatter in the yard made me whirl round. Alban was leading his horse across the yard, muttering to himself. He faltered as he caught sight of me, but led the horse purposefully forward, staring straight ahead as if he had not seen me, though I was sure he had.

'I understood that you were doing us a great service by keeping watch on the pinfold, Brother Alban. Surely you're not deserting your post.'

He hesitated, clearly wondering if he could pretend not to have heard me, but reluctantly stopped. 'Only a few carcasses left down there now. Villagers have seen Brother Nicholas's handiwork with a sword. They'll not be fool-hardy enough to tackle a knight of his skill. Not worth getting their heads lopped off for a scrawny haunch of meat.'

'Men whose families are starving might well think it worth the risk,' I said, but Alban merely grunted.

I stepped closer. Blankets and packs were tied high around the saddle to help keep him firmly seated on the muddy track. Plainly he wasn't riding out to inspect some local mill or tenant's farm. 'It is late to be riding out, Brother Alban. And you look set for a long journey. Where are you bound?'

'Brother Nicholas's orders,' he said dourly. 'Reckons there to be a good two hours of riding light left.' His voice lowered as he continued grumbling, but he seemed to be addressing himself. 'Could have waited till morning, get a full day in. What difference will an hour or two make? He's not the one'll have to sleep out.'

'Sleep out?' My stomach lurched. 'Is Brother Nicholas sending you to Buckland?'

I caught a twitch of Alban's mouth at my mention of the name. For a moment, I thought his shifty expression was because I had guessed correctly, but then the real reason dawned on me.

'You're not going to Buckland, are you? Where are you bound?'

Alban glanced behind him towards the guest lodging. He seemed to be considering whether or not to answer, then finally he shrugged. 'Clerkenwell, that's where.'

'But it is madness in this foul weather. Even if the horse doesn't get mired, half the bridges have been swept away and the rivers will be far too swift and swollen to ford.' I caught hold of the reins, trying to think of some way to keep him there. 'At least stay until morning. You'll need a full day's riding even to reach a road that is well travelled. Go blundering about the moor in the dark and you'll break your neck.'

He stiffened and I knew at once that I'd said the one thing guaranteed to make a man like Alban go. 'I've yet to put my leg over a horse that can throw me, Mistress. Flood, snow and storm, I've ridden in them all and there's never been one that's stopped me going wherever I've a mind to.'

He jerked the reins from my hand and led the horse around me towards the gate. Meggy was already struggling with the beam that braced it. The old gatekeeper seemed to be having much more trouble than usual in releasing it. Everything was swelling and sticking in the wet. Alban watched Meggy for a moment or two, then impatiently nudged her aside and thrust the reins into her hand, leaving her to pat and soothe the horse, as he wrestled with the beam, but it took even him an age to drag open the heavy gate.

I watched him lead the horse out on to the moor, sick with dread. There was nothing I could do to stop him. Our time was running out far more quickly even than I had feared.

Chapter 43

Sorrel

Todde lies in the mud behind the spoil heap. Blood pools around his thighs and the earth is too sodden to soak it up. It vomits it back. It will drink no more. Todde's belly is mangled, slashed by Gleedy's knife, which stabbed and twisted and stabbed again. Gleedy's boots are stained with scarlet as he viciously kicks and stamps on the dying man.

'Think to stop me following her, did you? I'll track her down and make her watch the dogs chew you up and shit you out. She'll not be weeping over your grave, Toddy. There'll be nothing left for her to bury.'

But I do weep. I scream at Gleedy to stop. I thrash at him with my fists. But though he hears my shrieks, to him they're only the cry of the owl, and though he feels my fists, it is only the buffeting of the wind.

A fox, a black fox, suddenly appears above Todde's body on the ridge. It stands motionless, its head turned towards me, ears pricked. We stare at one another, its brush streaming out in the wind like a flame from a blazing torch. I smell its animal scent. It grows stronger. It envelops me. And I know that the boot which slams into Todde's ribs and smashes his nose can do no more hurt to him now.

A tiny shriek jerked me back into another place. I couldn't grasp where I was, and I was too afraid to move. Giant flakes of snow were falling and swirling about me. One drifted down on to my face, but it wasn't cold. It was dry and scratchy. Leaves, that's what they were, not snowflakes. I was lying in a small copse, my body twisted between mossy rocks and snaking tree roots. Through the trees, I could just make out the smudge of a distant tor, black and jagged against a pale ghost light, which marked where the sun would shortly rise.

A weasel, slender and sinuous as an eel, bounded on to a moss-covered rock and stood on its hind legs, warily sniffing the air. My alien human scent hung between its hunting ground and the den it was making for in the roots of the twisted oak.

A mouse scurried through the undergrowth, trying to reach its nest before dawn, just one more rustle among the thousand whispers of the dried leaves. Only the weasel could smell it. The hunter was on top of its prey in a single leap, wrapping the muscles of its body around the mouse like the coils of a snake, squeezing the frantically beating heart. The mouse screamed. The weasel sank its fangs into the neck of its prey. The mouse shuddered, and lay still. The hunter bounded off towards another of its dens, breakfast dangling, like a hanged felon, between its jaws. They say our souls leave our bodies as mice when we dream. It was well for me the weasel hadn't noticed mine scurrying back.

I dragged myself upright in the gap between the mossy boulders, rubbing my stiff neck. As the breeze hit my back,

I shivered. My kirtle was soaked through from the sodden ground, but I was well used to waking to that.

I could hear the burble of running water somewhere close by. My throat felt as if it had been stuffed with old tree bark. I tensed, listening for any sounds of Gleedy's dogs. But they were probably back at the camp by now and he had more than likely set them on to poor Todde's corpse to obliterate the stab wounds. I gagged and tried not to think . . . tried not to think that Todde was dead because he'd protected me. I wanted Gleedy to pay and, somehow, I *would* find a way to make him pay for Eva, for Todde and for me too. I wanted to tear him apart. I wanted him to die pleading for his life and I wanted to hear the fear and pain in his voice, see them in his twisted soul.

Rage only increased my thirst. I clambered towards the sound of running water, though my legs were so numb I could barely stand. My feet kept sliding off the sodden moss, and my legs slipped down the gaps so that I was continually banging my ankles and knees on the rocks, but it was still so dark beneath the trees, I was more afraid of stumbling straight into the river.

As the first pink shaft of light penetrated the small gap in the trees, I saw a twisted rope of pearl-white mist threaded through the trunks and caught the glint of water racing beneath, spilling over the clawed roots of the nearest trees. But above the rush and gurgle of the stream, I was sure I could hear other sounds – voices, a high-pitched murmuring as if people were hidden behind the ribbon of fog, or even in the water itself. They were like the sounds on Fire Tor, but these were fainter, higher, like a host of soft-spoken women. I stopped, balancing precariously on a boulder. Were spirits watching me through the mist?

My tongue was glued to my teeth and there was a foul taste in my mouth, like the stench of wet dog. My belly ached for food. Maybe if I drank deep it would fill my stomach and stave off those hunger pangs, but I was afraid to go any closer. When I was a child, Mam had often warned me about the water sprites who lured people to the riverbanks with their singing, then reached out their long, icy arms and dragged their victims beneath the water to devour them in their slimy beds.

I peered through the billowing white mist. It seemed to glow with light of its own under the dark, twisted branches. Great beards of silver lichen hung from the twigs, stirring faintly in the breeze. As the wind swirled the edge of the fog, I thought I could see a dark shape moving, the outline of a head turning towards me. I jerked backwards. My foot slipped on the moss and I crashed down against the trunk of the tree, dashing the breath from my body.

I was fighting so desperately for air that, though I was dimly aware of something or someone moving silently towards me through the gloom, there was naught I could do to protect myself, save raise my arm to try to fend it off.

'You bang your head?'

I knew that voice.

Morwen vaulted like a cat over the boulder from which I'd clumsily fallen and crouched beside me, holding me up till I could drag air back into my lungs.

'Thirsty,' I gasped. I needed water so badly now that I couldn't think of anything else. Morwen hauled me to my feet and steadied me, as if I was a babe learning to stand, as we climbed over the rocks and roots to the river. The sky was lightening all the time, but the mist clung chill and damp to my face. We both knelt by the stream. Morwen cupped her hands in the icy water, tipping them towards my mouth, but she dribbled much of it down the front of my kirtle. I pushed her hands aside and bent forward cupping the water to my mouth, with my good hand, while Morwen grasped the back of my gown to stop me falling in. There wasn't enough water in the whole river to extinguish the fire of my thirst, much less fill my belly, but finally I dragged myself away and sat up.

Morwen reached into the front of her own ragged kirtle and pulled out a small piece of stringy meat, which she placed in my lap. I didn't stop to ask what it was, I sank my teeth into it. My belly was so empty, I couldn't stop myself gulping it down in lumps, which stuck in my raw throat for I'd barely chewed it in my haste.

I nodded at her, still sucking the last fragments from my fingertips. 'Can't remember when I last ate anything solid.'

''Bain't much. Taegan gave it me. Ma's been keeping me hungry after Ryana told her I'd taken you into Fire Tor.'

Shame and guilt burned my cheeks. 'I thought you'd saved . . . I'm sorry.'

I was aghast at my selfishness. No one had food to spare unless they took it from their own mouths. But the truth was, I'd been so eaten up by hunger I hadn't thought about where it had come from.

Morwen grinned. 'I like watching you eat. You came last night, close by the cottage.'

'How did you know?'

'Saw you when I was journeying. Found your mark when I got free.' She dug into her kirtle once more and held up the stone still bound with my hair. 'It fetched me here.'

'Got free?'

Morwen grunted. 'Ma and Ryana tethered me in the pen.

Ma used to tie us up in there when we were chillern, if we'd vexed her. Tell us the wisht hounds would come for us. She's not done it for a good long time – doesn't have the strength now unless that cat Ryana helps her.'

Morwen massaged her neck and, in the growing light, I could see the red ring about her throat. She'd been chained up like a dog. I glimpsed other marks too, a purple welt just showing above the top of her kirtle, and from the way she flinched as she moved, I guessed there were more on her back. Kendra and Ryana had done more than tie her up in a kennel.

'It's my fault, I shouldn't—'

She laughed. 'Never met such a one as you. I reckon if the stars came tumbling to earth, you'd be saying it was your fault for bumping into them.'

She listened without saying a word, while I told her all that happened in the tinners' valley. 'And I can't ever go back,' I finished.

She looked at me as if I was mad. 'Why would you want to? Brigid called you to her. She brought you here. She's been biding her time, waiting till you learned what you needed.'

'She spoke to me again.'

Resentment flashed across Morwen's face, though she struggled to push it away. 'What did she say?'

'Protect the boy. That's what she said. But I don't under-stand. What boy? You always seem to know what these things mean.'

A slow smile lifted the corners of Morwen's mouth, as if something she had been fretting over suddenly made sense to her.

'You know, don't you?' I said. 'You know who the boy is.'

360

Still giving me that strange look, she shook her head. 'Not yet,' she said softly, 'but I reckon I will. Tell me what Brigid showed you, what you saw when she told you to protect the boy.'

She listened patiently to the tale of the child atop the great pyre on the tor and her smile widened into a gap-toothed grin. 'Ma was wrong. I was sure she'd not looked at that smoke right, like I was sure that blood charm she gave you had no power. I know who he is now. I know his name!' Grabbing my hands, she dragged me to my feet, dancing around me in delight.

'I reckon it's almost time. The three sisters are come into their power.' She glanced up as a skein of geese flew honking towards the rose-pink dawn. 'But we'll have to find a place to hide till the hour comes. That Gleedy might decide to have another go at tracking you in daylight.'

'I want to kill him,' I said. My jaw clenched so hard I could barely get the words out.

Morwen laughed. 'Brigid will take revenge on him, never you fear. When Brigid's cubs are harmed, the great mother's more savage than a she-wolf. When her anger grows, there's nothing and no one can stand against her. You wait and see. When I went journeying, I saw—'

She broke off and tilted her head as if she was trying to see around something that was blocking her vision. 'The river's crying, can you hear it?'

'I thought it was a spirit, like in Fire Tor.'

'No, that's her, that's the river,' Morwen said urgently. 'It's her warning. When she cries like that it means death. It's beginning.'

Chapter 44

Hospitallers' Priory of St Mary

Although darkness had descended over the priory, fires were still blazing in the courtyard and the steam from boiling goats' heads mingled unpleasantly with the smoke from the wood and peats. The flames beneath the great iron pots and the torches burning on the walls lit up the yard with a demonic red glow, and the figures of servants and sisters emerged and vanished again into the eye-stinging fog like wraiths on All Hallows' Eve.

Brother Nicholas picked his way across the yard, slippery with mud, blood and the evil-smelling green sludge from the goats' stomachs. Although he was coughing violently, he was almost grateful for the dense smoke: it hid the stack of skinned goats' heads that had been heaped by the kitchen door, their sightless black eyes staring out at their kin already drowning in the bubbling grey water of the cauldrons.

For once, the smell of cooking meat was not making Nicholas hungry, quite the reverse, for the stench of blood and dung was equally powerful and he could not stop seeing those beasts lying scattered across the pinfold, their heads

362

almost ripped from their bodies and their guts spilling out into the mud.

An image of another pile of heads flashed unbidden into his mind, human heads, chopped from their bodies while their owners were still screaming for mercy, or muttering fervent prayers, which were severed long before they were finished. The ransom demanded had not been paid. Saracen prisoners were executed in the full sight of their friends, wives and children as the spotless sun blazed down and the azure sea sparkled behind them. Whatever men might boast by the firesides in England, there were some orders they were forced to carry out in war that were neither honourable nor glorious. Nicholas chided himself. He was growing soft here in this cold, grey land, or maybe it was old age creeping up on him. But he didn't want to admit that.

Through the smoke, he caught flashes of steel turned ruby in the firelight, heard the rapid chopping of an axe blade smashing through bone. Three or four servants were working on a trestle table erected in the courtyard, skinning and dismembering the carcasses, cutting away the chewed flesh the dogs had mauled and tossing what could be saved into the wooden tubs behind them. They would most likely be chopping, boiling, pressing and salting meat till dawn. With the flesh so mutilated by bird and hound, it had to be preserved within hours else it would turn foul.

At least with the coming of darkness, the birds had finally departed. Not even the smoke and fires had discouraged them. Every roof ridge and post in the priory had been black with squabbling ravens and crows, while dozens of kites circled and screamed overhead, constantly swooping to snatch meat from the table or peck at the pile of heads. The birds even clawed and stabbed the servants' hands and arms, trying

363

to steal the raw meat they were holding. They had spent more time shouting and lashing out to drive the feathered thieves away than they had skinning and cutting. But even as a maid fought off one bird, three more would be stealing from the barrels behind her. Now cooks, scullions and even the stable lad sweated, chopped and sliced at a feverish pace to make up for the time they'd lost.

Nicholas reached his chamber and barged in, slamming the door quickly before the smoke and stench could follow him. He didn't bother to light a candle before dragging off his boots. He was so tired he knew he'd probably fall asleep before he could snuff it out. From the tail of his eye he caught a glimpse of movement on Alban's bed. That idle bastard was already slumbering, no doubt with a well-stuffed belly.

'I'm not stirring from this chamber till noon tomorrow,' Nicholas announced. 'My bones are colder than a witch's dugs and my back's as stiff as the devil's prick. Christ curse this foul land and all those thieving villagers. I'd hang every last one of them by their heels till their eyeballs bled.'

It was only as he flung himself down on his own protesting bed that he remembered Alban should not be there. He was supposed to be well on his way to Clerkenwell by now. Had that witch somehow stopped him leaving?

'Alban? What in the name of Beelzebub and all his flies are you doing back here?'

Nicholas flung his boot towards the dim outline of Alban's bed. There was an explosion of squeaks and scrabbling claws as a horde of mice leaped off and bounded across the floor and up the walls. A plague of frogs, then flies, now these vermin! What next? Locusts? he thought savagely.

He'd told the prioress that the frogs were a curse sent by

God, a sign of heresy, and now that he had discovered the marks of the Inquisition on that man's body, he felt vindicated. Alban was even now on his way to deliver a report informing the Lord Prior of England that Johanne was harbouring a heretic. But just who was the man? A Cathar, a Waldensian? Or was it possible the pathetic creature who lay twisted in that infirmary was the remnant of a Templar knight, a foul sodomite, whose brethren had caused men to turn against not only the Templars but the Hospitallers as well. Nicholas had urged Lord William to send a group of men-at-arms without delay to seize Johanne and Sebastian and drag them both to Clerkenwell for questioning. They would soon discover the man's identity and the heinous sins to which he had confessed.

If Sebastian proved to be a fugitive Templar, Lord William would be aghast at the thought that he had been given shelter in one of the Hospitallers' own priories and profoundly grateful that Nicholas had uncovered the secret before anyone outside the order had stumbled upon him. It would certainly divert the Lord Prior and Commander John from Nicholas's failure to produce any definite proof that money was going missing.

Yet a persistent thought was buzzing at the back of Nicholas's head. One he had not even wanted to contemplate. There was another to whom Prioress Johanne had stubbornly given shelter, one accused of killing a priest. Ice water ran through Nicholas's guts as he again felt the boy's arm writhing, like a serpent, in his hand, the skin turning to scales beneath his fingers.

He had refused even to think about what had happened in that chapel, pushing it fiercely from his mind each time it edged towards him. He told himself that the boy had somehow witched his mind. He'd seen ebony-skinned magicians on Rhodes cast their staves upon the ground and watched the rods transform into serpents and wriggle away before the eyes of an awestruck crowd. Those men could make your very eyes deceive you, as if you had drunk far too much strong wine.

But seeing is one thing, touching is another, and what he had felt in his hand was no trick of the eye. It was nothing less than a demon, its foul form concealed beneath a child's soft skin, like a cankerous worm lying coiled in the heart of a peach. But he had not confronted that fiend, not sent it howling back to Hell. Instead, he had run away from the creature, like a stable boy fleeing the field of battle.

Nicholas knew he could not make any mention of that encounter in the report that Alban was even now carrying to the Lord Prior of England, not if he hoped to be returned to the Citramer again, as Commander of the English Tongue there. A holy knight of St John, who admitted he could not even confront evil in the form of a small child, would be fortunate to find himself in charge of a midden heap.

From beyond the walls of the guest chamber he heard a yelp of pain and a stream of oaths from one man, answered by raucous laughter from the others. Someone had probably slipped on their backside in the filth of the courtyard.

But something else troubled him now. The night that Sebastian had tried to stab himself, when the heretic had shrieked and raged, sending all the other patients and sisters backing away in alarm, the boy had sat motionless on his bed, like a puppet that had been laid aside and would not move again until his master took him up. Had the boy been hag-riding Sebastian, driving him into fits of terror as he had the old priest? But why would a demon torment a heretic? They were both the devil's servants. And there could be no doubt that Sebastian was a proven heretic: the Inquisition did not permit anyone to live who had not fully admitted their guilt. But the prioress herself had told him that Sebastian had been tormented by these fits of madness long before the boy had arrived. So, if the boy was not controlling the man, then . . .

Was the prioress not only harbouring a heretic but also a sorcerer? She was seen to have private, whispered conversations with Sebastian, to go to him when he was seized by the visions of the torments of Hell that awaited him or the evil spirits that surrounded him. Had Johanne forced Sebastian to conjure a demon to serve her in the form of the child? Was that why she had given the man shelter? Was this the payment she was demanding from him?

The boy had appeared as if by magic, the very night he and Alban had ridden in, and he had tormented the blind priest to death before Nicholas had had a chance to question him. It was the hosteller, Sister Melisene, who had first accused the boy of murdering the old priest, and she seemed a practical creature, well used to dealing with all manner of men. Was it possible that Prioress Johanne herself had commanded this demon child to kill the old priest to stop Nicholas discovering the truth?

Words and phrases swept through his head, carried on a swelling tide of fear, but the only one he could snatch out of the flood was *malum* – evil. Evil! Put a sword in his hand and he would gladly have fought a dozen armed Saracens singlehanded. He had been trained all his life to face such enemies without flinching, but demons, sorcerers, he had no weapons to fight those. And that terrified him.

The light from the fires outside filled his chamber with a

dull red glow and shadows slithered across the wall so that it seemed no longer to be solid, but rippling, dissolving in front of him. Smoke mingled with blood, and the sickly smell of boiling flesh pushed its way in through every crack and crevice. The clatter of bones being hurled into the pails, the chatter of the servants and chopping of knives and axes grew ever louder until he could hear nothing else. He could see the servants transforming into creatures with monstrous birds' heads and lizards' tails, the great open mouths in their bellies snapping at the mangled goats. And they were laughing . . . laughing at him.

Chapter 45

Prioress Johanne

'Vinegar for pickling has almost gone, Prioress,' Sibyl said, rolling her eyes balefully in the direction of Sister Clarice, leaving no doubt as to whom she blamed. 'And the salt's finished too. Ground up the last cat of it an hour since, and that was one I rescued from the floor of the pigeon cote. Had to scrape the bird shit and feathers off it afore I could crush it. Couldn't salvage any more than a pound or so fit for use. I suppose it's a mercy the cote is almost empty and birds won't be needing salt. But what am I to do with these? I can't even set them on the drying racks in this weather.'

She gestured towards several wooden tubs that stood against the courtyard wall. They'd been covered with planks that had had to be weighted with rocks to stop the ravens and kites, which were already massing in the early-morning light, finding a way in. Our cook's hair was straggling down beneath the cloth that bound it. Her face, hands and sacking apron were streaked with dung and rusted with dried blood. She, like the other servants, looked exhausted, but she was still chivvying and scolding any scullion she caught snatching

369

a few minutes' rest. They had worked until dawn, and now that the last goat had been butchered, the yawning servants were scrubbing the blood from the trestle tables and tossing gory axes and knives into a tub ready to be cleaned and sharpened, just as soon as they'd filled their bellies.

'And those,' Sibyl pointed through the dark doorway into the cavernous kitchen where skinned goats' legs lay piled on the long table, 'I can build smoking stacks in the courtyard if we can get enough dry wood or peats, but what use is smoking the meat if I've no salt? And before you say honey, Sister Clarice, there's not enough of that left after the pickling to sweeten the temper of a toad. We should've had more salt in the stores.' She glared reproachfully at Clarice.

Seeing my steward's eyes flash dangerously, I hurriedly stepped between them. 'None of us could have known we'd have to salt down almost our entire herd of goats, Goodwife Sibyl.'

'And those salt cats don't sprout out of the ground like turnips,' Clarice said tartly. 'Have you any idea of the price those thieving merchants are asking for them? The panners can't dry salt in the rain any more than you can dry meat. You'll just have to—' She broke off, giving me a sharp jab in the ribs. 'You might want to make yourself scarce. Brother Nicholas is coming this way and he doesn't look happy!'

The warning came too late. I tried to step swiftly into the kitchen, but my direct route was blocked by a table in the yard and I found myself trapped.

I had asked a servant to deliver small ale and a platter of boiled goat's meat to Nicholas's chamber well before the usual breakfast hour, and instructed her to inform the knight that the refectory was being used by the cook to press the head meats for brawn, there being no space left in the kitchens.

She was to tell him that his meals would be served in his chamber and the sisters would eat in their dorter until the refectory could be cleared. I had hoped in that way I might avoid him for a few hours at least, but it seemed my prayer had not been answered.

Brother Nicholas's voice rang out imperiously even before he'd reached me. 'Where is the boy, Prioress Johanne?'

'If Brengy is not in the stables, he will probably be in the kitchen with his sister, Dye, helping with the goat carcasses. Why? Did you want your horse saddled? Are you planning to leave us like Brother Alban?'

I was aware of Clarice's gaze upon me, and found myself torn between hoping we were about to be rid of our brother and dread that she had been right: he would try to ride to Buckland and deliver his report in person to Commander John. It was too much to hope that neither Alban nor he would get through to Clerkenwell or Buckland.

'I'm not looking for the stable lad,' Nicholas snapped, 'I visited the infirmary last night, but I didn't see the blind boy there.'

My stomach churned. Why had he taken it into his head to visit the infirmary? Was it to question Sebastian?

'It was most thoughtful of you to visit the sick, Brother Nicholas. I am sure that they were much comforted.'

All the time I was talking, I was trying to edge away, though it was difficult: that corner of the yard was not only greasy with blood, dung and the contents of the goats' stomachs, it was also littered with kegs, pails and the other tools of last night's butchery.

'But the boy was not in the infirmary and I wish to question him,' he repeated firmly.

'And as I have explained many times, Brother Nicholas,

371

the boy is not able to speak. It is likely he has been dumb from birth, and since he is also blind, we cannot even make gestures to ask him if he is hungry, much less ask him questions.' This time I pointedly turned away from him and, lifting a pail, moved it out of my path, deliberately setting it between myself and my brother knight. But as I took a pace towards the kitchen, I was startled to feel a hand grasp my arm and heard a gasp of outrage from Clarice. The knight's fingers dug into my flesh, but I refused to flinch. I stared down at my arm, then up at Nicholas, meeting his gaze full on, determined to say nothing until he had removed his hand. For a long moment, we glared at each other, neither stirring. Then he grudgingly released me, his face flushed, though from his furious expression, it was not with embarrassment.

'I demand to see the boy, Sister Johanne.' His voice rang round the courtyard, bouncing from the walls.

'*Prioress* Johanne,' I said. 'And you may demand all you wish, Brother Nicholas. I will not allow you near that child.'

'I know who that creature is and I know you have tried to keep me from him since the day he arrived, afraid no doubt that I would discover his real nature. Is that heretic you harbour also a sorcerer? Did he conjure that demon boy? Is that why you whisper with him?'

I tried once more to walk away, fearing that any answer I gave might endanger Sebastian still further, for Nicholas would twist whatever I said. As I turned, I glimpsed several of the sisters and servants gazing at us curiously from doorways and casements. Nicholas was not troubling to keep his voice low – indeed, he seemed determined that the whole priory should hear him.

'That devil's spring lies at the heart of all of this,' he

thundered. 'That's why you and your coven of sisters seek to stay here, because the well is the source of all the evil and corruption that infest this priory. Is that why the heretic was drawn here, so that he could use its malevolent power for his sorcery? I will see that well of yours destroyed stone by stone and filled with rubble, so that no one can ever enter that place again. And as for the sorcerer who lies in your infirmary, I will finish what the Inquisition started. Do you know the penalty for a pardoned heretic who relapses into his old sin? He is burned on the pyre, Sister Johanne, burned alive.'

Nicholas took a step towards me, which would have been far more menacing had he not tripped over the pail I had placed there and stumbled sideways, having to grab at my skirts, like a child in clouts, to avoid crashing down on to the filthy stones.

Flushing still deeper, he drew himself upright. 'You cannot hope to hide that demon boy in a place such as this, *Sister* Johanne. I will seek him out and I will send him screaming back to the devil, his master. And, mark this, if you dare to stand in my way, I will have you bound hand and foot to that heretic and dragged to the pyre with him. I will see the two of you burn in this life and in the fires of Hell to come.'

Though I had known from the moment he arrived that he was determined to have me removed as prioress, even I was shocked by the malice that contorted his face. He was a knight of the holy order of St John, a monk who had devoted his life to the service of God: how could he be filled with such hatred? I found myself shaking, unable even to summon the words to begin to defend myself. How could you reason with a man who thought that a blind child was a creature summoned from Hell? I was beginning to think it was Nicholas who was blind. The boy was pure innocence, entrusted to my care by St Lucia herself. The more Nicholas sought to harm him, the more I knew I must protect him. If I could guard this child, keep him safe, then St Lucia and the Holy Virgin would surely defend us.

'Prioress! Prioress!' Meggy was hurrying across the courtyard.

A man shuffled awkwardly behind her, seemingly unable to make up his mind whether to come towards us or to retreat. His gaze slid to the bloodstained table and the tub of axes and knives that were steeping in the pool of gore that had dripped from them. Flies were crawling over the tub and more were buzzing over the puddles of dung and blood in the courtyard.

The man's eyes darted briefly to Clarice, Sibyl and me, but he addressed himself firmly to Brother Nicholas, as if certain the knight must be in charge.

'Thing is, there's a body been found out on moor. Reckon it to be one of yours seeing as how he's wearing the white cross. You want him brought in here?'

Nicholas frowned. 'A knight of our order? Dead?'

'As salt pork,' the man said. 'No question of it. Dogs and foxes have been at him, birds too, I reckon.'

'If he is of our order, you may lay the body in our chapel,' I said, gesturing towards the door. 'But has the coroner given leave for it to be moved and brought here?'

The man eyed me warily, as if I was some strange talking bird, and when he did speak, he addressed himself to Nicholas again. 'No call to be fetching any coroner. Found the body alongside the river. Water flows fast and deep there and with all this rain . . .' He spread his hands, which were

374

almost black with ingrained dirt. 'Reckon he must have got lost in the dark, and stumbled into the water. Managed to drag himself out, but was too exhausted to move. He'd have lain there and died of the cold, I shouldn't wonder. Seen it afore a heap of times, I have, 'specially when men have had a drop or two more cider than is good for 'em. Hound belonging to one of our lads was sniffing around and found the body behind a great heap of tailings. We're not dumping waste there any more, see, 'cause we're working further along the valley.'

'We?'

'Tinners. That's where we found him, on tinners' land. So, you see, there's no call to be dragging coroner all the way out here. Natural death, it was, in as much as any can be called natural. Nothing for the coroner to be fretting himself over. But we thought it only right he be given a decent burial, if he was one of yours. We don't want any man accusing us of trying to hide a corpse. So, we fetched him here. Lost a day's work over it, we have.'

'No knight would go walking over the moor,' Nicholas said. 'If he was on a journey for our order he would have been riding. Where is his horse?'

'There you are, mystery solved,' the man announced happily. 'His horse must have thrown him off into the river. No crime's been committed, save by the horse, that is. Beast will be miles away by now. Still, if we should happen to catch it, I dare say there'll be a reward.' He looked Nicholas up and down. 'There's none in your order rides anything but the best blood. Worth more than most men earn in a lifetime, those horses of yours. And, like I say, times being what they are, a man can't afford to lose even an hour's work. For it's our poor wives and chillern that'll go hungry 'cause of it, though they didn't ask for any knight to go wandering into the river,' he added.

'When you have fetched the corpse in, go to the alms window and I shall instruct Sister Melisene to give you food enough for your family's supper tonight,' I told him.

'Food?' The tinner could not have looked more affronted if he'd been promised a flock of sheep and received only a skein of wool.

'Think yourselves fortunate to be getting anything,' Clarice said, eyeing him shrewdly. 'For I dare say you've already helped yourself to your own reward.'

A spasm of what might have been guilt flashed across the man's face under Clarice's steely glare, but it vanished rapidly and he turned back to Nicholas. 'Could have left him where we found him, 'stead of hefting him all the way up here,' he said plaintively.

But his efforts to appeal man to man were wasted, for Nicholas was loudly commanding us to fetch candles and a bier on which to place the body, as if he was in charge. Since we had no bier, I instructed the man to wait until the blood had been scrubbed from the trestle table and it had been carried into the chapel, then set before the altar ready to receive the body. When that had been done, two tinners lugged the tightly wrapped cadaver inside and dumped it, none too gently, on the rough wood. They slouched off towards the alms window, muttering that they should have buried the carrion under a spoil heap and spared themselves the effort.

Most of the sisters, who'd been listening to Nicholas shouting in the courtyard, now crowded into the chapel behind us, crossing themselves and staring at the bundle. Sister Fina hastened to light the candles on the altar, then pressed herself back against one of the pillars, holding it on either side as if she could not stand without support. I was on the verge of sending her out: I feared what the sight of a corpse might do to her. I knew she'd resent it, though, so I allowed her to stay.

I decided it might be wise for once to allow Brother Nicholas to have his way and take charge of the deceased. It was, after all, a brother knight who lay dead and Nicholas might recognise him. At the very least, he would be diverted from thoughts of demons and sorcery.

The head and shoulders of the dead man were encased in a filthy sack and lengths of soiled cloth had been wrapped around the body, bound tightly in place with lengths of straw rope, trussing it from neck to ankle. The tinners were plainly not prepared to waste a serviceable cloak or blanket on a corpse.

'I must discover who this brother is,' Nicholas said pompously, the moment the door closed behind the tinners. 'His preceptor will have to be informed without delay. He will want to send knights to collect the body for burial in his own priory.'

He motioned us back with his knife as if we were the fluttering wives of noblemen, who must be kept from unpleasant sights in case we swooned. Clarice raised her eyebrows at me, but I mouthed at her to let him get on with it. At least it was keeping him from the infirmary.

Nicholas set to work with his knife, sawing at the straw rope. From the tail of my eye, I saw Fina flinch as each band broke and the body beneath sagged, as if she feared that, freed from its bonds, it might leap up and attack her. Nicholas cut the final rope around the ankles and a pair of feet flopped out from beneath the cloth, revealing blue-white mottled skin and horny toenails.

'A brother of our order riding barefoot?' I said.

Clarice snorted. 'I dare say he was well shod when he was found, but those tinners wouldn't let a pair of good boots or hose go to waste. I wouldn't be surprised if we find half his clothes have accidentally fallen off in the river too.'

Nicholas took hold of the ends of the sack that covered the man's head and tugged, but the sack would not come off.

'Stuck to the skin,' he said. He tried again, almost jerking the corpse on to the floor in his impatience.

Only with Clarice's help, and a great deal of pulling, did the sack finally slide free. It gave way so suddenly that the man's head thumped back on to the wood. But it was not the crash that made those standing around cry out.

Nicholas's jaw tightened so hard that it was a wonder he didn't splinter his teeth. I realised I was doing the same. Most of the sisters were trying to disguise their hastily averted gazes by crossing themselves and murmuring prayers.

The face of death is rarely known for its beauty, but this face, or what was left of it, was enough to make the bile of even the battle-hardened rise in their throats. The nose, lips, tongue and part of one cheek had been chewed off, leaving a cavernous black hole and a mocking grin of teeth stained rust red by the man's own blood. The eyes had been pecked out and the skin of the forehead, which had been stuck to the sacking by dried mucus and blood, had peeled off the flesh beneath as the cloth had been torn away.

No one spoke. A long moment passed before even I could unclench my jaw to force out the words, 'Ch-Christ have mercy on his soul. This must be the work of wild dogs or foxes. For pity's sake cover his face, Brother Nicholas. Let us offer our brother some dignity in death.'

Nicholas picked up the stained, stinking sack and tried to drape it over the ravaged face. But Clarice tugged it out of his hand, letting it fall to the flags. She trotted to the chest containing the altar cloths, took out a small white linen manuterge and laid it over the head. She threw a defiant glance at Nicholas, as if daring him to protest at this misuse of a sacred object, but for once he was silent.

'We'll have to examine the rest of the body,' I said grimly. 'I fear even his closest friends would find it impossible to identify our brother from his face and it will be harder as each day passes. In my experience, decay is more rapid wherever there is a wound. Perhaps some item of his clothes or his scrip will help.'

Nicholas did not acknowledge that I had spoken, but he began silently removing the pieces of soiled cloth from the feet up, as if even he was reluctant to approach the head again.

'It would appear that for once you have been overly harsh in your judgement of the tinners, Sister Clarice. His jerkin appears to be still in place, though—' Nicholas broke off, as he lifted the sack covering the corpse's belly.

We could see at once why the tinners had been reluctant to strip anything more than the boots from the corpse, for even had they removed the black jerkin, they could not have sold it or given it away even to the most desperate of beggars. It was so badly shredded and mauled, it looked as if it had been thrown into a pack of hounds for them to fight over. And the dogs, if they had done this, had not merely savaged the cloth, but also the soft belly beneath it. The corpse had been eviscerated, the stomach, liver and guts torn out, leaving a gaping hole, black with dried blood.

'Tears of Mary!' Clarice muttered grimly. 'It seems those

379

tinners were right not to bother sending for the coroner. Only this man's ghost could tell you if he met his death by accident or foul murder. He could have taken a dozen stab wounds to the face or belly and there'd be no knowing it now. If it was the same pack of hounds that attacked our goats, there's someone hunting out there whom I'd not want to run into after dark.'

Several flies, which had found their way in through the holes in the chapel shutters, came buzzing towards the corpse and immediately crawled inside the belly. Nicholas flapped at them and quickly drew the filthy cloth back over the wound.

'We must get the corpse into the stone drying coffin until his preceptor can arrange to collect him for burial,' he said curtly. 'Otherwise this body, too, will begin breeding flies and all manner of flesh worms to infest the chapel again. And I mean to put an end to these plagues once and for all.' He glowered at me.

'But how are we to know which priory to send word to?' Now that the wounds were covered, Basilia had found her voice. 'He may have recently arrived by ship or have been making his way to a port to board one. In either case, his priory will not yet realise he is missing and be searching for him.' She gnawed her lip. 'If he had a scrip . . . or a purse.'

'If he had a purse you can be sure that's long gone,' Clarice said.

'Look!' Fina was still standing with her back pressed hard against the pillar. She gestured wildly towards the corpse. 'His hand . . . the right one, see!' Her words ended in a high-pitched shriek.

I glanced down. The man's arm had slipped, so that it was dangling off the table. I took a step closer and, pinching

380

the cloth of his sleeve, pulled the arm upwards. The skin was dark with pooled blood and smeared with dried mud, but that did not disguise the fact that the hand was missing the forefinger and half of the middle finger.

Nicholas gaped at it. 'Alban! But it can't be. He should be on his way to . . .' He lifted the linen manuterge covering the corpse's face and stared briefly at the mauled flesh beneath, closing his eyes and breathing hard as he dropped it back. Gingerly he lifted the edge of the cloth covering the gaping hole in Alban's belly.

'His belt, the scrip . . . they're gone! Those tinners, are they still here?'

Without waiting for an answer, which none of us in the chapel could have given him, he ran towards the door.

'Aren't you going to stay with us to pray for him, Brother Nicholas?' I called, but the only reply I received was the slamming of the chapel door.

I stared again at the corpse, trying to picture Alban as I had last seen him alive, wrestling with the beam on the great door. I realised he had not been wearing the large leather scrip. On such a rough track, it would have bumped against him constantly as he rode, irritating both rider and horse. Instead it had been strapped to his saddle along with his blankets and provisions.

If outlaws or tinners had taken his horse, they had all that Alban was carrying, including Nicholas's report. It was unlikely that any man who had stolen it could read. They would simply have burned it, with anything else that might incriminate them. And if the horse was found wandering by an honest man on the moor, he would recognise the Hospitallers' seal and would surely bring both beast and scrip to us. Either way, that report would not now reach Clerkenwell. Relief washed over me, swiftly followed by guilt that my deliverance had been at the cost of a man's life. I sank to my knees and tried to pray for Alban's soul.

Chapter 46

Hospitallers' Priory of St Mary

Brother Nicholas eyed the lump of bread with disgust. Even prisoners received larger portions than this. On the other hand, did he really want to eat any more of it? God alone knew what it had been made from, ground goat bone judging by its dryness. But he knew from experience that a diet of meat alone turned your excrement to rocks. Years of hard riding in sweaty armour had caused him enough problems with his backside without the pain that came from straining for hours over a draughty shithole.

Nicholas spooned some of the goats' liver and heart pottage into a bowl and crumbled the bread into the sour gravy. He told himself he must have eaten worse in the service of the order, though not much, but as his growling belly now reminded him, he'd swallowed nothing since that early breakfast of goat's meat. No one had had much appetite after they'd seen Alban's body, but now his head was throbbing and he felt dizzy with hunger. He'd have to shovel this pigswill down.

He stabbed his knife into another piece of what, from its

texture, seemed to be a lump of lung. God's teeth, it was rank. Not even the strong sauce masked it. Were they trying to poison him? The thought took hold and he felt the whole mess rising in his gorge.

He dropped to his knees and flung open the lid of his wooden chest, rummaging feverishly until his fingers grasped an object the size and shape of a walnut enclosed in a pierced silver case, which dangled from a chain. He had bought the bezoar years before from an Arab trader and had always carried it on his belt, but since he'd been living in Buckland, he'd not felt the need to arm himself with such protection until now. Holding it by the chain, he staggered to his feet and dipped the silver case in the remaining wine, then drained the goblet in a single gulp. He breathed more easily as the goat pottage settled itself in his stomach. If it had indeed been poisoned, the bezoar would render it harmless. But he'd certainly lost his appetite again.

Alban was dead. Would he be next? A brother of his order was even now lying mutilated in the chapel on the same table they'd used to hack those goats into bloody pieces. And he knew exactly who was responsible. That boy! That devil! That demon of the witch Johanne! She had commanded him to kill Alban just as surely as he had murdered the old priest. What other explanation could there be?

In all his years in the order, Nicholas had met few riders more skilful than Alban. On the journey to the priory, when a deep mud hole had brought the sergeant's rouncy crashing to its knees or when its hind legs had slipped from under it on a treacherous slope, Alban had not only kept his seat, as if his arse was nailed to the saddle, he had got the horse back on its feet and calmed it, before the beast had realised what had happened. Nothing less than a demon from Hell could have so spooked both horse and rider to cause a man like Alban to be thrown.

Nicholas knew only too well what demons could do. In the Holy Land, he'd seen tiny swirls of dust swell into mighty whirling djinn that flogged all in their path with whips of scorpion stings. They could pluck up a rider and his horse together, carry them through the air and fling them down a dozen miles away. He had seen a soft night sky fill with a thousand shrieking black imps that had flown at bands of men, fastening on to the eyes and flesh of horses and knights, sending the horses rearing and bolting in panic while their blinded riders lay crushed and trampled beneath the plunging hoofs. An innocent form could disguise fiends of such power and evil, that even the strongest warrior was powerless against them.

Nicholas wrenched open the door of the guest chamber, admitting a blast of icy night air, and peered out into the courtyard. Unlike the night before, the yard was unusually deserted and dark. Both sisters and servants, exhausted by the hours spent butchering and preserving the meat, had fallen into their beds almost before the last rays of the sun had vanished, some barely able to keep their eyes open long enough to pick at the boiled goat on their trenchers.

A few candles burned in casements, set ready in case anyone should need to rise in the night. Their faint glow flickered around the edges of the shutters. Nicholas's gaze methodically quartered every wall in turn, like a hound trying to pick up a scent. Earlier that day he had convinced himself that the boy had been hidden in the refectory, which was why the sisters were trying to keep him out. So, while they were in the chapel praying for Alban's soul, he had searched it but, to his disgust, had found nothing but dishes of goat meat being pressed into brawn, just as Johanne had said.

He'd waited until Basilia and the lay servants were occupied in preparing Alban's body, then slipped behind the screen in the infirmary, determined to question Sebastian, the conjuror of Johanne's demon. Nicholas would have been the first to admit he lacked the skill and finesse of the Grand Inquisitors. They understood that it was not enough merely to inflict pain. Men can grow inured to it. You have to break their minds and spirits, drag them down into the sucking mire of despair and hopelessness, so that they no longer even imagine there can be a Heaven. You must convince them that only you possess the truth, that everything they once held dear is a lie, that they are a lie. You must make them believe they are not even men. And an art like that is not mastered overnight.

But, still, Nicholas was only too aware that the memory of a battle could be more terrifying than the battle itself. Simply pressing his weight on an already twisted, dislocated joint or forcing open clawed fingers could reawaken the horror in Sebastian, remind him of what he had suffered and what awaited him again if he were to be delivered back into the tender mercies of the Inquisition. That might be sufficient to loosen his tongue.

But as soon as Nicholas had approached his bed, he'd known it was useless. Sebastian lay insensible, drugged to the point that Nicholas could have smashed his leg with a hammer, eliciting no more than a groan, much less a single word that made sense. Johanne's instructions, Nicholas had had no doubt. But she couldn't keep him asleep for ever, not without killing him, and the prioress needed her sorcerer alive.

Nicholas closed the door of the guest chamber and shuffled back across to the smouldering fire. He poked savagely at the sulky embers trying to stir them into a blaze, though at this hour, the fire should have been safely damped down for the night. He glimpsed a tiny movement on the floor and brought the poker thudding down with a great clang. He felt a satisfying crunch under the iron.

'Got you, you little imp.' He crouched, then straightened again, swinging the mangled remains of a mouse by the tail. He let it dangle for a moment, revelling in the proof that the swiftness and accuracy of his sword arm had not diminished, then dropped the tiny corpse on to the fire. The impudent creature had gnawed holes in his boots during the night. Well, the vermin had paid for its crime now. But, as if they were thumbing their noses at him, he heard the scurry of a dozen more in the rafters.

Nicholas threw himself down on to his bed, which groaned beneath his weight. It was the boy. He was drawing these plagues here. All the filth and evil in the land were crawling out of the ground towards him. Those foul creatures could smell the stench of the devil in the priory. Beelzebub, Lord of the Dunghill, was calling to his minions. Even the birds of ill omen flocked over the place where the boy was, hundreds gathering on the roofs and walls, waiting and watching over their master. That demon child was the curse that infected this place, a curse summoned by the witch Johanne and her sorcerer.

And she had surrounded herself with a treacherous sisterhood who thought nothing of cheating any man who crossed their path, like every woman Nicholas had ever met. They had continually lied to the villagers about the well. They had even tried to keep Nicholas, a brother in their own order, from discovering the truth of what lay down there. Lies came so easily to their lips that they didn't even hesitate or blush with shame. They—

The well . . . That was it! That was where they'd hidden the boy. Nicholas struck his head with his hand. How could he not have known it at once? Where had the frogs and flies swarmed to their demon king? Down in that cave! That was where the fiend would assume its true form. Why were the sisters trying so hard to keep himself and all the pilgrims from the spring, even though it was losing them money? Because they knew a demon had taken up residence down there. But no more! He would send that monster howling back to Hell whence he had come. And once he had defeated that devil, the sisters would have no weapon to send out against him, as they had against Alban and the priest. Then he would see to it that the whole coven of hags was dragged to Clerkenwell in irons.

Meggy stood in the doorway of her small hut, huddled in a blanket, blinking up at Brother Nicholas. She never removed her clothes when she was abed. In fact, often she did not trouble to lie down, preferring to doze in her chair close to the warmth of the fire. At her age, sleep came quickly, but did not linger long, so she was more than a little vexed to be jerked awake by a thumping on her door. She eased it open a crack, grumbling all the while that such shocks were not good for a body at her age.

'What is it? If you've a mind to go out, the gates are locked for the night and no one enters or leaves till the Prime bell.'

'I have no wish to depart,' Nicholas said. 'I have come for the key to the chapel and the well. And before you protest, old woman, many souls in this priory may perish if I do not succeed in my work tonight.'

Meggy took a step outside and peered across the courtyard towards the prioress's casement. It was in darkness.

Nicholas caught her arm and stepped in front of her, so that she was forced to pay attention to him. 'The prioress has retired for the night. It is I who demand the keys. As a brother of this order I have every right to enter the chapel and the well at any hour of the day or night I see fit. And as a knight of St John, I can, as easily as the prioress, have you dismissed and banished from this place. You would do well to remember that.'

Meggy pulled the blanket tighter about her shoulders against the cruel wind. 'If you want to spend the night freezing in the chapel that's naught to do with me. But you might have fetched the keys afore decent folks retired to their beds, 'stead of disturbing them in the middle of the night. Up all last night I was, 'cause of those goats. Not a whisker of sleep did I have, and here you are banging on my door, dragging me from my fireside, when I've only just managed to close my eyes. It's not Christian. Call yourself a holy knight? You ought to have more consideration.'

She bustled inside, emerging moments later with a ring of keys, which she thrust into his hand. 'You make sure you lock up after you and don't you go banging on my door again tonight. You can give me the keys back at a decent hour, when the sun's at least had time to wash his face.'

Nicholas edged into the chapel and closed the door quietly behind him. He did not want to warn the demon that he was coming. He lifted the lantern and peered around.

Five fat candles had been lit around Alban's body, which still lay on the rough wooden trestle beneath a long white cloth. Raw wool had been packed beneath it to absorb the

389

liquids dripping from it. But even though thyme and other dried herbs had been bound into the winding sheet, the stench of putrefaction was beginning to fill the chapel.

An image flashed into Nicholas's head. Bloated bodies lying strewn across a sun-scorched earth. The sky almost bronze above the shimmering heat haze. The deathly silence, save only for the head-splitting buzzing of the flies that covered the corpses in a dense black crust, and the flapping of the vultures' wings as they lumbered to the earth to stab at the swollen bellies. And that smell, the sweet, gagging stench of rotting flesh: it clung to your clothes, your hair, your skin; it slid down your throat and filled your nostrils and mouth till you could taste and smell nothing else for days, maybe for a lifetime.

Nicholas glanced up, trying to wipe the memory from his mind. He stared at the bowed head of the crucified Christ on the altar haloed by the soft light shining down from the oil lamp hanging above. Kneeling on the hard, cold stones, he bowed his own head and tried to gather his faltering strength for the battle that would take place in the depths below. The fiend, the beast of Satan, was squatting directly beneath the body of the man he had already killed. Nicholas could see it. Its great frog eyes bulging, unblinking. Its long snake tongue coiled, ready to lash out. Could it sense the presence of the knight above it? Was it preparing to take another victim? His hand slid towards the hilt of the sword hanging from his belt. Could this demon be defeated by steel? If he had been facing a man, ten men even, excitement would have borne him up, but he found himself gripped by something he had rarely known before a battle: a cold tide of abject fear.

He prayed fervently. He found himself repeating the same words over and over again, and that chilled him the more, for he could feel the demon crouching beneath him, sucking his breath from his body so that he could barely think, much less remember how to pray.

In the end, it was the pain from kneeling on the merciless stone that drove Nicholas, tottering, to his feet. He took up the lantern and advanced towards the well door. It was only as he struggled to fit the prongs of the key into the holes in the wooden bolts on the other side that he remembered he had not bolted the chapel door. He hesitated, then realised he would feel safer if he left it unlocked. At least if he was forced to flee, he would not be left grappling to open his only escape route.

He paused at the top of the steps, holding the lantern low so the light was cast as far down as it could reach, which was only the first few steps. Beyond that, the darkness rose up, reaching out to drag him down. He listened, but heard only the sound of his own heart thumping and his rapid breaths. No water splashed or even dripped. Although he knew the spring had stopped flowing, the silence was unnerving, ominous. Should he call out a challenge? Even as he opened his mouth, he knew the words wouldn't come. With one hand pressed against the wall, he edged down the stairs, but though he tried to tread lightly, the gritty mud on the soles of his shoes ground against the stone with each step he took, echoing through the granite till it sounded, even to his ears, as if a great scaly creature was clawing its way down.

As he descended, the walls began to shimmer with that green-gold glow. But it served only to remind Nicholas of what lay at the bottom: the monstrous poison-green beast. The glistening walls no longer seemed miraculous, but as if the bloated creature had slimed the walls of its lair as it passed up and down, like a slug leaves a shining trail wherever it crawls. He snatched his hand away from the wall, rubbing icy wetness on his breeches. Why had he not realised from the first that this unnatural light was a sign of evil? But the steps, though he knew they were solid, seemed to undulate beneath his feet, twisting in the eerie, flickering light, until he was forced to press his hand against the wall once more, just to keep from plunging down into the bottomless mire of darkness.

He paused on the steps as the lantern illuminated the entrance to the cave. Something was squatting in the deep shadow just beyond the glow of the candlelight. He froze, heart thudding, staring until his eyes hurt, watching for the slightest twitch of movement.

He grasped the hilt of his sword, but the stairs were too narrow to draw it. He should have had it ready in his hand. He was a knight of St John. It was second nature to him. The demon had bewitched him, was fuddling his mind, making him forget the most basic lesson that had been beaten into him long before his voice had broken.

He thrust the lantern forward so that the light pierced deep into the cave. Where the creature had been squatting, he now saw only the side of the coffin-like trough, covered with green moss. Where had it gone? He swept the lantern about, but the cave was empty. Had he been staring at the basin all along, or had the demon transformed itself and was hiding? But unless it had made itself as small as a spider, there was no crevice large enough to conceal it. Unless the beast was crouching inside the trough . . .

He raised the light high, trying to peer inside the long stone basin without leaving the comparative safety of the last step. The yellow candlelight showed only a rim of red mud, and above it, on the far side, a face. He had never seen the carving without its veil of water, but now that it was naked, grinning out at him, he realised it was a skull, with vipers writhing from the dark eye sockets and darting out from between its grimacing jaws. As he moved, so the snakes in the shadows moved too. The jaws of the skull opened wider and more vipers wriggled out, their tongues tasting the air. In his terror, every word of defence he knew against the forces of darkness fled from his brain. Raising his arm to shield his face from the devilish sight, he turned to flee.

It was then that the guttering lantern light caught something black behind him on the stairs. He saw the flash of steel and instinct made him jerk back even before his mind had registered that it was a blade. His foot missed the step below him and he crashed down. His head cracked against the wall, as the knife slashed towards his face.

Chapter 47

Prioress Johanne

I eased the door of the chapel open and stood on the threshold listening. When Meggy had come to my chamber grumbling that Brother Nicholas had roused her from her bed to demand the keys, I had sent her back to her gatehouse and hurried over at once.

I had told Sister Clarice that I had managed to persuade Brother Nicholas that Alban's body could not be taken to Buckland for burial until the first frosts.

'Being as wet as it is, I reckon that if it turns colder we're more likely to have snow than frost up here,' she had said. 'That means there'll be no moving him off the moor till spring.'

'The point is, we must stop the body being taken anywhere, now or then. If Commander John or the Lord Prior should learn that a Hospitaller was murdered here, we shall have the whole order riding in to investigate. I think even Brother Nicholas understands that he couldn't get a cart further than our gates without it becoming hopelessly bogged down. But he is demanding to take the heart to Buckland for burial at least, which he says he can do on horseback, whatever the weather. And I suspect he could, given his skill as a rider and his determination. Once there, he is bound to be questioned about how the man died. Commander John will not let Brother Alban's death go unavenged.'

'Aye, and that low-bellied viper will waste no time in tattling to Commander John all he thinks he's discovered that's amiss here, including my accounts, not that he's got a mote of proof,' Clarice had added indignantly.

'Then we had better see to it that Brother Nicholas does not leave this priory,' I had said. Missing money was the least of the crimes Nicholas would report, if he had the chance. Half the priory had heard what he'd threatened and those who hadn't had certainly learned of it by now.

I cursed myself. I had already given orders that a grave be dug and that Alban should be buried at first light. With the ground so sodden and the corpse so mutilated, it would decay rapidly in the earth, and if we could keep Brother Nicholas out of the way until the grave was filled, even he might balk at digging it up, especially if we could convince him the heart would have rotted. I had thought to let the body lie before the altar until dawn, for by rights a corpse should lie for three days as Christ's had done. The soul must be given time to move on, before the earthly remains are laid in the ground. Alban was a Hospitaller and he deserved that much at least.

But now I knew that I should have had Alban interred straight away. Nicholas was probably even now cutting out the heart. Why else would he have demanded the keys to the chapel at this hour? Which meant he had determined to set out for Buckland tonight. I had to prevent that, whatever the cost.

But as soon as I entered I saw that the chapel was empty, at least of the living. Had Nicholas already removed the heart? I crossed swiftly to Alban's body and drew back the cloth that covered it. The winding sheet was still in place, the cord still tightly bound around the neck, thighs and ankles. Just to reassure myself, I laid my hand upon the chest, feeling for any signs that the ribs had been broken open. Those, at least, seemed to be intact. Relief flooded through me, swiftly followed by guilt. I had thought so little of Nicholas that it had not occurred to me that he might simply have wanted to keep vigil and offer his prayers for the soul of our brother. Though even as that struck me, I confess I was shocked that his prayers should have been quite so perfunctory, for he must have left the chapel before Meggy had even finished telling me he was there. Otherwise I would have seen him crossing the courtyard. Most knights of our order would have remained kneeling in vigil till dawn.

I knelt too, to beg mercy on Alban's soul, though I had already spent some hours in prayer for him. But my prayers now were also brief for the hour was late and I would have to rise before dawn to see that the body was laid to rest as deep as possible in the earth. I was on the point of scrambling to my feet when I heard something that sounded like slow footfalls.

I rose swiftly, fearing that someone was behind me, but I could see no one. Stone amplifies and distorts sound, so I couldn't be sure of the direction, but as I strained to listen again, I realised it was coming from below my feet. The cave! I glanced towards the well door. The pool of light cast by the trembling candle flames that stood sentinel around Alban's corpse did not reach as far as the wall and the door lay in deep shadow. But as I edged towards it, I saw it was partly open.

If that was Brother Nicholas moving about, then what on earth was he doing down there? Certainly not collecting holy water, that was for certain, for there was no sound of splashing to indicate the spring was flowing again. A thought struck me. Was it possible *he* had caused the water to run red and had blamed the tinners for it? And had he somehow managed deliberately to block the flow? He'd boasted of his knowledge of how to poison water supplies. Was that what he was doing down there now, poisoning the holy water, so that the pilgrims would fall sick and our priory would be closed? Only that morning he had threatened to destroy the well, fill it with rubble so that it could never be used again. Was he even now carrying out his threat?

I had no weapons except the knife at my belt and I knew I was no match for a trained knight. But I could not stand aside and let him do this wicked thing. At the very least, I intended to catch him in the act and confront him.

Chapter 48

Hospitallers' Priory of St Mary

Brother Nicholas felt as if he was lying at the bottom of a deep, dark, water-filled pit, staring up into a small circle of sunlight. He couldn't move his limbs. He could hear voices, but the sounds were far off, muffled. Two figures in black hovered above him, locked together, struggling, fighting. He caught the flash of a blade. Then the small patch of sunlight shrivelled into a tiny ball and vanished. All was silence and darkness.

'Brother Nicholas, open your eyes.'

Something was crawling down his face. Flies? He tried to bat them away, but his arm had been turned to stone. He could scarcely lift it. A cold ring closed about his neck. Water! Water was trickling over his skin. Was he drowning? He forced his eyes open and pain seared through his head. Only as it subsided into a dull throb did his mind begin to grasp where he was.

He was lying on his bed in the now too familiar guest chamber. Sister Basilia's massive breasts almost slapped his chest as she bent over him to peel a sodden cloth from his forehead, immediately replacing it with another dripping icy water. He winced as she smoothed it across his brow, pressing it against the tender lump on the side of his head, which seemed to be the source of his pain.

'How are you feeling, Brother Nicholas?' Prioress Johanne was standing at the foot of his bed, her face illuminated from beneath by the candle set on the table. She looked like a talking skull.

Skull, where had he seen . . .? Vipers pouring out from between the jaws . . . Someone on the steps behind him . . . someone with a knife.

He struggled to sit up, but Sister Basilia pushed down on his shoulder with her not inconsiderable weight. 'You must lie still, Brother. You struck your head, and if you get up too soon, you'll feel dizzy and sick. We don't want you falling again and giving yourself another nasty little bump, now do we?' she cajoled, in the jolly tone that a mother would use when trying to divert a small child from crying over a grazed knee.

She was right about feeling sick, though. Nicholas was afraid to sit up again for fear that he would disgrace himself and vomit. He resolved to lie still, at least until the bed stopped rolling, like the deck of ship.

'What happened? I was down in the cave . . . How did I get here?'

'You slipped,' Johanne said briskly, 'and banged your head on the rock. Meggy helped me to drag you up into the chapel. It wasn't easy getting you up those stairs. If you hadn't been found, you might have lain unconscious in the well all night, probably for days. When I saw the chapel was empty, I was about to relock it. Only by the grace and blessed intervention of St Lucia was I moved to check the well first.

We must give thanks to her for that miracle. You could easily have died of the cold. What were you doing down there in the middle of the night, Brother Nicholas? The spring is dry. And you, above all people, must be very well aware of that.' Her tone had grown suddenly sharp and suspicious.

But Nicholas ignored the question. He had one or two of his own.

'I slipped because someone crept down behind me on the stairs. Someone who tried to stab me.'

'Stab?' Johanne gave a slight smile. 'It would appear you are still a little confused from the blow to your head. I am told our recollection of events is often jumbled, when we have been rendered unconscious. Isn't that so, Sister Basilia?'

The infirmarer nodded enthusiastically. 'Some men can't remember anything that happened on the day they were injured. One I tended thought it was still Lent when it was just a week from Michaelmas. And there was a woman who couldn't even remember her own name. Swore she'd never been married when her poor husband was standing right there with the half-dozen children she'd borne him clinging to his breeches. When she clapped eyes on him she—'

'I know exactly who I am,' Nicholas bellowed, though he instantly regretted it as a spear of pain shot through his skull. He tried to keep his tone level. 'I can remember with perfect clarity what happened down in that cave. Someone was standing behind me with an upraised knife. If I'd not slipped, that blade would, at this moment, be sticking out of my back, or I'd be lying in that well with my throat sliced open. I don't know who it was because her face was hidden in the shadow on the stairs, but I do know it was a sister in this priory. I saw her black kirtle.'

Sister Basilia's hand shot to her mouth and she gave a

strangled gasp, as if she was the one who was going to faint. 'Why would anyone wish to harm you, Brother? No sister in our order would ever do such a wicked thing to any living soul, much less to a brother knight. It's that bang on your head that's making you imagine such terrible things.'

But Nicholas was not listening to the infirmarer: his gaze was fixed on the prioress's face.

'Sister Basilia is right. I fear you misunderstood what you saw, Brother Nicholas, which is hardly surprising in the confusion. You may indeed have seen someone on the stairs carrying a knife but, I assure you, no one was attempting to stab you. It seems that while Meggy was in my chamber, explaining that you had borrowed her keys, Sister Fina was crossing the courtyard to the garderobe, when she caught sight of a light moving behind the chapel window. Knowing that the chapel should have been locked at that hour, she was naturally concerned that thieves had broken in and went, rather foolishly, to investigate, instead of rousing the lay-servants. She is keeper of the well and has come to believe that it is her responsibility to protect it. She says she saw the well door open and could hear someone walking down the steps, so she followed them, and pulled out her knife to defend herself, should she have need. As soon as you turned, she saw who you were and quickly withdrew so as not to disturb you. You must have slipped as she was climbing back up the steps. The floor of the cave is treacherous.'

Sister Basilia beamed with evident relief. 'There, you see? I knew there was no harm intended. Hardly a wonder Sister Fina should have been afraid that thieves and outlaws had broken in after what had happened to dear Brother Alban, God save his soul. It's my belief it was outlaws who set upon that poor man and killed him. Since this famine came upon us, they've grown so bold and reckless that it's not safe to cross our own courtyard after dark.'

She crossed herself, gazing anxiously at the closed shutter of the chamber, as if she feared that a band of bloodthirsty robbers might even at that moment be massing on the other side of the flimsy wood, preparing to attack.

The infirmarer might have been convinced by Johanne's story, but Nicholas was as far from reassured as it was possible to be. He knew now he had seen two sisters on the stairs, as he'd briefly regained consciousness, but neither had been rushing to his aid. One had been trying to hold back the other, he was sure. But what he didn't know was whose hand had been holding the knife.

Chapter 49

Sorrel

'Tonight, it'll begin tonight,' Morwen said. 'We must summon the spirits to help us.'

My whole body tingled. Though I'd no notion what would happen, I knew this was why Brigid had called me. I could feel a power growing inside me, like a flame that runs silent and unseen, burning beneath the thatch till suddenly the whole village is ablaze.

'Are we going to Fire Tor?' I asked her.

'Can't go there. Ma'll be waiting. She'll have set her curses on the tor to keep us out. She'll try to fight us and we've no time to waste dealing with her. It's Brigid we must serve now. We must go to the place where the spirits walked long afore they were driven into the shadows. They were strong in life and are even stronger in death. You'll see.'

I took her hand, which was warm in mine, and we clambered over the ridge in the dawn light, following the path of a surging river that ran along the bottom of the steep-sided valley. Streams and rivulets ran down the sides of the gorge into the river from tar-black bog pools and glistening rocks.

A brown buzzard watched us from its perch in a dead tree, jagged as a broken tooth against the swelling granite-grey clouds.

Morwen stared up. 'It'll be a duru moon tonight – that's when the door to the other worlds opens. Ma'll be at work too, but she'll not be able to stop us.'

As we came around the curve of the hill, Morwen gestured towards a long strip of dense woodland that hung above the river. 'That's where the spirits gather. My granddam told me that, hundreds of years ago, the tribes who lived in these parts brought their cunning women and men here to be buried. The oaks are sacred. They keep watch over the dead. No one ever cuts wood from these trees, or comes here unless they know the charms and the gift to bring, 'cause Crockern keeps his wisht hounds here and they guard it.'

She tugged me back towards the riverbank. 'Afore we go into the woods, we must wash. The old 'uns will be offended else.'

We stripped off our kirtles and left them by a small rowan tree just before the first oak. Morwen scrambled naked into the river. She arched her back and shivered in the shock of freezing water, but as soon as she found a place to balance herself against the strong current, she held out her hand to me. I slipped off the bank and down into the water. I gasped. It was so cold it sucked the breath from my chest. The current knocked my feet from beneath me, and I shot under the water, but Morwen clung to me, dragging me up. I was gasping and coughing, but we were both giggling. Our teeth were chattering like magpies.

Morwen ducked three times beneath the water and I copied her. We were rigid, our lips blue, our feet stabbed with knives of ice. The wind chilled our dripping heads, but we grinned at each other, though we were so numb we could scarcely move our lips. We hauled each other back on to the bank, squeezed the water from our hair and rubbed each other's limbs to warm them.

Morwen pulled some green reeds from the bank and I watched her tie them into the rough form of a doll. A brideog, she called it. She started to make one for me, as if I couldn't manage it. I snorted, snatched it from her hand and finished it myself by wedging it between my knees as I bound a strip of reed around the neck to make a head. I glanced up and saw her smiling, but it wasn't in mockery of my efforts.

She pulled out a few strands of her hair and bound it around her brideog, then tucked it into the fork of the tree that stood at the very edge of the wood, begging the oak of the sun to give us leave to enter. I did the same.

Morwen stood for a long time, inclining her head as if she was listening to a host of people. I tried to make out what she was straining to hear.

'The trees are talking,' she said. 'Don't need words, but you can hear them right enough, hear whether they're angry or content. Granddam used to say that if the trees are silent, that's when they're at their most dangerous. You must never enter the vert then. "Take heed of the silence," she always said, "for then the trees'll strike without warning" – a great branch crashing down on someone who's vexed them, a long-cripple striking out from its nest deep between their roots. The long-cripples in this wood are deadliest of all the vipers in England. No man or beast can survive their sting. The old oaks have their own ways of exacting revenge.'

The trees in this valley were barely taller than me, gnarled, stunted, twisted, like ancient dwarfs. They were almost bare of leaves now, but hung with long beards of silver-grey lichen.

Their roots slithered over thigh-high boulders that covered the ground so closely that in places you couldn't lower your foot between them. Rocks and roots alike were wrapped in a dense pelt of emerald-green moss, sodden and weeping.

We picked our way through the tangle of stone and wood, clambering over the mossy boulders and clinging to the branches to balance on them where the spaces were too narrow to squeeze between them. I pointed with my chin towards some flat stones laid on top of vertical slabs of rock. 'They look like little tables.'

'Tables where the dead eat,' Morwen said. 'Bones of the dead rest inside those. Long-cripples curl round them to guard them. Seen whole nests of them, big and little 'uns, slithering through the ribs and skulls.'

We'd reached a steeply sloped clearing, ringed by oaks standing so close together their branches had grown through and around each other, frozen in woody knots that could never be untangled. A huge rock jutted from the ground in the centre, broad at the base and narrowing to a point at the top, like a spear, reaching up as if it would impale the sky.

'That's the queen stone, that is,' Morwen said, padding towards it. I followed.

The boulders were smaller there, humps beneath the skin of shaggy moss that covered the ground, like the lumps on a toad. My skin tingled with cold, but for the first time in my life I welcomed its bite. The air inside the wood was chill, damp, but quite still, as if the wind was forbidden to enter this place, but the trees were still talking.

Morwen turned this way and that, as if she was trying to catch a whisper being tossed back and forth between these ancient souls, yet somehow I understood, as well as she now, that the language they spoke was deeper than any word or thought. The two of us squatted between the small boulders, gazing up at the stone. Towering ramparts of purple cloud were bubbling up over the moors, sucking the light and colour from the earth below.

She began to sing. The notes were soft, like the distant rushing of the water running unseen in the river below. I caught the tiny whisper of movement. A wren had fluttered down. It perched on the twisted, moss-covered root of a tree and regarded us. Lifting up its tail as if it was trying to imitate the huge rock, it suddenly burst into a short piercing trill of a song, its whole body trembling with the effort, then hopped towards one of the little stone tombs and vanished, as if it had walked through the solid rock.

'There,' Morwen breathed. 'That's the tomb of the one who will lead us tonight. Bran's bird lives with the dead, she knows. Cracky-wren tells all the secrets of the living to spirits and they whisper theirs to her. Now we wait for the moon. We wait for the door to open.'

Chapter 50

Hospitallers' Priory of St Mary

The clash of metal, and the screams of men and horses smash into Brother Nicholas's ears. Sweat pours down his face and chest. His hands are slippery with it. The Saracen is running towards him, a great curved scimitar raised above his head, glinting in the burning sun. He reaches for his own sword, but as he raises it, he sees he isn't holding a sword at all but the severed head of Brother Alban. The eyes open wide and the lips move. The swollen face is pleading with him, but he can't make out the words above the howl of battle. The deadly scimitar is slashing closer and closer. The Saracen is whirling it high in the dust-choked air. At any moment it will descend on Nicholas's skull, cleaving it in two. But he can't defend himself: his arms are full of bloody heads. More and more are being heaped on top. He mustn't let any of them drop. He has to carry them to safety.

Nicholas's yells woke him as he fought to climb up out of the pit of sleep, but it was some time before he could force his eyelids open and even longer before he could make his limbs move. They felt heavy, swollen, though from what he could see of them they looked normal enough. The bedclothes were sodden and cold, drenched in his sweat. His mouth and throat were as dry as a desert and his teeth covered with a sickly, sticky film. He groaned. Just how much had he drunk last night? He struggled to remember, but fragments of images and words were scattered haphazardly in his skull, as if marauders had broken in and smashed all that was inside. And, from the throbbing in his head, they were still in there, rampaging around with war hammers.

He staggered out of bed and over to the table, reaching for the goblet that was still half full of wine. He took a deep swig, rolling it around his parched mouth to moisten it. The wine was even more foul than usual, with a bitter-sweet taste, but maybe that was because his furred tongue was like something dug out from the bottom of a midden.

But he'd drunk less than usual, that much he did remember now. Besides, he'd been known to consume a whole flagon of wine and still manage to cut the heads off a row of straw dummies at the gallop, without missing a single one. He pressed his hand to his forehead as the grisly images from the night terror surfaced again in front of his eyes, and flopped down into a chair.

It was Sister Basilia who had brought the wine to his chamber last night. She'd poured it herself and insisted on warming it before handing him the goblet. Why had *she* brought it and not one of the scullions? The servants were abed – that was what she'd said. But . . . He turned to stare at the empty bed. Alban was dead, murdered by that demon boy. For a moment, he thought it had been another nightmare, but he knew it wasn't. And last night, down in that cave, one of the holy sisters in this priory had tried to kill him too.

Nicholas was suddenly aware of how chill the chamber felt. The fire was out, the ashes cold. How long had he slept? He began to pull on his clothes, clumsy in his feverish haste. His limbs still felt leaden, his back ached and his fingers kept losing their grip. He stumbled to the door, half afraid that it might be locked, but it opened easily. He shut it again and stood for a moment, staring at the wood, trying to calm himself. Of course they hadn't locked the door. What in the name of Lucifer had made him think they could or would? He was a knight, a warrior who'd faced the enemy in battle more times than he could remember. He'd been afraid, yes – any knight who said he wasn't was either an untried fool or a liar – but he'd never panicked. He'd always been able to think coldly and clearly, even in an ambush. What was happening to him? Was that foul demon even now witching his mind?

Nicholas turned back into the room and began stuffing what he could into a small leather scrip. He'd have to abandon his travelling chest and most of what he had brought with him, except his sword, of course. It was only as that thought struck him that he glanced over at the corner where it usually hung next to his cloak. It wasn't there. He snatched down his cloak, but it wasn't hanging under it. He pivoted on his heel, staring round the small chamber. Although he knew he would not have put the sword anywhere else that did not stop him searching for it, even in places that could not possibly contain it. He was finally forced to admit it was gone, and he felt as if someone had cut off his arm. Never had he felt so defenceless.

Up to that moment, he had still been resolved to cut out and carry Brother Alban's heart to Buckland so that it could be buried with the honour due to any in the Order of St John.

He hadn't particularly liked the idle, greedy swine and, truth be told, he was sure Alban had despised him, but every knight was pledged to ensure that if the body of a brother could not be returned for burial to their own priory the heart must be laid to rest there. But now Nicholas had only one thought in his head: to escape this vipers' nest while he still could.

He peered out into the courtyard. A couple of servants were crossing to the kitchen, looking as if they were performing some kind of strange and jerky dance, as they kicked out and flapped their arms to drive off the horde of kites and rooks that were pecking at the mud and filth on the ground. Keeping close to the wall, Nicholas made his unsteady way to the stables. Once safely inside the dim interior, he breathed a little easier, drinking in the familiar, comforting smell of horse sweat and dung. He moved towards the far end where he always made sure his horse was tethered, furthest away from any driving rain and wind. But the space was empty.

'You looking for something, Master?' Brengy, the young stable boy, emerged from behind the dun-coloured palfrey he was brushing.

'My horse! Where is it? Has someone taken it out?'

Getting no reply from the boy, Nicholas grabbed him by the back of the neck and dragged him the few paces to the empty iron ring on the wall to which he always tied his mount. 'The black rouncy, where is it?'

Brengy attempted to wriggle free, but the knight's grip was too strong.

'Blacksmith took him back to his forge to shoe him. Can't do it here, can he? How do you think he'd fetch a thundering great furnace and his anvil up here? Ow!' He squealed as Nicholas cuffed his head

'There was nothing wrong with his shoes when I last rode him.'

'Knocked one loose in the night. That ugly brute's always kicking at the walls. Keeps me awake half the night.'

'I'll kick you till you can't sit down for a month if you don't mend your manners. When's the blacksmith bringing my horse back?'

'When he's finished, I reckon,' Brengy said, earning himself another resounding slap around the head.

'I'll fetch him myself—'

'Young Dye said she saw you coming in here,' a voice called from the door. 'Now what are you doing loitering in a draughty stable when there's a good hot supper waiting for you?'

Nicholas turned to see Sibyl at the entrance, her hands on her broad hips. Brengy, taking advantage of his distraction, wriggled free and ran out of the stables as if the devil himself was flying after him.

Sibyl bustled forward. 'Now you come and see what I've cooked for you. A nice mess of Saracen.'

For one crazed moment, Nicholas thought she'd meant it. He was beginning to believe these women were capable of any horror. Then he realised she was babbling about sarcenes, a sauce dyed cherry red. She was still talking as she edged him back towards his chamber, as she might herd a goose towards the butcher's knife.

She opened the door for him. 'I know how much you like your rich sauces, Brother Nicholas, but don't you be telling the sisters I made this for you. There's scarcely any spices left in the store. But I thought you needed a good supper inside you after that nasty business. And you've not eaten for nigh on two days. You must keep up your strength,

412

else you'll end up like poor Brother Alban, God rest his soul.'

'I dined last night.'

The cook shook her head. 'Night before last, it was. Been sleeping like a bear in winter, you have. And a good thing too, if you ask me. No better physic for body and soul than a nice long sleep. But your belly must think you've forgotten where your mouth is. So, you make sure you eat every scrap. I've no bread to give you for sops, but I've put plenty of goat's meat in there you can use to mop up the sauce. Mind, it'll not taste quite the same as usual for I've had to use honey and herbs 'stead of sugar and cloves, and there's no flour. But I'm sure you've had worse.'

As soon as the door had closed behind her, Nicholas crossed to the fire, which, in the brief time that he'd been in the stables, had been rekindled. A pipkin of the dark red stew was keeping warm by the blaze.

Someone, that scullion probably, had plainly been charged with keeping watch on his door. He dared not risk trying again to leave until all in the priory were sleeping. If he could slide the brace back on the gate without the old gate-keeper hearing, so much the better, but if he couldn't, he'd threaten to kill her – he *would* kill her – if that was the only way of keeping her silent.

But he should put something warm in his stomach before setting out on the moor – he didn't intend to stop until he had put himself well beyond the reach of the priory. He pulled his spoon from his scrip and fished around in the sarcenes sauce. As the cook had said: there was a generous quantity of goat's meat in it. He scooped out a chunk.

Now that he'd smelt it, he found he was indeed ravenous. Hardly a wonder, if Sibyl was right and he had slept for nearly two days and nights. Was that possible? He'd never done it before in his life, not even after battles that had raged from dawn to nightfall. But the rest certainly hadn't refreshed him. Even now he was finding it hard to think clearly, as if his mind was drowning in a mire. But a thought was slowly unfurling and taking shape in his brain. No man sleeps for two days without waking at least once. That had been no natural sleep. Only dwale or some such potion could make a man slumber so deeply, or for so long.

He dashed the piece of meat on his spoon into the fire. Did they really imagine he was foolish enough to fall for that trick again? He seized the pipkin of stew and was on the point of opening the door and hurling both contents and pot across the courtyard in his fury, but stopped, smiling grimly to himself. Very well then, let them think he had eaten it. If they checked and found him deeply asleep they would reason he could be left for hours, and wouldn't bother watching his door or setting a guard on the gate.

He couldn't risk emptying the pot on to the fire. They'd smell the stench of burning meat. He searched for somewhere to dispose of it. His eyes lighted on Alban's chest, still standing in the corner. Pulling out the spare clothes, he tipped the contents of the pipkin into the bottom. His mouth watered and his belly pleaded as the aroma enveloped his nose. Quickly he shoved the clothes on top of the mess, arranged himself on the bed and lay in the gathering darkness, waiting for the door to creak open. Even as he lay there, he could feel the women standing on the other side of the door, a silent ring of black cats, watching their prey, just waiting for it to walk into their savage jaws.

Chapter 51

Sorrel

The clouds slid over one another, parting to reveal the rising moon then veiling her again. Waves of bone-white light and darkness lapped over the twisted trees. Snakes of mist slithered around their trunks and writhed through branches shaggy with lichen. Morwen and I sat in silence till the first ray of moonlight touched the stone in the centre of the clearing. Then Morwen stood up. I sensed that whatever she was going to do she must do alone. I didn't move as she took a tiny piece of dried meat from a small bag about her neck and chewed till it softened, then pushed with her tongue till it fell into her hand. She placed the morsel at the foot of the rock as carefully and solemnly as our village priest used to lay the Host on the paten.

'Flesh from a red cat, Mother.'

She blew on each of her palms and laid them over her eyes. I kept still and silent, watching. The moonlight washed over Morwen, turning her hair to silver, her bare shoulders to marble, petrifying her, until she was one more stone among the many. For a long time, she stood quite still. Then she drew her hands from her face, reached out to grasp my withered paw and pulled me towards the queen stone. We pressed our free hands to the rough surface. We were a circle of three now, three women, three rocks. And Morwen began to sing a chant that made my skin prickle. I understood without being told that I must want the spirit to rise, think it, will it. I knew if I let it, my hand could sink into the stone, like hot iron into snow, and I would be drawn into the very heart of the rock, as I had been pulled down into the heart of Ankow, but that was not where I had to go, not tonight.

I stared towards the stone slab where the wren had vanished. The tomb seemed to hang suspended, its mantle of wet moss glittering in the moonlight. The oak crouched over it and a coil of mist wrapped itself around it, as if they were determined to protect it. Then the moonlight vanished and the tomb became a deep, dark hole in the forest of trunks. And still Morwen sang.

A thread of mist trickled from the hole, like the wisp of smoke when a candle is snuffed out. The mist thickened, rearing up, whirling, though there was not a breath of wind inside that wood. It threaded up through the crooked branches, skull-white at first, then slowly glowing poison-green.

Chapter 52

Hospitallers' Priory of St Mary

The latch on the door of Nicholas's chamber lifted softly and he heard the soft pad of leather approaching his bed. He lay still, eyes closed, trying to slow his breathing to the steady rhythm of a man deeply asleep, but it was not easy – his body was as taut as a drawn bowstring. Was it Johanne, Clarice? It would be the easiest thing in the world for any of the sisters to smother him with sheepskin as he slept or plunge a dagger into his chest, if they thought him helpless with dwale. It might be weeks, even months, before the cart from Buckland was able to return and anyone discovered the two brothers were missing. Even when they did, if the sisters disposed of his body, they could easily claim he and Alban had set out on horseback to Buckland and must have been attacked by outlaws or swept away in a fast-flowing river when they tried to cross.

The footfalls came closer. Skirts swished against the leg of the bed. Suppose the sarcenes sauce had contained not a sleeping draught but poison? Would they think him already dead? Someone was standing over him now. He could hear

417

her breathing – short and shallow. Excited? Tense? Someone who was about to raise a dagger? It took all his willpower not to open his eyes.

Just as he thought he could hold himself in check no longer, the person softly padded away from the bed to the fire. He heard her raking and banking it down. At least they weren't planning to burn him to death, or more likely they just didn't want their precious priory to catch fire. Then came the clink of the empty pipkin as she picked it up. Finally, the soft rustle of skirts and the slap of shoe on stone as she crossed towards the door. He heard it open and felt the rush of cold air as she paused, watching him again till finally it closed behind her. Still he dared not relax, trying to maintain that steady, slow rhythm in his breathing just in case they were standing outside, listening.

Nicholas lay motionless on the bed, straining to catch the sounds outside – chatter in the yard, the distant clattering of pots, the creaking of the well rope. He was afraid of falling asleep, of lying there as vulnerable and helpless as a trussed chicken if they crept back into his chamber. He had to admit, grudgingly, one blessing of being so hungry: the ache in his belly was sharp enough to goad him into wakefulness.

How many hours had passed? Now he could hear nothing except the wind outside. Were they all safely asleep? Nicholas slid off the bed, trying not to let it creak, and tiptoed to the casement. He could see a flicker of lights in the crack beneath the shutter, which he hoped were the flames from the night torches on the walls. He eased the door open an inch and squinted out. The courtyard was deserted, silent.

He fastened his cloak about his shoulders and, keeping close to the walls, slipped around the yard towards the stables. He was certain that his own rouncy would still be missing, but he would not get far on foot across the moor. The horses pricked up their ears, stamping and snickering softly, as he entered. The only light came from the torches in the courtyard and he could barely distinguish the beasts from the blackness around them. He needed to get closer to find a mount that would bear his weight over such a distance, but only a fool would risk getting too close to the hindquarters of a strange horse for fear they might kick out.

Something creaked above him in the hay loft. Nicholas froze. The ladder cracked and swayed, as the stable lad descended. He leaped down the last two rungs and bounded towards the courtyard, clearly intending to raise the alarm. But Nicholas's training had not deserted him. He seized Brengy from behind in mid-stride, clamping one hand across his mouth and locking his neck tightly in the crook of his other arm.

He bent his head so that his lips almost touched the lad's ear. 'Listen carefully, boy. I have killed many men in my time and I can break your scrawny neck with a twitch of my arm.' He squeezed Brengy's neck harder to ensure his words were believed, slackening his hold only slightly when he began to choke.

'Now, when I let you go, you're going to saddle your fittest and strongest horse for me. And you'll do it quickly and silently. If you utter any sound or make any attempt to run, you'll be dead before you reach the courtyard. Do you understand?'

He loosened his grip a little more and the lad nodded as vigorously as anyone could, with the bulging muscles of a knight's arm beneath their chin.

Brengy, when released, worked swiftly, though he was shaking, and as soon as it was done, he thrust the reins of the horse towards Nicholas, plainly anxious to have his attacker gone. But Nicholas had not finished with him yet. Seizing the reins in one hand, he grabbed the lad by the scruff of the neck and dragged both horse and boy into the courtyard. The mud and filth in the yard mercifully helped to muffle the sound of iron shoes striking stone until they reached the gates.

'Hold the horse, boy. You move or utter a sound, I'll cut your throat.'

Nicholas had pulled aside the beam that secured the door, and was about to drag the horse and boy through, when Meggy burst out of the gatehouse. Nicholas's arm locked round Brengy's throat again.

'Get back into your kennel, woman, and stay there. If you call for help, I swear I'll snap this lad's neck.'

He dragged the boy through and, in a swift movement, swept him up and dumped him face down in front of the saddle before swinging himself up. Brengy lay across the horse, his head and feet dangling helplessly. Nicholas looked down at Meggy in the gateway, both hands pressed tightly to her mouth, as if she couldn't trust herself not to cry out.

'I'm taking the lad with me, till I'm sure that no one is following. Then I'll let him go. But if I'm followed, you'll be fishing his corpse out of the mire. And you can tell those hellcats they needn't worry. I'll be back, but when I return I'll have half the Lord Prior's knights with me and I'll see to it that they put every sister and servant in this accursed place in chains and flog the truth out of them if they have to.'

The moon was baiting Brother Nicholas or perhaps it was the clouds that were bent on mischief. He was attempting to follow the trail along which Hob had led them on the

420

night they had first laid eyes on the malignance they called the Priory of St Mary, a night that he now cursed with all his heart. Even when the moon was shining he could barely distinguish the boggy track from the mire around it, but it seemed that the clouds were watching him, waiting until he came to a bend or a place where the path was washed away. Then they flung themselves across the moon, plunging him instantly into a terrible darkness, so that even the horse faltered and kept trying to turn back.

'I hope you're praying men, Brothers,' Hob had said, ''cause you'll need more than a sword to protect you up there.' Had Hob known more than he'd told them that night? 'Once you cross into the deadlands,' he'd said, 'there's no coming back.' The carter had been talking about the tor, but he could as easily have meant the priory.

Brengy, lying face down over the horse in front of Nicholas, kept whimpering that he was going to be sick and that his ribs were hurting.

'Then I'll have to give you something to take your mind off it,' Nicholas said, bringing his riding whip down hard across the lad's backside with a savagery that was born as much from his own fear and frustration as a desire to silence him.

Brengy gave a yelp of pain and started to cough and retch. Nicholas was in no mood to have him vomit down his legs. The lad had served his purpose, keeping the gatekeeper quiet at least long enough for him to get out of sight of the priory. Nicholas's confidence was surging back now that he had escaped. None of the sisters would follow him out here. And if they did, what danger could a woman possibly pose to him out on the moor? Even without his sword, they'd be no match for a trained knight.

He seized Brengy by the back of the shirt, dragged him backwards off the horse and flung him down. He heard a cry as the boy hit the ground and derived a vicious pleasure from it. He wanted to smash the priory and everyone in it. Besides, the stable boy deserved it. He should be hanged for stealing a knight's horse and Nicholas would see that he was, just as soon as he returned.

He stared out over the black sea of the moor. The wind was gaining strength, peeling his cloak back, creeping in under it, like a woman seeking warmth. The horse had stopped again and was trying to turn, as if it was determined to go back to its stable. It was much smaller and lighter than his own rouncy and, like all the horses in the priory, was suffering from the meagre diet of mouldy hay it had been forced to endure these past months. Nicholas could feel it wheezing and heaving beneath him. He wasn't convinced it would have the stamina to carry him as far as Buckland, but as long as the beast got him off the moor and safely to an inn or monastery, where he could eat and sleep without fear of a knife being plunged into his back, that was all he asked of it. He could find a stronger mount to carry him on from there. But even the fleeting thought of food reminded him of how ravenous he was. He tugged on the reins and wrenched the horse round, kicking its sides to urge it on, though he couldn't even see the track.

But they had barely moved a few paces before the horse stopped again, lifting its head, ears laid back. Nicholas caught the faint sound of iron shoes hitting stone, the squelch of hoofs plodding through mud. Another rider was behind him. He *was* being followed! His right hand went unbidden to his side, the fingers expecting to close over the familiar hilt of his sword, as they had done a thousand times before whenever danger threatened. But they touched only the cloth of his cloak. After several moments of shocked disbelief, he remembered that his sword had been stolen from his chamber and whoever was riding down on him might well be grasping his own deadly blade in their fist.

Nicholas was as much unnerved by his own reaction as by the danger behind him. He had faced hails of flaming arrows, men brandishing glittering scimitars, howling for his blood. His heart had pounded in those battles, but his mind had, if anything, become sharper and clearer: he had been able to decide instantly where to hack through a line of warriors or to spot in a flash a man who had left himself unguarded and thrust death home. But now he was gripped with blind panic.

He slashed his whip against the horse's flank, trying to urge it forward. But the beast wasn't accustomed to such treatment and, already unsettled by the darkness and slippery track, reared and tossed its head, trying once more to turn towards the safety of its stables. Nicholas fought to bring it around. Not daring to risk the whip again, he kicked with his heels urging the horse on.

The sound of a hunting horn reverberated in the air. Short notes answered by the deep-throated baying of hounds. In daylight and in another place, Nicholas's blood would have pumped hot and full to the thrill of a chase, but in the darkness, he felt beads of cold sweat chilling his back. He hesitated, craning round to determine where the sound was coming from, but howls were bouncing from hill to hill until they seemed to be all around him. He tried to tell himself it was only a nobleman out for a night's sport. He could confront the man, even seek his aid. But the image of Alban's corpse reared up before his eyes. The face torn off by merciless teeth, the guts and liver ripped from the belly by slavering jaws that could crack open a cow's thigh bone. A pack of hounds could rip a man apart like a hare, and if these were the same beasts, they had already tasted human blood.

As the horn sounded once more, Nicholas's horse seemed to make up its mind that the dogs were behind it on the track. It veered sideways and scrambled the foot or so up on to the bank that edged the path. Before Nicholas could force it back on to the track, it was plunging down the hillside and across the open moor.

Nicholas had always prided himself on being able to master any warhorse, even the mighty destriers, capable of carrying a man in full armour, but he was used to horses that responded to commands of the legs, for a knight must have his hands free to kill and defend himself. Instinctively, he found himself using his thighs and knees to try to steady and turn the frightened creature, but that seemed only to madden and confuse it.

It careered across the dark hillside, splashing through pools and streams, stumbling as its shoes caught in heather and lurching violently as its hind hoofs slipped on mud. One moment it seemed as if it would plunge forward and snap its neck, the next fall sideways and break a leg. Nothing Nicholas could do calmed it, and he could only pray that exhaustion would bring it to a halt.

Somewhere the horn sounded again, a dark, deep throbbing that boomed back at him from every hill, and the baying of the dogs grew more excited and ferocious. Even as the horse ploughed on, Nicholas could not resist glancing behind him. A dense black tide was rolling down the slope, moving swifter than the horse. At first he thought a torrent of water

424

had burst from some lake or dam, but as one, then another leaped high and bounded over a rock or mound of grass, he realised they were hounds streaming down the hillside, their glowing red eyes flashing out of the darkness, like a forest fire running straight towards him.

Chapter 53

Sorrel

A glowing green mist spiralled out of the rock tomb and wove through the branches of the oak above, where long fronds of grey lichen hung like the rags of a winding sheet. Morwen's song was drawing the mist upwards. It was taking shape, like the birds and beasts in the fire in the tor, but this was no animal. It was a woman, hooded, draped head to toe in robes that billowed out from her as if they were caught in a wind I couldn't feel. The creature lifted her head. Her face was dead, a mask, a skull without flesh, as solid as moonlight. But peering out through holes in the cavernous eye sockets a pair of living eyes were trapped behind the bone, as if she was a prisoner, staring out through the bars of a cage. The eyes shone with a fierce, angry knowledge, a burning fury that the dust of a thousand years could not smother.

She turned those blazing eyes and looked at us, but though I knew her power, I was not afraid. She did not mean us harm.

Call them. Call them.

The words flew through the trees between us, but I couldn't tell if I had willed it, or Morwen or the spirit, for the words were living now, darting around the grove like a flock of starlings, and we all willed them. I could feel the heat from Morwen's hand pulsing through the rock, as if her blood was pounding through the veins of the stone.

Summon them. They will obey.

Somewhere beyond the woods, the wind was gathering strength, wailing across the sucking bog pools, shrieking above the thundering river, howling through the crevices in the tors, but inside the forest of oaks all was still. A cold white mist hung between the distant trees, shrouding the clearing, shielding the living and the dead.

Call them!

I didn't turn my head, but I could feel the others drawing near in their long robes, their eyes peering out from inside their bones. They inhabited their skulls like the weasels staring out from their dark tunnels, watching, willing, waiting. The spirits drew close, tangled in the gnarled branches, their hair the silver-grey locks of lichen, their fingers the clawed twigs. Others slithered between the arching roots, and crawled towards us over the mossy rocks. And still I was not afraid.

A shudder ran through the wood, a rumbling of stones and trembling of trees. There was a great fluttering of tiny wings as, from holes and crevices too small even to admit a mouse, a huge flock of wrens flew up into the oaks, melting once more into craggy branches in their stillness.

Someone has entered the wood. Someone has violated the sacred place. He is unclean.

Chapter 54

Dertemora

The horse was tiring badly now, and it might even have allowed Brother Nicholas to bring it to a halt, if he had tried, but with the hounds baying ever closer behind him, he urged the sweating beast on, willing it to keep moving. They were teetering down the side of a V-shaped valley, and Nicholas's only thought was to reach the bottom where surely there must be a track or at least a level way, so that he could spur the horse on and find rocks or trees in which he could take shelter. If he could just climb up into the branches or scramble on to a steep-sided rock, armed with his knife, he might at least be able to defend himself from the hounds.

But, as if it had been hiding, waiting to pounce, the babble and thrashing of water burst without warning on Nicholas's ears. He heard grinding and scraping as the swollen river dragged gravel over stones, and stones over rocks. Like a drunkard weaving down a street, water crashed against one boulder, only to fall back on to another and trip over the next. The horse veered away. Herded by the roar of the river on one side and the yelping of the hounds on the other, it

428

struck out along the side of the steep hill struggling to keep its footing in the mud and sodden grass.

The poor creature's breathing was so laboured it seemed its lungs would burst with the effort, but fear drove the horse on, slipping and stumbling, long after its strength had been exhausted. Even in his own panic, Nicholas knew it was a miracle the horse hadn't fallen already, and if it did and rolled on him . . . The image of himself lying there helpless with a crushed leg and that pack of dogs snarling over him finally goaded him into action. If he tried to rein the beast to a halt and the animal resisted, he'd surely cause it to come crashing down. He couldn't take that chance. In the dark, he couldn't distinguish anything on the ground, but he knew these hillsides were littered with rocks and boulders lying in wait to crack a man's skull, and found himself praying that he'd land in soft, thick mud . . . But what good would prayer do now? Nicholas swung his leg over the horse's back and hurled himself into the darkness.

He landed momentarily on his feet, but the slope was too steep and slippery for him to keep his balance and he found himself tumbling backwards, rolling and bouncing towards the torrent of water. He flung out his arms wildly, trying to grab anything that might stop him plunging into the river, but it was the very rocks he'd feared that saved him. His back smashed into a boulder, and he lay still, fighting to suck the air back into his lungs. But as he gasped, a savage pain stabbed through his side. He'd broken ribs often enough in the joust and on the battlefield to know exactly what had happened. It would be agony to move, but at least he could walk. He tried to tell himself he'd been lucky – better his ribs than a shattered leg or spine.

Water was roaring inches from his head, drowning all

other sounds, but he knew the hounds were still out there somewhere. Would they follow the horse or pick up his own scent? Though his body pleaded not to move, he could not indulge it. He was defenceless, lying there in the open. He dragged himself up against the boulder and stood for a moment, listening, until the wave of pain ebbed a little. Somewhere above the thrashing of the water came the throb of a hunting horn, but it was not calling the dogs back, it was driving them on to search and kill.

He rocked forward, trying to hear where the sound was coming from. He was sure the track he needed lay somewhere to his right, but the baying seemed to be on that side of him too. He turned away from it, and with his arm wrapped tightly about his ribs, he stumbled on, following the course of the river. It was in full spate and he knew he'd be swept off his feet in an instant if he tried to cross it, but if the hounds did attack, it might be his only chance.

The clouds peeled away from the moon and for a breath the valley was lit by a ghost light. Frost-white foam spun across the seething river and ahead lay a dark mass of grotesquely twisted trees, their branches black against the moonlight, writhing like the Gorgon's hair from the scalp of the earth. The sight made him shudder, but from the tail of his eye, he caught a glimpse of movement. Silhouetted on the rise above him stood a great black hound staring down fixedly into the valley. Three or four others breasted the hill and paused, scenting the air. Almost before his mind could comprehend what he was staring at, darkness had flooded over him again. He stumbled forward. He had to reach those trees. That was his only hope.

But the whole valley seemed to be conspiring to keep him from reaching them, as if a charm had been put on the wood to stop anyone approaching it. His legs were sucked back by the deep mud. Brambles sank their claws into his cloak and tried to fetter him. Rocks reared up in front of him, barring his way, and stones rolled treacherously from beneath his feet, bringing him crashing to his knees and driving waves of white-hot pain through his ribs. The roar of the water grew ever louder but each time he paused he heard – he thought he heard – the baying of the hounds. Was it simply the wind? He no longer knew. Pain and hunger were making him dizzy, but he forced himself on, clinging to the one thought that if he could reach those trees he would be able to defend himself.

As he struggled towards them, he could see the smudges of the stunted trunks that stood sentinel on the edge. Just a few more yards, he urged himself. He turned his head as he caught the howling of the hounds again. They were closer now, much closer.

A harsh *kaah* made him whip round. Something was bobbing on one of the upper branches of the closest tree. A rook, a crow? He'd disturbed a roosting bird – that was all. He ducked under the branches, and heard another loud *kaah*, this time from the tree beyond. Both birds were screeching, irritated at being roused.

The sudden flapping of wings made him glance up and he fell heavily over a moss-covered rock, banging his cheek on another. The moss cushioned the blow to his face, but he yelped from the agonising jarring of his chest. He struggled to stand upright, unable to find a place to set his feet. The forest floor around him was covered with massive boulders, so tightly rolled together or heaped on top of each other that there was hardly a gap between them, except where the trees had forced their way through.

431

Kaah! Kaah! More birds were appearing in the trees around him. He could hear the furious flapping of their wings. The branches were so low that their thick beaks were clattering inches from his face. This wood must be their roost. But the yelping of dogs dragged his attention from the birds. They were close now, so close he could hear the snapping of gorse and the rattle of stones as they streamed towards him. He scrambled desperately over the boulders, cursing as his feet repeatedly slipped into the deep narrow cracks between them, constantly hitting stone with knees or elbows, each time jerking his broken ribs till he could hardly bear to breathe. It was madness to try to move quickly – he could trap a leg or even snap it.

The clouds drifted from the moon, filling the wood with cold white light and sharp, twisted silhouettes. It touched the forest floor, and the shadows ran lightly across it, so that the great mossy humps seemed to move, like waves rearing up in a stormy sea. Tendrils of glowing mist slithered between the knotted roots and through the branches, not hanging as they should but creeping and writhing as if they were alive. Yet, the air was unnaturally still.

The whirling of bird wings forced him to look up. Crows, jackdaws, rooks and ravens were flying down and alighting on every branch around him, their beaks glistening silver in the moonlight, their eyes glittering inches from his own. He ducked away from them, instinctively trying to raise his arm to shield his face, but he couldn't lift it above his shoulder for the sickening jolts of pain shooting upwards from his chest. He was drenched in cold sweat and struggling to breathe. Then he heard it: the long vibrating note of the hunting horn. Except it wasn't coming from outside the wood but from inside its very heart.

Darkness flowed down over the trees again. Nicholas couldn't move. How could the huntsman have reached the wood ahead of him, and if he was here, where were the hounds? He tried to calm himself. The sound was being distorted – these rocks, these hills flung it around, so you couldn't tell where it was coming from.

Something flew straight into his face. Feathers covered his mouth and nose. Talons raked his skin. Though every blow sent pain shooting through his body, he beat it off and scrambled across the boulders, clawing up the steep slope towards the centre of the wood. He could no longer remember why he must get there, only that he could think of nothing else to do.

'Holy Virgin, make the clouds roll back! Give me light, any light,' he begged.

With abject relief, Nicholas realised that his fervent prayer was being answered. The clouds were sliding away from the moon, as if the Blessed Virgin herself had stretched forth her hand and was pulling aside the curtain. He was in a small clearing. The trees there formed a circle around a massive spear-shaped rock. But he registered the rock only dimly, merely as a backdrop to the two women who were standing in front of it.

The cold white light fell on their naked bodies, running down the curves of their breasts, trickling over their ribs, stark as the timbers of a wrecked ship, dripping over their flat bellies and pooling in the hollows of their thighs. Snakes of mist, glowing green as the walls of the well, coiled about their ankles, slithering around their legs. Nicholas gaped in disbelief. Were these women humans or sprites?

In spite of his pain and exhaustion, he could not wrench his eyes from their bodies, from where the fingers of mist were reaching up, probing, penetrating. His hands twitched as if they would reach out to touch them too. If these were sprites, he would willingly surrender to their enchantment.

'You shouldn't have come here.' The voice was all too human.

He looked at their faces, their wild hair hanging down in wet strands. He saw now that they were beggars, nothing more than common vagabonds or street whores, probably both. As the one who'd spoken turned a little, he glimpsed the livid welts on her hip and shoulder. She had probably been stripped and whipped out of the nearest town, though she'd not been flogged nearly hard enough if she was still flaunting herself.

Fear was ebbing away from him and anger bubbling up in its place, as he remembered exactly who had driven him out on to this accursed moor in the middle of the night. He stared at the women coldly, his desire for them instantly extinguished.

'Now, just what manner of game have we caught here?' he said. 'It would seem that someone is hunting these hills with a pack of hounds. Is it you they're seeking? Thieves, are you? Runaway serfs? Don't invent some lie. What you are doesn't interest me. But I will strike a bargain with you. Show me the way to an inn or somewhere I can shelter for the night and I'll see what I can do to call off your pursuers. I dare say a well-filled purse will convince them to lose you for good.'

He had expected the women to look alarmed that he had discovered their hiding place or grateful that he had offered them a means of escape. He was even prepared for them to try to wheedle some coins for themselves, but though it was hard to see their expressions, he could have sworn they were laughing. Perhaps they were simple or mad.

'Come now, my dears, you've nothing to fear from me.' He braced his arm against his ribs, trying not to gasp with pain as he talked. 'I'm a knight of St John. Not even the sheriff's men would dare seize you, if you were under my protection.'

But instead of begging for his help, the girl who had spoken threw back her head and began to sing. At least, it was a kind of singing, he supposed. The unearthly chant made his skin crawl, as if a thousand flies were creeping over it.

If the Virgin Mary had been holding up the curtain of cloud, she now let it drop and the grove was plunged into darkness again. The trees were crowding in, shuffling towards him, like evil old men, carrying their birds nearer and nearer. The raucous *kaah, kaah* was all around him, hundreds of wings flapping furiously, beaks snapping. Blindly, he tried to fight his way out, but could find no space wide enough to squeeze between the trunks. How had he come in? There must be a gap – there had to be! Where was it? Then he heard it. The blast of the hunting horn so close, so piercing, he knew the sound was coming from someone standing in the centre of the glade.

All at once he saw them, the great black beasts with their burning red eyes, standing in a circle around him, just beyond the ring of the trees. He saw the blue lights crackling from their coats, saw the long, pointed teeth flash white as they threw back their heads and gave that deep sonorous howl. They were slowly padding towards him, a merciless black tide, and he could no more turn them back than a man can stop a monstrous wave rolling towards a stricken ship. The pain in his chest was almost numbed by his abject fear, for even as he drew his knife, he knew deep down that not even his sword or a hail of flaming arrows had the power to save him from this foe.

Brother Nicholas's legs gave way and he sank abjectly to his knees, crawling frantically away from the women, away from the hounds. But instead of colliding with a tree trunk or stone as he had expected, his leg vanished into the gap between two rocks. He wriggled backwards, trying to ease his battered body into the shelter of a hollow. It was a small space, no bigger than a kennel, but just wide and high enough for him to squeeze himself inside.

He crouched there on all fours, the blessed solidness of rock covering his head, his back, his sides, like steel armour. Relief surged in his belly, and he gripped the knife with returning confidence and the growing excitement of a seasoned knight facing an enemy he knows he can defeat. He was protected on all sides, save the front, where he could freely wield his weapon. That was the only place the dogs could touch him, and the entrance was so narrow that they could attack only one at a time. Kill the first and second, and the hounds' own bodies would shield him from the rest of the pack. And once the beasts smelt blood, they'd more than likely turn on their own dead and wounded. He could fight these fiends and he could win.

He waited, every muscle in his aching body tense. 'Come on, you brutes, try to take me now. Who will be first to have their throat slashed?'

Through the demonic cackle of the birds in the trees above him, through the baying of the hounds that shook the pillars of Hell beneath, he heard the women laughing.

And then his back arched in agony as a dozen white-hot

stings stabbed into his legs, his sides, his neck. He stared down in disbelief as the sinuous bodies wriggled over his hands. Vipers! They were crawling over his shoulders, dropping into his hair, slithering down his face. He twisted and shrieked as their fangs struck and struck again, begging the Holy Virgin for mercy, but mercy was not granted.

When the first brilliant rays of the rising sun touched the tops of the hills, all that remained of the noble knight of St John of Jerusalem was dismembered, bloodstained bones. The birds had feasted well. Before anyone discovered them, the bones would be covered with moss, indistinguishable from the roots of the twisted trees and the rocks among which they lay scattered. Those who stumbled over the skull would think it another mossy boulder. Ferns would grow through those broken ribs, liverworts plant themselves in the eye sockets. The birds would rear their young, safe and warm, in nests lined with strands of grey hair.

Pick nothing up in that wood. Take nothing from it, for who knows whose remains you will hold in your hand? Do not disturb the resting place of the dead, for the hounds that guard it guard it well.

Chapter 55

Hospitallers' Priory of St Mary

Meggy drew her chair closer to her fire, prodding it to send the flames blazing upwards. Outside, the wind wailed like a soul in torment and monstrous shadows flickered across the courtyard walls. All the days she had lived at the priory, the old gatekeeper had prided herself that she had loyally obeyed whatever orders the prioress had given, even if she thought them foolish. She'd have laid down her life as willingly as any knight of St John, not for the order – she had little patience with that – but for Johanne and this priory. But though the prioress had given instructions that fuel was to be kept for the kitchens and the infirmary, tonight Meggy knew it was wise to disobey: the prioress might know all about the running of a priory but she was a babe in clouts when it came to understanding the ways of Dertemora. It wasn't the chill wind that drove Meggy to this small act of defiance – she was well used to feeling the cold and expected no less at her time of life. It was the hounds.

She'd heard the beasts baying across the moors and felt again their great rasping claws on her back and their fangs

438

snapping inches from her cheek. Her hand strayed unbidden to where the little bag had once hung at her waist before they had ripped it from her, almost cutting her in two. Save for that bloodstained rag, it hadn't contained much – her son's milk tooth and an iron nail her husband had fashioned into a little cross to keep her safe. It was all she'd got left of her menfolk . . . all she'd had, for those precious objects were now scattered somewhere among the heather and grasses of the moor.

She knew the hounds had chased to stop her taking that rag to old Kendra, though she'd no idea why. Still, she counted herself blessed. There were not many souls who'd come face to face with the wisht hounds and lived to tell the tale. Those spectral hounds were hunting their prey again tonight and Meggy was in no hurry to chance her luck twice. If Brother Nicholas was still out there on those moors then God help him, for Old Crockern wouldn't and the knight deserved all that was coming to him.

Poor young Brengy had still not returned. Dye had tearfully begged the sisters to search for her brother, though she was too afraid to go out on the moor in the dark herself.

But Sister Clarice had said firmly there was nothing to be done until cockcrow. 'If we start wandering around out there at night, one of us will end up in a bog or worse, and with the wind as strong as this, even with torches we might walk within a foot of where he's lying and not hear him even if he's able to cry out.'

Prioress Johanne had agreed. 'There is little point in starting any search tonight. Sleep will serve us better. The servants and sisters can set out at first light tomorrow. We've no idea where Brother Nicholas set Brengy down, if indeed he did. He might have decided to take the lad with him all the way to Buckland.'

The prioress had looked more drawn and anxious than Meggy had ever seen her, but she knew the poor soul had more on her mind than the missing stable lad.

Meggy had coaxed Dye out of her wailing by asking her to help dip new torches and set them blazing on the walls outside, telling her that their lights could be seen as far off as Exeter. All Brengy had to do was walk towards them from wherever he found himself. The gatekeeper promised to sit up and listen for the bell all night till he came home. Besides, she told herself, she'd never be able to close her eyes with Old Crockern's hounds howling out there on the moor. Privately, she wondered if poor Brengy would ever return. She wouldn't put it past that devil Nicholas to throw the boy into the mire, like he'd threatened, just from spite, though she'd never have said as much to Dye. No sense in setting her off again.

The sisters had long retired to their beds, but Meggy found she couldn't rest until she'd checked and rechecked that the gates to the priory were locked and braced. She'd pulled a charred stick from the fire and drawn crosses on the threshold and casement of her hut, and binding knot signs around the fire to prevent evil from entering. Alban's ghost, and maybe poor little Brengy's too now, would be wandering the moor, searching for the lych-ways, and it was well known that such lost souls who'd been snatched violently from life were drawn to the living. They would try to enter their cottages and even creep into the mouths of those who lay sleeping inside, so desperate were they to remain in this world.

But in spite of the wind, the distant baying of the hounds and her own fear, the old gatekeeper was exhausted, and the heat from the fire made her eyelids grow heavy, though she tried to resist sleep. She floated in that twilight between sleep and waking, noises from this world mingling with those from some place far off in her dreams, so that when the door of her hut creaked open, it seemed to her that the sound belonged in another realm.

Soft footfalls rustled through the bracken strewn on the beaten-earth floor. The flames bowed low in the breeze from the figure passing, then leaped up wildly. A small branch popped, and cracked open as the sap oozed out with a long, hissing sigh. Old Meggy jerked upright, almost over-toppling in her chair. The boy was standing not a foot away from her, his face half in darkness and half bathed in the ruby firelight. His head moved slightly from side to side, like a snake's, as if he was trying to sense where she was.

'What do you want this time of night? How did you get here?' Meggy demanded.

Even to herself she sounded angry, but the boy didn't flinch.

He tilted his face up, but his sightless gaze was fixed somewhere over her shoulder. Meggy half turned her head, fearing that something or someone was behind her, though she knew even as she did so that it was something blind folks did. They always said old Father Guthlac was looking at angels, but she was sure it wasn't any creature from Heaven the boy saw.

He took a pace forward, shuffling, feeling his way. He was learning how to move. Then his hand followed. It groped towards her and she wanted to draw back so he wouldn't touch her, but it seemed a cruel thing to do to a child. Instead, against her will, she found herself stretching out her own gnarled hand, touching the icy fingers. The boy immediately grasped it and began to tug her towards the door.

'Hold hard! Where do you think you're going this time of night?'

She couldn't imagine what the child was doing so far from the infirmary. Had he slipped out to use the garderobe and been unable to find his way back? But no one used the garderobe at night – that was what the pisspots in the chambers were for. If the child heard her question, he gave no sign. Although Meggy's arms were far stronger than those of most women her age, from years of toiling alongside her husband in the forge, she found she could not free herself from his grip.

The boy dragged the door open and the wind barged in, clanging together the worn iron pots dangling from the rafters, tumbling ropes and nets to the floor and sending the ash and smoke from the flames swirling, like a whirlpool, about the small hut. Meggy gave a cry of alarm. The wind often made mischief when the door was opened, but the gate lodge was sheltered behind the high wall and it had never ransacked her room like this before. It was as if her home had been plucked up and set down on the very pinnacle of Fire Tor.

'We'll be knocked off our feet, if we venture out there,' she bellowed, above the roar. 'You'd best spend the rest of the night in here.'

She struggled to slam the door, but either the wind or the boy was too strong – it must be the wind, surely. The grip on her hand tightened and, though she tried to resist it, she felt herself being pulled out into the darkened courtyard, as if her wrist was bound to a plough horse. She was punched and shoved by the gale and would have come crashing down several times, had the boy not clung to her, dragging her

442

towards the great oak gates. Shutters whimpered against the flailing wind. Pails were thrown across the courtyard. Broken twigs and chips of goat bone were dashed against Meggy's face, and now it had begun to rain again, great cold stinging drops that lashed her skin.

She fought to turn back for the shelter of her little hut, but the boy pushed her hand up against the oak beam that braced the gates. She did not have to hear him speak to know he wanted her to wrest it back and open it.

'You can't go out there, lad! There's a storm building and death hounds are hunting. I'll not open those gates tonight, even if the Good Lord himself comes a-knocking.'

He took her hand again, pushing it over and over against the brace. Still, Meggy tried to drag him away, but it was as if he suddenly weighed as much as a full-grown bull and she couldn't even lift him to move him aside. Then, above the roar of the wind, she heard the sound of the bell tolling. Someone was outside, begging for admittance. Brengy! Was that what the child had been trying to tell her? Had he heard the bell over the noise of the wind when her old ears could not?

She was already tugging at the beam, when caution stayed her hand. She had never opened the gate without checking first, and maybe it was only the fierce wind that was rocking the bell. She opened the shutter over the metal grille and peered out.

Two figures stood there, huddled against the driving rain. Neither was the stable boy – that much she could tell. But the torches outside had long been extinguished and the devil himself could have been standing before her gate and she'd not have known him from the archangel Gabriel. The pair came closer.

443

'Let us in, Meggy. Brigid needs us.'

It was a woman's voice, one she thought she knew, but it was muffled by the storm. The woman came closer, pressing her face to the iron bars. Her hair whipped up in wet strands about her head.

'It's me, Meggy, Morwen. Let us in. The wisht hounds are running. Brigid needs us. The boy needs us.'

Meggy hesitated. The prioress had forbidden Kendra and her tribe of daughters to set foot in the place, and Meggy had always carried out those orders faithfully.

As if Morwen heard her thoughts, she shouted, 'Ma's not with us. She fights against us, against the boy. Help us, Meggy.'

Meggy felt the child's cold fingers on her hand, so icy they burned. She glanced down. The boy was staring at the door, as if he could see right through it. Suddenly he pressed his face against her thigh, sinking, like a child weak with hunger, as if all the strength was draining from him and he could no longer stand. He staggered and she caught him in her arms. She lowered the boy gently to the ground, smoothing the hair from his cold little brow. Then she clambered to her feet, took a deep breath and heaved on the swollen brace beam, dragging it back.

Chapter 56

Morwen

Glancing fearfully around her, Meggy hurried us into the chapel and bolted the door behind us. She set the lantern on the floor, so the light wouldn't be seen through the casements, while she wriggled a great iron key into the door on the far wall. Sorrel edged closer to me and the boy, staring up at the statue of the bloody man hanging on the cross, as if she thought he might raise his carved head and shout for the black crows to chase us out of his house. I was afeared in that place too but not of the crows.

When I was little, and Ma was trading in the village, I'd sometimes slip away from her and peer in through the door of the church. I liked to look at the paintings of men and beasts on the walls, the colours as bright as yellow furze and the scarlet rowans on the hillside. But this chapel wasn't like that. It was a clearing in a dark wood with great pillars, like tree trunks, stretching up all round. I was never scared of the spirits of Fire Tor, or of the ghosts of the moor, but there were shadows slithering round these walls, dark, malevolent creatures who'd never lived in this world but meant to bring harm to any who did, if ever they could cross into this realm.

Old Meggy wrenched open the door and pointed down into the darkness. 'Bryde's Spring is at the bottom of those steps,' she whispered, though even if she'd shouted no one outside, not even a screech owl, would have heard her over the storm. But she didn't move aside to let us pass.

'Kendra said the boy must be kept from the well. She said if his eye opens . . .' Meggy trailed off.

'Aye, Ma spoke the truth of what she saw, but she doesn't understand the meaning of it.'

Still Meggy hesitated. Sorrel took a step towards her. 'Brigid sent the wisht hounds to stop you taking the rag to Kendra. They turned you back. She wants to protect the boy.'

The old woman's head jerked up. 'How do you know that? I didn't tell a soul . . .' She stared at Sorrel, tucking her thumbs beneath her fingers, as if she thought Sorrel might witch her. 'You got the gift, haven't you, like old Kendra?'

Slowly Meggy dragged her gaze from Sorrel. 'But even if I let you take him down there, it won't do you a mite of good, for the well's dry. Spring's stopped running. Some say it's the tinners have done it, but Sister Fina reckons it's . . .' She jerked her chin towards the boy, who clung to my hand.

I shrugged. In truth, I'd no notion what we were to do down there, only that I knew Brigid wanted the boy to be taken to her well. Like Ma said, if you asked what Brigid wanted of you, you must swear to do it, else you must not ask.

Meggy looked from me to Sorrel, then seemed to make up her mind. She stepped aside from the well door and,

446

picking up the lantern, held it out towards me. She said she'd stay up in the chapel and keep watch. But I think she was afeared to come down.

Sorrel and I crept down the stone steps, with the boy between us, me first, stepping sideways so I could keep hold of the boy's hand and guide him down. His legs kept buckling beneath him, but not 'cause he couldn't see. He was as weak as if he'd been starved for days.

The walls shimmered like glow worms on a summer's night, pigsey gold, Ma called it. Suddenly the boy crumpled on to the stone step, his head lolling against his chest.

I pushed the lantern up at Sorrel and knelt on the stairs below the boy, so that I could heft him over my shoulder. He made no sound. I didn't know if he'd fainted, but even through my kirtle I could feel the frog-cold of his body. Was he dying, dead?

I was feeling for the steps with my bare toes, trying to balance the boy and walk into the darkness. But then I could no longer feel a step below and as Sorrel came down behind me with the lantern, I saw that we were standing in the cave, just like I remembered from when I was small, save that there was no water. The stone trough lay empty and raw red, like the belly of a rabbit when its guts have been torn out. On a ledge above the well stood a painted statue of a woman grasping a long dagger, pointed down at the ancient stone carving of Brigid, as if she meant to gouge out the old mother's eyes.

I laid the boy as gently as I could on the rocky floor, his eyes were open, staring straight up, unblinking, but he didn't move, though I could see his little chest rising and falling in fluttering breaths, like a wild bird when you hold it in your hand.

Sorrel crouched beside me. 'There's not even a drop of water . . . What can we do?'

I closed my eyes. I was in Ma's cottage. A little girl lay on the floor and her granddam sat facing Ma across the hearth fire. I watched Ma clenching her fingers about the smoke, saw it sucked up into her fist.

'Brigid's closed the water in her hand. Only she can release it.'

There was no need for me to tell Sorrel what to do now. She knew better than me. She settled herself on the floor, and grew still. Sorrel didn't need to sing to open the door 'twixt the living and dead. But I sang, not to summon the spirits but to hold back those creatures of shadow that prowled above our heads. They were trying to enter, trying to cross into this world, and though the moon was hidden from mortal sight, it was a duru moon. They no more needed to see its light than I needed to see an open doorway to walk through it in the dark.

I could feel them massing, trying to find the cracks to slither through, trying to claw down the walls and ooze down the steps until they filled this cave with a darkness that would smother everything. I forced the song against them, trying to make it fill every hole, block every crevice in the cave, as I begged Brigid to hear us, to open her hand and let her spring flow. My knees were pressing hard against the boy's body. A shudder ran through him, like the death throes of a mouse when its neck is snapped. The child was dying, but Brigid wouldn't open her hand. She wouldn't let the waters run.

Sorrel scrambled to her feet. She clambered into the stone trough, then on top of the rim nearest the wall of the cave. Her feet planted on either side, she balanced precariously, steadying herself with her good hand against the rock. For a moment she swayed there, then lifted her hand and reached up to the painted statue. But she had no means of holding on. Before I could get to my feet, she was toppling over. She grabbed the wooden dagger in the statue's hand and dragged it with her as she fell. Both crashed on to the rocky floor of the cave. The head of the painted woman snapped off and bounced away, slamming into the lantern, sending it, too, spinning across the floor. The candle flame guttered wildly and blew out. We were in darkness, save for the green-gold glow of the walls that lingered for a few moments, then slowly began to fade.

'Sorrel, are you hurt?' I scrambled over to her.

She was lying on the floor. I felt her head, trying to see if it was bleeding or broken, but she pushed my hand away. 'Listen!'

Water! Water splashing on stone. The spring was running again! The statue was smashed. The well was Brigid's once more. In the darkness, we lifted the boy and carried him to the trough.

'We need to wash his eyes,' Sorrel murmured.

'No, you need to. Brigid called you to Dertemora for this.'

She didn't argue. The sound of the water changed as she cupped her hand beneath the trickling spring. Then I felt the cold drops fall on my hand as she poured the water over the boy's face. Once, twice, three times three.

As Brigid of Imbolc brings back the sun
As the Sun gives sight to earth
As the earth opens to the green mist
So may his eyes open to see
So may his eyes open to see
So may his eyes open to see.

The spring was gushing from the rock now, the sound almost deafening as it thundered down into the stone trough. I was drenched in a fine mist. Water was creeping up the side and starting to spill on to the floor of the cave. The moss on the walls began to glow, though no candle had been lit, softly at first like the first light of a winter's dawn, then brighter and brighter, like the summer's sun glinting on a pool. As I gaped at the walls, I felt the boy drawing out from my arms. I caught sight of Sorrel. She was staring over my shoulder towards where the boy stood behind me, her mouth open as if she had cried out, but I could hear nothing above the roaring of the water. I turned my head to look at the boy, but he had vanished.

Chapter 57

Dertemora

A crackling blue lightning flash split the dark sky above the tinners' valley. The thunderclap, when it came, rampaged around the hills, hurling itself from one side to the other, like a caged beast. Rain thrashed the bare sides of the valley, streaming down in torrents, dragging the mud and gravel with it.

Inside the storehouse, a woman pushed Gleedy's sweaty head from her breasts and struggled to slide out from beneath his slippery carcass. She froze, holding her breath, as Gleedy grunted and rolled over. In the dim lamplight, she watched a silver snail's track of drool trickle down his chinless face and soak into the straw pallet. Gleedy had drunk the best part of the flagon of wine but, even so, she was amazed he could sleep through this storm.

The woman pulled down her skirts and tiptoed across the floor towards the stores. There were stacks of tools, ladders and buckets to be had, but she knew that most of the boxes, barrels and sacks that had once contained dried beans, salted meat or flour were now as empty as a staved wine cask. The

451

last time Gleedy had dragged her to his bed, she had seen him take her payment of food out of the boxes hidden beneath the empty barrels, but she dared not risk waking him by shifting them.

A dazzling white flash of lightning pierced the gaps around the shutters and door, followed a few moments later by a long rumble of thunder. But, as if it was determined to have the last word, the wind roared back even louder and the rain seemed to redouble its efforts to drill through the roof. The woman had to get to her own hut. Her young son would be terrified there alone.

Gleedy's hounds, tethered near the door, were howling and barking loud enough to summon the devil from Hell. Usually a single growl or yap would be enough to send Gleedy scurrying to them, fearful that someone was trying to break in. She'd have to find something to toss to them to keep them back from the door so that she could slip out. He usually kept a sack of dried sheep's trotters close to his bed. She edged back, watching Gleedy for any sign that he might be faking sleep, then found the sack and took out two hoofs. Without planning to, she grabbed three more, stuffing them down the front of her kirtle to add to her cooking pot.

With another anxious glance at the slumbering figure, she hurried to the door and tried to open it quietly. But she had reckoned without the wind. Before she had pulled it more than a hand's width open, it snatched the door and hurled it back against the wall, ripping off one of its leather hinges. The wind charged in, sending stacks of tools crashing to the ground and empty sacks flapping through the air, like flocks of geese. Not even a drunkard could sleep through that.

Gleedy was on his feet with a bellow before his head realised what his body was doing. The hounds were leaping and pulling so hard on their chains that they were choking themselves. The woman threw the two trotters at them, but for once they were neither interested in food nor in any intruders. They were simply desperate to get into the shelter of the storehouse and out of the storm. Gleedy gave a shout of rage, but the woman didn't wait. She fled into the rain-drenched darkness.

Gleedy was halfway across the chamber in pursuit of her when a blast of icy air on his naked cods reminded him that he was clad only in a short shirt. He was torn between his need to force the door shut and his fear of anyone catching sight of him in the lantern light. A pile of iron pots crashed to the floor, and he ran to the door, trying to wrestle it shut, but it was hanging sideways by the one remaining hinge that was also on the point of ripping from the wood. Against the force of this wind, it would take at least two men even to get it upright and force it back into the doorway. Icy rain dashed against his face as if a man was tossing buckets of water through the hole where the door should have been. Though it did not entirely sober Gleedy, it shook him fully awake.

He abandoned his efforts and hastily pulled on his breeches and a cloak. Not even attempting to lace his hose, he thrust his bare feet into the boots and ran out into the storm past the howling dogs, heading towards the blowing-house. He intended to order whoever was working there to return with him and force the door back into place, before the wind wreaked any more havoc or those thieving tinners started looting his stores. And someone had better be there manning that furnace, or he'd see to it that by morning they were tramping the moor without so much as a shirt on their backs.

But, once outside, he found he could barely stand against

the gale, much less see where he was going. Rain, grit and shards of stone were flung into his watering eyes as if they were fired at him by a hundred bowmen. Water poured off the hillside, turning paths into streams and washing away great chunks of mud and stone, sending them slithering to the valley. The river roared down its diverted course, dragging rocks the size of a man's head with it, and even though the sluice gate, which dammed the lake, was closed, the ditch below it was rapidly filling with rain and the muddy water pouring off the land above.

Just in time Gleedy glimpsed a chunk of wood hurtling towards him. He managed to sidestep it, but slipped in the mud and crashed down on his back, landing in the water that was racing down the track. Not that the wetting made much difference, for he was already soaked, but the heavy fall shook him, while the wine and his recent exertions had, for the moment, robbed him of the strength to right himself.

Lightning sizzled down, like a blazing spear thrown to earth, causing Gleedy to squint up. Two figures stood on the edge of the lake above the blowing-house staring down into the valley. He saw them only for as long as a white flash lit the moor, but his mind held on to the image as darkness closed in again. He was sure he had seen two women up there, their hair and skirts whirling about them, their arms open, held up to the sky as if they were calling upon the heavens to throw down all their arrows, daring a thunderbolt to strike them. Had they run completely mad? The wind alone could knock them into the lake or send them plummeting down into the valley. Even a village idiot would have enough wit to seek shelter. He certainly wouldn't have ventured out even this far, had that bitch not let the wind break his door. She'd pay dearly for that when he caught up with her.

He dragged himself upright, cursing as he slipped again in the streaming mud. He wiped the water from his eyes and glanced back to where he'd seen the women. It was hard to distinguish anything through the rain, but he was certain they were still there. Was it even possible to stand up there against this? Maybe they weren't flesh and blood at all.

Eva! Could her ghost have risen? The other had only one arm raised – he was sure that was what he'd seen in the lightning flash. One arm – Sorrel? Had she, too, perished out on that moor? That was what he'd wished, what she deserved. But had she, too, returned from the dead to haunt him?

A cold snake of fear slithered down Gleedy's spine and curled itself inside his guts. Whatever was up there he had no intention of staying out here alone. He ran for the blowing-house, slipping and sliding all the way. Crashing to his knees, he struggled up again, ignoring the stinging and the warm trickle of blood running down his leg. He reached the door. It was shut! It was never shut! He pounded on the wood, though no one inside could have heard him above the thunder rolling around the hills. Eventually his fuddled, panic-stricken mind grasped at the memory that even this door had a latch. He groped over the sodden wood, like a blind man searching for lost treasure. Several times his fingers came within inches of it, but he couldn't remember whether it was high or low, much less see it. By the time his numbed hand struck it, his eyes were streaming, not just from the driving rain but with tears of fear and frustration. He dragged on the latch, leaning with all his weight against the wood. As the door swung open, the wind shoved it so violently that he fell head first into the building, almost dashing his brains out on one of the granite ingot moulds inside.

As he dragged himself to his knees, scrubbing the water from his eyes, two men rushed past him and fought to push the door shut against the storm. Gleedy felt a surge of relief and annoyance, relief to be safely inside and in the company of half a dozen men, and annoyed by the grins on the tinners' faces at the sight of him sprawling at their feet. Suddenly aware of the rain dripping from his hair and the mud clinging to him, his irritation was not assuaged by the realisation that he must look like a drowned cat fished from a well. The men silently returned to the furnace, warming their hands and glancing warily at one another.

Now that he was safely inside, in the light and heat of the blowing-house, the very notion that he had seen two vengeful ghosts seemed risible and he could hardly believe that he had allowed it to take such a hold of him. His anger at his own foolishness turned in a flash on those around him, as he gradually became aware that inside the blowing-house one sound should have been louder even than that of the raging storm, but it wasn't. The great waterwheel was silent, as were the huge bellows it pumped.

'Who gave orders for that wheel to be shut down?' he demanded.

The men glanced at each other. Then the stoker raised his head. 'Reckon it were me. Water's coming down at such a lick that if we hadn't disconnected the wheel it would've broken its shaft and been smashed to pieces.'

Gleedy wasn't stupid. He knew the stoker had done the right thing. Truth be told, he'd probably saved Gleedy's hide for, as he'd had cause to remind the tinners often enough, Master Odo had paid a fortune to build the blowing-house. If the wheel had been destroyed it would not only have cost a tidy sum to replace, but smelting would have been halted for weeks. Nevertheless, Gleedy was not in a mood to show gratitude, not when he'd seen them laughing at him.

'So, you think that if the wheel isn't running, you can sit on your backsides for days till the furnace heats up again? And I suppose you imagine Master Odo is going to pay you for doing nothing. There's an assay meeting in Tavistock in less than a month and if we don't have a full load for the assay master to test, then Master Odo'll not be a happy man, not if he's made to look a fool in front of the other tin owners. If he doesn't get his money, you'll not get yours. That I can promise you. So, if you can't use the wheel, you'd best pump the bellows by your own muscle, for if that smelting is ruined by the furnace cooling, it'll be your wives and young 'uns that'll go hungry and all those men out there too. And I reckon that if the tinners learn you've lost all they sweated to dig up, you'll find yourselves caged in that wheel, being forced to turn it by crawling.'

An angry muttering broke out. One man faced Gleedy, his face contorted in fury and his great fists clenched. 'Takes two men to pump those bellows. How are we supposed to stoke the fuel, load the heads and pour out the tin too? I've not hands enough, nor strength neither.'

Gleedy flicked his fingers towards the other four men in the blowing-house. 'No sense in them sitting idle watching.'

'We've been breaking our backs all day graffing. You can't expect us to work all night too. We're meant to be sleeping. Only came in here to get warm and dry 'cause our huts are so deep in water only the fish could sleep easy in there. Rain's flooding down that hillside. I reckon most of them will have collapsed by morning.'

As if to prove his words, another long growl of thunder rumbled round the valley and the rain redoubled its efforts to pound through the roof, drowning the tinner's words, so that he was forced to bellow. 'Every tinner and his brat in this camp will be making their way up here afore long. There'll not be room to hang a man then, much less keep that furnace burning. We'll have to bed down in the storehouse. That and this blowing-house are the only dry places left.'

Gleedy made a noise somewhere between a strangled croak and a screech, as he was suddenly brought back to the reason he had made his way to the blowing-house. The very idea of the tinners and their families wandering unchecked around his storehouse in the middle of the night was enough to cause an iron band to squeeze so tightly around his chest that he could barely breathe. His jaw throbbed with pain. He wouldn't have a bean or a pot left to cook it in by morning, if that thieving rabble got in.

'You and you.' He pointed at two of the more burly and skilful men. 'I need you to fix the hinges of the storehouse door. They've been torn away and it won't close. If a strong blast of wind gets in and under that roof, it'll lift it right off.'

Gleedy was infuriated to catch the half-concealed grins that darted between the tinners. Anyone would think they were amused by the thought of the storehouse being destroyed. They wouldn't be laughing if there was no food for them to buy next week, or a new pick head, when their old one snapped or was stolen. See if they found starving to death a cause for mirth. But even he knew that that argument wouldn't persuade them to help him tonight.

'It breaks my heart to think of those poor little children and their mothers, soaked to the very marrow, toiling up here only to find that there's nowhere to shelter from the storm,' Gleedy said dolefully. 'It'll be the death of some of them, I shouldn't wonder, if they should find themselves out in this bitter wind and rain all night.'

Morwen and Sorrel steadied each other against the buffeting of the wind and gazed down into the valley, watching the glimmers of silvery white that marked the lines of the foaming river and the ditch. Streams of water ran down the raw hillsides, like blood from a flayed back. Waves whipped up by the wind and the tumbling waterfalls raced across the black lake at their feet, crashing against boulders and splashing over the dam wall and sluice gate.

The feeble red and yellow pinpricks from the tinners' fires at the far end of the valley had been snuffed out by wind and rain. All the valley had been plunged into darkness, except for the plume of smoke that gusted from the blowing-house, lit from below by an unearthly red glow, as if it was rising from the fires of Hell.

It is time!

The heads of the two women turned as one, strands of wet hair writhing into the dark sky. Rain ran from their clothes, their skin, their fingers, their bare feet, gushing like twin springs into the lake. On the other side of the water, the blind boy stood so still that it seemed even the wind was afraid to come near him. Morwen began to sing, her voice rising into the storm above the roar. Other voices, unseen, joined hers, as if a thousand curlews had taken wing.

The boy crouched on the bare, bleeding hillside. He bowed his head and Sorrel held out her arm across the raging water. Slowly, like a new leaf unfurling, he rose, but he was growing taller, broader, his fingers thick and strong, his muscles swelling, his legs lengthening. Great beetle brows hung over dark eyes, craggy cheeks and a sharp, angular nose. Like an old tree awakening from the depths of a winter's sleep, the boy, an old man now, an ancient man, aged as the tor on which he stood, stretched his gnarled fingers across the lake. His voice boomed, like a thunderclap.

My land, this is my land!

Old Crockern's eyes were open and the lightning that flashed blue from them shot like an arrow across the water to the very edge of the lake. It struck the wooden sluice gate, shattering it into a thousand burning fragments. With a roar almost louder than Crockern's, the water of the lake surged over the edge, sweeping rocks and boulders and all before it, down, down into the deep valley below.

Gleedy watched the two sullen tinners struggling to hold the door of the blowing-house. He barged out in front of them, leaving them to follow. But the moment the three were outside, the wind charged into them, knocking them hard against the wooden door, as if it was trying to punch them back in through the cracks. The men stood for a moment in the lee of the wall trying to regain their balance. They wiped the lashing rain from their eyes and braced themselves to step out into the full force of the storm.

Gleedy, his arms wrapped tightly but uselessly around himself, shuffled from foot to foot, yelling at them to hurry. The tinners scowled and swore, not troubling to lower their voices, knowing the weasel would never hear them over the wind.

'When we get in there, I'll keep him occupied. You grab any food you find. Split it with you after.'

Gleedy was staring down the valley. He was sure he could hear men shouting, struggling to make themselves heard above the pounding rain and water surging through the wooden leats. He thought he could glimpse people moving along the valley below. If he didn't get that door back in place before that rabble got up here . . .

All three men glanced up as a great boom echoed across the lake above, and they were still staring as the lightning bolt sizzled through the blackness and the sluice gate burst apart. Burning fragments of wood arced scarlet through the black sky. The tinners dived for the shelter of the wall, covering their heads as burning wood showered down. But Gleedy, standing further out, seemed rooted to the spot. He stared as a plank somersaulted in the air, showering red and yellow sparks as it fell straight towards him. Only at the very last moment did his legs stir into life and he tried to run, but it was too late. The fiery wood struck him on the back, knocking him face down into the mud. Gleedy lay pinned beneath the burning plank. The flames blazed up into the darkness.

He screamed as fire danced up his back and down his thighs. Had his shirt and breeches not been sodden, his whole body would have been instantly engulfed in flames, but even so the heat was so fierce that his skin was bubbling, blistering, like that of a roasting piglet. But even as he struggled in vain to free himself, his cries were lost beneath a deafening roar.

A flood of water and boulders crashed down upon the blowing-house and the storehouse. It swept around the stone walls. The blowing-house stood its ground for a few moments, but even it could not withstand the force bearing down. Water, rocks and now the entire contents of the storehouse were hurled against its walls, with all the force of a siege engine, and the blowing-house, though sturdy, was no castle.

A corner shuddered and collapsed. The flood poured in and hit the red-hot furnace, which burst wide open, spewing steam, burning wood and molten tin into the maelstrom. The remainder of the blowing-house toppled sideways and caved in, severing the cries of the men trapped inside.

Below in the valley, the tinners stared up at the great wall of water sweeping down towards them out of the darkness, dragging men and rocks with it. Their minds were unable to grasp what was roaring towards them until the moment that the freezing tide hit them. Then the shrieks and screams of the men, women and children were drowned in the skull-splitting howl of that flood.

Gleedy knew only a moment of relief from pain as the icy water doused the burning beam, before he, too, was swept gasping and choking into the valley below, his helpless body battered and thrashed by the barrels, ladders, spades and iron pots all churning in the raging surge.

Chapter 58

Prioress Johanne

I hear the door of the chapel open and close, but I do not look round. I know who it is and why they've come. It is the darkest hour of the night, when all of the candles and torches are burned away and when the embers of the fires are buried so deep beneath their snowfall of ashes you think they can never be revived. Only the oil lamp hanging in the sanctuary still flickers, spilling a pool of blood-red light on the altar to trickle down on to the floor.

The priory has been at peace for more than three months, the kind of peace that steals over a dying man in the hour before his death, a calmness and resignation, when the fight to stay alive has finally been surrendered. And we, too, have surrendered to death.

In the cave below where I kneel, the waters have finally subsided. The night of the storm, when the well overflowed, the spring ran, like blood pumping from a wounded heart. Water rose up the steps and streamed out beneath the door, flowing across the chapel floor. We didn't discover it until the evening of the next day, for that night it rained so hard that the courtyard itself was turned into a lake, water pouring in under the doors of all the chambers, cascading down the steps into the kitchen and extinguishing every fire.

It was a month, maybe more, before the waters in the cave finally seeped away and the holy spring retreated to its bounds within the trough, flowing gently as it had before the boy came. It was only when the waters had retreated that I found the statue of St Lucia, which I had placed above the well to sanctify it and cleanse it of the old goddess. It must have been washed off the shelf in the flood. It lay in two pieces on the floor of the cave, the head snapped off as if the ancient goddess herself had hurled it down in a fit of rage. Blind and dumb now, St Lucia's painted eyes and lips had been washed away by the battering and rolling of the water. Her dagger was smashed.

The ancient stone face that gazes out beneath the veil of the spring is unmarked, unchanged, but our saint is broken, defeated, destroyed. The old goddess has won and we are forced to retreat, for the flood has weakened the foundations of the chapel. Great cracks have appeared in the walls. It is only a matter of time before it collapses. It will not survive another winter. *We* cannot survive another winter.

And now the day has come, the Day of Judgment, of reckoning. I have spent these past nights in prayer and repentance, but I do not know if I shall ever be forgiven. For I have stolen a man's life, killed him. Snatched a heretic from the Church before he could be brought to repentance and absolution. Sentenced him to everlasting Hell.

Know this, that it was my hand who stole the dwale from Sister Basilia's stores. It was my hand that poured the syrup into the Holy Blood of Christ taken from the tabernacle high in the wall of the chapel, for it was the only wine left in the priory that by some miracle the flood had not spoiled. It must serve as his viaticum to strengthen his soul for his journey into the next world, for there was no priest to anoint him with chrism or pronounce the final absolution. It was my hand that held the cup of wine mingled with dwale, not water, to his lips. My arms that cradled him and my lips that murmured soothing words to him as he slipped gently into the sleep from which he would never wake.

I cradled him against my breast as his heartbeat retreated into the far distance, as his breathing faded to the whisper of a babe. Held him as once, long ago, I had hugged him when the night terrors had woken him as a child. Had the boy glimpsed the torments that lay in wait for the man? Had he, even then, seen visions of the terrors the future held for him?

I know what foul things they had said of the Templars. Every vile act that the holy and righteous men of the Inquisition could imagine they had accused those knights of committing. Every foul demon the Inquisitors could name they had charged the knights with worshipping in ceremonies so depraved that even the devil himself would have blushed to witness them. They had tried to force Sebastian to confess that he had worshipped the head of a devil or a golden image of a dog-headed god. They had tortured him until he could not stand, then tormented him still more until his mind was smashed into shards that could never be repaired, leaving only the terrible memories that flayed him afresh every time he closed his eyes.

I had watched the Inquisition burn those Templars who would not confess. Every day I wake with the burning stench of their flesh in my nostrils and their shrieks in my ears. They say the men died bravely. They say they died as courageously

465

as the noble knights they were, singing praises to God. But no mortal man, no man made of flesh and blood and pain, no man condemned to those cruel flames dies like a knight in battle. They perish writhing and screaming until their throats are seared and their shrieks are silenced, but even that does not bring the mercy of death.

Sebastian did not burn. He confessed and was released, if you can call it release to send him out caged in such a twisted carcass of pain. But the confession was false. I knew my brother could never be guilty of any of those foul deeds. I was his sister, his twin. I had known him and loved him since the day our mother had birthed us. I did not need him to tell me he was innocent.

Our father had played a game of cross and pile, flipped a coin, one of us to be given to the Templars, the other to the Hospitallers. If the coin had fallen the other way, as I'd prayed as a child it would, Sebastian would have been safe. And I thought God had answered his prayers. I thought God had chosen my brother, blessed him, not me. A coin, just a coin on which our whole lives were to spin for ever.

Sebastian never knew an hour's peace after the Inquisitors let him go. He wept daily because he had confessed. He cursed himself for his weakness, because braver men had gone gladly to their deaths singing psalms. I tried to tell him that the crackle of the flames had not been drowned by their singing, as the legends say. I knew the truth of it. I'd tried to convince him that he had endured far more than many who had died. What good would his denial have done? The Inquisition, the kings and the bishops would never have believed him. They did not want to believe him. What would his death have accomplished?

But he knew only guilt that his brother knights were dead

466

and he still lived. *Could that pitiful existence be called life?* And I knew that next time they questioned him he would recant that confession. He would be presented as a gift from the Knights of St John to their masters, a burnt-offering, proof of their loyalty to Pope and Crown. But I have watched a thousand men burn nightly in my dreams, each with my brother's face. I could not let them take him. Can you understand that? Can you forgive me? Will he?

Holy Virgin, let me take his place in Hell. Let me suffer while he is finally at peace. And if Heaven will not open its gates to him, then let him be granted sweet oblivion.

Chapter 59

Hospitallers' Priory of St Mary

The knights from Clerkenwell arrived just as Brother Nicholas and Brother Alban had done, after nightfall, muddy, cold and hungry. Six of them. No carter this time, for though the frosts came and went, the ice had never lingered long enough to freeze the deep mud, and more rain had fallen, widening the already flooded rivers and deepening the puddles.

It was only when they were slumped in the refectory, devouring slices of cold goat's brawn, that their leader, Brother Roul, had insisted Brother Nicholas and Brother Alban should be asked to join them.

'Brother Nicholas left us three months ago,' Prioress Johanne told them. 'Our stable boy informed me that he set out in the middle of the night, taking one of our horses, since his own had cast a shoe. I imagine you will find him at Buckland.'

Brother Roul leaned forward, frowning. 'Three months? Even with the roads as foul as this and stopping nightly for shelter he should have reached Buckland in days, a week or two at the most. But Commander John de Messingham arrived in Clerkenwell less than a month ago, and he told the Lord Prior he had neither seen Brother Nicholas nor received any of the reports he had expected from him since he was dispatched here. Both Commander John and the Lord Prior are anxious to hear from him. They've become concerned that some disaster or deadly contagion has ravaged the priory, for there's been no word from anyone. It's why we were ordered here, to discover the cause. Has Brother Alban had word from Brother Nicholas since he left?'

'He's dead,' Sister Melisene blurted out. She paused in the throes of directing a couple of servants who were carrying in the straw-filled pallets that were needed for those brothers who would have to sleep in the refectory. She hastily busied herself arranging blankets, as if the words had not come from her.

'You believe Brother Nicholas has perished?' Roul asked sharply.

'My sister is referring to the passing of Brother Alban,' the prioress said, before Melisene had a chance to jump in again. 'He tragically died shortly before Brother Nicholas left. Indeed, that is why we assumed Brother Nicholas rode off in such haste, to convey his heart to Buckland for burial, since the state of the roads made it impossible to take his body there by wagon.'

In spite of their hunger, all of the brothers had stopped eating, their knives suspended in mid-air, as if they had turned to granite.

'But what manner of death was it?' Brother Roul demanded. 'Did he die of a fever?'

The other knights around the table now began to regard each other with alarm.

'I went to the infirmary,' one muttered. 'There was an old crone in the corner so yellow she looked as if she'd been dipped in saffron. Even the whites of her eyes were like mustard.'

The door opened and Dye edged in. She began to collect the empty trenchers. Roul heaved himself from the prioress's chair, which he had been occupying, and strode over, intercepting the scullion before she had a chance to reach the door. She backed against the wall, alarmed.

'You, girl, I warrant you know all of the gossip in this place. Can you remember back three months ago, when the two knights, Brother Nicholas and Brother Alban, were here? Did either of them fall sick?'

Dye's gaze darted towards her prioress, but the knight shifted his position slightly, deliberately blocking her view with his broad shoulders.

'Not them, Master. Always tell when a man or a pig is sick 'cause they can't stomach their meats, but the brothers must have been the fittest men alive – they ate enough for a dozen men and a dozen pigs too.'

The knights around the table roared with laughter and visibly relaxed a little.

'So how did Brother Alban die, girl?'

'Wisht hounds, that's what they say, Master. He was hunted down by the terrible black hounds who haunt these moors.'

Brother Roul swilled the sour, watered wine around in his mouth and spat it into the fire, but nothing seemed to remove the foul taste of the grave that clung to his tongue and crawled up his nostrils. He'd been outraged to discover that Brother Alban's corpse was not lying in the stone drying coffin but had been hastily buried in the sodden ground where it lay rotting in several inches of water. It confirmed his suspicions that there was much about the brother sergeant's death that Prioress Johanne and the other sisters were anxious to conceal.

He had learned that neither coroner nor sheriff had been summoned when Alban's corpse had been discovered, though plainly his death had been sudden and violent, and he did not for one moment believe the servants' tales of spectral hounds. To learn that one of the two Hospitallers, who'd been dispatched on the order of the Lord Prior to investigate the financial affairs of a priory, had met with an unnatural end, and to discover that the corpse had been hastily dumped in the mire without Buckland or Clerkenwell even being informed of his demise would have aroused the suspicions of a saint. And if that was not bad enough, it seemed that within hours of the corpse being discovered, a noble knight of the order had vanished in the middle of the night without even waiting for his own horse to be shod.

Roul had searched the knight's chambers himself and, with growing alarm, had discovered that not only had Nicholas abandoned all his clothes and possessions but had left his sword hanging on a peg near his bed. A sword was as dear to a knight as his right arm. He would no more set foot outside without it than he would lop off a limb and leave that hanging on the wall. Here was certain proof that Nicholas had not willingly embarked on any journey, not even as far as the nearby village, much less to Buckland or Clerkenwell. If his brother knight had left the priory at all, it must have been as a prisoner or corpse.

Roul had ordered Alban's grave opened the very next day, much against the protests of the village deacon, who warned of all manner of ills that would follow such a wicked desecration of the resting place of a man in holy orders. The sisters had withdrawn, leaving the grim-faced knights watching while Brengy, the stable boy, and an elderly manservant dug into the squelching soil. It was almost impossible to distinguish mud from the soaked and soiled winding sheet, and they only realised the spade had cut into the corpse's shoulder when a stench as foul as Satan's farts rolled up towards them. Brengy gagged and fled, but only managed to get a few yards away before he doubled over, vomiting so violently it seemed he might retch up his own guts. The knights, though they had encountered plenty of fresh corpses in their time, found themselves stepping backwards and gritting their teeth to avoid humiliating themselves by emulating the boy.

When some of the festering grave gases had dispersed, and with a cloth clamped to his mouth and nose, Roul, with a knight who had worked as a physician on the ships, examined the corpse. It was impossible to say what had finally killed their brother, but in spite of the putrefaction, one thing was evident: his heart had not been cut from his chest. Was that evidence that Nicholas had had a hand in his brother's death? Did he fear the corpse would bleed in the presence of its murderer and proclaim his guilt? Or was Nicholas also lying somewhere, foully slain, like his brother?

Brother Roul drew himself upright in the high-backed chair and studied the woman seated in the centre of the refectory. His five brother knights were ranged along the hard benches that had been pushed against the walls so that they might have something to rest their stiff backs on during the long hours of questioning that had been in progress since Prime that morning. The winter sun had long since vanished behind the high walls, and the fiery glow from its dying rays skimmed through the top of the casement, casting a blood-red puddle of light at the woman's feet.

Roul had sent for each of the sisters in turn, with those few servants he considered might have at least some wits, but neither coaxing nor threats had produced a tale from any of them that made sense. The sisters talked of plagues of frogs, flies and water turning to blood. The servants told wild tales of hellhounds, of a blind boy who was a powerful sorcerer, and even creatures called pigseys who, though they were invisible and barely taller than a man's thigh, were apparently able to spirit away strapping knights who were powerless to resist them. And between these fanciful tales, both sisters and servants had babbled about rampaging tinners and murderous outlaws, as if Dartmoor was to be found on the edge of the world among the isles of the dog-headed men rather than in the civilised realm of fair England.

Roul glanced at his brothers. Some were beginning to look glazed, others shifting on the creaking benches, trying to ease their numbed buttocks. He knew they were willing him to call a halt for the day, but he was determined to finish it. The Lord Prior had made abundantly clear what was expected of his emissary when he'd walked with Roul alone in the private walled garden. It was the only place Lord William could be sure they would not be overheard, for he knew well the maze of listening tubes, squint holes and concealed passages that riddled Clerkenwell, like worm holes in a ship's timbers.

'No scandal, no trial, no outsiders,' he'd commanded. 'Not a breath, not a whisper of any wrong-doing must leak out. Deal with whatever you find, Brother Roul. Deal with it decisively, but discreetly.' And as the knight had knelt for his blessing, he'd added, 'If the end is in God's cause, then the means will always be sanctified.'

Roul had bowed his head obediently. There had been many times when, as a young knight, his conscience had smote him over those means, when he had been jerked from his dreams by the cries of terrified boys or tortured old men, cries that years later still pursued him through the dark and twisting labyrinths of sleep into his waking hours. And as he'd lain in his bed trying to calm his breathing, he'd wondered if the living Christ could gaze down on the agony of His enemies with such solemn-eyed indifference as He did in his painted image on the walls of the churches as He watched the damned being clawed into Hell.

But later, when Roul had seen for himself what his enemies did in the name of their god, he had come to believe that it was not for a man like him to reason the cruelties of Heaven. And there was no question of not doing his duty now. If the order was disbanded and the Knights of St John arrested as the Templars had been, the women would be lost anyway. Better that they be sacrificed than thousands tortured. Besides, if they were guilty of the deaths of two of their brothers, not to mention stealing money from their holy order when it was most needed to defend Christendom from the Turks, then Christ Himself demanded their punishment.

'Sister Basilia,' Roul said.

The plump woman was staring up at the fragment of jewelled light still gleaming at the top of the narrow casement. She smiled at him in spite of the anxiety that was evident on her face, like a child who was eager to please but afraid she would not be able to do what was asked of her.

'We have been informed that on the night Brother Alban's

corpse was brought to the priory, Brother Nicholas went into the chapel, apparently to remove Brother Alban's heart. But it would appear he never had the chance to do so because he received a blow to the head. And you were summoned to the chapel to attend to his wound.'

'It wasn't a blow, Brother Roul.'

'It wasn't? You mean he had no head injury when you examined him?'

'His head was hurt, poor lamb. He had quite a nasty bruise here.' She tapped her temple to indicate the place, then frowned. 'Oh dear, perhaps it was this side,' she said, changing hands. 'It was over three months ago and I can't quite be sure. Now let me see. He was lying—'

Conscious of the audible groan from one of his brothers behind him, Roul hastily cut her off. 'You admit his head was bruised, Sister, yet you have just said he didn't suffer a blow.'

Basilia, thrown by the interruption, shook her head, apparently trying to clear her thoughts, making her chins waggle. 'Oh dear, I'm sorry, Brother. What I meant was that a *blow* makes it sound as if someone had struck him, which they hadn't, of course. He slipped . . . down in the well. The floor's always wet. I didn't see it myself, but that's what the Prioress Johanne told Brother Nicholas. She explained to him that he'd slipped and hit his head on the rocky wall. There are lots of rocks sticking out and—'

'The prioress told him? He didn't remember?'

'He was confused. People often are after they've knocked themselves out. Like I told him, I once had to physic a woman . . .' This time Basilia caught the exasperated expression on Roul's face and managed to stop herself. She took a deep breath. 'Poor Brother Nicholas saw Sister Fina behind him on the steps holding a knife. He told the prioress he was afraid our sister was going to stab him but, of course, she'd never dream of doing such a thing. She'd seen a light moving in the chapel. Sister Fina thought it was thieves who had broken in, but as soon as she realised it was only Brother Nicholas, she came back up the stairs. And that was when he slipped. Poor Brother Nicholas thought someone was trying to kill him, but it was all a mistake. Prioress Johanne was the one who found him. She and Meggy brought him up because it would have been no use me going down, not with my girth.'

She gave a nervous giggle, but Roul ignored her. In all the fog of these wild tales, he felt he had finally glimpsed the end of a thread, which, if he could grasp it, might lead him to the truth.

He leaned forward. 'So, let us be quite clear, Sister Basilia. Brother Nicholas swore that someone tried to stab him while he was in the cave, and three other people went down to the well that night besides him – Goodwife Meggy, Sister Fina and Prioress Johanne. None else.'

Sister Basilia's eyes flew wide. 'But he was mistaken, I told you.'

'Brother Nicholas claimed an attempt was made to kill him and days later he mysteriously vanishes during the night, leaving everything behind, even his sword. Perhaps our brother wasn't as mistaken as you have been led to believe, Sister.'

Even Brother Roul did not know quite what he hoped to find when he gave orders that the sisters' dorter, the prioress's chambers and the gatehouse should be searched. A bloody knife perhaps, a bloodstained kirtle, concealed chests of money and jewels that those at Clerkenwell suspected had been withheld from the responsions. But despite Lord William's absolution, even Roul realised he could not, in all conscience, convict any of these three women merely on the garbled account given by the infirmarer. He couldn't even swear that a crime had been committed, much less that one or all three of them were guilty of it.

Alban had been buried with indecent haste and without either the sheriff or coroner being summoned, which could, if the coroner pressed the matter, result in a heavy fine, but it did not mean the women had killed him or, indeed, that the sergeant had died by any human hand. As for Nicholas, Roul couldn't prove he was even dead, though he would have wagered his own life on it. No, he needed something more before he could act. And, as if God had heard his prayers and had sent an angel to deliver it straight into his hands, Brother Roul was to discover far more than even he could ever have dared to hope.

Chapter 60

Prioress Johanne

This will be my last night on earth and I will go to my death unshriven. I will receive no mercy, but Death is not merciful to anyone. He spares neither the good nor the wicked, the innocent nor the guilty. Why then should we expect more from men?

There are many things in my past I could confess to – deeds and denials, doubts and deceptions. They all line up, shouting and whispering their accusations. And they are right to shame me for I am guilty of them all, but not of what I have done to protect this priory, to protect my brother. If I had not done those things, I would not have sinned, and yet I would have caused the innocent to suffer. If you do what God and man declare wrong, but do it for good, is that a sin? *Thou shalt not steal. Thou shalt not lie. Thou shalt not kill.* They are crimes that condemn the body to the gallows and the soul to Hell. Yet if you steal to feed the hungry, kill to spare the innocent? Does God condemn me for that?

I will not say, 'I am guilty.' To kill is not the same as being *guilty* of killing. To kill is not the same as murder. Yes, I did

478

it – I lied, I stole, I killed – but I am not *guilty* of doing these things, for guilt means shame and regret. And I feel no shame, no regret, no remorse.

It was old Meggy who was the cause of my betrayal in the end. Forgive me, *betrayal* is too cruel a word. Poor soul, she meant only to protect us – that was all she'd ever tried to do. But in the end, it was her very loyalty to me that gave Brother Roul all the proof he needed to condemn me. They found nothing when they searched my chamber. They did not discover the little room behind the panel in which I'd concealed the chest of money, the true ledgers and even, in those last few days, had hidden Cosmas from Brother Nicholas. That room remains sealed. Only Sister Clarice knows of its existence.

They found nothing among Sister Fina's possessions. There was no evidence that she had tried to kill Nicholas that night in the cave, though she would have done it, poor creature, had I not wrestled the knife from her hand. She'd heard his threats to destroy her beloved well, and I think she would have killed a dozen knights to save it.

Finally they searched Meggy's hut. It took them a long time and they were losing patience. Both Clarice and Melisene had to hold the old woman back, while the knights threw her broken pots, torn blankets, rags and ropes into the courtyard in a jumbled heap. Her treasured possessions were only rubbish to them. It was almost dusk, when one of the knights, poking about with a stick beneath the thatch, caught something pale as it fell from the top of one of the rafters. When he carried it out into the dwindling light, we all saw what it was: a roll of parchment fastened with the order's seal, a report written in Nicholas's hand. The mice had nibbled the wax seal but sadly not much else. And I did not have to read those spider-black words to know of what I stood accused. Theft! Sorcery! Harbouring a heretic!

Meggy had stolen the parchment from Alban's scrip when he had left her holding his horse as he struggled with the gate. There had not been time enough for her to warn Sister Clarice of his departure, as she'd been instructed, and besides, she knew Clarice could never have bribed Alban. Had Meggy deliberately fumbled with the beam so that she could search his scrip?

But why had she kept it? Was she afraid to confess to the theft after Alban was killed or afraid to burn something she could not read? Or was it simply that our old gatekeeper could not bring herself to part with anything? I almost smiled. Fate had played a cruel jest on us all, for if poor Meggy had not been so diligent, that parchment would long since have been dust and ashes from an outlaw's fire blowing in the wind.

I can hear them outside the door, the rustle of their robes, their whispers so low I cannot make out the words, their breathing as they lay their ears to the wood to hear if I am sleeping. My heart begins to race and my stomach churns, even though I have knelt here for hours praying, trying to convince myself that I am not afraid to die – *should not* be afraid to die. We are taught that the saints even blessed the instruments of their torture, became protectors for the very things that brought about their death because they released them from the travail of this sinful world into the bliss of Heaven.

But did they, though? In those last few hours as they waited for their execution, did their flesh not shrink from the pain of it, their minds scream in terror of what death might really hold? Christ did. Had He less courage, less faith than they, or did they not understand what death was?

Maybe I have, after all these years, finally lost my faith. I know that I am no saint. But I have made my confession as truthfully as I can, if not to Brother Roul or to a priest, then at least to the image of Christ, who hangs on the cross above the altar. Up there His wounds perpetually bleed afresh in the flickering red glow of the lamp. Blood pours from His pale body, a spring, a river, a flood, but it does not reach me. It does not cleanse me or absolve me.

I kneel outside His light and His indifferent stare is fastened on something behind me. On the door? On the place that my executioners will enter? Will they meet His eyes and hesitate just for a moment?

My body stiffens as I hear the click of the latch, the creak of wood, feel the blast of cold air enter then swirl about me, like the vortex into which the whores and harlots are cast in Purgatory. In the past few days, I have lived this moment a thousand times. I've asked myself if, when they come, I should rise from my knees and turn to face them with courage. Make them face me, make them look into my eyes as they do this. And I will let them do it. To resist would be undignified, useless.

Shall I remain on my knees in prayer, so that the last thing I shall see is the painted figure of the one I have died for hanging in His death? Shall I keep my brothers from seeing the accusation in my eyes, spare them the pain of watching the life drain from my face? Can I do it? Can I simply make myself wait and not struggle, not plead?

I hear three sets of footfalls, soft and stealthy on the stones behind me, the faint jingle of the three sword belts, three breaths quick, shallow. I know my death will be at Brother

Roul's hand. He would not ask another to do what he could not. Two of them stop . . . wait. Do they pray? Pray for my soul or for their brother to give him courage? The other pair of boots advances, and I can feel him standing behind me, hear the pounding of his heart . . . or is it mine? The rustle of his sleeve as he hastily crosses himself. The mutter of a hastily spoken prayer, uttered so low I cannot tell if he is praying for his strength or my forgiveness. But Christ hanging above does not bend His gaze to look at either of us. Is this what He demands? Is this why He was born and was crucified? Is it? If I could be sure . . . Do it, do it now, quickly, before my courage fails me!

No, no, please, wait! Another hour, another minute, please. I am not ready. Save me! Blessed Virgin, save me. I am afraid to die.

His arm brushes against my veil as he drops the cord over my neck. It tightens against my throat, and he twists swiftly, he twists hard.

They buried my body out on the moor, under cover of darkness. If any shred of life still lingered in it, that act alone would have snuffed it out for they dropped me into a water-filled hole, smothered me in oozing mud. I would have drowned, had I still breath in my lungs. I think my corpse will rot quickly unless, of course, the peaty water preserves my remains as it has the corpses of those who were bound and cast alive with nooses about their necks to drown in the bog pools before Christ was ever carried to this isle.

They say I will burn in Hell. That's what they say, but the devil has not come for me yet, and neither have the angels. Only you came, only you spoke to me, summoned me and I am content to sit in your company.

482

Chapter 61

Morwen

Sorrel and me, we built the pyre between the great rocks on Fire Tor. Took many days to dry the wood around the fire we kept burning inside the cave. But there was smashed wood enough to find in the tinners' valley, scattered down the length of it as the waters sank back to the river, where they belonged.

Those tinners who'd escaped the flood had taken whatever they could carry away from the turf huts and fled even before the flood had retreated. But when the water was gone, there were good pickings buried under the mud and gravel for the villagers to scavenge, or so they reckoned. Soon as word got out, they were swarming over the valley, like ravens squabbling and flapping over a dead sheep, trying to snatch up all the treasures they could find to use or sell – iron pots, picks, kegs and nets. Most were buried in the mud and they had to hunt for them, trying to spot the tip of a spade or the spar of a ladder they could drag up from beneath the stones. There were curses aplenty when they went to the trouble of digging them out only to find them smashed, but they took them anyway: a new handle could be fixed to a spade or a staved-in keg could be burned on the hearth fire. What they really wanted was food, but the river had taken every bite as her toll.

They even stripped the corpses of the tinners and their chillern, stripping the filthy rags from them, cutting off a knife that still hung from someone's waist or wrenching off the sodden boots. Not the amulets or crucifixes, though – no one would rob the dead of those for fear their spirits would come looking for them. The bodies were left where they lay. The birds and beasts had already started picking over them for they were starving. It wasn't many days before there was nothing but hair and bones. When the water drained away, some corpses were left buried under mud and the waste gravel from the spoil heaps that had been washed down with them. Sometimes it was only when you trod on them that you felt a leg or face under your bare feet, *his* face.

Soon as we'd finished building the pyre on Fire Tor, we carried the corpse of Ankow out and laid it on it. Ma wouldn't dare come up here again, I knew that, not now she'd seen what we could do. We laid him facing the Blessed Isles, and I combed his flaxen hair over the hole in his skull, though there was no disguising the long gash across his throat. I took the hag-stone from his beard, which Ma had placed there, and the black river stone Ryana had laid on his forehead, and the bracelet of the flying thorn I had woven for his wrist. All those I would place on the new Ankow. This one must be set free to make his last journey.

We heaped more wood and dried peats over him, for the fire must be hot to eat through flesh, and as darkness fell, we set it ablaze. The scarlet flames darted in and out of the wood beneath, and then as the night wind gathered strength, they rose up through the pyre, crackling and roaring into the night sky. The glow turned the twisting smoke red and orange and blue as it spiralled upwards. We sat side by side, Sorrel and me, as the spirits drew close about us, crawling through the stones and slithering over the grass, the breath of their wings brushing our skin, the smell and taste of wood smoke and burning flesh filling our mouths and nostrils.

Below the tor we heard the soft pad of claws on stone, the panting and whining as the hounds gathered, their coats crackling blue as lightning, their red eyes glowing out of the darkness. Old Crockern's hounds were circling the tor. They were waiting for Ankow, waiting to take him home.

A shape was rising out of the smoke, gathering itself dense and dark as a shadow on a summer's day. Only its eyes lived, glowing like the hounds' eyes in the dark. It stood, head bowed.

'I loved her.' His voice was like the wind moaning through the rocks in the cave. 'I knew it was sin, for I had already a wife, but my bride wasn't of my choosing. It was her I loved and when her father sent her away, I had to follow. I was burning up for her. She was my life, my breath, my being. But when I found her, she was changed. She would not touch me. I had come so far, risked everything, and she would not even look at me. I only meant to take a kiss. I thought if she felt my lips upon hers, her body would remember our passion and I'd see the tenderness flow back into her eyes. But once I kissed her, I could not stop myself.

'I do not blame her for what she did, for the blow or the knife or for my death. I deserved to die. But I have been punished for my love beyond all imagining. I have been the slave of Death, and I have walked the lych-ways over this moor without rest or mercy, guiding the souls in misery and

485

torment to their rest, but never reaching the place of peace. I can bear no more. Release me, I beg you, have mercy, release me and let me rest.'

'Go,' I told him. 'Another has come to take your place. You are Death's bondsman no more.'

There was a sound like a great flock of birds taking wing and at once the figure's head lifted. He looked straight at us, then his words came like the voice of an ancient door closing. 'Thank you.'

The figure of smoke grew fainter and greyer, the edges dissolving into the sky, and all at once the hounds began to howl, a great mournful cry that rolled across the moor. One by one the pairs of burning eyes vanished. The pyre suddenly collapsed in on itself, sending a shower of golden sparks high into the sky as if stars were rising back to their places.

I took Sorrel's hand and we slipped into the cave. A corpse already lay on the wicker frame above a fire that emitted only smoke. It had been well prepared with herbs and honey. It would take several weeks of smoking before I could be sure it would not decay. But Brigid had guided us to it quickly, before it had started to rot. He was her choice and we would tend his corpse carefully, Sorrel and I.

His ghost, whimpering, pleading, terrified, was already cowering among the shadows of the cave, as the leather wings and claws of the spirits slithered over him, curious to see what we had brought them to play with.

'Let me go,' he begged. 'I was always nice to you, Sorrel, isn't that right? You're a good woman. I always said so. You'd not see a poor soul tormented. There's dozens died in that valley. You could take any of them. They deserve to suffer, thieves the lot of them, murderers too. Take them, let me go . . . What do you want with me?' he wailed.

'You are Ankow, the serf and bondsman of Death,' I said. 'And you'll do our bidding, till you come to carry us safe to the lych-ways and that will be many years from now.'

Gleedy gave a great howl of despair, but he was in our storeroom now. And there would be no release for him, not while we lived.

Epilogue

Dertemora

The firelight licks about the slabs of stone inside the tor. Its scarlet fingers probe the crevices, and all the secret places that only the phantasms know. Morwen sits facing Sorrel across the fire. The light is gentle on Morwen's ancient wrinkled skin and burnishes her grey hair to the tawny red it once was, the colour of an autumn leaf. And the face that smiles at Morwen through the smoke and flames seems as young as the one she first saw at the door of Ma's cottage, though many seasons have passed for them both since then.

The white cloth on the slab at the far end of the cave is black with the dust and dirt of decades. It billows and slides from the mounds, crumpling on to the floor as if a wind has stirred it, but though the wind is baying around the rocks outside it dare not enter here. Three figures lie side by side on the shelf, a holy family, a dead family – Gleedy, old Kendra and Ryana.

Kendra perished from old age and hunger the winter after the flood, cursing Ankow when he came for her and spitting venom to the end, poisonous as any long-cripple whose head sways in the stone wall. Ryana died from making herself pottage of hemlock having mistaken it for cow parsley. Morwen always said she couldn't tell mouse-ear from mugwort. She'd warned her not to eat it, but her sister would not take telling from Mazy-wen. But Morwen doesn't call upon their spirits to aid her. She has no need. She and Sorrel have all the power they want between them and it grows. Besides, she'd had enough of their malice in life, and death will not have made them kinder.

Taegan does not lie here. She ran off to live with Daveth and his brother. She has a brood of boisterous, red-headed offspring, grandchildren too, though the Black Death took some and famine took more, but Taegan and the brothers survived. And as to which brother fathered which of Taegan's sons and daughters, they neither know nor care. For they are brothers, and they have always shared the good things that come their way.

The cross on Father Guthlac's grave has been swallowed by the earth, as have his bones. He and the old gods had long been enemies, and he recognised his foe in that child. Old Crockern felled him, like a tree in a storm. The wind has no malice, but it will destroy anything that lies in its path, when it begins to blow.

Only the ruins of the priory stand now, and they are being eaten away by storm and rain, snow and frost, and by the villagers who, year after year, carry away more of the stone to mend their cottages and build their pinfolds. The ravens and buzzards nest safe on the broken walls, and foxes burrow beneath them. The villagers have reclaimed their well, and bring their children for Morwen and Sorrel to dip in its waters, for they are the true keepers of it now.

In the tinners' valley, the sores on the land are healing.

Grass and heather, sedges and gorse have crept over the wounded backs of the hills. The river lies quietly in her old bed, but scars will remain long after those who made them are forgotten, and deep welts will for ever mark Old Crockern's hide.

Forgotten, did I say? Yes, their names are forgotten, but they are not unseen. For if you are foolish enough to find yourself upon the lych-ways when night falls, stumbling between the sucking mires and black bog pools, straining to peer into the darkness; if you turn in fear at the whispering in the reeds and the voices in the rocks, you will glimpse flickering lights moving slowly ahead of you. And if you hold your breath and watch, you will see the silent host of men, women and children who follow those bone-white lights. Some are dressed in the white robes of monks, others in the black robes of sisters, some in beggars' rags, others in tinners' mud. You will see old village priests and women skull-gaunt with hunger, men pale with gory wounds, crones as wrinkled as time itself, or babes so young they have not lived a single day. But if you see them, do not speak to them. Do not follow them. They are the shadows of the dead. And once you cross into the deadlands, there's no coming back, Brothers, there is no coming back.

Historical Notes

From 1315 to 1317, the Great Famine ravaged Europe. It was caused by extreme wet, cold weather, which affected the whole of northern Europe from Russia down to southern Italy. Crops failed and livestock died, causing widespread starvation. Even King Edward II, passing through St Albans with his court, went hungry because there was no bread. Bands of people were on the move across Europe, hoping to find food or better conditions elsewhere. Children, babies and the infirm were abandoned on the steps of churches and monasteries, the elderly deliberately wandering off to die so that the young ones could live. There was a surge in violent crime and highway robbery as people became increasingly desperate. Frightening reports circulated, claiming that some were turning to cannibalism, but no one knew if they were true or merely rumours.

The Knights Templar

The Knights Templar were originally founded in the twelfth century to protect travellers making pilgrimages to Jerusalem. But over the following two hundred years they became the international financiers of Europe, lending money and amassing huge resources of wealth and land. They were answerable only to the Pope, and this, combined with their wealth and power, posed a grave threat to the kings of Europe.

Philip IV of France particularly feared their increasing influence, so much so that in 1307 he turned on the Templars in France. He arrested the knights and their commanders on the grounds of immorality, sorcery and heresy, charges the Pope was reluctantly forced to investigate. Over the next few years, many knights across Europe were tortured to induce them to confess to these and other crimes, including homosexuality, immorality with women and alleged bizarre secret rituals, including worshipping a 'head'. Those Templars who refused to confess or who subsequently recanted confessions made under torture were burned alive.

In England, King Edward II at first flatly refused to believe the accusations levelled against the Templars, or perhaps, given the accusations of homosexuality that had been made against him, was anxious to defend the knights. He resisted Philip's demands to bring the Templars to trial, and it wasn't until a papal bull arrived in December 1308, commanding him to take action, that he gave orders that the knights were to be arrested. Even so, it was only when members of the Inquisition landed on English soil in September 1309 to begin the ecclesiastical trials in London, York and Lincoln, that the real round-up of Templars began. This was two years after the first arrests in France, and by then a number of leading Templars had fled from Europe to England.

The Pope authorised the use of torture against the Templars arrested in England, because they were accused of heresy, though torture was technically unlawful under English law. But no one could be found who could do it effectively. They either accidentally killed the victim before he'd talked or were not practised in the art of breaking him down mentally as well as physically, so few confessions were extracted in that way. Most evidence presented at the trials in England was obtained from a Templar who had previously been arrested and escaped, and was believed to have been a spy carrying information to the Grand Master in France.

The Templar order was disbanded throughout Europe by the Pope, and its wealth, when it could be found, was declared forfeit to the Pope or Crown. Templar property was mainly handed over to the Templars' rivals, the Knights of St John.

Throughout their history, the Templars and Hospitallers were rivals for power and territory. They frequently clashed in the Holy Land, the Templars supporting the baronial side of any political disputes, while the Hospitallers supported the monarchy. However, some of the noble families of Europe placed sons and daughters in both orders as a way of gaining the maximum political influence and financial advantage. It also ensured they always had one of their offspring on the winning side. Having children in both orders was a way of hedging temporal and spiritual bets.

Knights Hospitaller

The order of the Knights of St John of Jerusalem, also known as Knights Hospitaller, originated in the founding of a hospital in Jerusalem in 1080, on the site where, according to legend, the angel Gabriel foretold the birth of St John the Baptist. It was established to provide care for poor, sick or injured pilgrims in the Holy Land. Hospitals in those days were not primarily places where the sick and injured were treated, although physicians and surgeons did work in them: they were principally intended to offer hospitality, a place where the elderly, the infirm, orphans, pilgrims and travellers could rest and be provided with safe shelter, good food and spiritual comfort.

In 1099, when Jerusalem was captured by the Christians during the First Crusade, the Hospitallers became a religious and military order under its own charter, charged with caring for pilgrims and the poor, and defending the Holy Land. The establishment of the order was confirmed by a bull of Pope Paschal II in 1113, and the Hospitallers' founder, Gérard, rapidly acquired territory and revenues for his order throughout Jerusalem, which became known as the Citramer, the heartland of the order. His successor, Raymond du Puy, established a Hospitaller infirmary near the Church of the Holy Sepulchre in Jerusalem and the care offered to pilgrims expanded into providing them with an armed escort, which soon grew into a serious fighting force.

By the mid-twelfth century the order was divided into military knights and those who worked with the poor and sick. But it was still recognised by the Church as primarily a religious order and was exempt from tithes and from obedience to all secular and religious authorities, except the Pope. At the height of their power in the Holy Land, the order held seven major forts and 140 other estates in the area, the largest two being their base in Jerusalem and lands in Antioch.

But by 1289, the Muslim forces were seizing more and more territory in the Holy Land, and in May 1291, the last remaining Christian stronghold of Acre fell, after a terrible month-long siege. The Hospitaller Knights evacuated to Cyprus, where they set up their base alongside the Templars with whom they had fought at Acre. But they became embroiled in the bitter politics of Cyprus, and Grand Master Guillaume de Villaret turned his sights on

Rhodes as their new homeland, which strategically was much better situated.

In 1306, Vignolo dei Vignoli entered into a pact with the Order of St John, offering the knights Rhodes, Kos and Leros in return for their help in securing his own lands in Rhodes. The Hospitallers made several attempts to take the island, eventually laying siege to Rhodes town, and in August 1309, it surrendered to them. Under their new grand master, Fulkes de Villaret, Rhodes became the new Citramer, where the knights had to adapt from being primarily a land-based fighting force to a navy, using their fleet of ships to fight the Turks. The order's lands outside Rhodes, known collectively as the Outremer, were organised into Langues, or 'Tongues', with bases in Auvergne, Spain, England, France, Germany, Italy and Provence, each administered by a prior. But the number of Tongues and the location of their administrative centres in Europe changed frequently throughout the Middle Ages as political boundaries and alliances shifted.

Since their foundation by Gérard, the members of the order had formed a fraternity of brothers and also sisters of the order. Both took the three monastic vows of poverty, chastity and obedience. All the members of the order, both male and female, wore black with a white cross until Pope Innocent IV ordered that the battle dress of the knights should be a red coat with a white cross. Anyone wishing to become a knight or sister had to be of noble or 'gentle' birth. Those wishing to join the order who were not of that rank became serving members. In addition, like all monasteries and nunneries, the priories of the order employed a number of lay servants, hired to do the hard manual work and wait on the knights and sisters.

As had happened with the Knights Templar, the vast estates

and wealth of the Knights Hospitaller gave rise to accusations that they were living in luxury rather than in obedience to their vow of poverty. Since the Pope was the protector of the order, and the otherwise powerful bishops had no authority over it, this resulted in many bitter conflicts between the order and the bishops of the various sees in which the Hospitallers had lands and priories. This being an age in which bishops maintained their own fighting men, both clergy and kings feared the wealth and military power of what they perceived to be an alien army in their midst, whose members owed no allegiance to anyone but the Pope, and when the Pope was in conflict with a particular bishop or king, the local authorities became distinctly nervous. Little wonder that some sought to crush the Hospitallers as they had the Templars.

The order lost Rhodes in 1522, but in March 1530, Emperor Charles V of the Holy Roman Empire and Spain gave them as their base the barren rock they were to turn into the fertile island of Malta. For this they paid an annual rent of a falcon each year – the Maltese Falcon. From this base, they continued to harry the Turkish Ottoman Empire, so much so that in 1566, the sultan launched the Great Siege of Malta, which the knights broke after four months, founding a new capital Valetta, named for their grand master, Jean de la Valette. They remained there until 1798 when they were ousted by Napoleon. In 1834, they founded a new headquarters in Rome, but continued to be known as the Knights of Malta.

Today, this Catholic order currently has around 13,500 members and 100,000 staff and volunteers, who work in hospitals all over the world. Thirty per cent of the members are now women, who are given the title 'Dame'. The order of the Knights of Malta is really a state without a country. It has formal diplomatic relations with 106 countries and states, and they produce their own passports, licence plates and stamps.

In 1540, during the Reformation in England, King Henry VIII confiscated the Hospitaller priories and land, including its headquarters in Clerkenwell. An attempt was made to revive the order under his daughter, the Catholic Queen Mary I, but it was lost again under the Protestant Queen Elizabeth I. But in 1858, during the reign of Queen Victoria, an order of the Knights Hospitaller, independent of Rome, was founded, which was known as the Venerable Order of the Hospital of St John of Jerusalem in the British Realm. A few decades later it was to oversee three charities – the very famous and familiar St John Ambulance Association (established 1878), St John Ambulance of Uniformed Men and Women (1888) and, returning at last to where the order first began, the Ophthalmic Hospital in Jerusalem (1882).

The Goddess Brigid

Brigid, Brigit or Brig, the exalted one, was a triple Celtic deity. She was goddess of poetry, spring, fertility, cattle and sacred wells, and she had two sisters, Brigid the blacksmith and Brigid the healer. Her festival was Imbolc, celebrated around 31 January/1 February, midway between the winter solstice and the spring equinox. The festival marked the transition between those months ruled by the crone of winter and those by the maiden of spring. It was celebrated by the lighting of sacred fires and the pouring of water. The goddess was the guardian of high places, such as tors, mountains and hill-forts. She was also strongly identified with cows, ewes and milk, which were of vital importance in Celtic society. In mythology, she is the creator of 'keening', which is first heard when she mourns her son slain in battle.

Brideog – pronounced *bree-jog* – means *little Brigid* or *young Brigid*. At the Celtic feast of Imbolc, long lengths of rushes or straw were twisted into the rough image of a doll, which was dressed in white and decorated with leaves, stones or shells to represent the goddess Brigid. The brideog would be sprinkled with water taken from a Brigid's Well, Bryde's Well or Bride's Well, and carried by unmarried girls in procession to a great feast where the goddess would be offered food, drink and fire, in gratitude for bringing them safely through winter, and asked to bring new life.

With the coming of Christianity, the Celtic feast of Imbolc became the Eve of St Brigid's Day, 31 January. On that night, unmarried women and girls would make a crib for the brideog and sit up with her. Young men would call and be offered food and drink, but had to treat the brideog as if she was a saint and the women with great respect. Before the girls went to bed, the ash in the hearth would be raked smooth and each girl would lay out a cloth in front of it. In the morning, they would examine the ash and cloths for any sign that St Brigid had walked over them. If she had, it was a great blessing, and any girl whose cloth she had marked would be married within the year. On St Brigid's Day itself, the brideog was carried from house to house by unmarried girls, who presented the head of each household with a St Brigid's cross.

Brigid's Cross – a woven cross traditionally made on St Brigid's Eve, 31 January, but originally associated with the Celtic goddess Brigid. It was woven from freshly pulled rushes. The newly made cross would be green, symbolising the coming of spring. The cross was woven in a sun-wise direction, and it is thought that in Celtic times it was intended to represent the sun and the hope that light and warmth would return after the cold and darkness of winter.

Today there are many elaborate versions of this cross, but probably the oldest style was the three-armed cross, or *triskele*, which was hung in byres and cowsheds to protect the animals, for in Celtic society wealth was measured in cattle, not land. There are also six-band interlaced patterns, square patterns, and a cross in a circle. A Brigid cross made with a 'binding knot', which keeps out evil spirits, was usually woven and hung in the home on All Hallows' Eve (Halloween).

But after the coming of Christianity, when many of the legends about the goddess Brigid were transferred to the hagiography of the sixth-century Irish St Brigid, Abbess of Kildare, the abbess became credited with having woven the first Brigid's Cross at the bedside of a dying chieftain. St Brigid's four-armed version of the woven cross gradually became the one most commonly found hanging over doors or hearths in cottages, having first been taken to the church to be blessed by the priest. The 'pagan' *triskele* was not brought to be blessed by the Church, but it continues to be used in byres in some parts of Europe to this day.

Brigid's Mantle – There is a traditional Irish blessing, *Faoi bhrat Bhríde sinn*, 'May you be covered by Bride's mantle,' and the old Gaelic title for Brigid was 'Brigid of the Tribe of the Green Mantles'. The goddess was thought to weave a mantle of green on her loom and spread it over the earth, banishing winter, bringing spring, and protecting all those whose hearths it covered.

When the goddess was transformed by the Church into a saint, the symbol of her mantle gave rise to a legend that St Brigid decided to build her monastery in Kildare, Leinster. She asked the King of Leinster to give her the land, but he refused. Brigid prayed, then begged him to grant her the amount of land that her mantle would cover. The King found her request so amusing that he foolishly agreed. Four virgin followers of St Brigid each grasped a corner of the cloak and walked away from each other. The cloak stretched as they walked until it covered the whole area St Brigid needed for the monastery with all its outbuildings. Awestruck, the King gave her the land. Brigid built her church near an ancient oak tree, sacred to the Druids, and close to a holy well, which was then dedicated to the saint.

The cathedral of St Sauveur in Bruges, Belgium, today houses a holy relic in the form of a piece of woollen cloth, which is said to be part of St Brigid's mantle and which is venerated on her saint's day, 1 February. Measuring 21 by 25 inches, it is a dark crimson-violet. Tests carried out in 1936 showed that it was dyed with iron oxide. Cloth of a similar weave and dye has been found in early Bronze Age burials in Denmark and Ireland. However, similar home-spun weaves and dyes were still in use up to the sixteenth century, so this fragment may have been made much later than the sixth century.

The earliest known record of this relic was written in 1347 and comes from the cathedral of St Donaas in Flanders. According to tradition, after the death of the Saxon King Harold at Hastings in 1066, his sister Gunhild fled to Flanders and presented this relic and her jewels to the Church there in gratitude for sheltering her. The piece of St Brigid's mantle was removed from St Donaas before its destruction during the French Revolution.

Dartmoor

In 1182, the name recorded in official documents is *Dertemora*, meaning *Moor in the Dart Valley*. *Moor* comes from the Old English *mor*, meaning bog or swamp, and *dart* from the Celtic, meaning *the river where oak trees grow*. Since the whole of the river is unlikely to have been lined with oak trees, even in Celtic times, it suggests that the oak groves that grew along stretches of it were considered special or sacred. Groves of ancient dwarf oaks, such as the mysterious Wistman's Wood, still survive on Dartmoor, their twisted branches hung with shaggy lichen, their gnarled roots growing over great moss-covered boulders.

Glowing Moss

Dartmoor is home to an increasingly rare luminous moss known locally as Goblin's Gold, and in other parts of England as Elfin Gold, because people passing abandoned rabbit holes, caves and ancient stone huts would glimpse something shining like gold in the dark interior; when they reached in to grab it, they found themselves clutching only a handful of wet dirt.

What they had seen was in fact a tiny, fragile, frond-like moss, *Schistostega osmundacea*. It forms dense mats covering the walls of caves or damp burrows, but grows to only around half an inch in height. It is found growing in caves, tunnels or in half-buried ruins where other plants can't survive because only a very faint light penetrates. Seen against a dark background, the moss shines with a beautiful green-gold luminosity and under flash photography can appear a vivid electric blue.

The luminous effect is due entirely to reflected light. The protonema of the moss have lens-shaped cells, which focus any available light on the chlorophyll granules. These absorb only the wavelengths of the light needed to photosynthesise, reflecting the rest of the light back towards its source, so the light seems to be radiating from the moss itself, which appears to glow. These 'lens' cells can move to within 45 degrees, to adjust to a shifting light, so that at times the glow from the moss appears to pulsate.

One location where it could still be found at the time of writing was at Yellowmead, on Sheepstor, Dartmoor, in a man-made cave, known locally as a potato-cave, but which was probably once an old tinners' tool store or stone bee-hive hut.

Land Measurement and Acres

By the fourteenth century, landholdings were recorded in *acres* and *half-acres*, not *hides*, as they had been in the Domesday Book. The word *acre* comes from Old English *æcer* meaning *open field*. An acre was roughly the amount of land a *yoke*, or two oxen, could plough in a day. But it was an estimated size used mainly for taxation and land sales rather than a measured area. In 1195, the monks of Thame exchanged two and a half acres of land for three and a half, but recorded that the second area was no bigger than the first.

By 1250, acres were increasingly being measured using *perches* (long rods). An acre was deemed to be four perches by forty perches. But this didn't clarify things much, because the perches themselves were not a standard length, varying from around 16.5 feet to 25.5 feet in different shires. This was a problem for anyone coming from another part of the country who was trying to assess the exact size and value of a landholding. A further complication was that, even in the same place, the length of perch used varied with the type of land being measured, so poor pasture or woodland would be measured with a longer perch than prime arable land, making an acre of woodland larger than an acre of arable land, so *acre* still really referred to the taxable value of the land rather than its actual size.

The River's Cry

If you are walking along a lonely riverbank out on the moor on Dartmoor it can be quite unnerving suddenly to hear a wordless singing coming from it, which rises above the general noise of the rushing, gurgling water. On several occasions, I've thought there must be a radio playing somewhere even though there are plainly no cars or people about. The phenomenon is due to the granite rocks and pebbles in the water, which amplify and distort sound.

When the River Dart is in full spate and this coincides with a north-westerly wind, a loud booming sound is sometimes heard, known as the 'river's cry'. It was a long-held belief that the River Dart claimed a human heart in tribute every year and the 'Dart's Cry' was the warning that one of those hearing it would shortly drown or die. Down through the centuries, there have been many tales of people hearing the cry, only to hurry home to news of an unexpected and tragic death in the family. But the river's cry has also saved lives when those hearing the booming scrambled out of the river or off the rocks in fright, only to see a huge wall of water sweep past them, which would have carried them to their deaths.

Pigseys

Pigsey or *pigsy* is an old dialect word for a *pixy*, also called *piskies, pisgies* or *pysgies*. The earliest published version of *The Three Little Pigs* in 1853 comes from Dartmoor, and in this version the heroes are not three little pigs but three little *pigseys* or *pixies*. Throughout this novel, I have used the older dialect form, *pigsey*, to help separate the medieval concept of these dark, supernatural creatures from the jolly models of grinning pixies sitting on toadstools that we find in souvenir shops today.

Pigseys were mythological little people, mostly invisible to humans, who lived hidden but parallel lives. In pre-Christian times, they were simply regarded as another race with magical powers, but with the coming of Christianity it came to be believed that they were the spirits of babies who had died before baptism and therefore could not enter Heaven, but nor could they go to Hell because they were too innocent. They were transformed into pigseys to live as close to humans as they could, though they could never speak to their families or show themselves. But in this form they could punish their neglectful parents by causing mischief and would also jealously torment their living siblings by pinching them black and blue at night.

In medieval times, pigseys were considered to be frightening and often malicious creatures, vengeful and quick to anger. They were thought to inflict painful illnesses on

504

humans, and bring disasters and chaos to farms, families and livestock. Pigseys would disguise themselves as bundles of clothes or lumpy sacks to lure children close, then snatch them and carry them off into a *pixy-house*, from which either the children never returned or were found wandering, lost and bewildered, weeks or even years later, believing they had only been away for a few hours. A *pixy-house* is the local name for a deep crevice or hidden natural cave on the moors.

Pigseys delighted in leading travellers into bogs and mires, known as *pixy-beds*, or sending them stumbling around, hopelessly lost, in the mist or snow until they died of exhaustion. Until the twentieth century, *pixy-led* was a term that conjured fear for it meant being completely lost and helpless. If you thought you were being pixy-led you could counter this by removing your coat or cloak and putting it on inside out to reverse the spell.

There are many places associated with pigseys on Dartmoor, especially Sheepstor, which has a cave among the rocks known as Piskie Cave, Piskie Grott, or Elford's Cave, so named because a member of the Elford family is said to have hidden from Cromwell's troops in this *pixy-house*. It is believed that the cave was once much larger, but rock falls have destroyed or sealed part of it and made the existing entrance even narrower, though it is still possible to squeeze in if you are slender.

Fire Tor

There are a number of *knocking caves* or tors on Dartmoor, from which the sounds of tapping, whispering human voices, wailing, music and singing can be heard. So much so that people through the centuries have believed these tors either to be the abodes of ghosts or pigseys or the entrance to Purgatory. Many have thought there were people inside and were so convinced they went in to investigate, but found the caves empty. The sounds are probably made by the wind whistling through the many crevices, and from water dripping or running unseen among the rocks, which echoes through the granite stone and hollows.

Holy Wells

There are many healing or holy springs and pools all over Devon and Cornwall. Some are known as Bryde's Well or Bride's Well, and were once dedicated to the goddess Brigid. Since the medieval Church was powerless to stop local people continuing to make offerings at these 'pagan' sites for good fortune or for healing, many were renamed and dedicated to Christian saints, and stories were constructed to explain how the saint had caused the well to bubble up. These legends often incorporate elements taken from Celtic and other pre-Christian mythologies.

The stone carving of the head or skull described in this novel, which lies behind the holy spring, was inspired by a carving that can be found on Sheepstor Church, Dartmoor; it has evidently been moved to the church from another site.

Frogs

In the Middle Ages, frogs were one of the creatures believed to be produced by spontaneous generation. This was thought true of a number of animals and insects whose juvenile form did not resemble the adult, such as flies, which were thought to be generated by corpses. Some people even advocated beating the corpses of calves to bring out the 'blood maggots', which would eventually turn into bees, while others said scornfully that this was foolish as it was well known bees were born from oxen, hornets from horses and wasps from the corpses of donkeys. Most were in agreement that frogs and toads were born from mud, not surprisingly because they would be seen in great numbers after rivers flooded in the spring.

In many ancient cults, they were associated with goddesses and venerated as symbols of regeneration and fertility. There are a number of holy wells in Devon and Cornwall, such as the one in Bovey Tracey on Dartmoor, where legend has it that little golden frogs were seen swimming in the clear water. These golden frogs were a sign that the well had been blessed or become a healing well, thanks to an act of kindness by a villager towards a beggar woman they had encountered. Originally, she was the goddess Brigid in disguise, in later centuries the Virgin Mary. But, like owls which were once sacred to ancient goddesses, when Christianity spread and the goddesses were demonised, owls became symbols of death, and frogs became symbols of evil because they sprang from mud and filth.

The passage quoted in the novel is from the New Testament, the Book of Revelation 16:13 – *And I saw from the mouth of the dragon and from the mouth of the beast and from the mouth of the false prophet, three unclean spirits like frogs. For they are the spirits of devils.* This verse also made frogs a symbol of heresy in the Middle Ages because they come 'from the mouth of the false prophet'.

In the later Middle Ages and during the witch trials of the sixteenth and seventeenth centuries, frogs were one of the animals that witches and sorcerers were most frequently accused of having as their *familiars* or *imps of Satan* to aid them in their spells and to spy on their neighbours. Lucifer and three of his imps are said to dwell in the form of frogs in Frog Well, Acton Burnell. While the imps are often seen mocking those who look into the water, the devil, true to his wicked nature, cunningly conceals himself, waiting to do mischief.

In the days of damp houses and wells, it must have been only too easy to discover a frog hiding somewhere in the home or garden of the alleged witch, and frogs would certainly have been seen in the sodden dungeons into which the accused were thrown. What more proof did you need that the 'witch' had been whispering to one of the devil's imps?

Black Hounds

The legends about the packs of wisht hounds that hunt the moors are unlike those of early accounts of the solitary 'Black Dog' or 'Black Shuck', which often appeared on isolated roads turning travellers back from danger and may have a different origin.

The talbot, or Norman hound, was brought to Britain with the Norman Conquest. It was a hunting dog bred for speed, strength and stamina, and was probably the size and build of the modern bloodhound. The Norman hound was a crossbreed, and one of the strains used in the cross was the Hubert, a huge black hound bred in the monastery of St Hubert in the Ardennes. They were so sought after as hunting dogs that they were presented as gifts to royalty. Huberts had 'red' patches over the eyes, and if some of these dogs, or strains bred from them, escaped and turned feral, hunting in packs, they might have contributed to the legends of the terrifying hellhounds or wisht hounds of Dartmoor, with their black coats and 'red' eyes. *See also Glossary – Wisht Hounds.*

Glossary

Agasted – a medieval word meaning *afraid* or *terrified*. It is still used in Devonshire dialect today.

Ankow, Ankou or Ankuo – was a legendary medieval figure found in many areas that had once been Celtic lands; belief in him in some parts continued right up to the last century. He was the servant or bondsman of Death, and was thought to be the last person to die in the parish in the previous year. Other legends say he was a prince who had foolishly challenged Death to a contest to catch a magical stag and lost, or that he was Cain who had slain his brother Abel and was doomed to collect souls as a punishment for bringing murder into the world.

Ankow was responsible for guarding the graveyard and collecting up the souls of all who died in that parish throughout the following year. He was sometimes thought to ride a black or skeleton horse, or drive a black cart. He guided the souls of the newly dead and helped them find the spirit paths, or lych-ways, along which they must travel. Ankow announced his arrival by a mysterious knocking sound or by an eerie wail or the call of an owl. Once he entered a cottage, he never left alone.

In times of plagues and deadly fevers, when people often concealed sick loved ones for fear they would be taken away, Ankow was said to ride through the villages and towns at night, marking the doors of infected houses with a red sign.

511

This could lead to families being walled up alive by frightened neighbours or even killed. It would be only too easy for someone to sneak out at night and mark the houses of those they suspected of being sick or against whom they held a grudge, and claim Ankow had done it.

Bait – dialect word meaning to feed a fire and also to be in a fiery mood or bad temper.

Blow-in – a derogatory name for an outsider, a newcomer, someone who was not born in the area or village.

Brideog – a crude doll made from twisted rushes or straw, representing the goddess Brigid. *For further details see Historical Notes – Brigid.*

Buddle – a rectangular surface or shallow trough with a sloping base used in tin streaming. Crushed gravel would be tipped in and washed with water. The heavy tin ore, the *heads*, would settle near the top of the slope. The lighter worthless material or gangue, known as the *tailings*, would settle at the bottom, or be washed off the buddle, and the mixed stone, the *middles*, would settle between. *Heads* produced the best quality tin, *middles* could also be used, but would need to be smelted twice, and the *tailings* were discarded. The skill lay in spotting where to draw the line between each.

Changeling children – with many medieval villagers living in small isolated communities, constant intermarriage between the same families for generations could result in children born with genetic problems. If these were serious enough to be spotted at birth, the newborn might be exposed out on the moors and left to die. But when a child who seemed healthy at birth later began to look, behave or develop in ways that were different from the other village children, it was said that the faerie folk had stolen the human baby and left their own offspring in its place. Parents were advised that if they beat or mistreated the changeling or even pretended to throw the child on the fire, the faeries would snatch it back and return their human baby. Other, kinder, remedies were for the parent to do something ridiculous, like boil water in an egg shell, which would startle the changeling baby into speaking and betraying its real parents, who would then be forced to return for it.

Chollers – Devonshire dialect word meaning *cheeks*.

Citramer – the Hospitallers' origin and spiritual heart lay in the Holy Land, and when that was lost, in Rhodes. So, no matter which nation they were from or where they served, they referred to the Holy Land or Rhodes as being *Citramer* or *home*, whereas their priories in England and mainland Europe were *Outremer* meaning *overseas*.

Clooties (also spelt *cloutie* or *cloughtie*) – These were rags or strips of cloth torn from the garments of people who were sick or seeking good luck that were dipped in the holy wells, then tied to a nearby bush or tree, especially a thorn or oak. The affected part of the body might first be washed using the wet rag, before the clootie was hung in the tree. If someone couldn't visit the holy well themselves, a relative might bring a clootie for them. Some people regarded the clootie as an offering to the goddess or spirit of the water, in which case the rag would be torn from a garment they valued.

In other cases, the intention was to transfer the sickness or bad luck to the clootie and leave the ill-fortune at the well, in which case the rag might be torn from a garment they hated or associated with the start of their illness or misfortune. As the rag disintegrated or eventually blew away, the ailment would vanish. If anyone removed a clootie belonging to someone else they would risk that person's illness or ill-fortune passing to them.

Even when a holy well was rededicated to a Christian saint the practice continued and it still does today, along with the custom of throwing coins (silver) into wells or fountains as offerings to the gods or spirits for good luck or to make a wish come true.

Cracky-wren or **Crackety** – are Devonshire dialect names for a *wren*. Some claim that they refer to the bird's tiny size, others that they derive from another of its dialect names, *Crackadee*, which imitates the sound of a wren's alarm call. The wrens' song is said to contain more notes than any other birdsong. This, together with the wrens' habit of nesting in caves and tombs, was the reason people believed the bird carried messages between our world and the world of the spirits or the dead.

Crockern – *See* **Wisht Hounds.**

Cross and Pile – a popular gambling game played by all classes, which today is known as 'heads or tails'. Two players each chose a side of a coin and bet on their chosen side landing uppermost when the coin was flipped in the air. In the Middle Ages, the game was known as 'cross and pile' because one side of a medieval coin was stamped with a cross or a Christian symbol.

Hammered coins were produced by placing a metal disc of a certain weight between two patterned dies, then striking the upper die with a hammer to stamp the pattern on the coin. The bottom die was called a pile, and by extension the reverse side of the coin, which became imprinted with the bottom die's pattern, also became known as the pile or pyl.

King Edward II was so fond of cross and pile that he was said to have borrowed money from courtiers and even his servants to keep playing.

Cross formée – a Greek cross with four slightly fluted arms or the thicker version – a *cross pattée* – appears the most likely to be the version of the cross that the Knights of St John had emblazoned on the front of their surcoats and at the top of their left sleeves during the thirteenth and fourteenth centuries, since this is the type of cross most often depicted on their seals and in carvings on their buildings from the thirteenth century. The original cross used prior to this period was probably the patriarchal cross, which has two cross-bars. The now familiar eight-pointed Maltese Cross, still used today by the St John Ambulance, was probably not adopted until the sixteenth century. But in the early history of this order there were often variations in design between countries.

Donats – wealthy lay men and women could become donats of the order of the Knights of St John, by making a single generous donation to the Hospitallers of money, land or property in exchange for spiritual benefits, while continuing

515

to live as laity. Donats could be buried in Hospitaller grave-yards and hoped their act of piety would shorten their time in Purgatory, particularly as the Knights of St John and their priests would remember them in their prayers and says masses for their souls.

Donats had to pledge that if they ever decided to enter holy orders, they would join the Hospitallers. A number did so in old age, which enabled them to be cared for when they were frail. But some waited until they were on their deathbeds to become fully professed members of the order. Often husbands and wives would both become donats and mutually promise that if one died, the surviving spouse would make a full profession and enter the order rather than remarry, usually to ensure their estate was maintained intact for children of that marriage. A number of wills survive from this period which contain such provisions. But it was also accepted that many donats would never want to become fully professed.

Duru – Old English word meaning *door*. A waxing gibbous moon was believed to be the doorway into other realms. It was a place between darkness and light, a time of beginnings. Different curses and charms were thought to be most effective when created at certain phases of a moon – waxing, waning, full or new – depending on what they were intended to do.

Egurdouce – it meant *sweet and sour*. It was sauce used with a variety of meat, including hare, mutton and beef, and also fish. Meat such as rabbits' legs and saddles were deep fried in lard, then laid in a dish and covered with fried onions and fried currants. A sauce of melted lard, red wine, vinegar, sugar, pepper, ginger, cinnamon and salt was made and seethed until it was thick, or thickened with egg yolks or breadcrumbs, then poured over the meat and served.

Garderobe – this was a feature of religious houses or wealthy manors and castles. It was a tiny room enclosing a lavatory, often built on an upper storey projecting from an outer wall, so that waste would fall through the hole beneath the seat into a pit, moat or river. Its height made it harder for thieves or invaders to climb up through the hole. If it was built in the middle of a complex on the ground floor in a monastery, a stream of water would usually be diverted from a nearby river to run beneath it and carry off the waste. Clothes were often hung in garderobes as the stench of urine and excrement was said to keep away moths.

Gleedy – the character's nickname is derived from *gleed*, an old word meaning a *squint*.

Graffing – ancient dialect word meaning *digging*.

Hag-stones – small holed stones or pebbles, which were thought to guard against evil. Hung on the back of a door, they prevented the entry of evil spirits or witches. Hung over a bed, they guarded against illnesses and nightmares. If a key was attached to them, the combination of the stone and iron was thought to be a powerful amulet against bad luck and protected the house from thieves. Many holed stones can still be found on doors in houses and barns today, and are still hung on key rings.

Hare's beard – one of the many old country names for mullein (*verbascum*). It was called this because the plant is covered with white hairs. When dried, it could be used as kindling and as candle wicks or tapers, hence other names such as *hag-taper* and *Our Lady's candle*. Witches were said to use mullein in their spells and it may be one of the nine herbs referred to in the Anglo-Saxon Nine Herbs Charm, but the plant was also thought to be very effective in warding off demons and night terrors. The juice was believed to remove warts and the leaves and flowers were infused to make a cough, cold and bronchitis remedy.

Horn gesture – this was made by tucking your two middle fingers under your thumb, while extending your index and little finger, like two horns, towards the person or object you feared. It was used to ward off evil, especially to protect against sorcery, or defend you from those you thought might be 'overlooking' you with the evil eye.

Imbolc – is Brigid's Day, celebrated around 31 January to 2 February, approximately midway between the winter solstice and the spring equinox. The origin of the word *Imbolc* is disputed. Some authorities claim it comes from the Old Irish meaning *in the belly*, and refers to the pregnancy of ewes. Other sources state that it meant to *ritually wash* or *cleanse* and some link the origin of the word to *milk*, particularly ewe's milk. During the Middle Ages, many of the traditions, images and beliefs associated with Imbolc became merged with the Christian festival of Candlemas on 2 February, which celebrated the ritual purification or cleansing of the Virgin Mary, forty days after the birth of Christ. *See also Historical Notes – Brideog and Brigid's Cross.*

Larks-claw – *Delphinium consolida*, also known as *larkspur*, *larks-toe* and *larks-heel*. It was used to pack wounds and treat the stings of scorpions. Oil from the seeds was extracted to kill lice. If tossed in front of any venomous beast, it was widely believed the creature would not be able to move until the herb was removed.

Livier – the living space for people. Dartmoor long houses often consisted of just two rooms built sideways on a slope. The livier, at the higher end of the slope, was where the family ate, slept and worked, and the room on the lower end was known as the *shippon* and that was where the live-stock were housed, especially during winter. The livier would have a central peat fire, but no chimney or windows. An open drain ran down through the middle of the shippon and out through the wall at the lowest end of the building to carry away animal waste. Both beasts and humans used the same door, and the partition between livier and shippon was often only a half-wall, so that the heat from the animals helped to keep the humans warm and the beasts, especially young or ailing ones, benefited from the warmth of the hearth fire in the livier.

Long-cripples – Devon dialect word for snakes, usually adders, but it can also mean dragonflies or lizards. Some leech or healing wells were given the name *long-cripple*, either because they cured snakebites or because they cured the same ailments as adder skins were thought to do, such as headaches and rheumatism. The groves of dwarf oaks on Dartmoor, especially Wistman's Wood, are home to hundreds of adders, which take shelter among the rocks and are said to be the most venomous adders in the British Isles.

Lungwort – *Pulmonaria officinalis*. Folk names include *Bloody Butcher*, perhaps because the flowers change from pink to blue like a butchered meat. It was also known as *Adam and Eve*, *Mary and Joseph*, *Mary's Tears*, *Spotted Dog*, *Beggar's Basket* and *Our Lady's Milk-sile*, because the white spots on the leaves were said to be the stains or 'sile' made by the drops of milk that fell from the Virgin Mary's breasts when she was feeding the infant Jesus on their flight to Egypt. The leaves resemble the shape of a lung therefore it was believed they cured lung conditions in both humans and livestock. Ointment made from the leaves was used to treat ulcers on the sexual organs. The plant was also said to banish sorrow and depression, and to 'comfort the heart'.

But to confuse matters, the green lichen, *Lobaria pulmonaria*, which grows on tree trunks and rocks, is also known as *lungwort* because it, too, is said to resemble lungs and was also used to treat ailments of the lungs, especially asthma.

Manuterge – from the Latin *manus*, meaning hand, and *tergēre*, to wipe. A small white linen towel used by the priest during mass for drying the hands after washing them in the *lavabo* (ewer and basin). Today it is often called the *lavabo towel*.

Mazy – local dialect word meaning *stupid* or *mad*. *Mazy-jack* was often used to refer to someone who was considered to be the village simpleton.

Pigseys – old dialect name for *pixies*. *See also Historical Notes – Pigseys*.

Pinfold – an enclosure, often circular, in which animals were penned for the night. Most medieval drovers' roads had pinfolds built along them at intervals where animals being driven to and from market could be kept overnight to prevent them straying and keep them safe from predators and thieves while the drovers slept. In Devon, the enclosure usually consisted of broad banks surmounted by a thick hedge, or wide dry-stone walls that had tunnel-like 'kennels' built into the hollow between the stones, so that dogs could stay dry and warm while keeping watch. On Dartmoor, there were also many Bronze Age stone circles and the remains of large Bronze Age circular stone-huts; farmers and drovers often turned them into pinfolds to save building one from scratch.

Responsions – each priory of the Knights or Sisters of St John was required to send a third of all their income from produce, rents and financial dealings to the central or mother house in their country. In England, this was Clerkenwell, north of London. Knights or paid agents then took the money to the procurator-general in Avignon from where it was sent to the treasurer at Rhodes. However, records show that during the fourteenth century the responsions from the English Tongue were not always dispatched to Rhodes, because the English Hospitallers were heavily in debt. In times of war between France and England, the King refused to allow them to be delivered, since this was giving money to England's enemies, not least because French-speaking knights were in the majority on Rhodes. At such times, money from the English order of the Hospitallers was given to the King to help in the defence of England.

Rouncy – (also spelt *rouncey* or *rounsey*) – an all-purpose horse, used for riding and battle. The huge *destrier*, capable of carrying a man in full armour with weapons was the most highly prized war- and jousting-horse of the Middle Ages, but the least common, and the destrier was not a good riding horse over long distances. The agile *coursers* were often preferred for hard battles fought at close quarters, but only wealthy knights could afford either of these. A poorer knight or man-at-arms would use a rouncy for fighting and distance riding. Often in the Middle Ages the nature of the expected battle would dictate the type of horse required, so if a swift pursuit was anticipated, the knights would be advised to bring rouncies rather than destriers. None of these horses were specific breeds; rather, the size, build and training of the individual horse determined what it was called.

Sarcenes – the full name of the dish was *bruet sarcenes*. A bruet was stew containing meat. A strongly flavoured meat, such as venison or goat, was boiled and drained, and the water it had been cooked in mixed with ground nuts to produce almond milk. A sauce for the meat was made from the almond milk, flour, cloves and powdered spices. It was boiled until thickened, then wine, sugar and salt were added, with a deep red dye made from alkanet root.

'Almond milk' was made from any kind of ground nuts that were available. The powder was kept dry, then mixed with a liquid, such as wine or stock, just before cooking to create a 'milk'. It was used in many sauces and puddings where today we would use dairy milk: animal milk soured quickly and wasn't available all year round, so it was mainly reserved to make butter and cheese that could be stored.

Scroggling – an old word for a tiny, shrivelled apple, which no one bothers to harvest because it is worthless; by extension, a person who is useless, good for nothing.

Shaggy mane – the edible fungus, *Coprinus comatus,* also known as Shaggy Ink Cap, because it makes good black ink. It often grows where animals have dropped dung, probably generated from spores the beast had ingested. If it is cooked after it has started to open it can dye all other ingredients black. Not to be confused with Common Ink Cap, *Coprinopsis atramentaria*, which is poisonous if alcohol is drunk with it or after eating it.

Simples – any herbs with a medicinal property.

Sledges – on Dartmoor, wooden sledges were not principally intended for use in snow, but were used to drag fodder, kindling or other supplies across the open moorland all year round. With their broad metal runners, they could be pulled over heather, rough grass, stones and mud much more easily than a wheeled cart. Old horseshoes were hammered into rough circles and nailed to the sides of the sledge, through which ropes or poles could be attached, allowing the sledge to be dragged by horses or people.

Strappado – a method of torture favoured by the Inquisition in which a victim's hands would be bound behind their back. Their wrists would be tied to a rope slung over a high beam and they would be hauled upwards, thereby dislocating their shoulders. Victims were often also repeatedly and violently dropped several feet in the air, but jerked to a stop by the rope before they hit the floor. This generally broke their arm and shoulder bones and caused serious damage to the spine. Weights might be attached to other parts of the body, such as feet and genitals, to inflict even greater agony and damage.

Todde – Old English, meaning *fox*. By the twelfth century it had become a nickname for someone who resembled a fox in some way, perhaps in hair colour, or was foxy, cunning or crafty. As with many early nicknames, it was eventually adopted by some families as their surname, usually spelt *Todd*.

Trapes – old dialect word meaning a *slattern*, *slut*, or *slovenly woman*.

Veckes and gammers – derogatory medieval terms meaning *old women* and *old men*.

Viaticum – the eucharist (bread and wine) given by a priest to the dying. It could be offered with or without extreme unction, which is the anointing of the sick with chrism (holy oil). Receiving viaticum formed part of the last rites in the medieval Church. Viaticum means 'provision for a journey', *via* meaning *way*. The journey is the one the dying person will make from this world to the life after death.

Whortleberry – *Vaccinium myrtillus*, commonly called a bilberry. It grows on low, wiry bushes. The fruit is blue with a strong sweet scent and flavour. The flesh and juice are red. They were known as *whimberries* in Wales and *whortleberries* in Devon. But many villagers on Dartmoor called them *hurts* or *urts*.

Will worth – cunning women believed a charm or curse would only work if the charmer firmly declared exactly what they wanted, really meant it and imagined it happening. In that sense, the physical charm or curse, whether it was a bunch of herbs or a curse written on lead, had no power in itself but became the focus of the cunning woman's willpower or wishes. *Will worth* meant to state your intention or your will aloud as you directed the charm or curse towards whatever you wanted it to affect.

Wisht Hounds – mythical beasts, otherwise known as *hellhounds*. *Wisht* originally meant to *bewitch* or *invoke evil*. Wisht hounds are a pack of huge black dogs with savage fangs and red eyes that hunt across Dartmoor at night, preying on lost souls and unwary travellers. After the coming of Christianity, they were also thought to snatch unbaptised babies and children from their beds and devour them, or drop their bloody corpses at the feet of their neglectful parents. To protect the baby from such a terrible fate until the infant could be brought for christening, which in winter or in remote areas might be some months, a piece of consecrated bread (the Host) was placed beneath the child's pillow.

The hounds' kennels are said to be in an ancient grove of twisted oaks, which still stands today, and is known as Wistman's Wood. Many of the stones in the wood are balanced such that they resemble dog kennels, and foxes, badgers and rabbits make homes in them.

As they run across the moor, the ferocious wisht hounds are followed by a lone huntsman swathed in black and riding a huge black or skeleton horse. He carries the hounds' 'kill' in a sack. Some say the huntsman is the devil himself, others that he is Old Crockern, an ancient god or guardian spirit of Dartmoor, whose face can be seen in profile on the rocks of *Crockern Tor*. It is he who releases the hounds from their kennels in Wistman's Wood whenever someone threatens the moor. *See also Historical Notes – Black Hounds.*

A Gathering of Ghosts

Reading Group Guide

- *'You can stamp and frown as much as you please, Mistress, but this is a battle I am going to win.'* Prioress Johanne rules the priory with a firm hand, but her authority is challenged with the arrival of Knight Brother Nicholas. To what extent is this book about power?

- The well sits at the heart of life in the priory – and is central to the mystery of the story. What did you make of the plagues? Were you surprised by the identity of the blind boy? Can we find an earthly explanation for the strange happenings?

- *Great grey clouds rose up, one behind another, like walls of stone, but a beam of dazzling sunlight, thin and straight as a golden arrow, slipped between them.* What did you make of the wild and remote Dartmoor setting? How does the myth-laden landscape frame the story?

- Compare the three first-person narratives – Sorrel, Johanne and Morwen – with the chapters that take place at the priory. Does this affect how we perceive the three different women? And what impression do we get of Nicholas?

- Discuss the theme of survival in the novel, and how it shapes the actions of the characters.

- *I saw black Ankow galloping across the moors on that skeleton of a horse, with his hounds baying at his heels. I knew he was hunting souls.* How can we understand the tensions between the different models of faith and tradition in the book – the conflict between pagan and Christian beliefs, magic, wisdom and ancient lore?

- How is the role of family presented in the novel? Think about Kendra and her daughters, the home Sorrel leaves, and the bond between Johanne and Sebastian. Is family something we're born into, or something we choose?

- Why do you think Todde wants to help Sorrel? How does fear influence the way people relate to each other?

- *Not all of our noble sisters enter the order entirely by their own choice, though they must swear that they do.* Discuss the sisters' different reasons for 'choosing' a life of servitude.

- *A Gathering of Ghosts* is set against the backdrop of a terrible famine which caused widespread poverty, desperation and displacement of thousands of ordinary people as they were forced to travel across Europe in search of food or better conditions elsewhere. What parallels can we draw with our world today?

About the Author

Karen Maitland travelled and worked in many parts of the United Kingdom before settling for several years in the beautiful medieval city of Lincoln, an inspiration for her writing. She is the author of *The White Room*, *Company of Liars*, *The Owl Killers*, *The Gallows Curse*, *The Falcons of Fire and Ice*, *The Vanishing Witch*, *The Raven's Head* and *The Plague Charmer*. She now leads a life of rural bliss in Devon.